The Rogue Narrative and Irish Fiction, 1660–1790

Irish Studies
Kathleen Costello-Sullivan, *Series Editor*

Select Titles in Irish Studies

Fine Meshwork: Philip Roth, Edna O'Brien, and Jewish-Irish Literature
Dan O'Brien

Guilt Rules All: Irish Mystery, Detective, and Crime Fiction
Elizabeth Mannion and Brian Cliff, eds.

Literary Drowning: Postcolonial Memory in Irish and Caribbean Writing
Stephanie Pocock Boeninger

Modernity, Community, and Place in Brian Friel's Drama, Second Edition
Richard Rankin Russell

Politics, Culture, and the Irish American Press: 1784–1963
Debra Reddin van Tuyll, Mark O'Brien, and Marcel Broersma, eds.

The Rebels and Other Short Fiction
Richard Power; James MacKillop, ed.

Science, Technology, and Irish Modernism
Kathryn Conrad, Cóilín Parsons, and Julie McCormick Weng, eds.

Trauma and Recovery in the Twenty-First-Century Irish Novel
Kathleen Costello-Sullivan

For a full list of titles in this series,
visit https://press.syr.edu/supressbook-series/irish-studies/.

The Rogue Narrative and Irish Fiction, 1660–1790

Joe Lines

Syracuse University Press

∞ The paper used in this publication meets the minimum requirements
of the American National Standard for Information Sciences—Permanence
of Paper for Printed Library Materials, ANSI Z39.48-1992.

For a listing of books published and distributed by Syracuse University Press,
visit https://press.syr.edu.

ISBN: 978-0-8156-3705-9 (hardcover)
        978-0-8156-3714-1 (paperback)
        978-0-8156-5519-0 (e-book)

Library of Congress Cataloging-in-Publication Data

Names: Lines, Joe, author.
Title: The rogue narrative and Irish fiction, 1660–1790 / Joe Lines.
Description: First edition. | Syracuse, New York : Syracuse University Press, 2021. |
    Series: Irish studies | Includes bibliographical references and index. | Summary:
    "Lines has crafted a study of criminal biography and picaresque or "rogue" fiction
    from 1660 to 1790 which demonstrates the central part played by these forms
    in the early history of the Irish novel"— Provided by publisher.
Identifiers: LCCN 2020048618 (print) | LCCN 2020048619 (ebook) |
    ISBN 9780815637059 (hardback) | ISBN 9780815637141 (paperback) |
    ISBN 9780815655190 (ebook)
Subjects: LCSH: English fiction—Irish authors—History and criticism. | Rogues and
    vagabonds in literature. | Outlaws in literature. | Criminals—Ireland—Biography—
    History and criticism. | Head, Richard, 1637?–1686?—Criticism and interpretation. |
    Johnstone, Charles, 1719?–1800?—Criticism and interpretation.
Classification: LCC PR8807.R68 L56 2021 (print) | LCC PR8807.R68 (ebook) |
    DDC 823/.50935269270899162—dc23
LC record available at https://lccn.loc.gov/2020048618
LC ebook record available at https://lccn.loc.gov/2020048619

Manufactured in the United States of America

Contents

Acknowledgments

The bulk of this research was completed as part of a PhD thesis in the School of English at Queen's University, Belfast. I am grateful to the Arts and Humanities Research Council for awarding me a doctoral studentship (2011–14). Shaun Regan was always encouraging and approachable, and his insightful feedback enabled me to shape my research into a thesis. The initial idea for this project came as a result of studying nineteenth-century Irish literature with Sinéad Sturgeon. I benefited from studying in the same school as Moyra Haslett and Daniel Sanjiv Roberts at a time when both were researching eighteenth-century Irish fiction. Ian Campbell Ross has been generous and proactive in scholarly exchanges. I learned an enormous amount from the annual gatherings of the Eighteenth-Century Ireland Society and Eighteenth-Century Literature Research Network in Ireland. At Syracuse University Press, Deborah Manion was a patient and accommodating editor. The *Eighteenth-Century Ireland* journal previously published part of chapter 4 in the form of an article, "Migration, Nationality and Perspective in Charles Johnston's *The History of John Juniper* (1781)." Thanks to the journal's literature editor, Clíona Ó Gallchoir, for giving me permission to reuse it in this book. Parts of chapter 2 were published in the book *Irish Literature in Transition, 1700–1780* (volume 1). I am grateful to Cambridge University Press and the series editors for allowing me to reproduce this work here. The people who made Belfast a friendly and stimulating environment are too numerous to list here. Thank you to Zosia Kuczyńska, Stephen Connolly, Manuela Moser, Emily McDermott, Caoimhe nic an Tsaoir, Matthew Reznicek, Padraig Regan, Tara

McEvoy, Caitlin Newby, Simon Statham, Matthew Williamson, and Romano Mullin for their friendship, support, and example. Particularly, I would not have finished this book without the encouragement of Sonja Kleij. In Belfast, I was lucky enough to spend a lot of time in the company of the late Ciaran Carson. Listening to Ciaran contemplate language was an experience which I am sure made me a better writer; he is much missed.

The Rogue Narrative and Irish Fiction, 1660–1790

Introduction

Genre and Ireland in Early Modern Writing

Bandit Country

In the years immediately following the 2016 referendum on the exit of the United Kingdom from the European Union, the prospect of a "hard border" on the island of Ireland brought back memories of the violence of recent decades in the North, and saw the return of an old phrase to public discourse.[1] The term "bandit country" was first coined in 1975 by Northern Ireland secretary Merlyn Rees to describe the staunchly republican and heavily militarized south of Co. Armagh, in a statement issued immediately after an Irish Republican Army (IRA) shooting that claimed the lives of three soldiers.[2] Rees's labeling of the present-day border region as violent and lawless had its roots in a much earlier period of Irish history, as is implied by the term "bandit," a now-archaic noun denoting not some paramilitary group or brand of helicopter, but bands of robbers who hid out in rural or mountainous areas. The term is derived from Italian (bandito), and was much used before 1800 in Ireland, along with its cognate terms tory, rapparee, and highwayman, to describe the criminal gangs that troubled the Irish countryside. The reputation of South Armagh as particularly prone to banditry was alive and well in the seventeenth century, when wooded, mountainous parts of the Ulster-Leinster border became fastnesses for bandits who, it was believed, had the support of the populace even as they were proclaimed as enemies to the Crown, their actions punishable by execution. Robbers such as Redmond O'Hanlon passed into national folklore, with their adventures

1

retold in novels such as William Carleton's *Redmond O'Hanlon, the Irish Rapparee* (1862).[3] A keen appetite still remains in Ireland for tales of outlaws, as indicated by popular history books with titles such as *Stand and Deliver: Stories of Irish Highwaymen*.[4] Fans of Irish music across the world can sample the songs of the Highwaymen and the Rapparees; the latter band's name, meaning "robber," is derived from the Gaelic *rapaire*, or half-pike, and entered the English language in the seventeenth century.[5] Irish highwaymen have become stars of the cinema screen: the Kilkenny-born Michael Martin (1795–1821) has been the subject of two Hollywood films, *Captain Lightfoot* (1955) and *Thunderbolt and Lightfoot* (1974), and the more recent film *Plunkett & Macleane* (1999) is based upon the life of James MacLaine (1728–50), a highwayman from Monaghan who rose to notoriety in London.[6] Indeed, even as such figures have traveled the world, banditry has retained its popular association with Ireland, and with regions such as the Ulster-Leinster border. In 2012, the *Irish Independent* newspaper marked an exhibition of paintings in Dublin on the Australian icon Ned Kelly by claiming Kelly as a representative Irish outlaw (by virtue of his immigrant background), assuring readers that he "spoke with an Irish brogue."[7]

Prior to featuring on cinema screens or museum walls, the figure of the Irish outlaw was formed by prose biographies and works of fiction, printed in English and published between 1660 and 1790 in London and Dublin. This book is a study of such narratives, which returns to their earliest roots and reveals the unexpected directions they took. The first accounts of O'Hanlon, MacLaine, and others were influenced by wider European traditions of stories about "rogues"—opportunistic, clever, and admirable characters who roved and robbed at will. The continued fame and reproduction of the Irish outlaw in a variety of media is often attributed to a residual skepticism of the law stemming from Ireland's colonial history. Between 1695 and 1705, what became known as the Penal Laws were passed, placing various social and economic restrictions on Irish Catholics in terms of the owning, leasing, and inheriting of property and the holding of professions.[8] In their defiance of the law, robbers can be framed as heroic rebels against the Crown, as seen in one modern biography of the eighteenth-century highwayman James Freney: "His striking at the very heart of Ireland's oppressors—plundering their secure and guarded homes, and sharing his spoils with the poor—catapulted him into the limelight and elevated him to the status of local hero and, eventually, living legend."[9] Yet the legendary status of the outlaw in Ireland cannot be seen simply as the product of past oppression; it need only be considered that the highwayman is an equally durable trope in England, where Robin Hood and Dick Turpin remain household names.[10] In fact, rogues in early Irish writing do not always figure in opposition to colonial authority, and are not always native Irish or Catholic. The rogue narratives studied here are more various than might be expected, their sources including the historical lives of men like O'Hanlon, but also French, Spanish, and English novels as well as non-narrative texts that imagined and anatomized a criminal underworld. Rogue-centered works of fiction are discussed here alongside biographies of real lawbreakers to demonstrate their closeness and interpenetration. These narratives reveal a fascination with the foreign and cosmopolitan in travel plots that repeatedly take the rogue outside of Ireland. The protagonists, who are female as well as male, are protean and adaptable, blending in seamlessly as they move through different cultures, penetrating elite society, acting as officers of the law, and sometimes reforming their morals. In the process, prejudicial stereotypes of the time about the Irish as a lawless, savage race are continually overturned.

It is well known that both criminal biographies and the "picaresque" novels of early modern Spain shaped the form and content of the novel in English. However, work focusing on Irish fiction before 1800 has been less in evidence—though existing surveys of early fiction about Ireland have revealed suggestive continuities. A prevalence of rogue and criminal tales is observable in the earliest Irish-focused works, published between 1660 and 1700. This study demonstrates the continuity of these seventeenth-century texts with the Irish novels that came later in the eighteenth century. It also reveals the influence exerted on fiction by popular biographies of real criminals. Famous rogues such as O'Hanlon were given lasting form in John Cosgrave's

A Genuine History of the Lives and Actions of the Most Notorious Irish Highwaymen, Tories and Rapparees (1747), which became a staple of lower-class Irish readers for the next century and was ripe for adaptation into novel form by Carleton in 1862.[11] This study will return Cosgrave's collection of criminal biographies to its rightful place among a host of contemporary narratives about Irish rogues. It reveals that a century before Carleton, Irish novelists such as William Chaigneau and Charles Johnston (sometimes spelled "Johnstone") adapted the short, popular biographies into longer and more expensive novels. In the process, from the mid–eighteenth century onward, the rogue narrative gave rise to fully fledged Irish novels that were informed and nuanced in their portraits of Irish life, people, and politics.

Early criminal and rogue narratives are, however, usually discounted from conventional accounts of Irish literature, due probably to their association with English legal, judicial, and colonial discourses tending toward a xenophobic view of the native Irish. Something of this condescension can be detected in the following passage, from a classic study of English prose fiction, Frank Wadleigh Chandler's *The Literature of Roguery* (1907): "Here and throughout the Irish novels, aside from the rogues that are studied, a host of picaresque traits and incidents appear. For the Irishman's love of defying the law, which leads to the drubbing of bailiffs, the outwitting of gaugers, illicit distilling, and smuggling, provokes many an amusing rogue scene, and his romantic delight in duels and abductions adds to the list."[12] The modern reader might take issue with the ascribing of a national unruliness to "the Irishman," but this characterization of the Irish novel is intriguing, if only because of the moment at which it was expressed. In 1907, James Joyce was still seven years from publishing his first work of fiction, *Dubliners* (1914). Joyce and the Irish novelists who wrote after him loom large in present-day definitions of Irish fiction, and have been used as orienting points by critics focusing on earlier periods of history. Terry Eagleton's *Heathcliff and the Great Hunger*, for instance, argues that "the Irish novel is only ambiguously realist," and maps a literary tradition of "largely non-realist works," from Jonathan Swift's *Gulliver's Travels* (1726) onward, culminating in Joyce's *Ulysses*

(1922).[13] But writing before the advent of Joyce, Chandler instead singled out Irish novelists for their "picaresque traits" and "rogue scene[s]." Chandler's account of "the Irish novels" begins with Maria Edgeworth's *Castle Rackrent* (1800), but if we look further back in time, taking advantage of the resources available to the twenty-first-century scholar, the significance of the rogue narrative in Irish fiction is even more marked.[14] This book will reveal that Irish rogue narratives are more than merely "amusing"; they engage with questions of identity and nationality, and with the political state and prospects of Ireland. Rogue narratives actually contest generalizations about Ireland as lawless—as a bandit country—by presenting versions of national identity that are complex, shifting, and ambivalent.

Early Irish Fiction

But what is "Irish fiction," and to what extent is it possible to read texts written centuries ago as either "Irish" or "novels"? Research on early Irish fiction has broken new ground during the last twenty years, returning many more works published before the 1800 Act of Union to the notice of readers. The current book has been made possible by this scholarship, and seeks to extend its scope. It must therefore grapple with the fact that its main texts were published in an era in which understandings of national identity and literary genre were very different from our own. This study begins with the work of Richard Head, born in Carrickfergus, Co. Antrim, in the 1630s, whose various and prolific output included plays, fantasy fiction, and rogue biography, all liberally interlarded with plagiarism and autobiography—though he wrote nothing that we would call a "novel." When dealing with such an author, who was moreover of English parentage and lived most of his life outside of Ireland, questions about nationality become as urgent as questions about the novel form.

Studies of the rise of the English novel had long afforded a place to such Irish-born authors as William Congreve, Jonathan Swift, Oliver Goldsmith, and Laurence Sterne, but the idea that a recognizably Irish novel might also have been developing in the eighteenth century was slower to take hold.[15] Well-known novelists such as Goldsmith and

Sterne did not utilize Irish settings in their fiction; many of their contemporaries, however, were writing novels that engaged more explicitly with an Irish context. These works included Sarah Butler's *Irish Tales* (1716), Chaigneau's *The History of Jack Connor* (1752), Thomas Amory's *The Life of John Buncle, Esq.* (1756–66), and Elizabeth Sheridan's *The Triumph of Prudence Over Passion* (1781). The significance of these novels was first pointed out by Ian Campbell Ross during the 1980s, and consequently many were given places in James M. Cahalan's *The Irish Novel: A Critical History* (1988) and *The Field Day Anthology of Irish Literature* (1991).[16] This existing work was augmented by the publication in 2005 of a pioneering bibliography, Rolf and Magda Loeber's *A Guide to Irish Fiction, 1650–1900* (2005), which uncovered a vast number of works that were by Irish-born authors, or set or published in Ireland. Moreover, from 2010, the Early Irish Fiction series from Four Courts Press has produced critical editions of several of the novels mentioned above.[17] The critical adage that Edgeworth's *Castle Rackrent* was the first Irish novel has thus been banished, with readers now able to extend their interest in Irish fiction as far back in time as the 1693 anonymous novel *Vertue Rewarded, or the Irish Princess*. The earliest-published fictions listed by the Loebers are Roger Boyle's *Parthenissa, a Romance* (1651) and Head's *The English Rogue Described, in the Life of Meriton Latroon* (1665)—a work that is, as its title implies, in the criminal narrative tradition, and which provides this study with a logical starting point.[18]

The expansion of scope as far back as the 1650s enriches the critical discussion only at the cost of problematizing the category of "Irish fiction." When assessing the relevance of a historical work to an Irish context, factors of authorial perspective, publication, and readership come into play. Loeber and Loeber write that the novel in Ireland begins as "an imported literary form, tied to the English language and . . . inspired by English and continental examples."[19] Works like *Parthenissa* and *The English Rogue* were written in English at a time when Irish was the usual tongue of the country's majority, and their language of composition reflected the Protestant, English roots of their authors. Both writers led peripatetic lives, and their national identity cannot be interpreted in singular terms. Boyle and Head's statuses were different—Boyle was the Earl of Orrery and a prominent politician, Head a London-based bookseller—but both would have been likely to emphasize their English ancestry and "would not have countenanced, perhaps even understood, the description of themselves as 'Irish writers,'" as Deana Rankin points out.[20] Elsewhere, Rankin has argued for the existence of a distinctive "Protestant English-Irish . . . literary voice" in the seventeenth-century writings of Head, Boyle, and others.[21] The impact of Head's time in Ireland on his writing is clear; he experienced the outbreak of the rebellion of 1641 as a child in Co. Antrim, and would draw upon this experience in the partly autobiographical *The English Rogue*.[22] The next chapter discusses the ways in which Head's fictions expressed the priorities and anxieties of the settler class, and argues that they also turn a skeptical eye on this class. Head's works are inevitably biased or limited in their view of Ireland as a society, being testament to how a recently arrived Protestant minority perceived their own position in a mainly Catholic and Irish-speaking country. Furthermore, the first works readable as Irish fiction were not directed primarily toward Irish readers, but to the larger audience available in England. Indeed, until 1730, works by Irish authors or concerned with Ireland were overwhelmingly published in London, as Moyra Haslett has demonstrated, based on Loeber and Loeber's *Guide*. Dublin-based readers were exposed to an increased amount of fiction after 1709, when Ireland's exemption from new copyright laws allowed the cheap reprinting of imported books. Original Irish fiction was scarce by comparison with English imports, but Haslett notes a trend from 1730 onward for novels by Irish authors to be printed first in London, then soon after in Dublin, implying the existence of a readership with an interest in homegrown works.[23]

Beginning with the fiction of the 1660s intensifies questions of genre as well as issues of nationality. Seamus Deane comments of the range of texts included in Loeber and Loeber's *Guide* that "to use the term 'novel' is in itself misleading, because although all novels are fiction, it is equally obvious that not all fictions are novels."[24] Indeed, works such as *Parthenissa* and *The English Rogue* belong to a period usually understood to precede the recognizable genre of the novel. Brean Hammond and Shaun Regan envision the British novel as emerging from "the mingling and mixing of different literary modes" in a process of "novelization" that is "carbon-dateable to the later seventeenth century." The earliest texts that Hammond and Regan discuss as novels hail from the 1680s and '90s, and critics have interpreted the earlier works of Boyle and Head alongside the precursor genres to the novel.[25] John Wilson Foster begins his survey of Irish fiction with Boyle's *Parthenissa* and Head's *English Rogue*, reading each as an "Irish exponent" of the modes or genres that constituted the early English novel—the heroic romances of France and Tudor England, in Boyle's case, and the Spanish picaresque, in Head's.[26] Foster thus joins the dots from the romance and picaresque to the novel, and from Europe to Ireland, an approach also evident elsewhere. The editors of *Vertue Rewarded, or the Irish Princess* discuss how the novel "contains its romance elements within the conventions of more modern fiction."[27] Attending to romance conventions has allowed critics to accommodate Irish texts within the broader development of the novel in Europe.

However, recent scholarship on early Irish fiction has attended more to romance than to the picaresque, the other contributory genre that Foster mentions. Critics of fiction generally concur that romance is the genre "most relevant to the novel's development," and is "a logical place to start if one is intent on finding liminal or originating moments."[28] In Foster's *Cambridge Companion to the Irish Novel*, a chapter on "The Novel before 1800" begins with a section titled "Uses of Romance," focusing on *Vertue Rewarded* and Butler's *Irish Tales*.[29] Similarly, *The Cambridge History of Irish Literature* (2005) uses Boyle's romances as its starting point in its discussion of prose fiction from 1690 to 1800.[30] The same volume features Head, but in the chapter on "Literature in English, 1550–1690," thus divorcing his output from the discussion of the novel that follows.[31] What, then, of the picaresque? At its simplest, the picaresque can be glossed as a rogue tale, being derived from the Spanish pícaro (rogue). This form was enduringly popular in eighteenth-century Britain and Ireland, disseminated in translations that inspired original fictions such as *The English Rogue*. This book will connect the picaresque-influenced narratives of Head and others to the novel, using Irish fiction as a prism through which to sketch this relationship. Firstly, the history of the picaresque must be surveyed, along with its development as a critical construct and usefulness in the context of Irish fiction.

The Picaresque

Critics often use picaresque interchangeably with rogue narrative (or tale, biography, or fiction); yet the terms "picaresque" and "rogue" do possess different histories, the former originating in Spanish, the latter in the popular culture of early modern England. As can be seen above, "picaresque" remains a common descriptive label in scholarship on Irish fiction. For instance, Derek Hand describes Chaigneau's *History of Jack Connor* as a "return to the picaresque world inhabited by *The English Rogue*."[32] Katie Trumpener positions Chaigneau, Amory, and Johnston as authors of a "nationally inflected picaresque" or "traveling fiction" in which the protagonist's movement enables the "survey" or "scansion" of different regions and nations.[33] Indeed, the term usefully expresses certain kinships between the fiction of Head, Chaigneau, Amory, and Johnston (such as travel plots), and it is still the standard means of discussing the kinds of writing that are this book's subject. However, I contend that the picaresque is a difficult and, finally, unsatisfactory fit in the case of early Irish fiction. This book's preference, as the title makes clear, is for rogue narrative, a term that more closely fits the Anglo-Irish contexts of these texts, and comes with less problematic critical baggage than the picaresque. Surveying recent scholarship, it becomes apparent that the term can only be applied to eighteenth-century fiction in a vague and qualified sense. Critics tend to define the picaresque according to certain formal characteristics derived from a canon of prototypical novels, thus resulting in those works most relevant to Irish writing being sidelined or discounted according to judgments that are, in the end, based on perceived literary quality. One of this book's intentions, then, is to advance the term "rogue narrative" as a more capacious and usable category. To this end, this section introduces influential definitions of the picaresque genre and glosses the debate over its extent.

The term "picaresque" is derived from the Spanish *picaresco*, the adjectival form of pícaro.[34] Spanish fictions about pícaros became a recognizable form with the anonymous *Lazarillo de Tormes* (1554). *Lazarillo* was followed nearly half a century later by Mateo Alemán's *Guzmán de Alfarache* (1599), which popularized the picaresque in Spain. *Lazarillo*, *Guzmán*, and Francisco de Quevedo's *La Vida del Buscón* (1626) are generally taken to be "the canonical texts" in the tradition.[35] The Spanish picaresque novels of the seventeenth century may be collocated on a basic level as biographical tales of low life, though they vary in length, narrative perspective, and tone.[36] Claudio Guillén has offered an influential definition of the shared "characteristics" of these Spanish works. Firstly, the protagonist is an orphan and vagrant whose homelessness leads to a narrative of peripatetic, wandering movement. The pícaro may work as a servant for various masters, observing different social classes and professions.[37] Beyond these plot features, the form of the picaresque has been defined on the basis of its satirical or outsider's perspective on society, its status as fictional autobiography, and its structure as an integrated, developing narrative that leads to a climactic final situation in the pícaro's life.[38]

By the mid–seventeenth century, many Spanish picaresque fictions were widely disseminated in translated form in France, Germany, and England. The first to appear in English was *Lazarillo*, translated by David Rowland and printed in 1576.[39] James Mabbe's translation of *Guzmán*, retitled *The Rogue*, was published in 1622 and it was this text that prompted a swathe of imitations such as Head's *English Rogue*. French novels influenced by the picaresque, meanwhile, included *L'Histoire de Gil Blas de Santillane* (1715–35) by Alain-René Lesage (sometimes spelled Le Sage).[40] *Gil Blas* became widely read in Britain and Ireland after its first translation into English in 1716.[41] The Scottish novelist Tobias Smollett published a successful English version of *Gil Blas*, and acknowledged it as a model for his first novel, *The Adventures of Roderick Random* (1748).[42] *Gil Blas* exerted a contemporaneous influence on Irish novels such as Chaigneau's *Jack Connor*; William

Chaigneau was from French Huguenot stock, and probably read the text in its original language.[43] *Gil Blas* was read and imitated across Europe, and had supplanted the Spanish originals in popularity by the early nineteenth century, according to Jenny Mander. In Ireland, Lesage inspired Charles Lever's *The Confessions of Con Cregan, The Irish Gil Blas* (1849). Around this time, the term "picaresque" began to be used to mean a type of narrative; Mander gives the first appearance of the term as 1810.[44] Walter Scott referred to *Guzmán de Alfarache* as "the most celebrated of the Spanish romances *a la picaresque*" in his essay on Lesage in *Lives of the Novelists* (1821–24).[45] The picaresque, then, was not a recognized type of fiction in the period covered by this study. It is evident, however, that Spanish rogue narratives had an impact on seventeenth-century fiction in English, before Lesage's French version rose to prominence in eighteenth-century Britain and Ireland.

The characteristics of the Spanish picaresque novels did not all endure intact in the journey from Spain to France, England, and finally Ireland. For example, the pícaro as petty criminal is transformed in *Gil Blas* to a more ingenuous hero who attains a comfortable status. Differences between the original Spanish works and their descendants have prompted much debate over the extent of the genre; as Peter N. Dunn writes, "The problem became visible when the picaresque narrative, like the pícaro himself, left home."[46] Studies of the genre from the perspective of comparative literature offer a precise and rigorous definition of its attributes. However, these approaches struggle to maintain the integrity of their definition while acknowledging the realities of the form's international dissemination. Critics of the 1960s and '70s constructed an international picaresque canon stretching from *Lazarillo* to Smollett.[47] A more recent exponent of this formalist approach is J. A. Garrido Ardila, who identifies the definitive English picaresque novels as Daniel Defoe's *Moll Flanders* (1719), *Colonel Jack* (1722), and *Roxana* (1724), and Smollett's *Ferdinand Count Fathom* (1753). These works serve as crowning proof of "a long process in which the picaresque genre slowly permeated English literature and was finally employed in the first half of the eighteenth century, engendering specimens of the picaresque genre."[48] This exemplifies the assumption, inherent in formalist surveys, of the enduring existence of the genre independently of place and time. It assumes that novelists perceived the various picaresque elements as part of a unified genre that could be "employed," but does not engage with the actual ways in which Defoe or Smollett accessed the picaresque, whether in Spanish, French, or English. It is important to remember that the conventions of the picaresque were not treated as sacrosanct, but freely refigured in other languages. As O. M. Brack and Leslie A. Chilton point out, "Picaresque narrative . . . was a new form lacking a snobbish literary pedigree, untrammeled by classically established rules, easily adopted by writers in various countries, and eagerly consumed by a variety of readers."[49] Adaptation and innovation, then, are to be expected in the history of a genre that was far from codified. As such, definitions of the Picaresque that include many qualifying characteristics cannot give an account of what seems, from today's perspective, most striking about the form—its eager adoption and consumption outside of Spain, leading to the discarding or transformation of those original attributes.

Close study of the descendants of the picaresque tends to put stress on the idea of an international picaresque genre. The case of Smollett is worth dwelling upon, as the Scottish novelist was a contemporary of Irish writers such as Chaigneau and Johnston. Smollett continues to be given a central role in studies such as Garrido Ardila's, but the picaresque has faded from view in criticism of Smollett himself. In the 1960s, the first wave of monographs on the picaresque elicited a debate among Smollett specialists as to the usefulness of the term.[50] John Skinner concludes that of Smollett's six novels, only *Ferdinand Count Fathom* includes a protagonist resembling the pícaro, and "even in the case of *Fathom*, one should speak at most of a 'soft' or pseudo-picaresque, if not simply of peripatetic narrative."[51] In Smollett studies, the picaresque would seem to have been a casualty of the shift in the 1980s from formalist to historicist approaches to eighteenth-century fiction.[52] Features of Smollett's novels long seen as hallmarks of the picaresque, such as their traveling, episodic plotlines, can now be placed in the context of "rapid, radical and deeply unsettling cultural change" and "colonial and commercial expansionism."[53] Recent critics such as Leslie A. Chilton recognize that "Smollett understood the picaresque tradition not as a model to be copied but as a set of rhetorical tools that could be used for a variety of purposes."[54] In approaching what we now call the picaresque, eighteenth-century novelists did not have access to a unified or overarching formal framework; they borrowed or referenced various elements of particular French and Spanish texts in diverse ways.

This study, then, takes place at several removes from the picaresque as understood through its Spanish origins, instead focusing on those mediated versions of the genre that were written later and in other languages. Head's *English Rogue* and Lesage's *Gil Blas* had a far-reaching influence on the popular fiction of Ireland, Britain, and France, yet standard literary histories still define these works simply as second-rate or watered-down versions of the Spanish picaresque. As Howard Mancing explains, studies of the picaresque often distinguish "true" examples of the form from "mediated" works that meet only some of the necessary conditions.[55] Skinner refers above to the "pseudo-picaresque," while Guillén uses the terms "strict" and "loose," or "*stricto sensu*" and "*sensu lato*."[56] There is little agreement on the texts belonging to each category. Guillén includes *Gil Blas* in the stricto sensu class, whereas Garrido Ardila discounts it because "it is empty of social meaning"; moreover, lambasting "its excess of gratuitous comedy."[57] The latter critic also decides that *The English Rogue* is not a true member of the genre because of the weakness of its satire: "The fact that the setting of [Latroon's] roguish adventures is England, where he is no outsider, renders the satire much less potent."[58] This aesthetic judgment echoes mid-twentieth-century critics of the picaresque such as Frederick Monteser, who referred to "that wretched effort which is *The English Rogue*," and Alexander Parker, who dismissed it as "not serious literature."[59] A recent survey by Walter L. Reed states that "no significant novelistic imitations or improvements" of the Spanish originals were written in English "before the third decade of the eighteenth century," and refers in parentheses to "the earlier and cruder English picaresque of Richard Head."[60] Such arguments result from definitions of the genre that, proceeding from acknowledged master-works such as *Lazarillo*, insist that satirical power, formal complexity, and integrated narrative form are its native qualities. This leads in turn to the conclusion, repeated in study after study, that Smollett and Defoe are the only British novelists who merit the status of pica-resque—a canon sustained by Garrido Ardila and Reed, publishing in 2015 and 2016, respectively. The restricted generic lineage of the pica-resque is thus incompatible with a central aim of this book: to further widen our knowledge of early Irish fiction through a focus on works that were missed by or excluded from previous surveys of the period.

Formalist accounts of the picaresque, in their insistence on a small canon of worthy works, appear ill-equipped to reckon with our ever-widening knowledge of British, Irish, and European fiction in the early modern period. It is not coincidental that a recent study of "the forgot-ten bestsellers of early English fiction" should reject the term. Simon Dickie draws attention to the abundance and popularity of comic fic-tion in the period between 1750 and 1770. Dickie admits that many of his chosen texts might seem picaresque, given their biographical travel narratives, but justifies calling them "ramble novels" instead because "this term—with its glance at the eighteenth-century diversion of the ramble or aimless excursion—seems better than *picaresque*, which was not yet used in this period and too easily connotes the bleak survival-ism of premodern rogue literature." Aside from chronological issues around the term, the picaresque connotes a prestigious literary lin-eage, whereas ramble novels were lambasted for their crude humor and formulaic, skeletal plotting, and thus quickly forgotten by later schol-ars. As Dickie admits, they are not the place to find the subtle satire or psychological acuity of a *Lazarillo*. Ramble novels, then, cannot be accommodated within conventional understandings of the picaresque, and have suffered from the same fate as the earlier criminal narratives of Head, being dismissed as "not serious literature." However, it is equally true of ramble novels that "[s]ome of the earliest Irish novels are exercises in this genre," including Chaigneau's *Jack Connor*.[61] This study will follow Dickie's use of the term "ramble novel" to discuss several works of comic fiction published after 1750, and will contend that they were key texts in the development of a distinctively Irish kind of novel.

My overarching concept of "rogue narrative" is intended to be more basic and neutral than "picaresque," in dispensing with requirements such as satirical weight and narrative complexity, while retaining a focus on the rogue protagonist, and on themes of crime, vagrancy, and wandering movement that proceed logically from that choice of character. Dunn defines the "identity" of a picaresque work as "the autobiography of a runaway," but stresses that this "identity (as we would expect) is the ground upon which differences are inscribed, while the differences rather than the identity are the vehicles of meaning."[62] The basic "ground" of similarity identified here is the use of the rogue combined with Irish characters and settings. The meaning of particular plots or characters derives ultimately, in each case, from the text's own historical moment. My purpose more widely will be to argue that Irish rogue narratives should be part of the history of the novel, not necessarily for their literary sophistication or membership of a foundational genre, but for the unique dimensions of eighteenth-century life that they present to us. Spanish and French iterations of the picaresque have an important role to play in Irish literature, and this study adds to our knowledge of the contact between these national traditions across two centuries. But the flexible idea of a rogue narrative will allow us to explore forgotten or belittled corners of early fiction in depth, and to read texts that draw upon multiple genres and traditions, without constant recourse to a strictly defined and all too well-known center.

Early Modern English Rogue Literature

Writers such as Head combined the Spanish picaresque narrative with a homegrown form of popular literature: compendiums of lore about the activities of beggars, fraudsters, and thieves, now called criminal anatomies or cony-catching pamphlets, or grouped under the general heading of rogue literature. As Paul Salzman explains, these anatomies provided an "enormous reserve of incident, lore and language which writers of picaresque fiction could use."[63] In the sixteenth and early seventeenth centuries, anatomies flourished in a context of public anxiety about vagrancy and crime. The standard anatomy is not narrative in shape, but simply gives information and cautionary advice about the different types of crook that readers might encounter. The rogues constructed by these texts found their shadowy real-life analogues among the most vulnerable in society: the poor, unemployed, and homeless, including migrants from Ireland. Consequently, the anatomies also functioned to shape the attitudes of English readers toward Ireland and its people. In early modern English writing, rogues become a figure for Ireland itself: just as the criminal exists on the margins of civil society, Ireland represented the outer fringe of British power and the incipient empire, and just as rogues are anatomized, the strange customs of the Irish become the object of study and—it is hoped—of reform. Seventeenth-century rogue narratives took their form from the picaresque, but they reflected earlier anatomies in their image of the Irish as criminal, mobile, and protean. In this rogue literature, despite its purportedly nonfictional status and emphatically English xenophobia, we can see the first hints of a developing Irish novel.

English criminal anatomies began with *The Highway to the Spital-House* (c. 1535–36) and reached their highest popularity between 1590 and 1620 with the works of Robert Greene and Thomas Dekker.[64] The first appearance of the word "rogue," said to originate from the "cant" language of thieves, has been traced to two influential anatomies, John Awdeley's *The Fraternity of Vagabonds* (1561) and Thomas Harman's *A Caveat or Warning for Common Cursitors* (1566).[65] Craig Dionne and Steve Mentz write that "rogue . . . became a catchall term for a variety of social deviants and outcasts, from rural migrants to urban con artists."[66] Kathleen Pories points out that "vagabond" was the standard term previously, and that calling the vagrant poor "rogues" functioned to criminalize them by imagining their status as a chosen career and implying their natural villainy.[67] Indeed, Linda Woodbridge rejects the "highly prejudicial" term to describe the real subjects of rogue literature, preferring "vagrant."[68] Anatomies represent rogues fancifully as "an anti-society," in A. L. Beier's phrase, with its own linguistic code or cant.[69] Harman's *Caveat* classified thieves and vagrants into classes and warned readers of their frauds and tactics: "palliards" were apparently beggars who feigned injury "for gain and to be pitied," while "fraters" forged "letters patents" to gain access to poor relief.[70] Harman also includes a dictionary of cant words, and such lists became a common feature of rogue literature, appearing also in fictions such as *The English Rogue*.[71] Through such tactics, the anatomies distanced criminals from law-abiding society, conjuring a threatening subclass who were immune to reform or to the reader's pity. This marks the difference between English rogue literature and the picaresque. Lazarillo de Tormes is represented as a pitiable vagrant who eventually lifts himself out of poverty, and the reader can identify with his ingenious efforts to climb the social ladder. But in English rogue anatomies, the reader is distanced from vagrants and vagabonds, who are rendered as undifferentiated types, belonging to a distinct, outlandish, and menacing sphere.[72]

Of course, this rogue society was technically within the borders of English society and subject to national law. As a result, rogue literature put forward a particular and selective discourse of English identity or "rhetoric of nationhood" that excluded its marginalized subjects.[73] For Hal Gladfelder, it is "that impulse to demarcate a world construed as foreign to the experience of their intended readers" that is most typical of criminal anatomy.[74] The inclusion in anatomies of the Irish and gypsies alongside thieves and fraudulent beggars associates criminality with foreignness or ethnic otherness. Harman's *Caveat*, for instance, refers to the presence of "above an hundred of Irishmen and women that wander about to beg for their living" in the southeastern counties of England, migrants "that have come over within these two years."[75] Such migration was episodic in the period, rising sharply in times of crisis in Ireland such as the rebellion of 1569 and the famines of 1628–29. Beier finds that the Irish "tended to arrive *en masse*" and traveled through England in large groups, adding to their visibility and exacerbating sectarian and national prejudices against them. A vagrancy statute of 1572 ordered that any Irish people arrested for the crime should be dispatched to their country of origin, and an act in

1597 "provided that dangerous rogues should be banished overseas," mostly to the American colonies.[76] The exclusionary tactics of anatomies fueled the public's distrust of migrants, in a climate of harsh penal responses to vagrancy which included the literal removal of supposed rogues from the nation.

The discourse of English identity drawn upon in rogue literature was exclusive and discriminatory toward groups such as the Irish. Yet at the same time, these texts blur the boundary between anti-society and civil society by elucidating the alleged ways and codes of criminals to readers. In Brooke Stafford's reading, anatomies thus raise the possibility that rogues can be "incorporated" into English society, and can be compared to colonialist treatises on Ireland such as Edmund Spenser's *A View of the State of Ireland*, written in 1595–96 but not published until 1633. Spenser likewise imagines the "translation" of the native Irish into a larger English whole, putting forward schemes to foster English culture, language, and practices in Ireland. But the reformation process is not unidirectional, as Spenser also observes how past generations of English settlers in Ireland have learned Gaelic, taken on local customs, and strayed from their English loyalties.[77] In the style of the anatomy, Spenser distinguishes several classes of troublesome Irish, one being the "woodkerne," or forest-dwelling bandits, who are to be put to work on the land: "Therefore are those Kearne . . . to bee driven and made to imploy that ablenesse of bodie, which they were wont to use for thefte and villainy, henceoorth to labour and industry."[78] The Irish can be integrated into English culture, and the English can likewise take on Irish customs. The distance or strangeness of the criminal sphere that vagrants or the Irish inhabit cannot be taken for granted, because their culture emerges as amenable and accessible to its civilized, English opposite.

The malleability of the Irish rogue in early modern English literature reflects the uncertain status of Ireland itself in relation to English power. Paul Brown examines the "discourse of colonialism" in early modern rogue literature and descriptions of Ireland. Brown identifies two discursive strands of "masterlessness" and "savagism" in early modern English anatomies. Masterlessness was the property of rogues or vagrants, "wandering or unfixed and unsupervised elements located in the internal margins of civil society." Savagism meanwhile denoted "alien cultures on the external margins of expanding civil power."[79] The people of Ireland could be (and were) viewed as savages abroad, but given the closeness of Ireland and the consequent realities of immigration, they were also readily framed as masterless rogues within the borders of the nation. Ireland was claimed for the English monarchy by the 1541 Crown of Ireland Act, meaning that it could be seen by the English both as a distant colony and as a neighboring kingdom.[80] It was, in Brown's terms, a "semiperiphery" between the "core" of Britain and the "periphery" of the New World. Spenser and his contemporaries viewed it as an ongoing problem in need of a solution, a land persistently troubled by rebellions in which conquest was incomplete. This uncertainty over the country's status as a subject kingdom meant that "the Irish were seen as both savage Gaels and lapsed civil subjects." If the Irish were masterless then they were merely "lapsed," and could become mastered, whereas there was no such hope for the "savage."[81] Early modern Ireland could thus be seen as both core and periphery, raising questions about whether its people were capable of being civilized, and whether they belonged within the nation or were destructive to it. The subclasses of masterless Irish represented in criminal anatomies perpetuated such questions by framing the Irish as an outlandish people while also incorporating them into English culture. The processes of transformation imagined by early rogue literature are moral, judicial, and colonial. The protean aspect to the rogue was expanded in later narratives, in which deception and pretense become central strategies by which rogues are characterized.

Seventeenth-century rogue narratives feature a fascination with the foreign, derived from their roots in the picaresque and in anatomies of the masterless and savage peoples of the colonial peripheries. Imitations following in the wake of Mabbe's *The Rogue* included William Melvin's *Sonne of the Rogue* (1638), *The Dutch Rogue* (1683), *The Irish Rogue* (1690), and *The French Rogue* (1694). Leah Orr identifies "the use of the title formula 'The [nationality] Rogue'" as a clear echo of Head, and notes that these works "combine an English version of the picaresque tradition with English nationalism," as seen in references that imagine native rogues outdoing their foreign competitors.[82] A prefatory verse to *The English Rogue* invokes the Spanish works as well as French authors Rabelais and Charles Sorel:

> What Guzman, Buscon, Francion, Rablais writ,
> I once applauded, for most excellent wit: . . .
> Henceforth Translations, pack away, be gone;
> No Rogue so well writ, as our English one.[83]

The opening of a later edition of Head's text boasted that "Guzman, Lazarillo de Tormes, and all others Remarkable for such like Villanies, are compell'd, as being out-done, to strike Sail."[84] Both passages use similar, xenophobic imagery of the European translations being ejected from the country. The rebuttal of the picaresque here is complex, involving claims to originality and the repudiation of rival products in the market, as well as attempts to exploit the patriotism and anti-Catholicism of readers in the context of international and imperial rivalries.[85] Yet, despite their bullish patriotism, rogue narratives were interested in and absorbed by other cultures. The translations of the picaresque by Rowland, Mabbe, and others presented themselves as informative accounts of Spain, and a similar rhetoric of explanation occurs in *The Irish Rogue*, which devotes a chapter to "a pleasant account of the Rogueries, Character, Manners, and Customs of the Native Irish."[86] Laura Rosenthal notices that fictional rogues are often "exoticized" or "non-English," reading them as figures for an unruly "global commerce" in their threat to the nation's wealth and property. Indeed, Head's "English" rogue is a key instance of the exoticized rogue, born in Ireland, and given a name, Meriton Latroon, that recalls the Spanish ladrón (thief).[87] This study analyzes the treatment of Irish nationality in the range of rogue narratives published after Head's foundational text, pointing out that the protean quality of characters such as Latroon overturns anti-Irish stereotypes, and that these works associate criminality with English and Protestant, Gaelic and Catholic characters alike.

The galleries of homeless vagrants featured in anatomies invoke the mass migration and displacement caused by civil war and instability in Ireland. Head echoes these texts in the account of Latroon's childhood, which quickly takes a grisly turn after the 1641 rebellion breaks out and the narrator's English father is slain by rebels. Latroon's experience during the rebellion recalls the origins of the rogue narrative in the literature of vagrancy: "It was now high time to flie, although we knew not whether; every place we arriv'd at we thought least secure, wherefore our motion was continual . . . The terrour of the Irish and Scotch, incomparably prevailed beyond the rage of the Sea, so that we were resolved to use all possible means to get on Shipboard. At *Belfast* we accomplisht our desires, committing our selves to the more merciful Waves."[88] Fiction, history, and autobiography are synthesized here, as the text invokes the experience of many in the 1640s, when a wave of Protestants fled from Ireland to Britain as refugees. As Beier reflects, "It would be a remote place indeed that did not witness the passage of some Irish beggars in the 1640s."[89] Two of these beggars may have been the young Richard Head and his mother; and, twenty years later, the adult author wove the story of Irish rebellion, displacement, and destitution into his work of fiction. The Irish vagrants that were caricatured in anatomies a century previously now trudged through the pages of the novel.

My central category of "rogue narrative" thus invokes a context in early modern English popular literature. In the sixteenth and early seventeenth centuries, anatomies grappled with the country's diverse and ever-changing population of poor, jobless, and rootless people. Rogue literature contributed to the criminalizing of these vagrants in public perceptions and official procedure. This new literature of the "rogue" exoticized vagrants as a distinct mass, undifferentiated and menacing. But this move, essentially fictionalizing as it was, created a space for other possibilities, such as the moral improvement of the rogue and the crossing of the boundary between criminal and law-abiding societies. This ambivalence in the literature took a particular form when it included the Irish as rogues. This was because Irish vagrants came from a country that was both overseas and a subject kingdom, and could thus be viewed as savages from the empire's outer reaches or wayward outlaws within the state, or even a workforce of model citizens (as Spenser projects). It is these early modern English anatomies that give Head and his successors their distinctive mix of cosmopolitanism and xenophobia. Similarly, international migration and hybrid nationality will continue to preoccupy the Irish rogue narrative until the end of the eighteenth century.

Criminal Biography

The life story of a real, named criminal, usually printed upon the offender's death, was a form closely related to rogue fiction and the anatomy. From the mid–seventeenth century to the mid–eighteenth century, British and Irish readers were exposed to an increasing range and variety of criminal biographies, issued singly in pamphlets and in larger compendiums. These biographies provide valuable glimpses of the lives of society's poorest, and have been used to illuminate the political attitudes of rural Catholics by Niall Ó Ciosáin, and those of London's Irish community by Peter Linebaugh.[90] But equally, the lives of their subjects were often freely fictionalized in terms recalling the picaresque, a tactic evident in one biography of the highwayman James Hind, which was titled *The English Gusman* (1652).[91] I will discuss how criminal biographies framed their real Irish subjects as literary rogues, attending to modulations in the representation of nationality and to differences between texts printed for London and Dublin audiences. My approach to the Irish criminal biography seeks to reinsert these texts into the history of fiction, establishing their role in the emergence of the Irish novel.

Criminal biographies are underpinned by the realities of migration between Ireland, Britain, and mainland Europe. The Irish who feature in their records were usually those who ended up in London, as the writing and publication of criminal biographies was bound up with the judicial system centered on the capital. A serial publication of biographies of offenders hanged at the Tyburn gallows, known as the Ordinary of Newgate's *Accounts* and written by that prison's resident cleric, began publishing in 1676 and continued for most of the next century.[92] Linebaugh has calculated that 14 percent of those recorded in the Ordinary's *Accounts* were born in Ireland.[93] In the 1640s, permanent Irish communities began to develop in areas of London such as St Giles in the Fields, and by the eighteenth century, such communities were well established and had a reputation for crime and vagrancy.[94] Equally, biographies illustrate routes between Ireland and Europe. A biography of the Dublin-born highwayman James Carrick describes its subject entering military service in Spain, "where he indulged himself in all the Extravagancies of the Country."[95] Catholics made such journeys for opportunities that were not available in their home country, serving in army regiments or studying for the priesthood at dedicated "Irish colleges." Many members of Gaelic noble families also found safe haven in the Catholic nations of Europe after they were dispossessed of their lands and titles in successive Tudor and Cromwellite waves of conquest.[96] During the 1679–81 Exclusion Crisis, opponents of the Catholic heir to the throne, James, Duke of York, claimed the existence of Catholic plots against the life of King Charles II. Fears of a so-called Popish Plot were stoked by the various informers who came forward in Britain and Ireland. These soon infamous figures became the subjects of opportunistic biographies, which have been read by Kate Loveman as "rogue narratives." Loveman highlights the mixture of biographical fact and fiction in these texts and the issue of trust in how readers judged informers and their accounts.[97] Biographies of Irish informers included a text about the Limerick-born David Fitzgerald, *The Wild-Irish Captain, or Villany Display'd* (1692), which is discussed in detail for the first time in chapter 2. Like many other Irish people whose lives became biographies, Fitzgerald came to public attention when living in London. His tale exemplifies how the criminal biography can provide a distinctive perspective on religious and political relations between Britain and Ireland.

Criminal biographies became still more popular after William of Orange's revolution (1688–91), which deposed the Catholic, Stuart King James II, and secured the monarchy in Protestant hands. After the Treaty of Utrecht in 1713 and the accession of George I to the throne in 1714, a wave of riots and criminal activity gripped England. As prosecutions soared, biographies increased in volume and variety, boosted by celebrity cases of the 1720s such as Jack Sheppard, known for his ingenious escapes from prison, and the "thief-taker" Jonathan Wild.[98] Standalone biographies of individuals such as Sheppard were sold alongside collections of lives such as Alexander Smith's *The History of the Lives of the Most Noted Highway-Men* (1714) and Charles Johnson's *A General History of the Lives and Adventures of the Most Famous Highwaymen* (1734). Both included several biographies of Irishmen, and Cosgrave's *Irish Highwaymen* was modeled on Smith's text.[99] This study will consider the complex view of nationality that transpires in criminal biographies about the Irish, which were often printed and set in London, but then adapted for Dublin readers in the mid–eighteenth century.

Criminal biographies were not simply journalistic records of lawbreakers, but drew upon established literary discourses through which criminality was represented, including anatomies and the picaresque. Lincoln B. Faller's distinction between two types of criminal biography is useful in grasping the diversity of these texts. Biographies of murderers were modeled on spiritual autobiographies, and tended to be didactic in tone and to emphasize their accurate recording of particulars. Biographies of thieves such as Fidge's *English Gusman* were less moralistic and more comic, imitating the picaresque.[100] The criminal biographies of the Irish that appeared from 1680 to 1750 were predominantly of the comic type, reflecting a trend observed by D. W. Hayton in which by the late seventeenth century the Irish were regarded as "figures of fun," as earlier antipathy toward Ireland's "wild" denizens modulated into patronizing amusement.[101]

This study will read biographies of real criminals alongside picaresque-influenced fictions such as *The English Rogue* and *The Irish Rogue*. In the period under consideration, "criminal biography and crime fiction . . . are often barely distinguishable," according to Patrick Parrinder, and Jerry C. Beasley similarly contends that "probably few readers in the early eighteenth century cared very much about fine distinctions between the picaresque as an established literary form and the popular criminal stories," instead perceiving an "interesting variety of rogue narratives."[102] Criminal biographies sold for relatively cheap prices, usually between sixpence and one shilling, and *The English Rogue* and *The Irish Rogue* were priced similarly on first appearance.[103] Rawlings points out that prices of sixpence and above "would surely have seemed expensive" to laborers, and concludes that "the core of the readership" for the criminal biography comprised the middling sort.[104] In comparison, novels by Smollett, Amory, Chaigneau, and Johnston retailed for around six shillings.[105] The pricing as well as the content of early rogue-themed fictions, then, suggests that criminal biographies were their immediate equivalents, not Irish novels in general. John Richetti includes criminal biography, "picaro-prankster stories," and "whore biography" under the umbrella term "criminal narrative," and points out that a comic, bawdy, and amoral tone is common to all three types of text.[106] Critics writing after Richetti have productively considered biographies of "whore" figures independently of other kinds of narrative, driven by an interest in their depictions of female sexuality and economic agency.[107] This study, interested instead in representations of the Irish, follows Richetti in reading whore biographies, criminal biographies, and rogue fictions together. The usual prices of these texts (sixpence to a shilling), along with their style, imply that they were seen as similar types of prose narrative in the period in question.

By the 1740s, original biographies of Irish criminals were published in Dublin, and the exploits of robbers and rapparees only became more popular with Irish readers as the century went on. In England, however, the appeal of the criminal biography began to wane at around the same time, and middling-sort readers became less likely to identify with the lower-class offender, as Andrea McKenzie among others has argued. A decline in the publication of criminal biographies is observable by 1770, and the Ordinary of Newgate's *Account* appeared last in 1772.[108] I will argue here, however, that the same kinds of vicarious gratification found in these texts were also available in the longer and more expensive novel in the mid–eighteenth century. Connections between what Richetti calls the criminal narrative and novels were discussed by early critics of the picaresque such as Parker, and in more recent studies: Michael McKeon argues that Henry Fielding "parodies the distinctly modern form of the criminal biography," and Beasley points out that Smollett "exploited the conventions of all kinds of rogue narrative, including criminal biography."[109] Existing work, however, displays a persistent tendency to restrict its enquiry to the more canonical British novelists. Defoe looms large in Faller and Gladfelder's treatments of criminal narrative, while a study by Erin Mackie widens the field to include Samuel Richardson, Frances Burney, and William Godwin.[110] Very little work exists on criminal and rogue strands in the Irish novel—possibly owing to a sense that such modes have little to offer Irish literature, given their association with English judicial and imperialist discourses. But this book will contend that the criminal narrative was a fertile form for Irish novelists writing between 1750 and 1790.

The Novel, 1750–1790

In the 1740s, the narrative of rogue mobility was imbued with a new impetus and currency by the appearance of popular novels such as Smollett's *Roderick Random*, the same author's translation of *Gil Blas*, and Fielding's *The History of the Adventures of Joseph Andrews* (1742) and *The History of Tom Jones* (1749). All of these novels feature a rogue-hero who is amenable to virtue rather than an incorrigible outlaw. These materials were combined with the earlier criminal narratives to form a new kind of Irish novel. The successful works of Lesage, Fielding, and Smollett were followed by a spate of what Dickie calls ramble fiction, among which were novels by Irish authors such as Chaigneau and Johnston. These novelists utilize the rogue narrative template, but from a patriotic standpoint that counters easy prejudices against their nation. As a result, taken together, these Irish novels have much to tell us about the development of a self-consciously Irish kind of fiction in the eighteenth century. They also shed light on the cultural history of masculinity, on interactions between Irish fiction and the dramatic stage, and on the political and cultural identifications of Irish Protestants in this era.

The volume of new fiction rose sharply in the 1740s, which was "a period of especial interest in the new novel form" inspired by the success of Fielding and Richardson.[111] As part of the boost to fiction publishing, more works by Irish authors were able to enter the market, including Chaigneau's first and only novel, *Jack Connor*.[112] Amory authored three works of fiction, *Memoirs of Several Ladies of Great Britain* (1755) and the first and second volumes of *John Buncle*, issued in 1756 and 1766. More prolific than either, Johnston began his career with *Chrysal, or the Adventures of a Guinea* (1760–64) and published five more novels between 1762 and 1786. Dickie has emphasized the volume of comic fiction that was written between 1740 and 1770, attending particularly to comic, biographical "history" or "adventure" novels with travel-based plots. A proportion of these "ramble" novels centered upon the adventures of young men in the style of *Tom Jones* and *Roderick Random*.[113] Indeed, *Jack Connor*, *John Buncle*, and Johnston's last two novels, *The History of John Juniper* (1781) and *The Adventures of Anthony Varnish* (1786), belong in this category. These Irish ramble novels will be placed in conversation with criminal biographies in my third and fourth chapters.

Readers at midcentury were exposed, in Dickie's words, to "piles and piles of droll narratives about sailors, orphans, rascally apprentices, and Irish fortune hunters."[114] "Fortune-hunting," or the courting of well-situated brides under false pretenses, was a charge often leveled at the Irish in the period. Literary caricatures of the fortune-hunting Irish can be found from the turn of the eighteenth century in plays such as George Farquhar's *The Stage Coach* (1704), but *Roderick Random* and *Tom Jones* were instrumental in introducing this character to the novelist's repertoire.[115] In the words of Joep Leerssen, "[I]t was especially in the novel that the Irish fortune-hunter led his most tenacious existence."[116] Derek Hand identifies the "fortune-hunter novel" as a popular midcentury form, instancing texts such as *The Adventures of Shelim O'Blunder, Esq., the Irish Beau* (1751).[117] This book builds upon these previous studies by attending to a wider range of novels, by comparing English and Irish representations of the fortune-hunting motif, and by pointing out overlaps between novels and biographies of people who were also accused of this offense, such as MacLaine. Novels such as *Jack Connor* and *Shelim O'Blunder* take place in a higher social echelon than tales of thieves and robbers, and are centrally concerned with defining Irish masculinity and gentility in relation to stereotypes of criminality.

As such, the research presented here contributes to understandings of masculinity in eighteenth-century literature, which have—again—tended to draw their examples from well-known British novels. Recent studies by Rosenthal and Mackie have read both novels and criminal narratives in terms of masculine prestige, highlighting how the figure of the disreputable rogue relates to that of the polite gentleman. Rosenthal illuminates the representation of sex and economics in *Tom Jones* by reading Tom's character in terms of the criminal masculinity found in fictions such as *The English Rogue*.[118] Mackie charts relationships between the ideal of the gentleman and the figures of the rake, highwayman, and pirate, arguing that all of these types, law-abiding or not, embodied aspects of prestigious masculine conduct. The novel at midcentury might be seen as endeavoring to furnish readers with virtuous images of men, beginning with Sarah Fielding's *The Adventures of David Simple* (1744, 1753) and Richardson's *Sir Charles Grandison* (1753–54) and reaching its apogee in the sympathetic, caring "men of feeling" presented in Oliver Goldsmith's *The Vicar of Wakefield* (1766), Henry Brooke's *The Fool of Quality* (1766–70), Laurence Sterne's *A Sentimental Journey* (1769), and Henry Mackenzie's *The Man of Feeling* (1771).[119] Dickie comments however that such "well-known sentimental or didactic novels . . . were surrounded, if not swamped, when they first appeared, by playful 'lives' and 'adventures.'"[120] Ideal characters such as Grandison were outnumbered by the tricksters and fortune hunters of the ramble novel. The popularity of novels centering on amoral, self-interested characters troubles the assumed rise to cultural prominence of sensibility in the middle decades of the century. Similarly, recent critics have questioned paradigms of politeness, refinement, and manners through a focus on the gentleman as an unrealistic or context-dependent construct.[121] In a study of elite male behavior,

Vic Gatrell points out that "[s]lumming it" in brothels and taverns was a usual pursuit: "Privileged young bucks consorted with rough low people habitually."[122] Critics of masculinity are now keen to collapse oppositions between the "polite" gentleman and the "low" laboring-class male. Attention to Irish writing is worthwhile here, precisely because the status of the Irish gentry was particularly vulnerable to being questioned or libeled in xenophobic terms. Irish claims to status in a wider British context were seen as suspect because they originated in a kingdom where the landowning stratum had experienced repeated dispossession, influx, and recomposition along ethnic and religious lines, without parallel in Britain. Representations of Irish rogues and fortune hunters have much to tell us about masculinity and the limits of politeness in this period, by adding dimensions of ethnicity and religious background to the discussion.

It is established that Irish dramatists in the eighteenth century actively contested the mockery of their nation in earlier English plays through the writing of pointedly honorable and heroic Irish characters. The Irish fiction of the same period can shed light on this process of amelioration and its underlying cultural context. David O'Shaughnessy describes a "considerable theatrical tradition," beginning with Farquhar and including Thomas Sheridan and Charles Macklin, "that sought to challenge the assumptions of . . . the pernicious Teague or ignorant booby, and advance ideas of Irish civility."[123] What Leerssen terms a "cautious amelioration of the stage-Irishman" took place between 1740 and 1760 in plays such as Sheridan's *The Brave Irishman*, first performed in England in 1746, and Smollett's *The Reprisal* (1757). Macklin's *Love à la Mode* was performed at Drury Lane Theatre, London, in 1759. In *Love à la Mode*, an eligible Englishwoman is courted by Jewish, Scottish, and Irish suitors, with the latter, Sir Callaghan O'Brallaghan, proving himself the best match by maintaining his suit even when her family are bankrupted. For Leerssen, it was Macklin's plays that led to a decisive shift in characterization, or "sentimentalization" of the Irishman, so that "from the 1760s, virtually all Irish characters on the British stage are sympathetically characterised."[124]

Macklin made his intentions explicit in the prologue to *The True-Born Irishman*, written for its London performance in 1767:

> Hibernia's Sons from earliest days have been,
> The jest and Scandal of the Comic Scene; [. . .].
> A lovely Bard this partial Law reviews,
> When social Justice fires his Feeble Muse.
> A home-bred Character he vows to draw
> In fair defiance of the Gothic law.[125]

Irish fortune hunters correspondingly fell from fashion in drama; O'Shaughnessy notes that by the early 1780s, Irish villains were virtually absent from the stage.[126] The contextual factors underpinning this shift in dramatic representations can be speculated. Is the rise to prominence of more Irish dramatists simply responsible, or did broader relations between England and Ireland play a part? Studies of Irish characters in eighteenth-century drama date back to J. O. Bartley's *Teague, Shenkin and Sawney* (1954), but no such survey has been attempted for the novel.[127] As will be shown here, several years before the influential plays of Macklin, Irish novelists such as Chaigneau and Amory were countering the idea of Irish villainy in their plots; fiction, then, did not simply take the lead from onstage trends. Rather, Irish novelists of the 1750s were innovative and outspoken in a wider British print context of anti-Irish caricaturing, evident from the volume of fortune hunter novels.

A sense of national belonging played a role in the readiness of novelists from Ireland's Protestant minority, such as Chaigneau, Amory, and Johnston, to intervene in such debates. Hand comments that the "observable increase in Irish-themed novels after 1750 can be attributed, perhaps, to a growing sense of confidence in Anglo-Irish society particularly, as the community became more embedded and grounded in the Irish world."[128] The development of a sense of Irish identity, usually termed "patriotism," among Protestants of English ancestry, can be observed in the first half of the eighteenth century. By the 1750s, a class that had at the turn of the century tended to define itself against Catholics and via its ancestral link to Britain had come to see itself instead as an "Irish interest" distinct from the "English interest."[129] The political and economic interests of the trading, professional, and landowning classes took precedence over culture, language, or tradition, in a climate in which the autonomy of the Irish Parliament to govern in Ireland's best interests was severely restricted by laws imposed from London. Protestants would have felt more secure after the defeat of the pro-Stuart Jacobite rebellion in 1745, especially given that the unrest did not spread to Ireland. Hayton points out that the period 1745–90 was both "the heyday of Protestant patriotism" and "the zenith of Protestant self-confidence," after the defeat of Jacobite hopes and before the Irish republican ambitions of the United Irishmen in the 1790s.[130] The climate of patriotism is evidenced in the fact, noted by Haslett, that Irish novels such as *Jack Connor*, *John Buncle*, and *Chrysal* "share striking defences of Ireland from common prejudice." Haslett reads this "challenge to prevailing representations of Ireland and the Irish" as part of the general experimentalism of the novel at this time.[131] As will be revealed here, this challenge often took place through plots of mobility focused on Irish men, who were either gentlemen or those attempting to rise to a more secure financial position.

The story charted in this book, then, is that of Irish writers adapting and renovating a prejudicial English discourse. A substrate of cheap, crime-themed fictions and biographies is reformed into an incipient Irish novel. The first two chapters accordingly focus on the criminal narrative from 1660 until 1750, whereas the third and fourth chapters turn to novels by Irish authors published between 1750 and 1790. The first chapter surveys the Irish writing of Head with a focus on his best-known and most enduring work, *The English Rogue*. It reveals how this writer dealt with his native country's traumatic history of rebellion in 1641, civil war, and Cromwellian invasion. The chapter considers all four parts of *The English Rogue* (1665–71) and surveys Irish references in the many later editions (1672–1786). I argue that in this work, criminality is characteristic both of the rebellious native Irish and of the English colonial adventurer. Recent literary histories still position Head as a second-rate imitator of the continental picaresque. Head is recast in this chapter as the originator of a tradition in Irish literature. The second chapter broadens out to address a range of pamphlet-length lives of Irish criminals published between 1680 and 1750. It brings together imitative picaresque tales like *The Irish Rogue* (1690) and biographies of notorious figures such as *The Wild-Irish Captain* (1692) and a 1725 account of Jonathan Wild. It compares these London-published works to narratives originating in Dublin, including a 1682 life of Redmond O'Hanlon and Cosgrave's *Irish Highwaymen* (1747). Although the English texts are more xenophobic and sectarian in their views of Irish Catholics, commonalities in plot and characterization unite English and Irish texts, together with an interest in international migration. It ends with a section on narratives about Irish Protestants, demonstrating how this class could also be represented as rogues, firstly in a fiction about a high-society courtesan, *The Secret History of Betty Ireland* (1740), and then in biographies of the highwayman MacLaine (1750).

Chapter 3 reads a range of ramble novels concerned with Ireland, published between 1750 and 1770, in relation to the criminal narratives that served as their precursors. The chapter's main case study is Chaigneau's *Jack Connor*, which is given a key role in contesting national prejudices and vindicating Irish masculine civility and social mobility. My argument compares this innovative novel with contemporary British fictions, which were in the main content to mock the Irishman as a fortune hunter. Furthermore, *Jack Connor* is placed in a wider context of Irish narratives such as *The Life and Uncommon Adventures of Capt. Dudley Bradstreet* (1755), Amory's *John Buncle* (1756), and *The Adventures of Patrick O'Donnell* (1763). The chapter reflects on how and why Irish novelists worked within or altered the crude and limited terms of the fortune hunter story, and draws parallels with contemporary developments in drama. The fourth chapter discusses two novels that represent a late flowering in the rogue narrative, authored by one of the most widely read Irish novelists of the eighteenth century. Johnston's *John Juniper* (1781) and *Anthony Varnish* (1786) are the least studied of this novelist's works, yet also the most concerned with Ireland. The chapter focuses on the representation of the Irish community in

Britain in both novels, and considers Johnston as an Irish diasporic writer living and writing in London and Calcutta. It charts how the novels responded to political developments in Ireland, Britain, and North America, with a particular focus on their responses to popular dissent and the ongoing repeal of certain penal laws. Johnston's two novels of the 1780s are testament to the endurance of the Irish rogue narrative, and its potential to adapt to new historical moments. To find its origins, we must go back more than 120 years, to the immediate aftermath of the restoration of the monarchy in 1660, and to a London-based bookseller and miscellaneous writer.

1

The Irish Writing of Richard Head

Scholarly assessments of Richard Head have long failed to appreciate his originality and significance as a writer. Chandler's foundational *The Literature of Roguery* set the tone: *The English Rogue* is "inferior in every way to the Spanish novels" because "it attempts no study of character or manners" and because of its unoriginality: "It is a mere debased copy that stole right and left three fourths of its matter from what was of least worth in its models. That it failed to reproduce more than the crudities was due to the brutality of its authors."[1] Chandler here originates two unproductive, yet durable, complaints against the text. The first is that it measures up poorly against the Spanish picaresque novels that it set out to imitate, and the second is that it is a somehow roguish work: scurrilous, plagiaristic, and hastily composed for financial motives. The use of plagiarized material in Head's output subsequently became a focus of scholarship on the author.[2] But *The English Rogue* is far more than a digest of other books; some of its most vivid parts are those in which Head drew upon personal experience, basing episodes in the rogue's life on his years in Ireland. My intention here is to take another approach to the text and its origins, emphasizing its importance in the early history of Irish fiction. *The English Rogue* will be placed in the context of the several other works that Head published featuring Irish settings, including a play, a whore biography, and fanciful travelers' tales of enchanted islands. These diverse works are all united by their debt to (and creative use of) the rogue literature tradition; and taken together, they form a sustained and original contribution to seventeenth-century Irish writing.

What follows will attest to the value of *The English Rogue* not as an attempt at a picaresque novel in English, but as a rogue narrative that—distinctively—reckoned with the matter of Ireland in the early years of the Restoration, and did so with some authority. Head was born in or around 1637 to an English couple living in Carrickfergus, Co. Antrim. His father, an Anglican chaplain, was killed during the rising of 1641, causing the family to emigrate. This sequence of events was attested to by Head's first biographer, William Winstanley, who claims to have known the author personally.[3] Head dramatized his early years in the first chapters of *The English Rogue*, and I will argue that that this Irish beginning frames the semiautobiographical text, remaining relevant to the story of a displaced and wandering rogue long after the action has left Ireland. It is established that the author spent some years in Dublin in the early 1660s, and he employed Irish settings and references throughout his writing. His first published work, the play *Hic et Ubique, or The Humours of Dublin* (1663), used his time in that city as material, and Ireland is the setting of Head's criminal narrative *The Miss Display'd* (1675). Between 1673 and 1675, Head also published three short works in the imaginary voyage or traveler's tale genre, all of which evoke or play on the legend of Brasil, a mythical island off the Irish coast. The representation of Irish places and peoples in Head's drama and fiction has been discussed productively by scholars such as Christopher Wheatley, Deana Rankin, and Barbara Freitag.[4] This chapter builds upon this criticism by means of a more thoroughgoing focus on Head's longest and most popular work, *The English Rogue*. The most detailed and balanced readings of *The English Rogue* offered to date are those that have dispensed with the comparative framework of the picaresque: Paul Salzman comments on the work's satiric energy, ambivalent moral stance, and formal complexities, and Parrinder places it in the context of English national identity. For both, however, the Irish scenes are interludes rather than material for analysis.[5] Two recent articles on *The English Rogue* by Leah Orr and Betty Joseph signal a growing interest in the text, though neither mention its Irish aspects.[6] Instead, this chapter will read *The English Rogue* through its various Irish scenes and references, in the context not only of Head's personal experience of Ireland, but of English and Protestant views of the place and its people.

The first two sections of the chapter focus on *The English Rogue*, placing this text in the context of the seventeenth-century Protestant settler culture into which Head was born. Works such as *Hic et Ubique* and *The English Rogue* participate in discourses of criminality specific to Ireland's Protestant class, presenting the Irish as wicked and rebellious, and imagining that English incomers might decline to a similar state. Early modern colonial views of Ireland encompassed self-interested, ambitious optimism about the country's "improvement" alongside fearful pessimism that it was a hostile place doomed to strife. Head, I will argue in the first section, realizes the terms of this colonial discourse through the form of the rogue narrative. The pushy, aggressive acquisitiveness of rogues is at times explicitly linked to that of colonizing agents. And equally, as the second section shows, the fatalism about morality in criminal literature—all rogues will lapse from virtue, most will end up hanged—allegorizes the future prospects of Ireland as viewed by the distrusting foreign power. Yet the implacable roguishness of Head's characters has the effect of undercutting any assumed binary between civilized and savage peoples; the processes of colonialism, plantation, and improvement are recast as petty crime. As such, Head's rogue narrative can be distinguished from contemporaneous English treatises on and descriptions of the neighboring kingdom.

Rogues survive by assuming various guises, and *The English Rogue* appears to us today as a protean and excessive text, the work of at least two authors, running to four parts that exist in many and varying editions. The original part 1, published by Henry Marsh in 1665, lacked the official imprimatur of a license and was popular enough to go through three further editions in 1666. Head was forced to expurgate some of the sexually explicit passages, and a corrected, licensed edition appeared in 1667. The 1667 version included some additional material, including a new second chapter on the history of the 1641 rebellion.[7] Head promised a sequel at the end of part 1, but then apparently refused to write further volumes after speculation that the tale was based on his own life. The publisher of part 1, Francis Kirkman, then took up the role of author, penning a part 2.[8] However, Head and Kirkman seem to have collaborated on parts 3 and 4. The consequently sprawling length and fragmented plot of *The English Rogue* are treated by Chandler as evidence that "Head and Kirkman were poor-devil hacks who set pens to paper for hire alone."[9] Both writers traded as booksellers in London, and Chandler's descriptions of them as "hacks" is imbued with lofty disdain for the author for hire. The third section discusses the later parts and editions of *The English Rogue*, returning to the dubious reputation of the authors, though in less judgmental spirit than Chandler. I contend that in parts 2–4, Head and Kirkman elided the Irish qualities of the rogue Latroon in order to distance the character from the original author. The more than usually complex publishing history of the text is a consequence of its popularity, which fueled the production of many new, abridged editions throughout the seventeenth century and into the mid–eighteenth century. The later editions and their varying renderings of the rogue's story will be surveyed in this section to illustrate that Head's rogue proved adaptable to new circumstances. The chapter closes with a discussion of several fictions published by Head between 1673 and 1675 that pick up on and modify aspects of *The English Rogue*. This last section emphasizes not only the range but the creativity of Head's engagement with rogue literature traditions, and the author's distinctive and recurrent fascination with Irish settings, characters, and plotlines.

Englishness in Head's Writing: Degeneration and Colonialism

The English identity that is evoked in *The English Rogue* and Head's other works is specifically that of those Protestants who moved to Ireland in the seventeenth century. Head's exposure to the cultural milieu of Restoration Dublin seems to have inspired his first known work, the play *Hic et Ubique, or the Humours of Dublin*. In the early 1660s, the author moved to Dublin to escape debts incurred by his gambling.[10] During this period he wrote the play, which was "Acted privately, with general Applause" in a tavern in the city's Quays in

1662, and then published in London in 1663.[11] *The English Rogue* also draws upon Head's experiences of the Irish capital, as Latroon makes a similar journey from London to Dublin. *Hic et Ubique* engages with the English view of Ireland in the years after the Restoration as a place where opportunities could be sought and fortunes made. For this reason, the play provides a useful introduction to the Irish context of *The English Rogue*. In both texts, as will be revealed, English settlers in Ireland do not prosper, encountering poverty, bodily deterioration, and illness in an acerbic reversal of the contemporary mood of optimism. Their fortunes evoke old fears about the influence of the Irish climate and culture on newcomers. Both the play and the fiction enact the blurring of English and Irish identities, and illustrate the aptness of the rogue as a figure for the questions of civility and progress with which the English in post-Restoration Ireland were preoccupied.

Hic et Ubique concerns a group of penniless, avaricious, and resourceful English adventurers newly arrived in Dublin, emulating the situation of their author a few years previously. The characters, who have names such as "Phantastick" and "Contriver," formulate unlikely and fruitless schemes to earn a crust. Their aspirations are read by Wheatley as a satire upon the vogue for improvements in industry and agriculture among Ireland's elite.[12] The attitudes and hopes of the English in Ireland in the mid–seventeenth century are well described by T. C. Barnard as an "amalgam of idealism, utility and careerism."[13] Contriver plans to transform the Irish wilderness, in the hope that "the King will confer on me little less than the title of Duke of Mountain, Earl of Monah, or Lord Drain-bog." Phantastick's intentions in Dublin are less utilitarian and more self-indulgent: "Had I so much money as thou speakest of . . . I would keep open house for all roaring Blades, and one part of my pastime should be to make 'em drunk." The adventurers soon find that fortunes are not easily made in Ireland, however, as they run out of money. Phantastick notices the poverty of a fellow Englishman: "I can hear hither thy belly grumbling out complaints against my mouth . . . I see thou hast no luck at contriving thriving maxims."[14] Although they have been contriving their own advancement, they are anything but thriving, and Dublin is thus revealed to be a land of penury rather than opportunity for the English adventurer.

The economic decline of the English in Dublin parallels a decline in their health, as Phantastick falls ill with a "distemper."[15] His fate evokes the belief that Protestant settlers in Ireland would succumb to Irish cultural mores. In the seventeenth century, new generations of English immigrants recalled the errors of past colonists who had adopted the language and cultural practices of the Irish. Spenser's *A View of the State of Ireland* decried the twelfth-century Old English settlers for "taking on them Irish habits and customes, which could never since be cleane wiped away, but the contagion hath remained still amongst their posterityes."[16] Spenser's conception of Gaelic culture as a "contagion" is linked to the common belief that Ireland's climate was unhealthy, as expressed by his contemporary, Fynes Moryson: "In Sommer it hath lesse heat then England, which proceeding from the reflection of the sunne uppon the earth, is abated by the frequent Boggs and lakes, (which together with rawe or litle rosted meates, cause the Country diseases of Fluxes and Agues fatall to the English)." Elsewhere in his "Of the Commonwealth of Ireland" (1617–20), Moryson raises the possibility of the English assimilating to Irish customs: "These new Colonyes should consist of such men, as were most unlike to fall to the barbarous Customes of the Irish."[17] The process of degeneration that Moryson and Spenser warn against comes to pass in *Hic et Ubique*. The English merchant Thrivewell ascribes Ireland's unwholesome, "rainy or windy" climate to divine causes; namely, "the windy god Aeolus, and phlegmatic Luna": "The natives yield submission to the god, for which the goddess punished 'em with an hereditary disease, called the fundamental thorough-go-nimble. I sure hath been troubled with it four or five days—."[18] The punchline here that Thrivewell has himself caught the Irish "disease" expresses more serious worries that the English would succumb to "barbarous Customes." As Wheatley and Kevin Donovan note, *Hic et Ubique* is a "humours comedy" in the style of Ben Jonson, in which the traditional humors of personality govern human action. The "Humours" mentioned in the title can be interpreted as the greed and self-interest of the adventurers.[19] As the play goes on, however, the energy of rogues is debilitated by poverty and illness. Thrivewell blames his "disease" on the "phlegmatic" goddess Luna, alluding to the humor that was supposed to cause apathy, and thus implying that lassitude is another of the "Humours of Dublin."[20] The play's narrative of the economic and bodily failure of the ambitious newcomer evokes the process of cultural transfer between native and settler cultures which was a subject of fear in English writing.

The idea of degeneration is foundational to the narrative of *The English Rogue*, in which worries about the proximity of Irish culture are also evoked through a preoccupation with the physical environment, with land and weather. Head's account of the 1641 rebellion describes close social relations and intermarrying between Irish and English in the years preceding the rising, observing how "many *English* [were] strongly degenerated into *Irish* Affections, and Customes, and many of the better sort of *Irish* studying as well the Language of the English."[21] The infant Latroon, born in Carrickfergus to English parents, becomes a case study of this process. In the preface to the uncensored 1666 edition, Head declares that his rogue is more than a match for his picaresque competitors: "I will not say that he durst vye with either an *Italian*, *Spanish*, or *French Rogue*; but having been steept for some years in an *Irish Bogg*, that hath added so much to his *Rogue-ships* perfection, that he out-did them all."[22] The idea of the country shaping the rogue's character is returned to when the narrator Latroon recalls his birth: "There is no fear that *England* and *Ireland* will, after my decease, contend about my Nativity, as several Countries did about *Homer*, either striving to have the honour of first giving him breath. Neither shall I much thank my Native Country, for bestowing on me such principles as I and most of my Country-men drew from that very Aire; the place I think made me appear a Bastard in disposition to my Father. It is strange the Clymate should have more prevalency over the Nature of the Native, than the disposition of the Parent" (7).[23] Picaresque fictions often ascribed significance to the pícaro's place of birth in this way. Lazarillo de Tormes was born in a mill above "the River called Tormes, whereof I took my surname . . . I may truely report the River it selfe, to be the place of my Nativity."[24] Guzmán reveals that his mother was a prostitute in Seville, and then dubs the city "a mother of Orphans, and a shelter for Sinners."[25] Latroon says of his parents that they "could neither flatter, deceive, revenge," whereas he can "dissemble and sooth up his adversary" with ease (7–8). As with Guzmán's reference to Seville as a "mother," the parental role is handed over to Ireland itself, which has rendered Latroon a "Bastard in disposition to my father." The text's repeated focus on Ireland's climate and boggy landscape exemplifies seventeenth-century understandings of how a person's disposition was formed, in which significance was ascribed to the climatic and astrological conditions of the place and time of birth. Before the nineteenth century, it has been argued, "[n]ature and nurture, or heredity and environment, were not yet seen as oppositions"; the native environment could have a determining effect.[26] *The English Rogue* captures this very different understanding of self-formation and inheritance in the account of the rogue's birth into a corrupting Irish atmosphere. The country's "principles" of flattery, deceit, and revenge are ascribed ultimately to the land and "Clymate," which conditions both the native population and the Irish-born child of English parents. Ultimately, climate stands in for what settlers saw as the savage culture of the Gaelic Irish; that culture is disembodied and thus absolute and unavoidable, part of the "very Aire."

In *The English Rogue*, as in *Hic et Ubique*, the English in Ireland quickly decline into sickness, vice, and poverty, and this evokes the financially straitened circumstances encountered by Richard Head himself around the time of his move to Dublin. Latroon becomes a servant to a tradesman in London, and in time gains "an House and Shop of mine own, very well furnisht" (193). However, his "exorbitant manner of living in Drinking, Whoring, Gaming" soon dissipates his profits, and he ends up fleeing to Dublin—another of the overlaps between the narrative and Head's biography (195). The city is described as a magnet for fugitives: "If any knavishly break, murder, rob, or are desirous of Polygamy, they straightway repair thither, making that place, or the Kingdom in general, their Azylum" (214). This passage implies an inevitability to Latroon's failure to live within his means or the law. In criminal narratives, the material prospects of rogues are usually dismal; Rawlings hypothesizes that middling-sort readers would have been disturbed by narratives about the socially mobile poor, relying as they did upon a large manual workforce of servants and apprentices.[27] But in *The English Rogue*, the plot of Latroon's economic decline is personal as well as conventional, as it is based on Head's time in Dublin. Latroon hopes to repair his fortune in Ireland, but soon falls back into his old habits. Losing ten pounds at the gambling table, he reflects: "By that sum I thought to have purchased Mountains in *Ireland* (and indeed there is too great plenty of them there,)" (217). When Latroon's money runs out, he suffers the same poverty and illness as the English adventurers of *Hic et Ubique*. Suffering from "the Itch and *Bunniah*, or Flux, (the two grand Epidemical distempers of *Ireland*)," he wastes away to "a mere walking *Skeleton*, my skin only serv'd as a mantle for my bones" (221–22).[28] This passage recalls Spenser's oft-quoted account of the victims of the Munster famine of 1582, who "looked like anatomies of death" and "spake like ghosts crying out of their graves,"[29] especially given Latroon's later comparison of himself to a ghost: "My voice sounded so hollow, as if I had spoken in a vault . . . others of the wiser sort believed me to be some *Spectrum*, or Apparition" (223). Furthermore, in his description of the emaciated rogue's skin, Head was surely aware that a "mantle" was a traditional Irish sleeveless cloak. The garment became mythologized as one of "the most visible signs of Irish cultural difference" in the seventeenth century, according to Helen M. Burke.[30] Spenser saw mantles as a disguise that enabled crime, calling them "a meet bed for a rebell, and an apt cloke for a thiefe."[31] The destitute rogue is described in terms recalling English images of Ireland's natives, and seems literally to don an Irish cultural identity, added to later on when he reveals the ability to speak "a little Irish" (230). Degeneration in *The English Rogue* is material or financial, but also bodily, and parallels and symbolizes the subject's assimilation into Gaelic culture.

But despite its narratives of decline and impoverishment, the text actually undercuts the logic of degeneration because Latroon's English side does not correspond with his better nature; the English in this text have no monopoly on virtue. An assumption of superiority lay behind what Barnard calls "the doctrine of improvement" as it applied to Ireland's people, who were to be the subject of "assimilation" to English habits of "civility."[32] The historiography of the 1641 rebellion reinforced the binary opposition of the two peoples, idealizing the Protestant victims as martyrs and imagining the rising as "a dramatic showdown between the saints and the Antichrist."[33] Head's writings, however, overcome this binary, incorporating both nationalities within the scope of the criminal underworld that was his subject. Just as *Hic et Ubique* depicts adventurers from London as rogues, *The English Rogue* presents English settlers in the terms of rogue literature. This is evident when Latroon sets off into the countryside around Dublin. In an extended analysis of this passage, Rankin notes similarities to past English histories and travel accounts, and maps the geography of Latroon's trip "into the Wicklow mountains, to the very edges of the Pale." Rankin concludes that Latroon is "firmly characterized as 'English,'" his adventures motivated by "fantasies of erotically inflected conquest."[34] Indeed, his encounters with locals are characterized by sexual opportunism and violence. He attempts to seduce a beautiful young woman, and when she rejects his advances, forces himself upon her. Three men hear her screams and repel Latroon with "a Flail" and "long Poles": "Pox on them they made me out of conceit with love for six weeks after" (230–32). The rogue suffers further poetic justice when he asks a man the way and is directed into a treacherous river: "I plung'd over Head and Ears, and had not my Horse been strong we had both perish'd." The Irishman's bad advice is interpreted as an example of the "causeless revenge they frequently exercise towards the *English*" (234). To Rankin, the confrontation here with "Ireland in the raw" functions to polarize English and Irish.[35] But importantly, the two peoples appear united in self-interest and malice; no binary of civility versus savagery can be sustained. The tropes and expectations of the rogue narrative undercut the terms of improvement or degeneration.

Head frames Latroon's preeminence in vice as a consequence of his Irish birth, but the English reveal themselves as rogues in the lawless terrain of the colonial frontier. In Ireland, Latroon occupies what

Brown would term the "semiperiphery" of the Pale around Dublin, but he ranges further afield after he is sentenced to transportation to Virginia toward the end of part 1. After undergoing shipwreck and run-ins with pirates, he washes up in India and is thankful to meet with a crew of English merchants. Brown's analysis of the colonial discourse of rogue literature looks westward to Ireland and America, both key imperial peripheries in the early seventeenth century.[36] Yet the East India Company, founded in 1600, was expanding in the same period in the subcontinent. Philip Lawson has called the 1660s "a golden age of English trade with the East," as the company's profits rose after the renewal of their charter in 1657. Latroon is taken to Surat, the location of an East India Company trading post founded in 1608, and then joins the English in nearby Swalley-Road, both ports in what is now Gujarat (86–87 [424–25]).[37] With his new companions, the rogue explores the Indies, marveling at the predictably barbarous customs and lascivious mores of the natives, in passages adapted from the fourteenth-century travel accounts of Sir John Mandeville.[38] Reaching Mauritius, he notes that the "Isle abounds with what the use of man shall require," including the "*Palmeto*" tree: "The chiefest commodity that this Tree produceth, is the wine which issueth from it, pleasant, and as nourishing as *Muskadine*" (102–4 [440–42]). The text imagines the Indies in terms of natural plenitude, a reminder of the earlier scenes in Ireland that elicit Latroon's desire for abundant land and sexual gratification.

But as before, fantasies of pleasure are interrupted by risk and danger. When the merchants move on to the port of Bantam in Java, Latroon becomes a rogue trader, buying precious stones on credit from a Chinese merchant, or "Bannyan," and then making himself scarce (111–12 [449–50]). He lives to regret this trick, however: "I went ashore; and walking with others of our Boats-crew in the same *Row*, (where most of our men were us'd to resort, because of the liquor that was there to be had, and a Whore to boot) a fellow came to me, with this Bannyan I cheated, and both of them with Creases, (a kind of Dagger of about a foot and half long) would have stab'd me, had not my friends prevented them, by striking up their heels, and afterwards with their own Creases stab'd them to the heart. After this, we could walk very quietly without any disturbance, going any where without any danger" (116 [454]). Again, the colonialist discourse of rogue literature struggles to maintain its exclusive and xenophobic construction of English identity against barbarism. The English merchants, "impowered by the East-India Company" to "Traffick" in Bantam (111 [449]), share their acquisitive movement, not to mention their drinking and whoring, with Latroon, a thief transported to the colonies who goes on to cheat the natives. On the periphery of empire, English and Chinese seem much alike, resorting to the same violent tactics. The Company's charter forbade them from using armed force to pursue their business interests, but in practice, their position was strengthened by clashes with rival European merchants; for example, the battle against Portuguese ships at Swalley-Road in 1615. The company was more than a peaceful commercial interest, and the dramatic knife fight is a reminder of tensions between English merchants and natives. In 1637 the Courteen Association was set up as a competitor to the royally sanctioned company. These newcomers resorted to tactics of freebooting and piracy, which led to native hostility and refusal to trade with the English.[39] Given this recent history, Head's association of his rogue with the company is not at all incongruous. For all its unashamed borrowing from Mandeville and lurid descriptions of oriental customs, Latroon's voyage to the Indies is more than a sensational, plagiarized supplement to the narrative. Ranging to the margins of empire, *The English Rogue* highlights the lawlessness of both colonizers and natives.

Just as English criminal anatomies associated their subjects with the peoples of the imperial periphery, Head's rogue narrative displayed an interest in imperial travel. Latroon can move seamlessly from Dublin to Bantam, petty theft to colonial trade, and Ireland and the East Indies thus become similar as venues for exploitative enterprise in which violence is a constant possibility. Head's ability to turn the English abroad into rogues makes his fiction distinctive in a context in which criminality was seen as characteristic of the Gaelic or Catholic Irish. Head uses the imagery of degeneration to construct his rogue's identity, alluding to fears that the English would go native in Ireland. The tropes of the settler's poverty and the unhealthy climate employed in *Hic et Ubique* recur in *The English Rogue*. It is initially stated that Latroon is a rogue because of his exposure to Irish culture. But later scenes complicate and reverse this equation; in rural Ireland and the East Indies, his experiences reaffirm his English, rather than Irish, identity through contact with strange and hostile peoples, and thus render the English colonial traveler as a self-interested rogue, seeking to appropriate wealth and exploit others.

Irishness in *The English Rogue*: Rebellion and Fatalism

The end of part 1 finds Latroon married to an Indian woman and supporting himself by trade with the locals. But Head wards off the possibility that he has changed his ways in an epilogue addressed to the reader which forecasts further crimes: "I left him [Latroon] in the East-Indies, and shall e're long discover what further progress he made there in his Cheats, not omitting the descriptions of the Places, wherein he perpetrated his Rogueries" (129 [467]). The rogue's durable criminality is suggestive of contemporary beliefs that the Irish could never live peacefully under English rule. The text opens with the 1641 rebellion, an event that troubled Protestant notions of progress and harmony and seemed to confirm a pessimistic, fatalist view of the native Irish. In the anxious, post-Restoration years in which Head wrote, connections were often made between the small-scale criminality of rogues and recent rebellions and upheavals. Parrinder points out the "conscious affinity between rogue fiction and Royalism" and compares Latroon in the Indies with "the defeated Cavaliers in exile from the Commonwealth" during the Interregnum.[40] I will argue here that the political import of the rogue is less English and more Irish than Parrinder suggests; his significance is rooted in the catastrophe of 1641, an outbreak of sedition that loomed large not only in the life of Head, but in English and Irish cultural memory.

The idea that Latroon's Irish origins are fatal, his career predetermined, is implied by the imagery of degeneration that Head uses: "the Clymate" and the "very Air" of Ireland are ever-present and

uncontrollable phenomena. The possibility of enlightening the sup-
posedly barbarous Irish was a central concern of early modern colonial
writing on Ireland. The still-authoritative medieval history of Ireland
by Gerald of Wales, *Topographia Hibernica*, had confidently stated that
primitive Irish customs would fade after their subjection to English
law. But John Derricke's *Image of Ireland* (1581) combined a "Calvinist
discourse of predestined damnation" with a "proto-racialist discourse"
to construct Irish Catholics as a people who could not be won over to
civil ways or the Protestant religion.[41] Spenser's *A View of the State of
Ireland* ascribed English difficulties in colonizing and subduing the
country to stubborn cultural practices rather than racial hostility. The
"evils" of Ireland consist, for Spenser, of "three sorts: The first in the
Lawes, the second in Customes, and the last in Religion." Spenser then
enumerates the dangers and errors of Gaelic culture, such as wearing
mantles. When these ways had been eradicated by military force, and
English law imposed, the Irish would live peaceably: "Evill people, by
good ordinances and government, may be made good."[42]

   The events of 1641, however, would belie such optimism. The
rebellion began with an effort by Catholic gentry in Ulster to capture
English garrisons, motivated by grievances including the confiscation
of Catholic-held estates during the Ulster Plantation thirty years previously, and by fears that their religious freedom was being increasingly delimited by the Dublin parliament. Their campaign against the
settlers quickly spread beyond Ulster and enlisted discontented sup-
porters of all classes. The rebellion gained the character of a sectarian
purge in subsequent accounts that concentrated on its bloody violence.[43] For English commentators, the outrages of the rebels seemed
to provide unanswerable proof of continued Irish savagery. Sir John
Temple's influential history *The Irish Rebellion* (1646) fell back upon
the staunchly Protestant fatalism of Derricke. Temple's history capi-
talized on and fueled the horror of sectarian murder felt in England,
and was reprinted for example in 1679, when public fears of a "Popish
Plot" were at their height. Kathleen M. Noonan suggests that Temple's view of the Irish "became the dominant one for more than 200
years" in England.[44] The same author has also revealed how accounts

of Protestant martyrs or "martyrologies" adopted stories from Temple, thus disseminating his opinions to a broader audience, beginning in 1651.[45] Head, ever alive to such trends in publishing, inserted a chapter titled *"A Short Account of the General Insurections of the* Irish, *Anno,* 1641" into the 1667 edition of *The English Rogue*, and like the martyrologies, this chapter used material from Temple's history.

The inserted chapter blames Catholic teachings for the worst excesses of the rebels, remembering how the "Irish Landlords, Tenants, Servants" of the English "destroyed them with their own hands. The Popish Priests had so charged and laid such bloody impressions in them, as it was held according to their Doctrine they had received, a deadly sin to give an English Protestant any relief" (14). The passage corresponds with the following in Temple's history: "The Priests had now charmed the Irish, and laid such bloody impressions on them, as it was held, according to the maxims they had received, a mortall sin to give any manner of relief or protection to any of the English." *The Irish Rebellion* presents 1641 as the latest manifestation of "the ancient malice of the Irish to the English," which is seen as an essential trait, rather than a grudge motivated by the memory of past conquests. Temple relates how the Elizabethan colonists tried all "fair meanes" in their "hopes of civilizing the people," but "the matter then wrought upon was not susceptible to any such noble forms . . . irreligion and barbarisme, transmitted down, whether by infusion from their ancestors, or natural generation, had irrefragably stiffned their necks, and hardned their hearts."[46] This language recalls conventional descriptions of irretrievable rogues as "hardened," as well as McKeon's distinction between "Matter" and "spirit" to describe the tension between vice and reform in picaresque narratives. The story's "Matter" consists of the actions and misdeeds of the rogue, and "spirit" is represented by moments of epiphany or susceptibility to virtue, which are derived from the influence of the spiritual autobiography.[47] Histories like Temple's, then, described the Irish in the terms of criminal literature, which were easily transferable into Head's picaresque narrative. *The English Rogue* echoes Temple's view of Irish barbarism as a "natural" inheritance, describing how the rebels pursued "the

English, which they designed as sacrifices to their implacable malice, or inbred antipathy to that nation" (8). The malice of Irish toward English, or Catholics toward Protestants, is "inbred" and cannot be placated, implying little hope for future peace. One influential subtext for Head's rogue narrative is Temple's view of the native Irish as a people who are "not susceptible" to civilizing influences. It remains to be considered whether Latroon remains unregenerate throughout the course of the narrative, but his Irish beginning is certainly not a promising one.

That said, the early chapters of part 1 do leaven Temple's fatalism with images of concord between English and Irish, reflecting a post-Restoration desire to heal division. Head reproduces a passage from *The Irish Rebellion* about the decades before 1641, in which Ireland experienced "fourty Years in peace," and "all those ancient Animosities, Grudges and Hatred, which the Irish had ever been observed to have unto the English, seemed to be deposited and buried in a firm Conglutination of their Affections" (11).[48] Although Head and Temple both go on to lament the breakdown of peace and the revival of ancestral violence, Head then raises the possibility that "peace and tranquility" might continue. The author writes that he has "purposely omitted" "many horrid things" from his account of the rising, "desiring to wave any thing of aggravation, or which might occasion the least Animosity between two, though of several Languages, yet *I* hope both united in the demonstration of their constant loyalty to their Soveraign *Charles* the Second" (15). This opinion is not borrowed from Temple, who wrote before the Restoration, and the passage implicitly also departs from *The Irish Rebellion* in refusing to include inflammatory accounts of "horrid things," whereas Temple's history derived much of its impact from "atrocity stories" of rebel violence.[49] Also not derived from Temple is Latroon's recollection of himself and his mother being saved from the rebels by their Catholic servant, who "imploring their mercy with his howling *Chram a crees*, for *St Patrick a gra*, procured my Mothers, his own, and my safety" (8–9). For all his stereotypical exclamations, his merciful intervention complicates the idea of unanimous Catholic barbarism, attesting to the existence of intercommunal ties. Head's representation of the rebellion, then, evidences a desire to discourage "Animosity" and foster "loyalty" to the king, reflecting a conciliatory, post-Restoration context of peace in Ireland. Head had satirized Irish Protestant ideologies of improvement and progress in *Hic et Ubique*, but the glance toward the kingdom's future in the early chapters of *The English Rogue* is more public-spirited and optimistic.

However, any prospect of Latroon's reform is collapsed in the course of part 1, in which a connection emerges between the disturbances of rogues and sedition. The text sometimes hints at the didactic structure common in criminal biographies that Faller calls the "criminal-as-sinner myth." In this plot, the protagonist descends into wickedness before eventually feeling guilty, confessing his or her misdeeds, and arriving at a state of "social reintegration and grace" before being executed.[50] Near the end of part 1, Latroon is thrown into Newgate for highway robbery and expects the death sentence. He undergoes visions of his "eternal punishment hereafter" that impel him to make a "faithful promise and constant resolution to lead a new life" (43–44 [381–82]). He then confesses to the chaplain: "The obdurateness of my heart was able to hold out no longer" (56–57 [394–95]). At this point, providence rewards the contrite rogue, whose sentence is altered from hanging to transportation (65 [403]). But he is not a convict for long, escaping his keepers after a shipwreck and ending up in the East Indies. After he swindles the Chinese merchant, he reflects, "I had now forgot what promises and vows, I made to Heaven, (when in *Newgate*, and sentenced to be hang'd at *Tyburn*)" (113 [451]). A sense of inevitability emerges, recalling the pessimistic view of Ireland's future prospects that transpired after 1641. Indeed, Latroon describes his crimes in terms recalling the larger offenses of rebels against the state, reflecting that "one turbulent spirit will even dissentiate the calmest Kingdom . . . such was *I*, that could not be contain'd within my due limits" (121 [459]). His attempts to appropriate wealth are seen as offenses against the "due limits" of status, recalling the threat posed by property crime to the middling-sort readers of rogue literature. A laudatory epigraph to the 1666 edition used similar language to explicitly state the link between rogues and rebellion:

What! More Rogues still? I thought our happy Times
Were freed from such, as from Rebellious Crimes.
But such will be; i'th'best of Times we find
The worst of men; the Law can't lawless bind.
It must be so, since Nature thought it fit
To give some nought but Lands, to others Wit,
But no Estates, bestowing such a mind
That can't within due limits be confin'd.[51]

The rhetorical first couplet compares Latroon's career to tumultuous events on a national scale, suggesting that the threat of further risings troubles the "happy Times" that were hoped for after the king's return. The "Rebellious Crimes" alluded to here are not just those of Catholics in 1641, but also Cromwell's seizure of power, as Harold Weber observes in his reading of the epigraph.[52] Nonetheless, the lines acquire a particular significance for Protestants in Ireland, given the events of the first few chapters. Rogues seek the "Lands" and "Estates" of the powerful, recalling the plantation and confiscation of Catholic lands in Ulster. Latroon's claim in the text's first pages that his Irish upbringing taught him how to "revenge" and made him "a Bastard in disposition to my father" thus becomes freighted with significance. The rebellion was interpreted and justified as a large-scale act of revenge against the planters of Ulster, and Latroon's father is "a Protestant Preacher" who is "barbarously murdered by the Rebels" (17). The outrages of 1641 are thus focused into a quasi-oedipal narrative as the son of a man killed by rebels grows up to emulate their outrages.

Ireland, then, is relevant beyond the first few chapters of part 1; the history of Irish opposition to English rule frames Latroon's career to an extent not previously realized. Rankin, for example, reads the text's beginning as constituting the limit of its concern with Irish affairs: "After these early forays into the complexities of nature and nurture, of origins and survival, the remainder of Head's picaresque romance retreats from the question of Ireland."[53] However, Latroon's robberies and frauds are themselves reenactments of rebellion within the terms of the text. At one moment set in London, his roguery is perceived, at least by his victims, as explicitly Irish. While working for a trades-man, Latroon is having an affair with his master's wife. One night, the tradesman hears the woman leaving her bed for Latroon's, and superstitiously fears that there is an "evil Spirit" in the house. Later, he describes what he imagined he saw: "Scarcely had mine eyes recovered the top of the Bed-cloaths, when I saw standing by me, a composition of meer bones, with a shrowd thrown over his shoulders, like an *Irish Brachin*, or a *Scotch Pladd*" (177–79). "*Brachin*" seems from the context to be an early use of the Scots *brechan* (cloak, plaid) rather than a ver-sion of the Irish *brat* (mantle).[54] Either way, the vision of a skeletal man shrouded in an "*Irish*" garment recalls the earlier, Spenserian descrip-tion of Latroon's hunger in Dublin: "I was a meer walking *Skeleton*, my skin only serv'd as a mantle for my bones." This episode is ostensibly humorous, mocking the cuckolded master, but it also has more dis-turbing implications for the projected English reader. For the trades-man, and by extension London's commercial classes, the Irish are the stuff of nightmares, in their emaciated poverty and their subversive intentions. Sleeping with his master's wife, the rogue is transgress-ing the "due limits" of class as well as marital restraints. The episode conveys an anxiety about the proximity of the Irish, who seem to encroach even into the bedrooms of law-abiding Londoners. Indeed, Irish migrants were increasingly present in London when Head was writing. The wars of the 1640s swelled the city's Irish population with refugees, and Noonan has shown how prejudices hardened as a result, via a study of the decline in poor relief meted out to Irish migrants. Partisan accounts of the 1641 rebellion also became popular reading material in England, reinforcing suspicions of Catholic hostility.[55] For Head's fictional tradesman, and implicitly for his readers, the Irish connote both petty vices and larger terrors, such as the rising that displaced so many of them to England—a memory that was, of course, doubly present for Head, given his own history. In his pseudoautobio-graphical fiction, the country of the rogue's birth haunts the narrative, resurfacing with the persistence of a trauma.

The national identity of fictional rogues is often represented as hybrid, a tactic stemming from efforts to exploit and rival the picaresque by presenting readers with Anglicized "Gusmans." The complex, English-Irish identity of Head's rogue Latroon is very much in this tradition. But the rogue is not "Anglo-Irish" in any stable, dual fashion, but English *or* Irish depending on the setting and—crucially—whom he is interacting with. To the people of Wicklow or the East Indies, he is an Englishman, a mobile, acquisitive incomer. But to the settled, prosperous English, he is an outsider; the London tradesman sees him as a mantle-wearing Irishman. The tradesman does not know that Latroon was indeed born in Ireland; still less that his family were Protestant victims rather than Catholic aggressors in the 1641 rebellion. In the knee-jerk reaction against the foreigner, such complexities are elided. But the scene suggests that a disobedient servant can uncannily *become* Irish in the dark, just as masterless men were seen as a nation in themselves. *The English Rogue* is a powerfully suggestive text when it comes to the manifold significances that the rogue came to acquire in Restoration England, as a savage outside the state, foreigner within it, and rebel against it. The "*Irish Brachin*" that Latroon wears has undertones of the pessimistic view of Irish culture, as a pernicious custom that cannot be extirpated. Just as the Irish retain their natural hostility and malice, the rogue is not amenable to civilizing and spiritualizing influences. Of course, Latroon is mostly perceived by others as English, and in other rogue narratives that will be considered here, Irishness often proves a temporary, disguised, or sublimated identity. In the later volumes of *The English Rogue*, the narrative itself was distanced from its Irish beginnings in a fashion that, I will argue, functioned to separate the text's original author from his criminal creation.

The Further Adventures of the Rogue: Later Parts and Editions

The second part of *The English Rogue* appeared in 1668 with Kirkman as the sole author, after Head distanced himself from part 1 due to the storm of speculation that the crimes detailed therein were based on his own life. However, Head then seems to have collaborated with Kirkman on parts 3 and 4 (both 1671), probably due to financial necessity.[56]

The present analysis has focused on the first volume thus far because it includes the fullest treatment of Latroon's Irish background. Parts 2–4 do not feature Irish settings or characters, being preoccupied by the interpolated tales of a gang of men and women encountered in India. The effect of this change of emphasis is to retreat from the questions of nationality and identity discussed thus far. Further editions of the four volumes were still being printed as late as 1786, demonstrating the lasting appeal of Head and Kirkman's fiction. These editions are often heavily abridged, testifying to the involvement of many different editors and printers after Head's death in 1686 and Kirkman's in 1680. Attending to the text's diverse iterations, a pattern can be discerned in the treatment of the Ireland-set episodes, testifying to the amelioration of English views of the Irish.

Though Latroon sometimes adopts a reflective tone during part 1, in the later volumes the narrator's progress is replaced with the miscellaneous material of criminal anatomy. In parts 2–4, Latroon travels by ship from India back toward England, a journey that proves to be little more than a frame for the interpolated tales of the ship's crew. Kirkman's preface accurately describes part 2 as "a considerable account of the greatest *Knaveries* and *Cheats*" of various "Trades," including his own business of bookselling, "which will be of very great use and consequence to any person."[57] The difference between part 1 and the later volumes is indicated by their titles. While part 1 is titled *The English Rogue Described, in the Life of Meriton Latroon, a Witty Extravagant*, parts 2–4 all follow the formula, *The English Rogue Continued, in the Life of Meriton Latroon and Other Extravagants*. In part 1, Latroon is what McKeon calls a "spiritualizing narrator," pausing to critically assess his moral state and lament his lapses into vice.[58] But in the later parts, the "Matter" of rogue literature takes over, with episodic and unconnected tales crowding out Latroon's relation of his own exploits.

Different editions of parts 1 and 2 set up various possibilities for the character development of the rogue, but these are not followed through. In an epilogue to the 1666 edition, Latroon expresses his contrition and the hope "that the reading of my life may be in any ways instrumental for the reformation of licentious persons."[59] This epilogue implies an end to the action, hence why it was discarded in 1667, by which point Head and Kirkman evidently saw the sense of continuing *The English Rogue* into further volumes. The later epilogue forecasts that Latroon would continue to commit "Rogueries" in "diverse Countries" before returning to London and meeting his demise in the Great Fire of London, "in which by just Vengeance he lost what he had unlawfully gotten, with his most nefarious and wicked life" (129 [467]). In this starker trajectory, reform is absent, with the rogue remaining hardened to the end in the manner of Spanish pícaros such as Lazarillo or Buscón. However, the promised death by fire did not come to pass either because part 4 lacked any closure, promising instead to "in short time give you greater pleasure and satisfaction, in the Continuation of our Extravagants adventures, which shall be fully finished in a Fifth and Last Part."[60] This fifth volume never materialized, leaving *The English Rogue* as an open-ended fiction. The authors seem to have initially planned a return to home ground for Latroon, as seen in the 1667 epilogue to part 1. Kirkman's preface to part 2, meanwhile, promises to "bring him again to his native countrey of Ireland, and so to England."[61] The description of Ireland as his "native countrey" is intriguing, given my broader argument about the importance of the rogue's Irish birth for his future course of life. But the overarching narrative of return never came to pass because the interpolated tales crowd out the protagonist and displace him to the margins of the story. As such, the four volumes of *The English Rogue* reinforce, intentionally or not, the mood of fatalism set up in part 1; Latroon emerges as a static criminal who is figuratively outside the law and literally beyond the bounds of the state.

The formal differences between part 1 and part 2 no doubt reflect the change in authorship from Head to Kirkman, but exchanging Latroon for "Other Extravagants" also seems to have been an attempt to avoid any further sullying of Head's reputation, while keeping the popular rogue narrative in the market. Kirkman writes that Head was "deterred" from adding further installments to *The English Rogue* because "he had reaped a great deal of ignominy by writing of that; for many people were so ignorant, as to believe that it was a true and exact account of the Authors life; especially after they had upon acquaintance or inquiry found that he was indeed guilty of some petty waggeries which are therein recited." Kirkman ascribes the "ignominy" suffered by Head to "ignorant" interpretations of the text but also admits the unhelpful "waggeries" of the author: "We suppose him guilty of many female frauds, his inclination leading him to be a lover."[62] Existing biographies of Head mention his marrying before the flight to Ireland, though they contain no hint of any "female frauds." But other factors might well have had a negative impact on how Head was perceived. Winstanley, who was acquainted with Head as well as being his first biographer, wrote in *The Lives of the Most Famous English Poets* that the author's return from Dublin had seen him rebuild his business, only to gamble his money away again. *The English Rogue* had also run afoul of the licensing authorities in 1665, after which the printers were threatened with imprisonment and Head went into hiding.[63] Winstanley remembers that the first edition was "too much smutty . . . so that he was fain to refine it, and then it passed stamp."[64] In his preface to the 1666 edition, Head reflected ruefully that "for some few years, the World and I have had a great *falling out*; and though I have used all *probable* and *possible* means, we remain as yet *unreconcil'd*."[65] This chimes with Kirkman's account that in the wake of part 1, "many people . . . lookt upon [Head] as a dangerous person, and shunned and avoided his company, lest they should be damaged thereby, or at leastwise scandalized."[66] Some readers may have been trusting enough to believe that the hyperbolic exploits related by Latroon had all been committed by Head. But even if they did not, the author's gambling, failure in business, run-in with the licensing authorities, and alleged "female frauds" constituted abundant reason to be "scandalized" by him.

The unlicensed *English Rogue* went into second, third, and fourth editions in 1666, followed by the licensed edition of 1667, all of which were published by Kirkman.[67] Given the popularity of the first part, the incentive for writing a second was clear, and so Kirkman's statement that Head did not want to be involved seems questionable. It is possible that Kirkman simply seized the initiative and wrote a second volume before Head got around to it; his account in the preface could then be read as a way of legitimating his own position as author, or even as a means of distancing the enterprise from its disreputable founder. Such speculation is given weight by Head's claim, in the preface to his *Proteus Redivivus* (1675), that he intended to write a "second Part" all along, but "the Cudgels were snatcht out of my hands before I had fairly laid them down, I intending to have had but one more bout at the same weapons, and so have compleated the Rogue."[68] If Head did have qualms about having his name attached to the text, they were temporary, as he rejoined Kirkman to write parts 3 and 4. However the later parts came about, sources agree that part 1's first readers connected the criminal narrative with Head's own history, and the author's reputation in the 1660s provided more than usual reason for this connection. It would not have helped matters, then, that Head had actually drawn on his experiences in Ireland for sections of part 1. The autobiographical basis of the fiction's Irish episodes was made more obvious by Head's publication of *Hic et Ubique* in 1663, a play about his time in Dublin. Of course, the notoriety of Head and his book might in fact have benefited the authors by arousing the interest of more readers, lending the product a scandalous appeal. But the contents of the later volumes imply that Head and Kirkman wanted to delimit any hint of Head's life and times in parts 2–4, thereby avoiding the proliferation of rumors and misconceptions about the original author. By 1668, it was evidently safer to scale back the difficult Irish elements of the rogue narrative by keeping Latroon in the Indies and foregrounding a crew of English rogues. In the first chapter of part 2, Latroon gives an account of "my fore-passed life" and "those several accidents that had formerly befallen me," beginning with his "rougeries when but a boy" and running away from home, but not mentioning his birth in Ireland or the rebellion.[69] In the reception of *The English Rogue*, the Irishness of the rogue and of the text eventually became a problem, because it led back to the life of its author, and as a result, it was marginalized or discarded in parts 2–4, thus foreclosing the questions raised by the original text about national identity.

The four parts were published first as separate volumes, but had their most enduring life in abridged versions drawing from all four parts. The first of these was *The Life and Death of the English Rogue, or, His Last Legacy to the World* (1679), a chapbook that renders Latroon's life in just thirty-eight pages. In this abbreviated narrative, the rogue's Irish birth is given little import, there is no mention of the 1641 rebellion, and the Dublin scenes are also elided.[70] In 1688, an abridgement of the four parts that exceeded two hundred pages was published by one J. Back for a price of one shilling.[71] This text provides a closing point to the inconclusive fourth part, in which Latroon finally gets back to London and repents of his sins. Orr's study of the abridgements to *The English Rogue* calls this text "the most important early abridgement" and "probably what most readers knew as *The English Rogue*," rather than the 1665 part 1 or other editions. The 1688 text had reached its seventh edition by 1723, which was still affordably priced at a shilling, and a version printed in 1759 also survives.[72] This version shifts the onus for Latroon's roguery from the Irish climate to his parents, in particular his father, no longer a pious chaplain but a rake who spends his way through his wife's inheritance in England "by running into all manner of Profuseness and Disorder," then flees to Ireland to lie low. He soon dies of unrecorded causes, providing the excuse for a return to England, the widow's native country.[73] The account of the rebellion and the passage about the criminalizing effects of Irish air are elided from these editions. Latroon does go to Dublin in the 1688 abridgement, suffering disease and hunger and taking his ill-fated trip into the countryside.[74] No longer present, however, is the narrow escape from drowning after following the Irishman's directions. In the original, Latroon interprets this interaction as an example of the "causeless revenge they frequently exercise towards the *English*, naturally hating us with a perfect antipathy" (234). The omission of such anti-Irish passages in later editions, along with the account of the rebellion, produce a less negative and fatalistic portrait of the Irish people.

A different version of part 1, published in 1741 and titled *The English Rogue, or the Life of Jeremy Sharp, Commonly Called Meriton Latroon*, gave the rogue a more Anglicized name and identity. *Jeremy Sharp* retains an account of the rebellion, perhaps in order to capitalize on the renewed public interest that would have surrounded the hundredth anniversary of this event, but it is differently weighted. Originally, Head wrote (quoting Temple) of "many *English* being strongly degenerated into *Irish* Affections, and Customes."[75] In 1741, the mention of degeneration is replaced with the more neutral "they adopted one anothers Customs and Manners." This version avoids the detail of the father's murder by rebels, having him die instead of "Terror" and "Fatigue" aboard the ship for England. The 1667 edition shows Ireland as a locus of crime even after the rebellion, when Latroon refers to Dublin as "*Divels Inn*," a hellish refuge for robbers and debtors (214). In *Jeremy Sharp*, this is softened to "I made my entry into Dublin, a place which I found shelter'd more rogues than myself." The river-crossing scene is also reworded; whereas in Head's original, the Irish "naturally hat[e]" the English, in 1741 "[s]uch mischief is sometimes in the hearts of those Savage Wretches, against those of their own Species, who have given them no offence."[76] The polarizing terms "Irish" and "English" are excised, and Latroon and his enemy are now one "species." Renamed Jeremy Sharp, Head's miscreant is flattened into an unambiguously "English rogue." The later editions of part 1 render the rogue as less tied to his birthplace, and Ireland itself as less criminal.

Though most of the eighteenth-century editions were abridged, a full and accurate version of part 1 was published in 1786 as *The Original English Rogue; Described in the Life of Meriton Latroon*. All of the Ireland-set scenes were included, and only minor changes were made to the whole; for example, the omission of the dictionary of thieves' cant. *The Original English Rogue* also includes an abridged part 2, making up around a third of the page count, but none of part 3 or 4.[77] The edition's reliance on part 1 illustrates Orr's argument that the most successful and enduring part of *The English Rogue* was "the narrative of a single life," not "the digressions about other characters and places" that make up most of parts 2–4.[78] *The Original English Rogue* further demonstrates the presence and influence of Head's rogue tale throughout the eighteenth century. The seventeenth-century part 1, with its vivid accounts of the 1641 rebellion and Head's time in Ireland, was still known and read, at least in England, more than a hundred years after its first appearance. Indeed, the later chapters of this study will demonstrate that rogue narratives were far from crude historical curios in the 1780s; new fiction was being written that fitted this pattern, and retained an interest in Irish affairs.

In Head and Kirkman's second, third, and fourth volumes, the rogue is transformed from a complex, "English-Irish" character to a static narrative device. It has been argued here that the sidelining of Latroon reflects a desire to delimit the text's autobiographical content, perhaps as a result of the controversial reputation Head had acquired by 1668. Latroon's time in Ireland mirrored the life of the author, thus inviting readings of the whole as confessional; and so the absence of Irish references after part 1 can be read as part of the distancing of author or text from scandal. But soon, the original authors were no longer in charge of the content of their text, which took on a variety of forms in abridged editions over the next hundred years. Later editors excised or softened parts of the text that might reflect badly on Ireland or imply that the Irish were particularly villainous. As the outrages of the 1641 rebels became less compellingly present over time, a climate of peace in Ireland doubtless contributed to these changes to the view of the neighboring island received by readers of one popular fiction.

Debtors and Bawds: Head's Fiction, 1673–1675

In the 1670s, Head continued to be active in London publishing, issuing a number of works in the rogue literature tradition. These ranged from criminal anatomies such as *The Canting Academy* (1673) and lives of hanged criminals like *Jackson's Recantation* (1674) to three tales of sea voyages: *The Floating Island or, a New Discovery* (1673), *The Western Wonder or, O Brazeel* (1674), and *O-Brazile or the Enchanted Island* (1675). The legend of Brasil (spellings vary) is usually assumed to have its origins in Irish folklore, though Freitag finds that an island with this name first appeared on fourteenth-century maps produced by Mediterranean seafarers, arguing that Brasil was first and foremost a "cartographic error."[79] Head's fiction does at least demonstrate that by the mid–seventeenth century, writers from Ireland were taking an interest in the myth. Only the last two voyage narratives feature

Brasil directly, but all three are stories of mercantile men who set out in search of economic opportunities. The protagonists of *The Western Wonder* sail to "Montecapernia," an evident allegory for Ireland.[80] *O-Brazile* is framed as a letter written from a Derry merchant, William Hamilton, to relatives in London. Hamilton relays the travels of Captain John Nisbet of Killybegs, Co. Donegal, who discovers the titular island off the northern coast of Ulster in the course of a trading mission to France.[81] My interest in these texts lies not so much in their representation of imaginary islands (or Irelands) as in their characterization of the adventurer, who is, in *The Floating Island* especially, a profligate and debt-ridden rogue, a farcical figure who undercuts the possibility of colonial ambition being realized. Characteristically, then, Head interwove the traveler's tale with the strategies and concerns of criminal literature. The contemporaneous *The Miss Display'd* (1675) is a biography of an Irishwoman whose career as prostitute and brothel keeper takes place mostly in Dublin. In this text, nationality is represented as complex or plural in a manner comparable to *The English Rogue*.

The first of Head's sea voyage fictions, *The Floating Island*, has been mostly dismissed or treated with bafflement by readers today. Freitag devotes less than a page to it, concentrating instead on *The Western Wonder* and *O-Brazile*.[82] Jonathan Scott calls *The Floating Island* "a spoof travel narrative of still less subtle hue" than similar contemporary works, while for Margaret C. Katanka it is "a weak satire on voyages of exploration."[83] *The Floating Island* is not a carefully constructed or unified piece of fiction, but it is of interest in its anomalous blend of genres, and can inform readings of the rest of Head's corpus. The text forms a bridge between tales of crime such as *The English Rogue* and the fantasies of an Irish Brasil that Head also authored. Its central conceit is that the travelers are not actually going anywhere, voyaging only within London, from Lambeth ("Lambethana") to Ram Alley ("Ramallia"). The diminished scale of *The Floating Island* is of a piece with the means of the travelers, who style themselves "the poor and distressed Society, called the *Owe-Much*, or *Bankrupt*," and who seek nothing more than to escape their creditors: "the enlarging of our

Territory by Discovery, and plantation in parts habitable and agreeable with our debitory disposition."[84] The adventurers wind up at Ram Alley and also stop at "the *Dutchy Liberty*," the Savoy or Duchy of Lancaster, both districts of London that constituted refuges or sanctuaries from arrest.[85] In the latter setting, the protagonists "put ourselves under the Protection of this place," where "a poor *Debtor*" is protected from "the merciless hands of his cruel *Creditor*."[86]

The fiction here comes close to reality, given Head's repeated brushes with insolvency: the loss of his bookselling business and withdrawal to Ireland, followed by gambling problems upon his return, necessitating a turn to writing for a living.[87] Head had of course already utilized his time in Dublin as a plotline in *Hic et Ubique*, and he again made use of a narrative that was near at hand in *The Floating Island*—with remarkable candor considering the notoriety that he had endured as a result of *The English Rogue*. *The Western Wonder* is structured on a similar but less overt narrative of enforced travel, as the narrator confesses that he and his shipmate "were both so *indebted* to the place wherein we were, that we only wanted a wind to Sell the Countrey." Their eventual destination, Montecapernia, evokes Ireland, Head's real-life refuge, with its landscape of "hills, mountains and boggs" and a people that "retain something of the relicts of Popish ceremony."[88] If nothing else, noting Head's continual, even compulsive reliance on autobiographical material constitutes a corrective to stock views of him as a serial plagiarist who was content to reproduce the works of others.

The satire of *The Floating Island* is twofold, directed at colonial projectors and also—on a more overt level—at the improvident lower middling sort of Head's home city. The preface claims, "I have only lash't the Debauchery of a fop-jaunty Suburbian; it being indeed a shame the City should be made by every Capering Fancy, the continual Subject of insufferable abuses."[89] The global voyage is diminished to a mere rogue's scheme, dreamed up by desperate and hapless men. Yet the portrait of the adventurer is notably more sympathetic than that found in *The English Rogue*. Guilty only of debt, the Owe-Much Society do not compare to Latroon, who commits theft, rape, and murder in Ireland and the East Indies. *The Floating Island* offers a comic exposé of Head's home city, with emphasis placed on the diversions on offer, as the travelers gamble, drink, and watch bearbaiting at "Ursina," or the new Southwark bear garden (though insolvent, the Owe-Much Society seem to possess ready money for these kinds of activities). We are encouraged to root for the debtors in their efforts to elude the law, which are described with tolerant humor rather than moral censure. A concluding section on *"The manners and dispositions of the* Ramallians, *with their* Religion, Laws *and* Customs" constructs the fugitives of the Ram Alley sanctuary as a nation in themselves. Different classes of resident are named and itemized in the style of the criminal anatomies of Harman and Dekker: "He that walks up and down a room smoking while the rest of the company is sitting, is stiled a *Peripatetick*." The anatomy is usually seen as a limited form in its conjuring of the underworld of rogues as irreducibly different and threatening to the reader, in contradistinction to the empathy of the picaresque. In *The Floating Island*, however, emphasis is placed on the pastimes of ordinary Londoners, not the crimes of an alien subclass— for instance, "a parcel of merry wives [who] frequently meet at a Tavern or elsewhere to drown the troublesome thoughts of having pevish [*sic*] aged impotent husbands."[90] *The Floating Island* should be recognized as a more than usually sympathetic anatomy of the Restoration London that the author knew, its pleasures as well as its dangers, and one that was given the distinctive gloss of a colonial voyage narrative.

Sanctuaries from arrest such as Ram Alley and the Savoy were highly appropriate settings for Head to choose, being zones where the usual laws did not apply and certain freedoms were permitted. "Ramallia" is an imagined foreign country that is really at the center of the home nation, where the norms and practices are at once both strange, escapist fantasies (for instance, a group of bankrupts who are somehow able to carouse endlessly) and the everyday leisure pursuits of London. As such, it is an apt illustration of the closeness of the "masterless" cultures of rogues imagined by the criminal anatomy as existing *within* the state, and the "savage" cultures constructed by ethnographies as *outside* the state, at the peripheries of empire. Ramallia is not, in the end, so far from Ireland—also a refuge from creditors, a place associated with escape, opportunity, affordable living, and sensual pleasure in other texts by Head such as *Hic et Ubique*, *The English Rogue*, *The Western Wonder*, and *O-Brazile*.

Following the Brasil narratives, Head returned to the rogue narrative with *The Miss Display'd*, a biography of a fictional Irish prostitute. The narrative is largely plagiarized from an earlier work of fiction, Nicholas Goodman's *Hollands Leaguer* (1632), the tale of the brothel keeper "Dona Britanica Hollandia," set in the land of "Eutopia." As pointed out by both Rankin and Katanka, the principal alteration that Head made to his source material was to transfer the action from "Eutopia" to Ireland.[91] As with *The Floating Island*, then, Head chose a realistic location with autobiographical overtones over a fantastical and allegorical setting. Cornelia is brought up in rural Ulster, the daughter of an "English Gentleman" and a mother who is "all Irish" and "became a Protestant, because her Husband (so intended) was of that Persuasion." She goes to Dublin to work as a lady's maid, but is seduced by her master, a knight. She begins to earn money through prostitution under the influence of the experienced "private Bawd" Polyandria. After some trouble with an unintended pregnancy, she rises to running her own brothel in Dublin, though this is closed down by the authorities. After a brief marriage, she goes to London and continues her career. The text ends thus: "She is now Arrived to a great height of unexpected glory . . . I hear she is now gone to *Paris* with one of her Gallants, to the intent, by her language and deportment she may pass for an *Outlandish Miss*."[92]

With the account of Ireland given in *The Miss Display'd*, Head moves away from the narratives of degeneration offered in *Hic et Ubique* and *The English Rogue*; Cornelia does not slide into illness and poverty or owe her criminal career to an encounter with Irish culture. She moves in increasingly affluent circles until the final view of her ensconced in London high society: "Her Boys are in Livery, her House splendidly furnish'd."[93] Rosenthal notes that the form of the whore biography allowed female criminals to acquire wealth and status to a degree not seen in stories of male rogues, who usually live more straitened lives, reflecting the latter form's roots in picaresque and vagrant literature.[94] The social milieu of the whore biography is more similar to that of Restoration plays focusing on aristocratic rakes and libertines. Raymond Gillespie compares *The Miss Display'd* to contemporary comedies of libertinism and reads the text as a protest against the effects of unchecked commerce on the city and social relations. Ultimately, for Gillespie, the story has some moral weight or charge, despite its licentiousness and the absence of punishment for the successful Cornelia.[95] For Rankin, meanwhile, the distinctive aspect of *The Miss Display'd* is the "cultural hybridity" of Cornelia,[96] described in Head's opening words as "*a notorious* Irish-English Whore." Cornelia is of mixed heritage from the beginning, and her identity seems to grow increasingly complex at the end, with the move to Paris "to pass as an *Outlandish Miss*." Head writes in the preface to Cornelia's story that "*I could not compleat it, since she is yet living, and gone into* France *to learn Language*"[97] (though no sequel ever appeared). She sets up her brothel in Dublin in the intermedial space of the port, "commodiously placed, both for her home-bred Customers and foreign visitants." The Irish city is represented as cosmopolitan: "Her Ears had heard all Languages that were charming, her Purse had received all Coins that were tempting."[98] Rankin notes the text's reliance on travel and lack of closure, finding that Cornelia "escapes confinement, and comes to rest neither in the novel, nor in Kilkenny, nor yet in Dublin."[99]

To elaborate upon Rankin's conclusions, it might further be pointed out that here, unlike in *The English Rogue*, criminal identity cannot be read as a cipher for either English or Irish identity; it seems to multiply identities beyond the duality of opposed colonial stereotypes. Whereas Latroon sometimes emulated the English traveler and sometimes the vengeful Irish rebel, Cornelia seems more various, a type of the city that admits "all Languages," or of the trader who accepts "all Coins." Her national identity is deferred into the hypothetical future of her "intent," into a realm of pretense and passing, and into the generically foreign or "*Outlandish*." In this, Cornelia is in part modeled on Goodman's Dona Britanica Hollandia, a cipher for Elizabeth Holland, the keeper of the Holland's Leaguer brothel in

Southwark, which operated between 1603 and 1632.[100] In Goodman's fantasy, Holland is "named *Britanica Hollandia*, by reason of some near allyances betwixt [her parents] and the Neather-lands," framing the text as an allegory for the ongoing Thirty Years' War between the Netherlands and Spain.[101] The Spanish flavor of "Dona" hints additionally at the picaresque tradition underlying the whore biography. Goodman's exoticized, Spanish/Dutch/English brothel keeper is updated by Head, writing some decades later, into an Irish/English woman headed for Paris. *The Miss Display'd* can productively be compared to later rogue narratives that also narrate Irish travel to Britain or the continent, and which represent national identity as provisional and plural.

Conclusion

Richard Head wrote the first known work of fiction to be set in Ireland. This has only really been recognized in the past fifteen years, since the Loebers's bibliographical survey provided a basis for such claims. It is still tempting to read *The English Rogue* as evidence of the limitations inherent upon what we now call "Irish fiction" in the seventeenth century. It lacks narrative drive, tending to lapse into anatomy-style episodes; it is only partially set in or concerned with Ireland; and its messiness and inconsistency reflect the peripatetic life of its author, and perhaps of his class in general. Two points can now be made that provide ways of reorienting our perspective on *The English Rogue* in order to emphasize achievement rather than failure, possibilities rather than limitations. Firstly, Head was consistent and innovative in his desire to tell Irish stories, and secondly, this crude and shocking, yet keenly read fiction kick-started a trend for Irish rogue narratives that endured for more than a century.

The English Rogue was only one example of Head's use of Irish material, maintained across more than a decade in works in several genres, from *Hic et Ubique*, written and performed in Dublin in the early 1660s, to *The Miss Display'd* (1675). No other seventeenth-century writer compares to Head in this respect. The frequency of Irish settings is both marked and remarkable in the sense that Head was throughout these years a fairly notorious figure, troubled by the conflation of his past life with the crimes narrated in his fiction. For all that, his works engaged closely with his own experiences, firstly in Ulster in the years leading up to 1641, and then in Dublin. Ireland emerges in these works as a place of strife and violence, but also a site of financial opportunity, freedom, and pleasure. In Head's imaginary, it was connected to the remote, undiscovered island, to the refuge or sanctuary from arrest, and to zones of urban libertinism such as the brothel. Ireland is a rogue place, where the usual limits and laws do not apply, and Head's interest lies specifically with the rogue adventurers and incomers who settle there. Head thus makes a substantial and original contribution to the early modern English construction of Ireland as lawless, which relied on the idea of native Irish barbarity. With his fiction, the possibilities of the Irish rogue narrative are for the first time realized.

Later editors of *The English Rogue* treated Head and Kirkman's four volumes as raw material to be altered, revised, and reassembled, rather than as a unified piece of fiction; nevertheless, the manifold editions of *The English Rogue* hint at ameliorations in English attitudes to Ireland across almost a century. Equally, the original works borrowed from and plagiarized texts such as Mandeville's *Travels* and Temple's *The Irish Rebellion*, and combined the conventions of the picaresque with autobiographical details, canting dictionaries, and accounts of the offenses of booksellers and printers. But the rogue narrative did not simply provide a receptacle for plagiarized and miscellaneous matter; it was an appropriate form for Head to work in, given his evident concern with Irish degeneration and consciousness of recent conflicts in Ireland. The conventional moves of picaresque fiction, the fatal birthplaces and narratives of decline into vice and poverty, become a means of evoking the perspective and position of the Protestant English in Ireland.

The unrepentant criminal Latroon stands for the native Irish, in the cynical view that hardened after 1641 under the influence of historians such as Temple. The English Irish rogue is a threatening, revenant-like presence for the metropolitan middling-sort readership of criminal narratives. In a context of comparative peace, he makes 1641 present again, embodying the persistence of anti-Catholic suspicions. Although he was formed in Ireland, he cannot be confined to a foreign land across the Irish Sea, as he preys upon victims in London. Moreover, with his Protestant parents, he embodies English vulnerability to Irish ways. After part 1, the rogue is transformed from a potentially moral first-person subject to a static narrative device, as the techniques of the criminal anatomy take over. That said, Head's fiction does contain less simplistic versions of criminal identity. The scenes set in the East Indies depict the brutality of English merchants, undercutting colonial pretensions to civility. And in his later *The Miss Display'd*, Head retells the criminal life not in terms of degeneration into Gaelic ways, but of pluralized nationality. The unpredictable course of Cornelia, who begins as an "Irish-English whore" and ends as an "*outlandish Miss*," resembles several criminal narratives published after 1680 that imagine Irish identity as shifting, and which are addressed in the next chapter.

2

Ireland in Popular Criminal Literature, 1680–1750

Seventeenth-century picaresque tales like *The English Rogue* coexisted with biographies of real criminals, and the boundaries between fact and fiction often became blurred. After 1680, an ever-increasing volume of criminal biography is observable. Perceived "crime waves" in the 1710s and 1720s provided continued appetite and material for biographies, which began to be compiled together into collections of famous rogues' lives.[1] This chapter provides a new angle on the heyday of criminal narratives through a focus on Irish stories, giving due attention to publications from Dublin as well as London editions. Most of the texts discussed are based on the lives of historical offenders, although their stories are often freely fictionalized. The chapter begins with a seventeenth-century fiction written in imitation of Head, *The Irish Rogue*, and also takes in biographies of two of the most famous highwaymen of the century, Redmond O'Hanlon and James MacLaine. Their stories are placed alongside a fascinating range of lesser-known characters—from "Betty Ireland," an eighteenth-century equivalent of Head's "Miss Display'd," to Irish informers during the Popish Plot and a Hibernicized version of the famous thieftaker Jonathan Wild allegedly descended from Irish immigrants.

Parts of this chapter were previously published as "The Popular Criminal Narrative and the Development of the Irish Novel," *Irish Literature in Transition, 1700–1780*, vol. 1, ed. Moyra Haslett (Cambridge: Cambridge University Press, 2020).

From its beginnings, English criminal literature gave its rogues a flavor of the exotic, as seen in anatomies featuring Irish migrants and gypsies and in picaresque translations presenting themselves as informative descriptions of Spain. The period under consideration here saw more fictions following the formula set out by *The English Rogue*, such as *The French Rogue* (1694), *The Scotch Rogue* (1706), and *The German Rogue* (1720).[2] The foreign rogue figure often provided a vehicle for xenophobia, and this is the case in the three English narratives of Irish criminals with which this chapter begins. Following the first section on *The Irish Rogue*, the second section examines two biographies: *The Wild-Irish Captain* (1692), on the informer David Fitzgerald, and *The Life and Glorious Actions of the Most Heroic and Magnanimous Jonathan Wilde* (1725). These three anonymous, London-published texts are at times crude in their anti-Irish stereotyping, and have understandably only been the subject of brief asides in previous literary scholarship. Here, all are analyzed in detail for the first time, to demonstrate the tension that arises in criminal narratives between the stereotypical national character and the unique rogue character. Such texts reveal a contradiction within criminal literature, which on one hand attempts to frame criminals as exotic and alien, but also has the potential to construct them as more multifaceted or sympathetic characters. Gladfelder argues that the criminal narrative, as a compound of disparate genres including the picaresque, was characterized by "hybridity or shifting between extremes." Criminal narratives register an "awareness of the insecurity of personal identity, of the permeability and multiplicity of the self."[3] In the texts to be analyzed, fictional "Irish" rogues shed signs of their nationality, blend into other cultures, and often prove indistinguishable from the English.

Criminal narratives were equally popular reading material in Ireland, and many Dublin-published works of biography and fiction from the same period have survived. Most were reprinted versions of English texts, but some original stories of Irish-born criminals were published: a pamphlet about O'Hanlon was issued in 1682, the year after his death. The third section will show that this corpus of Dublin criminal biographies sustains the idea of the rogue as national arche-type. Such texts can be contrasted to English representations because they accord some prestige to the Gaelic Irish identity of their protago-nists. The 1682 pamphlet on O'Hanlon and Cosgrave's later book *Irish Highwaymen* idealize native Irish Catholic rogues as representatives of resistance to colonial law. The chapter adds to previous critical anal-yses of the politics of Irish criminal biographies by attending more closely to the conventional features of rogue literature present in these texts. For instance, they utilize plots of international travel and con-ceive of character as hybrid and shifting; as a result, their rogues can-not consistently figure as Irish. These works, I will argue, share more than has been realized with the English criminal narratives already mentioned.

The last section continues to draw parallels between fiction and biography through a focus on narratives from mid-eighteenth-century England. *The Secret History of Betty Ireland*, a fictional life of an Irish woman, has been called a "forgotten bestseller."[4] *Betty Ireland* is a useful counterpart to the texts considered already as a depiction of a female criminal who is moreover from a wealthy Protestant fam-ily. Midcentury criminal narratives demonstrate that Protestants were vulnerable to stereotypes of the "rogue Irish." *Betty Ireland* can be profitably read alongside biographies of MacLaine, who came from a middling-sort Protestant family and presented himself as a gallant gentleman. As I will show, the criminal biographies that appeared upon his death viewed MacLaine in a more dubious light, and this was primarily motivated by his attempts to rise socially—that is, by class-based rather than national prejudice. With MacLaine, fortune hunt-ing became central to the Irish rogue narrative, recasting the rogue in terms of a threat to inherited wealth. The texts included in this chapter, then, cover a broad span of time, and present a range of sub-jects—Catholic and Protestant, elite and lower class, male and female. They are repeatedly resistant to national and ethnic stereotypes, dem-onstrating changing attitudes to the Irish criminal in both English and Irish contexts across nearly seventy years.

Rogue Fiction after Head: *The Irish Rogue*

The Irish Rogue or, the Comical History of the Life and Actions of Teague O'Divelley was published in London in 1690 and sold for one shilling.[5] It narrates the titular hero's upbringing and exploits in rural Ireland and then in Spain and France. *The Irish Rogue* has been treated dismissively in studies of early Irish literature, and it can be faulted for displaying little knowledge of Ireland, relying instead on durable English preconceptions. But a detailed reading of this fiction reveals an unexpectedly positive representation of the Irish central figure. Like *The English Rogue*, it makes manifest a tension between national types and the protean individual who can embody several different nations. And in this regard, *The Irish Rogue* establishes patterns in the representation of Irish nationality that are echoed in later fiction.

Derek Hand's assessment of *The Irish Rogue* can stand for critical consensus on the text, being both brief and inaccurate on details such as the subtitle: "Novels such as the anonymously written *The Irish Rogue: or the Further Adventures of Teague O'Divelly* [*sic*] (1690) reproduce negative attitudes towards Ireland and Irishness from the vantage point of British metropolitan power."[6] Certainly, the author of *The Irish Rogue* makes full use of the available stereotypes, beginning when O'Divelley informs us that his father was a "Tory, living by the length of his Sword."[7] "Tory" is here used in its original sense to mean a robber or bandit, derived from the Irish *tóraighe* (pursued, wanted). Many tories in Restoration Ireland were descended from Gaelic families dispossessed in the Elizabethan or Cromwellian conquests.[8] *The Irish Rogue* also refers to the 1641 rising in grotesque imagery designed to highlight the savagery and sectarianism of the Catholic rebels, referring to "the Grand Rebellion of 1640" as a time "when the massacred Protestants fat served for Consecrated Candles to light the Shrines of the Popish Saints."[9] The misdating of the rebellion to 1640 is symptomatic of the text's vague, distorted, and stereotype-led sense of Irish history, a good demonstration of John Gibney's point that in England, "1641 became part of the pantheon of foreign popery . . . in English terms the recollection of 1641 had an element of abstraction to it by virtue of distance."[10] The text also includes a section on "the Inclination of the Irish," who apparently "are naturally Contemners of all other Nations, and carry a kind of an Irreconcilable hatred to the English."[11] The preconception that the Irish were proud, defensive, and unfriendly toward other nations was common in late seventeenth-century England, as Hayton notes.[12] The text's reliance on stereotype rather than firsthand knowledge is evidenced when its views on the Irish national character are said to be derived from "an old author, *viz. Stainhurst*," the sixteenth-century travel writer Richard Stanyhurst.[13] At such points, *The Irish Rogue* imagines Irish national characteristics as absolute and ineluctable. The lawlessness of past tories and rebels is perpetuated by the career of the rogue protagonist, and can stand for the whole nation, who are imagined as an unremittingly hostile people.

The Irish Rogue locates the source of crime in Ireland's conflicted history, feeding into existing English prejudices. But the framing of the criminal as typical of his nation is difficult to sustain. As the narrative develops, O'Divelley's advertised Irishness becomes sublimated, particularly when he leaves Ireland. The rogue is a fugitive from justice after a robbery and a daring escape from jail. Boarding a ship to Spain, he reasons, "all the World being my Home, I knew not but my Adventures might prove as successful there as any where," imagining himself as a citizen of the globe, rather than of any specific country. He makes himself at home when he arrives in Cadiz, speedily learning Spanish: "I soon . . . could understand most words in the *Donish* Discourse." He also acquires new clothes and "appeared a Don at all points, Mounted and Armed." This persona is convincing enough to fool the natives, as he is accosted by Spaniards "desirous to be entertained with the News of the Court."[14] O'Divelley's skillful assimilation is an example of how he contradicts, rather than reinforces, Irish stereotypes, an inconsistency that is admitted in the preface: "You may be apt to imagine, a Native of Ireland (considering those people by nature are dull) could not be guilty of so much Ingenuity."[15] Later, he travels to Paris, where "I changed what Silver I had into Gold and Jewels . . . and feasted nobly, entertaining the Sparkish Ladies, and trying the difference of Nations."[16] His passing as Spanish and French is unexpected given the text's earlier claims that the Irish are unreceptive to other cultures, being "naturally Contemners of all other Nations." O'Divelley's skill at "trying the difference of Nations" might not accord with Irish stereotypes, but it is characteristic of criminal literature. Indeed, the rogue emulates his predecessor Latroon, whose name has a Spanish flavor, and who absorbs putatively Irish ways and behaviors as an infant, despite his English family. A similar transformation is effected in biographies of Thomas Dangerfield, a thief and Popish Plot informer who was styled "Don Thomazo" (or "Tomazo") in the titles of two accounts.[17] Dangerfield was of English parentage but, according to one biography, "put his name into the Spanish garb, to which he was most accustom'd in his travels."[18] O'Divelley's skillful adaptation to other cultures is thus to be expected in criminal narratives, but it also complicates the singular definition of his nationality set up in the text's title and references to "the Irish."

Taking account of the influence of the picaresque on *The Irish Rogue* complicates readings of it as straightforwardly anti-Catholic. O'Divelley's travels take in only Catholic nations, and as such, his journey might be taken as exemplary of the religious, economic, and military connections between Ireland, France, and Spain in this period. Migratory and trade routes between Ireland's west coast and ports such as Cadiz were well established by the seventeenth century, and significant numbers of young men traveled to study for the priesthood at continental Irish colleges.[19] In 1690, the French army recruited three regiments from Ireland, thereby establishing the Irish Brigades.[20] Given this context, O'Divelley's travels could be read as underlining the association between Irish Catholics and Britain's rivals in Europe, thus implying treachery or sedition from the text's perspective. However, the choice of Spain as a destination may not have been politically motivated in this way. Translations of the Spanish picaresque were popular at this time, and were cited as influences in biographies such as *Don Tomazo*: "The Cheats and cunning Contrivances of *Gusman* and *Lazarillo de Tormes* have been made *English*, out of the *Spanish* Language, as well to instruct as to delight."[21] *The Irish*

Rogue betrays its knowledge of *Lazarillo* by copying an episode from the picaresque novel about a pardoner selling fake papal indulgences. In both versions, an accomplice of the pardoner pretends to doubt his wares, and then to be stricken by divine vengeance, in order to impress a watching crowd.[22] For the writer of *The Irish Rogue*, a sojourn in Spain, a country popularly associated with amusing tricksters, may have been simply part of the protagonist's picaresque education. The "*Donish*" O'Divelley is readable as a treacherous and mobile Catholic Irishman, but also as a hybrid rogue produced by the popularity of the picaresque in English fiction at this time.

Teague O'Divelley probably takes his name from an Irish character who featured in two plays by Thomas Shadwell. Comparing the plays with the fiction reveals that the latter presents the Irish more positively, even though the works emerged from similar English and anti-Catholic contexts. Shadwell's plays *The Lancashire Witches* (1682) and *The Amorous Bigot* (1690) both featured "Tegue O Divelly," a villainous Irish priest. The earlier play ends with O'Divelley being arrested as a conspirator in the Popish Plot that had panicked the nation in 1678, after Titus Oates's allegations about a Catholic conspiracy to raise rebellions on both sides of the Irish Sea.[23] Fears of revolt in Ireland remained high throughout the 1680s, although Hayton's study of English attitudes to the Irish in this decade identifies an "ongoing process by which dread was being gradually replaced by derision."[24] Fittingly, Shadwell's plays exemplify both outlooks. The title of *The Amorous Bigot* sums up O'Divelley's double significance: he is a menacing religious "bigot," but also a laughable "amorous" priest whose desires for women are thwarted at every turn. In *The Lancashire Witches*, he conspires to rape the heroines, Theodosia and Isabella, declaring, "fait and trot I have a great need too, it is a venial Sin, and I do not care." But under cover of darkness, the priest mistakes an old witch for "de pretty Wenches," and is left crying "O phaat have I done?"[25] His nefarious intentions and comic failure distinguish this scene from the later fiction. In *The Irish Rogue*, O'Divelley is more attractive to women than Shadwell's priest, and thus overcomes the binary of "dread" and "derision" in the anti-Irish discourse of the time.

For example, when posing as a Spanish don in a noblewoman's castle, he reveals a hitherto unsuspected refinement, discoursing at length on the merits of her collection of paintings. Her passions are aroused: "Finding me thus free and discerning, she came closer, leading me into her Closet, and there discovering her Wants."[26] In stark contrast to Shadwell's plays, O'Divelley in *The Irish Rogue* is a rakish seducer who is allowed to possess the "discerning" tastes of a gentleman. The rogue derives his more positive aspects from the expectations of the criminal narrative. The seventeenth-century "stage-Irish" plays of Shadwell and others, with their British settings, position Irish characters as outsiders and relegate them to the roles of villain or butt of jokes.[27] The criminal narrative, in contrast, allows the Irish to occupy the central role, affording room for character development. Criminal lives style their protagonists as cautionary figures, but there is an extent to which they also glamorize rogues because of their intelligence and freedom from moral and legal restraints, as Richetti acknowledges.[28] This ambivalence in criminal literature allows *The Irish Rogue* to represent the Irish in a more complex way than is possible in contemporary drama.

The Irish Rogue reiterates contemporary English prejudices when it presents the Irish as violent and primitive, but its protagonist exceeds this crude definition of Irishness. O'Divelley's intelligence, attractiveness, and refinement make him a more positive figure than would seemingly be allowed by the text's view of his nation. His European travels and facility for languages and disguise estrange him from stock ideas of the Irish as savage, dull, or risible. Existing assessments of *The Irish Rogue* as a crude production, then, pay insufficient attention to its representation of identity within the frame of a picaresque criminal narrative. Moreover, the xenophobic aspects of the text did not prevent it gaining a readership in Ireland, where it was reissued in 1740. The tale evidently required some editing to fit the tastes of midcentury Irish readers; the rogue's name, which combines the anti-Catholic slur "Teague" with the satanic "O'Divelley," was altered to "Darby O Brolaghan." A claim in the original that the Irish are "the most superstitious of all nations" was excised.[29] When the rogue falls in love with a young girl, a footnote in the Dublin edition reads, "Here the author very judiciously describes the Irish beauties, who are perhaps in general the most lovely creatures on earth."[30] But the bulk of the text, including the travels of the rogue through Spain and France, was left unchanged. This picaresque travel plot enables the rogue's identity to be presented as contingent and outside the restrictive terms of anti-Irish prejudice.

Nationality and Migration in English Criminal Biographies, 1692–1725

Unlike *The Irish Rogue*, both *The Wild-Irish Captain* and *Jonathan Wilde* are based on identifiable criminals. Both titles employ the pejorative national category of "the wild Irish" (the second through punning on its subject's surname), which is glossed by Leerssen as "the Irish inhabiting the wild countryside."[31] Spenser's *A View of the State of Ireland* presents Gaelic agrarian practices such as "booleying" or "pasturing upon the mountaine, and waste wilde places" as not only primitive but dangerous, as they take place outside of the reach of English rule. Spenser describes the rebel as "a flying enemie, hiding himself in woodes and bogges."[32] English criminal narratives depict the Irish similarly through imagery of wilderness. O'Divelley confesses that "in searching after my Pedigree, I found it . . . intangled amongst the Bogs and Mountains."[33] In Ó Ciosáin's words, *Jonathan Wilde* perpetuates "an image of the Irish as brutal or barbarian" that was "general in England, particularly after the rebellion of 1641."[34] *The Wild-Irish Captain* describes the father of Fitzgerald as "one of the Cut-throats in the Irish Massacre of never dying Memory"; that is, the 1641 rebellion.[35] But the subjects of both texts fit awkwardly within the textual frame of the "wild" (native, Catholic) Irish; Fitzgerald was from a Protestant background, and Jonathan Wild was English. Both of these biographies thus exemplify an inconsistent, unstable sense of national character similar to the rogue fictions already discussed. Due partly to the international movements of their plots, the Catholic, Jacobite, or rebellious aspects of the rogue fall by the wayside as each narrative unfolds.

The Wild-Irish Captain was published in London in 1692, but owes its existence to the political climate of the Popish Plot years. In 1679, informers in Ireland began to follow the lead of Oates and allege that the kingdom's Catholics were planning an uprising that would be assisted by a French invasion. One of those who claimed the existence of an "Irish Plot" was David Fitzgerald, a tenant farmer from Limerick who went to London in 1680 to testify before the House of Lords and remained there, eventually becoming the subject of *The Wild-Irish Captain*. Fitzgerald's life and activities during the Popish Plot years (1678–83) have been elucidated in a 2007 article by Gibney, which however does not mention the 1692 biography, stating that Fitzgerald "fades from the historical record" in March 1683.[36] Criminal biographies of informers like Dangerfield and Fitzgerald formed a part of the "hundreds of titles" that fueled public hysteria about the Popish Plot. These texts characteristically link individual criminal lives to the security of the nation, reflecting the "heightened interest in a more individualized definition of current events" found in late seventeenth-century writing by J. Paul Hunter.[37] But the representation of Fitzgerald as a rebellious malcontent and figure for the Irish Plot becomes problematic because of the known details of his life. The English biography's incorporation of Fitzgerald within the menace of Catholicism reiterates the assumptions and biases of the Popish Plot years. That said, the text ultimately reveals the ambivalence of Fitzgerald's loyalties.

The Wild-Irish Captain attempts to cast its subject as an archetypal rebel whose informing was only ever a guise for sedition, framing him in terms of a static and pejorative national identity. This portrait of Fitzgerald was simplistic, as can be illuminated by Gibney's article. The biography labels Fitzgerald "a Zealous and Vehement Romanist" who was apparently jailed as a "Malecontent" after William III became king in 1689.[38] However, Gibney finds that Fitzgerald had "strong links to the distinctive Protestant colonial elite of Munster." Fitzgerald came to official attention in Limerick by claiming that a Catholic uprising and French invasion were imminent, allegations that were communicated to London in pamphlet form in October

1679. Gibney convincingly places these warnings in the context of the prejudices and fears of Protestants in Munster, a province that was vulnerable to coastal attacks from the south. The biography, however, associates Fitzgerald with the nebulous Catholic threat. Commentators in London came to distrust Fitzgerald in 1681, when he withdrew his original allegations about a Catholic plot.[39] He was accused of secretly acting on behalf of "the Popish Party" in a 1682 pamphlet that attacked the "Irish witnesses": "Though some of them (not all) did now call themselves Protestants, yet even those pretended Converts remained Papists in their Hearts, or at least, were still Irish Men, that is, implacable Enemies to the English." The pamphlet accuses Fitzgerald of sowing dissent by trying "to lay the plot at the Protestants doors," targeting his libels not at the Irish, but at prominent English politicians.[40] The pamphlet and the biography, then, attack Fitzgerald in similar terms, lambasting him as a treacherous "Popish" radical. However, Gibney concludes that Fitzgerald reneged upon his original anti-Catholic rhetoric for pragmatic reasons, due to the growing possibility of a Catholic heir to the throne, rather than an "implacable" antipathy toward the English.[41] Assuming that the informer must be a conspirator, *The Wild-Irish Captain* ignores the contingent motives that underlay Fitzgerald's conduct.

The Wild-Irish Captain is not only a partisan account of the Irish Plot, like the 1682 pamphlet, but also a criminal biography, with space for concerns beyond national security. After covering Fitzgerald's rise to prominence, it goes on to record his subsequent career of delinquency in London. The text thus illustrates the figuring of national news through individual lives, a trend that led to the ordinary life becoming of interest in itself, as Hunter argues.[42] After Fitzgerald's allegations are discredited, he is "cashiered from his higher Post of a State-Evidence, nevertheless, not to lie idle . . . he rambles about the Town in the Port of a Gentleman, and maintains his Character only by a little innocent Forgery, Cheats, and Imposture." The reader is regaled with details of "a prank he played on an Inn-Keeper at Charing Cross."[43] Gladfelder discerns a tension in the criminal biography between its "endorsement of the prevailing social and political orders" and its concentration on the "irreducible and arbitrary particulars" of individual histories.[44] This formulation aptly describes how *The Wild-Irish Captain* reinforces "the prevailing . . . orders" by attacking Fitzgerald, but is ultimately unable to reduce its real subject to a one-dimensional Irish rebel.

Fitzgerald's informing, as described in the biography, is often self-serving rather than subversive. During the reign of the Catholic King James (1685–88), he accuses the marshal of the King's Bench Prison, one Glover, of "High-Treason against the King" in order to secure the post of marshal for a friend. After William of Orange's revolution in December 1688, he continues "threatening to swear High Treason again at every turn." As the narrator observes, "It would be worth ones while to know what he means by Treason." The narrator's confusion admits the inconsistencies of Fitzgerald's position, with his indiscriminate accusations of treason. When he is thrown into prison as a Jacobite, the other prisoners doubt his radical credentials: "In this Confinement, though sometimes succor'd with some Popish Relief, being a zealous and vehement Romanist for that little Religion he had occasion for, yet the remembrance of poor Oliver Plunket, and some other very black Bars in his Scutheon . . . a little shorten'd their Doles, and curtil'd their Charity[.]"[45] Oliver Plunkett, the Catholic archbishop of Armagh, was executed in 1681 after informers alleged that he was involved in the Popish Plot.[46] Here, "the remembrance" of Plunkett's fate disqualifies the informer Fitzgerald from acceptance by Catholics. Fitzgerald emerges as a lone, friendless figure, lacking the protection of his fellow (Jacobite) inmates, while being criminalized by the new Williamite state. The biography tries to define the informer as a Catholic Jacobite, and to explain his actions via larger contexts of nation and religion, but its protagonist eludes and vacillates between identifications according to personal whim and necessity.

Given the complexity of Fitzgerald's allegiances and the self-interested nature of his conduct, it comes as little surprise when the onetime criminal takes up a role within the judicial system. Fitzgerald becomes the "Marshal of the King's-Bench" Prison, upon which the narrator reflects that he will fit in among the "Vagrants, and Varlets,

Poultrons, and what not, [which] have all along occupied the Place."[47] Marshals and other officials within London's judicial administration were seen as dishonest because they commonly bought their positions, and thereafter concentrated on making back their outlay through extortion and bribery.[48] This moment in the biography well illustrates the unpredictability of characterization found in this form. Gladfelder has analyzed the way in which the "racializing of deviance" in criminal literature characteristically gives way to the "blurring of the boundary between the deviant and the normal." This "blurring" is signified by the exposure of corruption in unexpected places, such as within the justice system.[49] This happens in *The Wild-Irish Captain* when the titular rogue collaborates with the authorities as an informer, and afterward becomes a prison official.

The boundary between lawbreakers and law enforcers is unsustainable in these two biographies, and in *Jonathan Wilde* this blurring leads to the collapse of the implied distinction between the wild Irish and the English. *Jonathan Wilde* is also concerned with official corruption, being loosely based on the life of a thieftaker. As private investigators, thieftakers occupied a similar liminal position to informers and marshals. They worked alongside constables on cases that were of interest to the Crown, but their success in catching offenders and in returning stolen goods depended upon alliances with thieves, as was the case with the real Wild.[50] This biography purports to disclose the Irish descent of Wild, who had recently been executed at the height of his notoriety. There is no evidence that Wild was Irish—he was born in Wolverhampton—and Gerald Howson, the thieftaker's modern biographer, comments on the "self-confessed fantasy" of this text, calling it a "curious production" compared to the several more accurate biographies that appeared in 1725.[51] The thieftaker may have evoked the stereotypes retailed by this text because of his surname, with its suggestion of the phrase "wild Irish." Despite its lack of concern for realism, the text was typical of criminal biographies in its brevity, at sixty-three pages, and price, at one shilling. *Jonathan Wilde* gives an account of several generations of "Wildes," ending with Jonathan himself. Wilde's ancestors are robbers who "lived in a Cave on the Mountains of *Newry*" and are "Natives of *Ireland*, or rather of the Mountains aforesaid." The text's last word on Wild is as follows: "This monster's destruction is *Tyburn*, as before has been proved by his Ancestors."[52] A rereading of this pseudobiography reveals that the crude verdict of this ending is belied by the transformations in identity that take place earlier in the generational narrative.

In this biography, Jonathan's ancestors are figures of Gaelic separateness and resistance, but later generations come to represent the English legal system. The sixteenth-century "O Neal Wilde" heads a company of robbers in Ulster who "bid open Defiance to all Government" and battle "Forces" sent by "the Lord Lieutenant of Ireland."[53] O Neal's name, "Defiance," and eventual capture and execution are all suggestive of the wars of Hugh O'Neill (1550–1616) and the Gaelic earls against the Elizabethans, which ended in defeat in 1601 at the Battle of Kinsale (although Kinsale did not prove the end for O'Neill himself, who spent the remainder of his life in European exile).[54] The text makes no reference to Irish history after this point, however. O Neal's son Patrick emigrates to England and becomes a bailiff, a trade that he passes on to his son, the father of Jonathan. The account of the Wilde family implies the domestication of the sixteenth-century Gaelic nobility from opponents of colonial rule to mediators of English law, as shown by a scene of Patrick's son, O Haro, and his fellow bailiffs "drinking a Health to their Wives, King and Country." Like David Fitzgerald, the Wildes take up official roles, and manifest political sympathies that are unexpected given what has gone before. The Anglicization of the Irish clan continues when O Haro marries a woman from York. Their son, Jonathan, is half-Irish and half-English, a position between nationalities that is analogous to his status between law-enforcing and criminal, savage and civilized spheres.[55]

As a story of an Irish criminal, *Jonathan Wilde* tries both to imagine a primeval Irish past and to ground itself in the familiar urban settings of London-published criminal literature. At the outset, the Wildes are dwelling in a mountain cave, a setting that underlines their status as primitive. O Neal Wilde then settles in the town of Armagh and becomes head of a gang of thieves. As the narrator describes the tactics of O Neal's gang, London place-names unexpectedly intrude into the narrative; for example, when a thief "dress'd up exactly like unto a Baker, and away he goes through the Strand, Fleetstreet, Cheapside, &c." The narrator warns the reader about "Fencers" and "Ratling Coves," and then admits: "These two last sorts of thief were not in being in Armagh, at the time when O Neal Wild entered into Conjunction with the aforesaid Assembly; and therefore the Reason why I mention them here, is in regard to those that have and may suffer by such an infernal Crew, which now in London . . . are many in Number[.]"[56] The effort to categorize types of thief links this passage to the criminal anatomy, and demonstrates how both anatomies and biographies utilized metropolitan and present-day settings in order to advertise their utility to readers "that have and may suffer by such an infernal Crew." This effort disturbs the text's intention to represent the Gaelic past as the source of crime. When O Haro becomes a bailiff in London, the narrator digresses on the corruptions of this office, exposing how bailiffs imprison and extort money from debtors. In the eighteenth century, bailiffs had the power to detain the insolvent, even when very small sums were owed, in private prisons called "spunging houses."[57] The narrator allows that the material on bailiffs is "something foreign from the design of this history, yet it may add something to the Advantage of Mankind," assuring the reader that "the Practices in Spunging-Houses at this day, are exactly the same with that erected by O Haro."[58] This section is separated from "the design of this history," and "foreign" to the story of the Irish Wildes. The aims of the criminal text, to warn urban English readers of timely and pressing dangers, lead to the foregrounding of the London underworld, pulling against the narrator's intention to explain Jonathan's crimes via his ancestral Irishness.

Like *The Wild-Irish Captain*, *Jonathan Wilde* sets out to root the origins of crime in Irish descent or culture, thus distancing it from the text's own viewpoint and context; but this project breaks down when "wild" Irishmen come to represent the English legal system. Both biographies emerge from a London in which the moral distinction between criminals and officials was hard to gauge, and their subjects progress naturally into law-enforcing roles without becoming less felonious. *The Wild-Irish Captain* and *Jonathan Wilde* move easily between Ireland and criminal locales closer to home, such as the King's Bench or the spunging house. Given the similarity between these cultures, the idea of the Irish as uniquely depraved becomes unsustainable. In the London-published criminal narratives surveyed in the last two sections, pejorative verdicts on the Irish national character are belied by the attributes of the central rogues themselves. *The Wild-Irish Captain* attempts to frame Fitzgerald as typical of Ireland, but this attempt is hindered by his singularity and complexity as a real subject who does not act in the ways that the text prescribes for him. The concept of the "national rogue" comes up against the fact that these criminal narratives derive much of their entertainment value from the protean identity of their protagonists, who possess mixed nationality, as in *Jonathan Wilde*, or pose successfully as other nationalities, as in *The Irish Rogue*. The conflict between national typicality and rogue identity is also evident in criminal biographies published in Dublin, as the next section will demonstrate.

Dublin-Published Criminal Biographies, 1680–1750

Several biographies of Irish criminals were published in Dublin between 1680 and 1750. Ó Ciosáin has provided the most in-depth treatment of these texts, finding that they represent Irish rogues as heroic figures of resistance to English encroachments. Dublin-published biographies highlight the descent of tories and highwaymen from the dispossessed Gaelic nobility: "The ideological context of these texts, therefore, and the principle that legitimizes a challenge to authority, is nobility of blood and the rightful ownership of land." Irish highwayman biographies are distinctive in their elevation of the Gaelic aristocracy in an era in which criminal literature more commonly demonized and mocked the native or Catholic Irish.[59] The present section nuances Ó Ciosáin's illuminating readings of Dublin highwayman biographies by attending to moments of variation in their depictions of identity. Highwaymen in these biographies move unpredictably between cultures and allegiances, operating skillfully between the polarized national and religious communities of late seventeenth-century Ireland.

Criminal literature was read as avidly in Dublin as it was in London between 1680 and 1750. Local and newsworthy crimes were retailed through broadside-length crime reports and gallows speeches.[60] Longer biographies, some derived from the Ordinary of Newgate's *Accounts*, were also available to readers.[61] Unlike the reports and speeches, most of the criminal biographies to appear in Dublin were reprints of London-published texts, not original works.[62] In 1735, the Dublin publisher George Golding advertised as for sale texts including "English Rogue," "Spanish Rogue," and "French Rogue."[63] Around 1740, an increase in the publication of original criminal narratives is observable, going hand in hand, James Kelly argues, with the dwindling popularity of the court reports and speeches.[64] Cosgrave's *Irish Highwaymen* is thought to have been first published in the 1730s or 1740s, though the earliest surviving edition, the third, dates from 1747.[65] The last page of this edition lists under "Books Printed for Country Dealers" both "ENGLISH Rogue, or Witty Extravagant" and "*Jonathan Wild* and His Accomplices," two titles that further suggest the availability of English criminal narratives in Dublin in the middle of the century.[66]

Before 1730, original criminal biographies were little in evidence in Ireland; however, one anonymous seventeenth-century text deserves attention. *The Life and Death of the Incomparable and Indefatigable Tory Redmond O Hanlyn*, published in Dublin in 1682, seems to have been an anomaly, precipitated by the death of a well-known figure. O'Hanlon has been described as "one of the most formidable tories in the kingdom." His Gaelic family were deprived of their hereditary estates in Armagh after Cromwell's invasion in 1649. He became the leader of a band of robbers in Ulster from 1674 until he was shot by an accomplice in 1681.[67] *Redmond O Hanlyn* mainly emphasizes the heroic side of the tory, summing him up as "bold, but not cruel, sheding no mans blood out of wantonness." He apparently donates some of his takings to those in need, and is lauded as "our *Irish Robin-Hood*." He is described as superior to other notorious rogues: "The Spanish Gusmond, the French Duval, and the English Rogue, were but

Puisnes in the Profession, not worthy to be mentioned in one Calendar with our *Irish* Grandee."[68] The reference to O'Hanlon as "our *Irish* Grandee" accords prestige to his family lineage while assigning him a national significance. The heroic status of tories in the eyes of the Catholic majority seems to have been cemented by their ancestry and their defiance of English-imposed law. In actuality, not all tories were of old Irish noble descent, and they seem to have robbed Catholics and Protestants indiscriminately, but they were supported and sheltered by the tenant class.[69]

The hero of *Redmond O Hanlyn* is a culturally hybrid character, comparable to fictional rogues such as O'Divelley or Head's Latroon and Cornelia. Latroon is born of English parents but assimilates easily into Irish culture, as seen when he reveals the ability to speak "a little Irish."[70] According to the 1682 biography, O'Hanlon possesses a similar linguistic facility: "It was his good Fortune to be Educated in his Youth in an English Schoole, where he attain to so complete a Perfection in that Language." We are also told that he disguises himself as a soldier in order to go about his business unsuspected, and his ability to speak English aids him in this pretense. For example, he eludes pursuing soldiers by posing as one of their number: "[H]e espy'd an English House not farr from the Road, and thither he hasted, and alighting confidently at the Gate, desired to speak with the Gentleman of the House, who civilly saluting him, Hanlin with great assurance told him, that he commanded a Party in Chase of the famous Tory Hanlin . . . he begg'd the favour of him to suffer him to take an Hours Repose in his House[.]"[71] The conventional rogue's skills of disguise and eloquence enable O'Hanlon to pass as English. In mid-seventeenth-century Ulster, "relatively little English seems to have been understood beneath the level of the ruling stratum," but the situation was changing quickly.[72] Raymond Gillespie writes that "by 1700 Ireland was, in large measure, a bilingual society."[73] The later seventeenth century saw the "disruption, penetration, settlement and commercialisation" of Gaelic-speaking areas by a new wave of Anglophone incomers, to the extent that English became "the necessary tongue."[74] In this sense, the biographer's version of O'Hanlon, given the typical linguistic versatility of the rogue, becomes a figure for the realities of Anglicization.

A life of O'Hanlon partly based on that of 1682 was placed first in Cosgrave's 1747 collection of biographies. Little is known about Cosgrave, who seems to have authored no other works and who does not appear in dictionaries of members of the Dublin print trade.[75] His Irish nationality can be intuited from asides in *Irish Highwaymen* such as "as it is customary with my Countrymen."[76] Highway robbery was uncommon in rural Ireland by the time Cosgrave was writing, due to harsh measures passed to suppress the activities of bandits from 1695 onward. Despite the decline in tory activity, their lasting appeal as antiauthoritarian figures can be inferred from the popularity of *Irish Highwaymen*, which was frequently reprinted, reaching its tenth Dublin edition in 1782.[77]

Ó Ciosáin argues that such texts maintained a wide readership because they represent tories and rapparees as heroic figures of resistance to colonial power. The robber band or gang is represented as a power structure mirroring that of the state, and "the legitimacy of this opposition is derived ultimately from the social position of the bandit himself and his command of an alternative structure."[78] The popular success of texts like *Irish Highwaymen* is undoubtedly explained by their conjoined themes of ancestral injustice and resistance to the law. However, the interpretation of Cosgrave's protagonists as figureheads for an oppositional culture ignores some of the vexed and ambivalent aspects of the rogue in fictionalized biography. Cosgrave's O'Hanlon usurps the role of the "Justices of the Peace" in Co. Armagh, styling himself "chief Ranger of the Mountains." But later, he is given "the Kings Protection for three years," during which "he remained . . . very inoffensive in the Country, and kept company with some of the best Gentlemen in the Kingdom." O'Hanlon is represented as both resisting the imposition of state power and accommodating himself strategically to it. A similar situation transpires in Cosgrave's biography of the cattle thief Peter Delany, who is also of an old "Irish" family: "Notwithstanding he was so great a Rogue, he was . . . very diverting in Company, and could behave before Gentlemen very agreeably."

Delany "gained the Favour of some of the leading Men's Sons in the Country, who endeavoured to get him reprieved."[79] The politeness of Cosgrave's bandits signifies their noble, old Irish lineage, but also blurs boundaries in Delany's case, securing him favorable treatment from the "leading" families of Ireland, a state in which political power was monopolized by Anglicans after the Jacobite defeat and imposition of the Penal regime. In Cosgrave's *Irish Highwaymen*, the rogue is distinctively made into a figurehead for older, oppositional loyalties, but equally, his verbal aptitude and mobile adaptability comes into tension with his national significance.

Cosgrave adapted many of the lives featured in *Irish Highwaymen* from earlier publications, including several London-published collections.[80] Smith's 1714 compilation, for example, provided Cosgrave with the story of Richard Balf (also spelled Bauf), and the 1719 second edition was the source of William Macquire's life.[81] Ó Ciosáin has compared the English originals with Cosgrave's versions by drawing upon Faller's typology of fictional criminals, which featured the violent and savage "brute" and the gallant "hero" alongside the buffoon. Smith and Cosgrave treat the Irish in opposing fashions, with the former representing Irishmen as brutes, whereas in *Irish Highwaymen*, the hero is "by far the dominant figure."[82] Both collections, then, attempt to make the Irish rogue into a national exemplar. But this agenda is undercut by the fact that, as Faller notes, "few . . . criminals are consistent enough to be all of one type; they shift from one to another quite freely."[83] In *Irish Highwaymen*, Patrick Flemming is a case in point, "having the name of . . . a violent Rogue and barbarous Murderer," but then becoming more heroic when he robs "the Primate and Bishop of Raphoe": "Because they made no Resistance, he used them very honourably, doing no further Damage, after borrowing what Money and Bills they had."[84] The dichotomy of savagery and civility, so often invoked to define the Irish, is present in the brutes and heroes of these biographies. But if the same rogue can act both honorably and savagely, then these qualities lose their exemplarity. Thus, *Irish Highwaymen* takes on the conventions of earlier criminal biographies, which problematize the notion of the criminal as a national archetype.

Cosgrave's collection follows its English models by utilizing travel narratives that sideline the Irish origins of the rogue. This can be seen in the life of the highwayman James Butler, which closely resembles that found in a London-published collection of 1742 that retailed for one shilling.[85] In both Cosgrave and his likely source, it is the international mobility of Butler that makes him hard to interpret as a representative "Irish" rogue. In Cosgrave's account, he enlists in "Lord Galway's regiment" and travels to Spain, then deserts to fight for "the Spaniards." But his allegiances are temporary, as he leaves the military and drifts between various employments, becoming a "Mountebank," a "Conjuror," and then joining a company of "*Banditti*" or Italian robbers. His wandering takes in Italy, France, and Holland before ending in London, where he is eventually executed for highway robbery. The Irishman passes easily between various countries and underworlds, finding accomplices everywhere he goes, as with the Italian "*Banditti*," or in "Paris, where he soon found Means to introduce himself into *Cartouch's* Gang." Butler learns to speak European languages, "both Spanish and Italian" in Cosgrave's version, emerging as a cosmopolitan figure.[86] His travels reflect the form's impulse to exoticize and hybridize criminals, as well as the trope of returning the rogue to his picaresque roots in Spain. Butler's ability to acquire languages and operate with equal success in many countries makes him comparable to the protagonist of *The Irish Rogue*. Though, unlike O'Divelley, Cosgrave's Butler is based on a real person, his resourceful and mobile character is indebted to the picaresque tradition. Even as Irish rogues are made into figures for their nation in criminal narratives, their nationality is obscured beneath other associations as a consequence of their itinerant histories, during which they seem to belong more to an international criminal stratum than to one specific country.

Two further biographies illustrate the prevalence of travel in *Irish Highwaymen*. James Carrick and John Mulhoni were accomplices who, like Butler, both fought in European wars and robbed in London. The Dublin-born Carrick joins the army as an ensign and is posted to Spain, where "he indulged himself in all the Extravagancies of the Country, rioting in Wantonness and Debauchery." When the war ends, he goes to England and takes up highway robbery—until, "another of his Comrades being taken, he withdrew himself to France for more Safety. Here he also pursued the old Sport." For his part, Mulhoni joins the navy and "served several years in the Mediterranean." He then returns to Ireland and "in Conjunction with *James Carrick*, they committed a Number of Robberies."[87] In this account, Mulhoni and Carrick migrate to London together and become part of a gang. These two biographies are both clearly based on the same London-published collection from which Cosgrave's life of Butler is derived.[88] In both accounts of Mulhoni, for example, he dies "very penitent according to the Principles of his Religion," being a "*Roman Catholick*."[89] However, Cosgrave's few additions are revealing. The 1742 collection relates how "the daily Instances of the Seizures of Highwaymen, and the constantly hanging them, so discouraged" Mulhoni and Carrick that they abandon the highways around London.[90] Cosgrave renders the passage as follows: "But the daily Instances of the Seizures of Highwaymen, and constantly hanging them, together with the small favour *Irishmen* are shown by *English* Juries, insomuch that it became a Proverb, *An* Irishman's *Name is enough to hang him*, I say, all this, considered together, discouraged our *Irish* Heroes so much that they no longer adventured to survey the high Roads on horseback."[91] The biography adds a critical reference to "*English* Juries" and also signals an awareness of its Dublin readership by referring to Mulhoni and Carrick as "our *Irish* Heroes." Even as settings shift and narratives are borrowed from earlier texts, then, these biographies occasionally reveal a specifically Irish perspective—here, when addressing the treatment of migrants in England.

The criminal narratives addressed so far in this chapter are united by the fact that they turn to the criminal's Irish background in order to provide what Faller calls "an etiology of crime" and explain why their subject turns to illicit ways. English criminal biographies in this period sometimes blamed a criminal's misdeeds on their undesirable parents, implying that vice was inherited, or alternatively, instanced a thief's poverty as the determining factor.[92] In *The Irish Rogue*, *The Wild-Irish Captain*, and *Jonathan Wilde*, vice is motivated by the subject's Irish savagery, which is a national rather than an individual inheritance. Conversely, in the Dublin-published biographies of O'Hanlon, the tory's crimes are precipitated by his family's reduced circumstances, and thus, by poverty. In either case, the criminal's Irish background is put forward as an explanation for his course of life. In the former view, the rogue is a "wild-Irish captain"; in the latter, "our *Irish* Grandee." But beyond their rationales for crime, these criminal narratives highlight the limits of nationality, raising the question of how Irishness is constituted. In Cosgrave's *Irish Highwaymen*, moral states are erratic, meaning that qualities that are constructed as nationally characteristic, such as savagery or civility, are freely adapted and shed during these unpredictable narratives. The works analyzed thus far share a loose conception of identity in which signs of cultural belonging such as language and political sympathy can vary. Tropes of the criminal narrative such as disguise, travel, and social mobility ultimately make the rogue seem less Irish, or challenge the definitions of the Irish made available by the texts themselves.

Religion and Class in Midcentury English Criminal Narratives

When criminal literature turned its attention to Ireland in this period, it usually focused on the Catholic Irish. In the narratives read thus far, Catholicism constitutes a part of the quintessential Irishness that is ascribed to rogues—even when the historical subject did not fit this frame, as with David Fitzgerald in *The Wild-Irish Captain*. Irish nationality was often assumed in England to be coterminous with Catholicism, and all of the criminals featured in Cosgrave's *Irish Highwaymen* were of native Irish or Catholic extraction. By the 1740s, Ireland's Anglican elite had begun to think of themselves as Irish, rather than insisting on their (often English) descent, and were viewed in Britain as such.[93] This expansion in the concept of nationality registers in criminal literature. Works such as *The Secret History of Betty Ireland* and two biographies of MacLaine, both published in 1750, incorporate their Protestant subjects within anti-Irish discourses of national criminality. These midcentury criminal narratives also inaugurate a process of transition in the social milieu and modus operandi of the rogue, who is transported from low into high society, to perpetrate frauds and deceptions in the marriage market, which are less likely to end in capital punishment, but are held to be even more despicable.

Betty Ireland was first published in London in 1740 or 1741 and in Dublin in 1742 and remained in print throughout the century. Ten editions are recorded before 1800, one of which, from 1765, was the "sixth edition" and priced at an affordable sixpence.[94] The male rogues of the criminal narrative are often presented in national terms, and the female protagonists of whore biographies were no different. *Betty Ireland* carries the following epigraph: "*Read* Flanders Moll, *the* German Princess *scan, / Then match our* Irish Betty *if you can.*"[95] Betty Ireland is immediately placed alongside infamous women whose names connote the foreign. The assumed surname of Daniel Defoe's heroine evokes the Low Countries as well as the Flanders lace that she steals during one of her exploits.[96] The "German Princess" was Mary Carleton, a Canterbury-born thief who, according to Alexander Smith, pretended that her parents were nobles from Cologne.[97] The heroine of *Betty Ireland* is also given a national alias in place of a real name. As the narrator tells us, "I have avoided to make mention of her Sir-name, in the room of which I have substituted that of the Country wherein she was born."[98] *Betty Ireland* is an example of how the prostitute narrative commonly "exoticized" its heroines, in the view of Rosenthal, by association with non-English cultures, including the subjugated peoples of Britain's colonies. Through these associations, and through their practicing a form of illicit or "infamous commerce," prostitutes "served as disturbing reminders" of "networks of global trade [and] colonial exploitation."[99] Betty might represent the Irish, but whether she is a figure for the exploited or colonized is debatable, given her upper-order status. She is the granddaughter of an English peer and daughter of a captain in the Williamite army, and possesses "the Advantages of the best Education," details that imply a Protestant background.[100]

Betty Ireland demonstrates how the subjects of criminal narratives depart from conventional social attachments such as family when they commence crime, and can even become estranged from their nation. Betty's licentious career begins when she abandons her role as a mother for the temptation-filled cities of Dublin and, subsequently, London.[101] For Rosenthal, the prostitute's national associations are transitory qualities in the open and fluid world of urban commerce in which they participate: "These characters function, perhaps unexpectedly, as both morally condemned, sexually objectified, and/or exoticized 'others,' but also as reference points for a range of readers faced with a newly commercialized culture."[102] Rosenthal's linking of exoticism and commerce well describes the way in which Betty conceals her origins in order to secure clients in London: "She looked upon the Playhouse as the best Market for her; and she went several Nights to the Pit in a Mask, before she could meet with anything to her Advantage. At last, she was accosted by Lord C——, who was . . . captivated with her Wit and Humour[.]"[103] This scene is possibly modeled on the opening passages of Eliza Haywood's *Fantomina, or Love in a Maze* (1725), in which the heroine attends the playhouse in disguise as a "prostitute" in order to win the esteem of men, including "the accomplish'd Beauplaisir," who is impressed by her "turn of Wit, and a genteel manner in her Raillery."[104] Lord C—— is keen to know more of Betty, and makes enquiries at her lodgings, but the landlady "could not give his Lordship any Satisfaction on that point; she believed her to be a Stranger to the Town." Betty cultivates an alluring mystery, hiding her background as a newly arrived Irishwoman. Lord C—— comments on her ability to "metamorphose yourself into as many Shapes as Proteus," [105] again recalling Fantomina, throughout which the heroine pretends to be several different women to maintain her allure for Beauplaisir, from the playgoing courtesan to a chambermaid. *Betty Ireland* can also be compared to an Irish predecessor, Head's *The Miss Display'd*. Cornelia runs a brothel in London where "all her entertainments (Proteus like) were full of variety and changes."[106] As in the narratives about male rogues considered earlier, female identity becomes "Proteus like" in the whore biography when the subject commences her trade. *The Miss Display'd* and *Betty Ireland* imagine the business of prostitution in terms of the elision of origins, enabled by the myriad variety of urban life.

Betty might conceal her Irish roots in the public realm, but *Betty Ireland* nevertheless registers the expansion of Irishness by the mid–eighteenth century to include Protestants of English descent. This is revealed by a comparison with the mid-seventeenth-century fictions discussed in the previous chapter. Protestants in seventeenth-century Ireland saw themselves as "the English in Ireland," as opposed to "the popish natives."[107] For Head, parentage dictates nationality, as the title of *The English Rogue* indicates. Cornelia's father is "an English Gentleman" in Ulster, and her mother is "all Irish," leading to the daughter being described as "a notorious Irish-English whore."[108] English ancestry, no matter how far removed, is of large significance, and the mother's relations are said to "never suffer any of their Family to commix, or Match with any of English Extraction."[109] But by the 1740s, Betty can be dubbed "Betty Ireland" because of her birthplace, and despite her English family. Though Betty hides her origins in London, she is still framed in specifically Irish terms. She runs into a former client who "accosted her in a very rough Manner, exposing her as a Bawd . . . *Betty*, who wanted not a native Assurance, brazened it out to the last Degree."[110] Betty's confident "Assurance" was a quality that "came to be connected particularly with the Irish" in plays of the period, as noted by Hayton. Before the Williamite Wars, these stereotypes were leveled purely at the Catholic Irish, but as the eighteenth century wore on, Ireland's Protestant ruling class increasingly came to claim an identity separate from the English, founded on their separate political and economic interests. Accordingly, the descendants of settlers were increasingly presented as Irish in English literature.[111] Betty's Irishness is emphasized at the end of the story, when she returns to Ireland to open and run a theater in Cork—a suitable career given her facility for disguise.[112] She also associates with other Irish criminals in England, such as Will, "an Irish Gentleman, who lived by his Wits." The narrative relates how Will "began, with the Assistance of Betty, to play the common Cheat," swindling tradesmen out of clothes and valuables.[113] Betty and Will's "common Cheat[s]" link them to the lower-class rogues of earlier criminal narratives, but their status shows what Hayton calls "the gentrification of the Irish stereotype."[114] The gentrification of the Irish rogue is also observable in several novels published after 1750 that will be the focus of later chapters.

A successful midcentury fiction about the Irish, *Betty Ireland* would seem to be a product primarily of English discourses, given that it first appeared and was republished most frequently in London; the only known Dublin imprint is that cited here. However, in the 1750s, satirists in Dublin would appropriate the character of Betty Ireland as a figure for her country, writing from a "patriot" perspective that sought greater autonomy for the Irish Parliament. Several allegorical fictions about the predicament of "Betty Ireland" were published between 1752 and 1756 in response to the so-called money bill dispute in Parliament over whose right it was to decide how a surplus of revenue should be spent, the Irish House of Commons or the Crown. These include Sir Richard Cox's *The True Life of Betty Ireland* (1753), an allegory about the difficult relationship between Betty and "her elder sister Blanch of Britain."[115] These works do not share the criminal content of the original *Secret History of Betty Ireland*, instead featuring elite protagonists and country estate settings in a fashion reminiscent of Swift's allegory of Anglo-Irish relations, *The Story of the Injured Lady* (1746).[116]

The gentrification of the Irish rogue at midcentury is encapsulated by the career and profile of James MacLaine, who was dubbed "the gentleman highwayman" due to his high-society connections in London. MacLaine acquired a reputation for genteel refinement among his admirers, but criminal biographies view his social mobility more dubiously. In seeking to expose him as a fraudulent pretender to status, they predictably fall back on attacking his nationality. MacLaine was born in Co. Monaghan and was the son of a Presbyterian minister, Thomas MacLaine. Arriving in England around 1743, he committed his first armed robberies in 1748 or 1749 on the outskirts of London with his accomplice William Plunket. He was arrested in July 1750 and hanged on October 3. During this brief period, he became a celebrity, the subject of many newspaper reports, visual prints, and prose accounts, and a visitors' attraction during his confinement in Newgate.[117] Robert Shoemaker and Tim Hitchcock argue that

MacLaine actively manipulated his image to earn the sympathy of the public, in part through his well-mannered and remorseful behavior in the dock.[118] One of the criminal biographies, *The Genuine Account of the Life and Actions of James Maclean* (1750), observed that "he has so far wrought Himself into the Esteem of Persons of Rank, that they have not only been induced to contribute to support him in Splendor while under Confinement, but to sollicit and use their utmost Interest to save him."[119] The *Genuine Account* was published in the same year as another biography, *A Complete History of James Maclean, the Gentleman Highwayman*, which was priced at one shilling.[120] Also extant is a first-person account of MacLaine's last days, Reverend Fifield Allen's *An Account of the Behaviour of Mr. James Maclaine from the Time of his Condemnation to the Day of his Execution* (1750), priced at sixpence. Allen, a Presbyterian minister, presents MacLaine as repentant and his family as pious and respectable: "Upon my saying, I had heard that his Father was a Minister in *Ireland*, he burst into a sudden Flood of Tears; and said, Yes, Sir, my dear Father, was a Minister of the same Denomination with yourself, who, as long as he lived, took care of my Education and Principles."[121] Allen's positive depiction of MacLaine suggests that his middling-sort Protestant origins were what distinguished him from the thuggish Irish rogues described in earlier English collections such as Alexander Smith's, underlying his image as the gentleman highwayman. Indeed, all three texts make much of MacLaine's devout family, including interpolated letters to the robber from his brother Archibald, also a minister in The Hague, functioning as a kind of documentary proof of his inchoate virtue.[122]

The two full-length biographies of MacLaine that appeared in 1750, however, stand apart from the public adulation of the robber, reacting skeptically to his claims to be a gentleman. The *Genuine Account* does so through Irish stereotyping, as seen when MacLaine "addressed" a superior "with the natural assurance of ——," and is later said to be part of "a gang of Irish Rapperees [*sic*], gamesters, fortune-hunters, or brothers in iniquity, which infest the court-end of town."[123] Irish gangs were known to operate in London; for instance, the group of "footpads" around James Carrick and John Mulhoni (both familiar from Cosgrave's *Irish Highwaymen*), comprising "thirty-two known members," many of them immigrants from Ireland.[124] The notoriety of Carrick's gang in the 1720s, Shoemaker argues, led to a popular perception that "street robbers" who operated on foot were a particularly brutal and disgraceful type of thief, as opposed to the horse-riding highwaymen.[125] The biography's assertion that MacLaine was part of an Irish gang, then, would have invoked negative connotations for the London reader, placing him squarely in an underclass milieu, as opposed to the genteel connotations and connections that MacLaine came to possess at the height of his fame.

Like the fictional Betty Ireland, the Protestant criminal MacLaine is very much eligible for anti-Irish stereotyping, and this has a reactive and class-based element, seeking to reestablish social hierarchies and reject the immigrant. Hitchcock and Shoemaker reflect that "[n]ot everyone was taken in" by MacLaine's claims to gentility, and point out the condescending tone of both biographies as proof.[126] In the *Genuine Account*, after coming to London MacLaine is said to dress "in a very grand Manner . . . but was always slighted by People of Sense and Discernment, who can always discover in the most dazling [*sic*] Dress, Assurance and Insolence from good Breeding."[127] *A Complete History of James Maclean* was published later than *A Genuine Account*, after the robber's death. In its assessment, MacLaine's main weakness was "an immoderate Desire of appearing a gay, fine Gentleman." The biography concludes: "Thus ended this famous Man, in whose Life we may observe, that he had but one predominant Foible, that is, an extraordinary itch for a gay Appearance, and that to maintain this, he had from his Infancy proposed to himself no other Scheme but by seducing some Woman of Fortune to marry him."[128] It is true that English highwaymen were also liable to dismissal on grounds of their suspect gentility, especially after 1750, as McKenzie shows in an analysis of several biographies.[129] Skepticism of the gentleman highwayman at midcentury can be situated within changing attitudes toward violent property crime and increased class consciousness among the middling and upper orders.[130] But in the case of the decade's most famous highwayman, there was a crucial element of English xenophobia to the reaction; as an Irishman, his claim to gentility was made still more frail or liable to attack than his English contemporaries.

In the biographies of MacLaine, fortune hunting becomes a major part of the Irish rogue narrative for the first time. While the *Genuine Account* concentrates on robbery, devoting more than two-thirds of its page count to MacLaine and Plunket's career on the road, the longer *Complete History* expands upon his life prior to 1748, and stresses "his favourite Scheme of Fortune-Hunting."[131] His "favourite Scheme" is associated implicitly with his nationality, as the women he targets are often Irish; he is pictured "depending for Support on the famous Miss —— his Country-woman, then in high vogue," before a different "noted Lady of Quality, likewise of his Nation" acts as his "Female Keeper."[132] Young, lower-class men who provided sexual services to wealthy women were termed "stallions," and Rosenthal finds that such men "were often imagined as exotic—frequently Irish," making them similar to their female equivalents in whore biographies. MacLaine's treatment of women, then, found parallels in social commentary more broadly in the 1740s and 1750s, when male prostitution was seen as a particularly prevalent vice to be excoriated. Crucially, the fortune hunter was "a more dangerous version of the ordinary stallion" because of his ability to actually possess his wife's property.[133] It is telling that in the *Complete History*, MacLaine's various marital plots are never successful. Early in the narrative, he moves from Monaghan to Dublin in search of "Fortune by Marriage," but cannot insert himself into the requisite circles and returns to his family in disgrace. Later, Plunket and MacLaine attempt to inveigle their way into the esteem of a young woman living outside London, pretending that MacLaine is an Irish "Lord" and Plunket his footman. But after "near three Months," "they had succeeded no farther than they did the first Week," and the scheme is abandoned when her father dismisses the protagonist as "a sharping scoundrel, and no Lord."[134] One intention of the *Complete History of James Maclean*, then, is to expose MacLaine as originally or foremost a kept "stallion" and failed fortune hunter, who then turns in financial desperation to robbery.

Eighteenth-century readers clearly found a degree of vicarious pleasure in stories of thieves such as Latroon, O'Divelley, and O'Hanlon, but the fortune hunter was an altogether more despicable figure, not eligible for romanticized treatment or empathy. The glamorized image of the highwayman represented certain masculine ideals, bravely daring to rob his victims without subterfuge, face-to-face, and treating women courteously.[135] Stallions and fortune hunters could also be admired for their sexual attractiveness, with "the potent labouring-class or immigrant, exoticized male" being opposed to "the effeminate peer."[136] But the *Complete History* imbues MacLaine with no such prestige, representing him as foppish, a "mere Beau," "powder'd Beau," and "feather'd Beau."[137] In both biographies, he is said to be too timid to lead the way in robberies, instead deferring to Plunket.[138] It is claimed in the *Genuine Account* that "he behaved with the utmost Pusillanimity, confessing with continued Tears" during his trial.[139] Fortune hunting is thus framed as unmanly in the narratives of MacLaine, in contradistinction to highway robbery, which requires toughness and bravery. Fortune hunters threatened the very basis of elite society, rather than simply augmenting it, like Cosgrave's highwaymen who are "diverting in Company, and able to behave before Gentlemen very agreeably." They could supplant rightful heirs, appropriating the wealth and property upon which power depended. The lives of MacLaine thus differ in tone from whore biographies such as *Betty Ireland*, which celebrate their heroines. Female courtesans can access high society, but they lack the gendered power of male rogues to exploit the marriage market. It is MacLaine's ambition, not his robberies, that condemns him in midcentury criminal biographies.

†

In England during the late seventeenth and early eighteenth centuries, texts about Irish Catholic criminals joined the many other narratives that tried to displace the phenomenon of crime beyond the borders of the nation. Narratives from the 1690s revived memories of Catholic rebellion in 1641 and engaged with more recent hysteria about an "Irish Plot" to present the Irish as violent and untrustworthy, and such views were still current in narratives of the 1720s. However, the attempt to essentialize fictional Irish criminals comes into tension with common strategies of characterization within the genre, which highlight cultural adaptability and hybridity. In *The Irish Rogue*, the protagonist sheds signs of his nationality and contradicts English stereotypes by assimilating into other cultures. *The Wild-Irish Captain* attempts to present David Fitzgerald as a participant in the factitious Irish plot, but encounters a contradiction between its political agenda and the particular life of its subject, which resists being shaped in this way. *Jonathan Wilde* sets out to explain a criminal's course of life via Irish ancestry, but the Wildes soon prove indistinguishable from the English. Gaelic Ireland is presented as lawless and primitive in these two biographies, but the charge of Irish inferiority is troubled by the revelation of English criminality. The implied superiority and civility of the English is not amenable to the criminal narrative's milieu of urban corruption. When Irish rogues become officers of the law, any attempt to exoticize and distance crime collapses.

Criminal literature published in Dublin between 1680 and 1750 was often based on English material, with narratives such as *The Irish Rogue* and *Betty Ireland* being reprinted in Dublin, and Cosgrave writing a collection of biographies modeled on London-published originals. Irish criminal narratives did not simply copy their English models, but are distinctive in their idealization of highwaymen, who are presented as noble rather than brutish, and become figures of opposition to the colonial elites. While the criminal career of O'Divelley or Fitzgerald is presented as a manifestation of the inherent nature of the Irish, the misdeeds of Cosgrave's highwaymen are responses to dispossession and plantation. Nevertheless, this chapter has argued that English and Irish representations of rogues from 1680 to 1750 have something in common, as both define their criminal as Irish, but also allow movement between cultures and allegiances. *Irish Highwaymen* suggests the limitations of national interpretations of rogues in the criminal narrative. Violent Irish criminals invite a context of pejorative stereotypes, and noble or principled robbers seem to attest to the prestige of Gaelic lineage. But in the end, both interpretations are subverted by inconsistent characterization that swings between the poles of brute and hero. Instead of standing for the Irish, the characters considered here are better read as representatives of an underworld that encompasses Ireland, England, and beyond. Rogues break with conventional social attachments such as nationality when they begin their lives of crime, and travel between nations, integrating into different societies, which are presented as similar in their criminal dimensions.

Such strategies are shared by the whore biography, in which a character like Betty Ireland abandons her familial role and sublimates her Irish background. Midcentury English criminal narratives testify to the expansion of conceptions of Irish nationality to include Protestants by the 1740s. The fiction *Betty Ireland* and the biographies of MacLaine attest to how traits and stereotypes usually applied to Catholics, such as "assurance," protean identity, and deviousness, were extended to the Protestant Irish in the eighteenth century. This was contingent upon the gradual shift in the self-image of Ireland's Protestants, who dispensed with the exclusive self-classification of "the English in Ireland." But the insistence that Protestants are Irish was also, in a sense, exclusive, coming from the perspective of an insular and class-conscious English society that was prone to stigmatize those from Ireland as outsiders through the familiar slur of an association with crime. This explains why MacLaine was labeled an "Irish Rapperee" in one biography. Biographers found it hard to attack MacLaine's respectable, middling-sort Presbyterian family, but they scorned his Irish "assurance" nevertheless, and reserved most derision for the aspect of his life that was seen as the most shameful, unmanly, and disquieting: fortune hunting. At midcentury, the fictional Irish rogue moves decisively into a higher social echelon, acquiring a different primary career. Many novels about Irish fortune hunters began to appear from the 1750s onward, and it can be argued that the life of MacLaine, as disseminated by the biographies, was one influence on this phenomenon. After 1750, the Irishman's social mobility was a recurrent plotline, a source of scandal in the English novel, and a problem that the Irish novelist needed to address.

3

Crime and Irishness
in Ramble Fiction, 1750–1770

On April 1, 1758, John Cartaret Pilkington announced to the world that his memoirs were soon to be published under the attention-grabbing title "The Adventures of Jack Luckless." The proposals issued for the book listed subscribers such as the archbishop of Canterbury, and Pilkington had good reason to hope for public interest in his life. He was the son of two noted Irish writers, Matthew and Laetitia Pilkington, known not only for being part of Jonathan Swift's Dublin circle but also for their scandalous divorce in the 1730s. His autobiography was an attempt to trade on his family's achievements, but also to participate in midcentury fashions for biographical fiction. "The Adventures of Jack Luckless" promised a "picaresque" tale of adventure and misfortune, as Norma Clarke points out, though the memoir was eventually published in November 1760 under a different title, *The Real Story of John Cartaret Pilkington*.[1] The reasons for the change can only be speculated, but it is nevertheless intriguing that Pilkington initially chose to frame his life with a whimsical pseudonym, Jack Luckless, in a title recalling Smollett's *Adventures of Roderick Random*. For this Irish author in the 1750s, memoir and the novel were not all that far apart. The two titles given to this one book are emblematic of a tradition within Irish writing that existed at the boundaries between scandalous autobiography, criminal biography, and fiction. This chapter pursues correspondences between the criminal narratives analyzed already and novels of the 1750s and 1760s that spun plots about itinerant Irishmen. The established motifs of crime, migration, social mobility, and pluralized identity remain central to Irish ramble novels, as will be shown through a reading of William Chaigneau's *The History of Jack Connor* (1752) alongside several contemporaneous works of fiction.

An early work of novel criticism, *An Essay on the New Species of Writing Founded by Mr Fielding* (1751), identified a "new kind of Biography" inaugurated by Fielding's *Joseph Andrews* (1742) and broadly defined as realistic and comic, against the excesses of heroic romance.[2] A porous boundary existed between the "new" comic fiction and the established genre of criminal biography. Francis Coventry's novel *The History of Pompey the Little* (1751) labeled the present day a "*Life-Writing Age*" in which "[t]he lowest and most contemptible Vagrants, Parish-Girls, Chamber-Maids, Pick-Pockets, and Highwaymen . . . think themselves authorized to appeal to the Publick, and to write Apologies for their Lives."[3] The inclusion of "Pick-Pockets, and Highwaymen" within the fashionable "*Life-Writing*" undercuts the idea of this "species of writing" as either new or "founded by" Fielding, directing our attention instead to interactions between longer and more expensive works of imaginative fiction and the shorter, cheaper criminal narratives that were already widespread. As I will demonstrate, English ramble novels reused the clichéd figure of the Irish fortune hunter and shared a narrative of transgression and punishment with the older criminal biographies. That said, contemporaneous Irish novels made more original use of the rogue narrative, depicting Irishmen who achieved real and deserved material success. The most significant of these is Chaigneau's pioneering *History of Jack Connor*.

In 1988, James Cahalan described *Jack Connor* as one of "several little-remembered novels by Protestant Irish writers" that appeared "[s]omewhere in the shadows" of eighteenth-century Ireland.[4] Since then, the novel has attracted a modicum of scholarly attention, and many of its contexts, Irish and otherwise, have been elucidated. A modern scholarly edition, published in 2013 and edited by Ian Campbell Ross, confirms its importance to early Irish fiction. Lesage's *Gil Blas* is now highlighted as an influence upon *Jack Connor*, and the novelist's heritage is a factor in his use of this model. Chaigneau (1709–81) was born into a French Protestant, or Huguenot, family that had emigrated to Ireland. He became an army agent in Dublin Castle.[5] Although Chaigneau utilizes both French and British models, *Jack Connor* manages to remain a distinctively Irish work. Haslett discusses *Jack Connor* as an example of experimental Irish fiction during the 1750s; for instance, in its tendency to digress into political and economic debates, or "incorporation of extra-fictional discourse into the novel."[6] Indeed, the novel draws upon the genre of tracts concerning economic improvement that dominated publishing in Dublin at the time, as Catherine Skeen has shown.[7] *Jack Connor* is often read as an Irish exponent of the picaresque, and its plot exemplifies many of the genre's features.[8] Jack Connor is raised by poor farmers in Co. Limerick, orphaned at a young age and adopted by a benevolent landowning family with the unsubtle name of Truegood. Leaving Ireland in his teens, he works as a servant for several masters in London and France. He pursues love affairs and associates with rogues and robbers, though his moral decline is arrested by the influence of friends. He joins the army and fights against the Jacobites in the 1745 rebellion. Having risen to the rank of captain, he is finally reunited with the Truegoods and wedded to a daughter of the family; as the novel ends, they are purchasing an Irish country estate. Rather than reiterating similarities with picaresque forebears, this chapter reads *Jack Connor* in relation to texts from its own historical moment: the ramble fiction that it exemplified, and the Irish criminal narratives discussed already.

The first section demonstrates that Jack's moral reform is correlated with the confirmation of the hero's loyalty to Britain in the wake of the 1745 Jacobite rising, and furthermore, places *Jack Connor* in relation to several rogue narratives from 1750s Dublin that associated crime with Jacobitism. Jack eventually achieves a material prosperity characteristic of midcentury novels such as *Tom Jones*, and the second section examines the significance of his rise to the status of a landlord. *Jack Connor* addresses questions of moral conduct through its ensemble of exemplary masculine types, such as Truegood, and cautionary images of criminal men. Chaigneau's narrative draws an opposition between the Irish gentleman and figures such as the highwayman—in similar style, I will argue, to a little-known ramble novel from the 1760s, *The Adventures of Patrick O'Donnell*. However, these ideal depictions of Irish masculinity take place within, and cannot entirely extricate themselves from, the context of criminal narratives. The third section reveals that Chaigneau's patriotic and publicly engaged novel also contains a countervailing theme of privacy. Jack is framed explicitly as a private individual, and also keeps aspects of his identity private or masked—thus being readable in the terms of rogue literature. The fourth section moves from *Jack Connor* to fortune-hunter novels, demonstrating how their plots are nuanced by factors of nationality, religion, and class. These formulaic fictions are used to illuminate the depiction of fortune hunting in one of the most original and striking Irish novels of the century, Thomas Amory's *The Life of John Buncle, Esq.* (1756). While not readable as a conventional rogue narrative, *John Buncle* reveals an anxious awareness of prejudices toward Irish men.

Crime and Jacobitism in Irish Rogue Narratives, 1750–1755

In the 1750s, ramble fiction combined with the existing tradition of criminal tales, thus imbuing the rogue narrative with a new popularity. Yet Dickie, in a chapter-length discussion of the comic "ramble" style, mentions "criminal biography" only to distinguish it from the ramble novel, in that the former focuses on "active con men" and the latter on "witty survivors who drift into crime." This agency-based difference, however, conceals more basic similarities between the two types of fiction, such as the comic tone, focus on vice and low life, and plot of wandering movement. Several of the texts that Dickie discusses are about prostitutes (for example, *Betty Ireland*), and still others are fanciful histories of real people.[9] This section compares *Jack Connor* to narratives about Irish criminals, particularly those published contemporaneously in Ireland, and highlights strategies shared by these texts, such as the parallel between the crimes of rogues and the transgressions of the Jacobite rebels in 1745.

One previously mentioned work that was almost contemporary with *Jack Connor* is illustrative of the overlap between ramble fiction and criminal biography: *The Adventures of Shelim O'Blunder, Esq.* (1751). Dickie reads *Shelim O'Blunder* as an example of the "male-centered ramble novel," though it was priced similarly to the criminal narratives discussed already, costing one shilling. At only forty-eight pages, it was a good deal shorter than the novels of Chaigneau or Amory, which sold for six shillings.[10] A narrative of unsuccessful fortune hunting in London, *Shelim O'Blunder* announces its purpose to offer "salutary Advice, or friendly Caution to the *Fair Sex* of *Great-Britain*." Shelim, from Tipperary, is in need of money and is encouraged by like-minded fellows to head for England in search of a bride. There, he is enlisted into the "Society of *Fortune-Hunters*," a detail that recalls the gangs and networks that rogue literature had claimed to expose since the earliest anatomies. Shelim claims to be descended from "an ancient and honourable Family," but the document by which he legitimates his suits is rejected as "a forged, pretended Title, to an Estate in an unknown Country." The narrative ends with him "deservedly cag'd" for the crime of debt.[11] The hero's marital aspirations and their ignominious failure recall the biographies of MacLaine, and the texts share a tone of condescension toward the Irish immigrant who presumes above his station. His eventual relegation to debtor's prison is the clearest sign of the endurance of the stock criminal plotline into midcentury ramble fiction.

Chaigneau drew upon the same set of established conventions to produce a very different kind of novel, turned toward moralizing and socially useful purposes. Ross points out that *Jack Connor* might have been first read as "rogue fiction or even criminal biography," and its third Dublin edition, published in 1753, was bound with the memoirs of a Kilkenny highwayman, *The Life and Adventures of James Freney* (1754).[12] Several decades later, portions of the novel were borrowed into the plagiarized life story of a real Irish pirate, the similarly named John Connor.[13] Indeed, Ross argues that Chaigneau may have written *Jack Connor* to provide Irish readers with an improving alternative to these kinds of popular criminal lives.[14] A stock plot of Irish criminality is one of the strands that Chaigneau weaves into his novel. His itinerant life begins when his parents are evicted from their farm in Co. Limerick. The Connors become beggars and "wander'd through many

Counties."[15] Several of the criminal narratives already surveyed begin in the same way. The infant Latroon and his family are displaced by the 1641 rising, whereas in *The Irish Rogue* the narrator and his mother "strolled the Country, till I became a lusty Lad." *The Wild-Irish Captain* relates that Fitzgerald's family "lived . . . as *Itinerants*, in plainer *English* dependents upon Charity for their Bread." Lastly, Alexander Smith's biography of the Irish highwayman Dick Bauf records that "his Parents being wandring Strollers, he was carried at their Backs, thro' so many Countries."[16] Accounts of "strolling" Irish families in criminal narratives reinforced the notion that Irish migrant laborers were idle and would not settle to regular work.[17] However, the eviction of the Connors is viewed more sympathetically in a context of economic uncertainty and tenant poverty: "The Transition from an *Irish Farmer* to a *Beggar*, is very *natural* and common in the Country" (45). Nevertheless, the trope of exile during infancy, foreshadowing the itinerant life to come, links *Jack Connor* to a recent tradition of narratives about Irish criminals.

If Jack's mobile life as a servant is characteristic of the European picaresque, then his travels in several countries are readable in relation to the Irish criminal narrative. Jack journeys through England, France, and Spain, the same itinerary as the fictional O'Divelley in *The Irish Rogue* and real highwaymen like James Butler and James Carrick in Cosgrave's *Irish Highwaymen*. On his journeys, he comes into contact with the Irish diaspora in Catholic Europe; for example, when he meets an Irish Brigades soldier in Paris, which leads to a further encounter with his long-lost mother, now living in Cadiz and married to an Irish merchant (214–19). Like earlier rogues, Jack is aided in his travels by his facility with language, speaking "*French* with great Fluency" (86–87) and winning the "Love" of his first employers, the Champignons, "by Songs, and a thousand *Irish* Stories" (99). He impresses his next master with "a *Latin Sentence*; and some *judicious* Observations . . . that surpriz'd the young Gentleman" (101). It is here that Jack differs from the rogues of criminal literature, his Latin representing the gentleman's education that he has received at a Protestant charter school in Portarlington. Nevertheless, his mobility, bilingualism, and adaptability construct him as a rogue because they lead him into illicit conduct. Jack can be interpreted as a rogue primarily due to his numerous sexual relationships, which begin in Portarlington when he falls in love with his French tutor, Nannett. When Jack's schoolmaster Mr. Johnston discovers their affair, he banishes the boy from his school and from Ireland, a plotline recalling *The English Rogue*, in which Latroon's mother, "perceiving my Lecherous inclinations, by my night-practises with her Maid, resolved to send me to a Boarding School."[18] In the account of Jack's romantic life, boundaries between the merely immoral and the illegal become blurred. Johnston discovers "the happy criminal Pair lock'd in each other's Arms," and subsequently threatens to "send you [Jack] to *Prison*, and have you *hang'd*" (91–92). Johnston's labeling of Jack as a "criminal" is suggestive of the larger overlap between the criminal narrative and the novel, both forms interested in mobile and eloquent protagonists.

The sexual conduct of Jack becomes yet more illicit because it is associated with French libertinism, thus connoting the allure of the Jacobite cause. A pattern of Jack's intimacy with French women is established with Nannett, and continues when he becomes an apprentice in London and falls for Tonton, the daughter of his Huguenot master Champignon (100). The plot of the young apprentice being lured away from his duties by a woman is familiar from the criminal biography, and has been noted by Rawlings.[19] Jack then moves to Paris, where his kindness to his landlady's daughter is "repaid by *Madelain* in *Caresses*, and by every Freedom except the *last*" (110). The landlady, Mme Commode, then informs him that the "Daughter of a *rich* Banker of *Paris*" is interested in him, and introduces him to the heiress's "Companion," Mlle Fardé. Jack courts Fardé at great expense, but eventually discovers that there is no heiress, and that Mme Commode is "but of the middling Order of *Bauds*. You are her *Dupe*," in the words of a friend (111–13). Jack thus has cause to comment on the immorality of French society compared to England: "*Libertinism* reigns here in a much higher Degree. The *French* have a Way of varnishing their Vices, and making them more dangerous and catching than our aukward Manner" (118). The idea of French libertinism as "dangerous and catching" to the unwary Irishman has clear political implications at this point in the eighteenth century. For Irish Catholics, France represented an alternative to their disempowered status, as the home of the exiled Stuart line, which British and Irish Jacobites still hoped could regain the throne. French forces had assisted the Jacobite rising in Scotland in 1745, seven years before the novel's publication. Recruits continued to travel to enlist in the Irish Brigades of the French army, which in McBride's phrase "remained the focal point of Catholic fantasies and Protestant alarms."[20] The novel contains an account of the rising that conceptualizes Jacobites as led astray by a foreign power, as expressed in the words of Colonel Manly, a character loyal to Britain's Protestant monarchy: "Can we be so stupid as not to see the *old*, the *stale Trick* of *France*? And must some of us always fall into so weak a Project?—Poor deluded Men! But thank God, we still have *Honour* and *Wisdom* sufficient to convince them of their Errors" (197). As the Irishman Jack is led into vice and then duped by French women, so "deluded Men" fall for the "trick of France" and lend their support to the Jacobite cause.

However, Jack is ultimately rescued from the temptations of crime and affirms his loyalty to Britain, a plotline that distinguishes *Jack Connor* from earlier criminal narratives about the Irish. The novel accords a decisive importance to values of education and virtue that are associated with the Church of Ireland. As a child, the protagonist is adopted by Lord Truegood, who appoints the steward Mr. Kindly to tutor the boy, and then sends him to Johnston's school, thus "breeding him up in *virtuous Principles*" and "giving him a *new Birth*" (72). In criminal narratives, the personality of the rogue tends to be innate, with subjects defined in childhood as "a Boy of a ready Wit" or "by Nature vitiously inclined," to take two examples from *Irish Highwaymen*.[21] Conversely, Chaigneau makes it clear that Jack's intelligence is derived from reading "*History, Voyages, Poetry*" at school, which "gave him a Facility, and a *genteel* and *easy* Turn of Language" (86). The school that Jack attends is lauded as a forerunner to the institutions set up by "the *Incorporated Society, for promoting English Protestant Schools in Ireland*," which was established in 1733 (62).[22] The principles of Jack's education remain with him during his later travels and adventures. After narrowly escaping arrest for his part in a highway robbery in London, he reads a letter from Kindly that urges him to *"repent of your Faults,"* and consequently "promis'd to himself an entire Change of Conduct" (167–68). Jack's reform is unusual when compared to the texts already surveyed in this book. An ending of spiritual betterment is common in the criminal biography, but lives of Irish rogues tend to avoid this pattern, instead evidencing the "disorderly and disjunctive" narrative that Faller ascribes to the influence of the picaresque.[23] *The English Rogue, The Irish Rogue*, and *The Wild-Irish Captain* end with the criminal still alive and unrepentant. *The Irish Rogue* concludes with its first-person narrator at large in London, but "being given up to a Rambling Genius, it cannot be expected I shall long continue in one place." Two more of the Irish criminal narratives considered in the last chapter, *Redmond O Hanlyn* and *Jonathan Wilde*, conclude with their subject's death, his moral state unaltered.[24] *Jack Connor* resembles such tales of Irish criminality, with Jack even taking up the trade of highway robbery for a brief spell, but Chaigneau departs from the picaresque pattern by demonstrating through Jack's example that the Irish rogue is capable of correction. Elsewhere, Jack speaks out against the tendency in the London press to charge crimes "to the Account of *Ireland*, when perhaps some other Part was entitled to the *Honour*." This critique of the stereotyping of "*Hibernians*" is of a piece with the novel's transformation of the Irish rogue narrative (106). Jack is able to arrest his decline into crime, making what he calls "an almost miraculous Escape" thanks to the influence of his education (168).

If Jack's crimes in France had connotations of radicalism, his moral correction then leads to his enlisting to fight against the rebels in 1745, and distinguishing himself at the Battle of Culloden (196–203). The rogue's reform is thus narrated in explicitly politicized terms. The narrative of moral improvement functions to repudiate Jacobite sympathies and advertise the loyalty of the Irish to the Protestant church and the Hanoverian royal line. The 1745 rebellion was generally supported among Irish Catholics, but no insurgency transpired, due in part to an absence of foreign aid, and afterward the threat of violent uprising felt by the Protestant elite receded into the past.[25] For Leerssen, "the '45" was a pivotal event in altering Protestant attitudes in Ireland toward the Catholic populace, who came to be regarded as fellow Irish citizens rather than as a rebellious subclass.[26] The crisis of 1745 proves to be the prelude to reconciliation between the criminal and society in *Jack Connor*. The novel includes a letter written by an English traveler in Ireland that charts just such a progression from anxiety to conciliation in Protestant attitudes toward Catholics. The author, a Mr. Villeneuf, sketches past Irish rebellions and claims that "the Resistance they made, and the Blood they shed, struck that Sort of *Horror* and *Hatred* in our Ancestors, that is handed down to their Posterity" (192). But he goes on to assure readers that Irish Catholics are now "*quiet* and *amenable*," meaning that the "*Hatred*" stoked by past violence is now thoroughly outdated: "Whatever might have been the Reason for holding the *Irish* in Contempt, even to *Hatred*, I can truly say, those Reasons must have, long since, ceas'd. They are now *Members*, and very useful Members to our *Body*" (195). The usefulness of the native Irish proves the error of past stereotypes: "The common Opinion of the *Laziness of the Irish*, is not strictly Just" (193). The sentiments expressed here in this letter belie Hand's opinion that *Jack Connor* represents "an Irish world that is itself inherently debased," in which "the idleness and sloth of the Irish are much remarked upon" as the root of their poverty.[27] *Jack Connor* instead reiterates the Irish "patriot" attitude that the underdeveloped condition of the country proceeded from mismanagement, with Villeneuf's letter commenting that "[t]he Error, I think, lies in the Generality of the *Landlords*," who are said to be too often absent from their estates (194). *Jack Connor* is a Protestant Irish fiction of its time, in its sense that rebellion is now unlikely and the Catholic Irish are acquiescent and useful subjects. Chaigneau can thus dismiss preconceptions about the innate inferiority of the native Irish, in the letter and in the optimistic narrative of the rogue's reeducation.

Villeneuf declares that Protestants once held "the *Irish* in Contempt," but they are now admitted as "Members to our *Body*." This trend maps onto fictional views of Irish rogues from the 1660s to the 1750s. Seventeenth-century criminal narratives were alive to the memory of the 1641 rising, which underpins their view of the Catholic Irish as violent and barbaric, most obviously in Head's foundational *English Rogue*, which devotes a chapter to the rising and includes episodes such as Latroon's journey through the Wicklow countryside, where malicious locals beat him up and attempt to drown him in a river. The two fictions from the 1690s, *The Irish Rogue* and *The Wild-Irish Captain*, also evoke memories of atrocities committed by rebels in 1641. Attitudes had relaxed after 1745, and new and original Irish biographies had emerged that did not partake in xenophobic caricaturing; for instance, the collection by Cosgrave. The conditions were created for narratives foregrounding the reclaiming of the Irishman from Jacobitism. Thus, when Chaigneau's *Jack Connor* represents Jack flirting with France, before giving up such vices and confirming his fidelity to Britain at Culloden, it takes place very much in the terms in which Irish transgression was understood in the criminal narrative.

Rogue narratives published in Dublin in the decade after 1745 tended to associate criminality with Jacobitism, allowing us to glimpse the interests of readers for whom the rising, even though it did not reach their shores, was made present through exciting tales of political tumult. One biography, *The Life of Nicholas Mooney* (1752), adopts the same tactic as *Jack Connor* and represents the reform of Mooney, who fights with the Jacobite armies, as a progress from sedition to loyalty.[28] In a criminal-as-sinner narrative, Mooney is enlisted to the Protestant faith as an index of his spiritual betterment.[29] Ó Ciosáin argues that the religious overtones of *Nicholas Mooney* are the reason for its lack of success with Irish readers, pointing out that it was reprinted only once, by Methodists in London.[30] More successful were biographies such as *Irish Highwaymen* or *James Freney*, which resisted plots affirming legal or state power. One further text exemplifies the rising's continued presence for readers: *The Life and Uncommon Adventures of Capt. Dudley Bradstreet* (1755), an autobiographical work published only in Dublin. The eponymous Bradstreet was a government spy from Tipperary who infiltrated the Jacobite armies in 1744 and 1745. His memoir reveals his undercover heroics, love affairs, and failed business ventures, and is comparable both to the fanciful lives of notable people identified by Dickie and to rogue literature. Bradstreet's many petty crimes include peddling gin on the streets of London, a "Scheme . . . directly opposite to the Laws of England," and advertising a gourmet feast that never takes place in order to raise money from ticket sales.[31]

Dudley Bradstreet can be contrasted with both *Jack Connor* and *Nicholas Mooney* in that service to king and country during the '45 is in no way opposed to the general criminal tenor of the life. Bradstreet is employed by a secretary to the Duke of Newcastle to infiltrate the armies of Charles Edward Stuart in their march toward the capital. Under the guise of an English nobleman, Bradstreet claims to have convinced the Jacobite commanders to retreat to Scotland, though this has not been corroborated by modern biographers.[32] Bradstreet's correspondence with Newcastle and King George II is included, and while it predictably advertises his loyalty to the Hanoverian line, it is motivated primarily by desire for payment for his services. Recompense is slow to arrive, and Bradstreet returns to scheming and fortune hunting. Unlike other Irish rogue narratives, then, Bradstreet's memoir does not emphasize reform and makes no attempt to imbue Protestantism or loyalty with spiritual or moral authority. Bradstreet is active in the defense of the realm while remaining a rogue. The mechanisms of justice are presented as shams when Dudley is convicted of harboring rebels in a fake trial, set up in order to make him appear convincing as a spy. After spending a fortnight in jail, he states baldly: "When my Time was elapsed, I got out, and may say, with other wretches accustomed to gaols it did not make the least reformation in my morals."[33] The blurring between lawbreakers and state agents evident here is reminiscent of criminal biographies of thieftakers, informers, and bailiffs such as *The Wild-Irish Captain* or *Jonathan Wilde*.

Dudley Bradstreet invokes the genre of the gallows speech, popular with Dublin readers, when it includes a detailed description of "the Trial and Execution of the Rebel Lords" William Boyd, fourth Earl of Kilmarnock, and Arthur Elphinstone, Lord Balmerino, on August 18, 1746, on Tower Hill, London; Bradstreet claims to have been "upon the Scaffold when two of them were beheaded."[34] Kilmarnock and Balmerino are represented as "unfortunate" gentlemen who share "a most affecting Embrace, and bid an eternal Adieu to each other." Balmerino "was a strong, robust, martial Man" who shows "Chearfulness" and "Composure" until the last moment, even giving the executioner some money. Representations of condemned criminals as game in the face of death were conventional, but the tolerant representation of two leaders of the rising is striking when compared to *Nicholas Mooney* and *Jack Connor*. It is possible that Bradstreet was keeping in mind the possibility of a Catholic readership in Dublin that would have less patience with politicized assertions of triumph over Jacobitism. Indeed, the narrator assures readers that he "never swore any thing against" either lord, "or any others concerned in the Rebellion."[35] The text's perspective is that of an interested spectator, nonjudgmental but not impervious to the tragic aspects of Kilmarnock and Balmerino's deaths. Shouldering his way onto "the Scaffold" to witness the scene, Bradstreet shrewdly exploits Jacobite regrets about the failure of the rising, general public interest in these events, and the popularity of gallows literature in Dublin.

Elements of *Jack Connor*—such as the hero's early poverty and his travels, sexual intimacies, brush with highway robbery, and eventual spiritual betterment—all encourage the view that the novel was informed by popular rogue narratives, including those published in Dublin or about Irish criminals. Ross posits that *Jack Connor* was written to provide Irish readers with what Chaigneau saw as a more correct alternative to those available in criminal biography. Whatever Chaigneau's attitude to rogue literature, his only novel exploited the undiminished appetite for such narratives in both Britain and Ireland, and did so successfully, as can be gauged from its second London edition in 1753, and several later Irish editions, including a "fourth edition" published in 1766.[36] English readers, used to amoral Irish tales such as *Betty Ireland* and *Shelim O'Blunder*, could receive *Jack Connor* as more of the same. Irish readers were exposed to a range of original Irish-authored narratives by 1755, meaning that particular styles and preoccupations can be identified. Comic, irreverent stories were more popular than moralizing ones featuring reform, and the novels

and memoirs by Chaigneau, Mooney, and Bradstreet catered to public
interest in the events of the '45. Taken together, these texts imply the
continued existence of a Dublin readership sympathetic to Jacobitism,
who were to be dissuaded from political error, or for Bradstreet, simply entertained.

Masculinity, Social Mobility, and the Novel Form

The existence of so many popular fictions that invited readers to identify with men who stole, lied, tricked, and even murdered implies that
masculinity, and its relationship to morality and law, was a contested
subject in the mid–eighteenth century. Masculine prestige and moral
rectitude were far from synonymous; critics of fiction such as Rosenthal and Mackie have discerned parallels between the figure of the
gentleman and those of the libertine or robber, who secure admiration
because of their energy and freedom from norms. Novels of the 1750s
and 1760s register these competing representations of ideal masculinity by trying to separate immoral or lawbreaking men from virtuous ones. Richardson's *The History of Sir Charles Grandison* (1753–54)
epitomizes the early eighteenth-century view of the gentleman as
polite and refined, rather than emotional, as in the "man of feeling"
novels of the 1770s and 1780s.[37] *Sir Charles Grandison* is "probably the
most influential articulation of the ideal gentleman in the eighteenth
century" for Mackie, but the novel can be read as struggling against
the widespread assumption of elite male libertinism: "Just as its hero
devotes a good deal of his time *not* becoming embroiled in duels, so *Sir
Charles Grandison* dedicates much of its narrative to establishing . . .
that this hero is not a libertine."[38] Chaigneau adds an Irish dimension
to understandings of masculinity at this point in time, by promoting
a brand of masculinity based on refined manners, but also on qualities
of publicly engaged responsibility and staunch political commitment
to the existing political order. As will be demonstrated in this section,
the novel achieves this through its form: a progressive narrative of
Jack's education in various societies and contexts, in which he comes
under the influence of ideal and criminal secondary characters. Jack is
an exemplar of good Protestant schooling, but also of a more general

concern with male morality, seen in the range of rogues, rakes, and gentlemen that he encounters. Jack's good fortune is conventional to the ramble novels of the time, with their romance-influenced endings, but Chaigneau is keen to demonstrate that Jack is a worthy recipient of his happy ending, in the process attesting to the possibility that this poor and obscure Irishman might both exemplify real virtue and achieve material success.

A formally innovative Irish novel, *Jack Connor* features numerous interpolated tales and variations in register, incorporating discourses ranging from economic and moral improvement to rogue literature. This formal strategy was commented upon by the *Monthly Review*: "But the merit of this work consists less in the entertainment it may afford as a novel, or the satisfaction it may give to the lovers of satire, than in those parts where the author digresses into useful lessons of moral- ity, and where he introduces certain conversation-pieces; from whence his younger readers may draw proper hints for their improvement in politeness."[39] The novel's digressions and interpolations are often "les- sons of morality," contributing to the formation of Jack as a character and the promotion of virtuous principles to the reader. Connections between masculine conduct, education, and written texts are signaled early in *Jack Connor* through Jack's course of reading at the Portar- lington school: "Accounts of the *Lives* of *great Men* of all Nations," but also "*Gil-Blas, Scaron*, and other Books of that Tendency." If great men's biographies provide ideal exemplars, then the French picaresque tales of Lesage or Paul Scarron are not to be emulated, although they are permitted as an evening's diversion (85–86). Indeed, *Gil Blas* is an important formal model for *Jack Connor*. Like Jack, Lesage's hero spends most of the novel as a servant before eventually finding a place among the elites. As Gil journeys from the criminal underworld to the royal court, the novel abounds with the interpolated tales of the people he meets, which nuance our interpretation of his character. The histo- ries of thieves like Don Raphael or Scipio, for example, are reminders that Gil has remained comparatively virtuous.[40] In both novels, these secondary characters function as good and bad influences for the pro- tagonist, as when Jack briefly considers highway robbery. In need of money, Chaigneau's hero is persuaded to join up with two robbers, but holding up a coach makes him feel guilty and cut ties with his accomplices (163–66). This scene mirrors an episode in *Gil Blas* in which Gil and his master Don Alphonso join up with a pair of highwaymen and are involved in the shooting of a rival gang, but their better natures eventually prevail and they leave.[41]

Several interpolations in *Jack Connor* provide evidence of the impact of criminal literature on the Irish novel. When Jack joins "a Society of *Footmen*" in London (156), the reader is provided with a list of "their principal Resolutions"; for example, "that no Member, when accompanying his Master or Mistress in their Visits, shall attempt to open or hold the Coach Door" (161–62). The narrative here emulates the criminal anatomy, itemizing the rules of the fellowship of servants, and claiming to have the "publick Use and Benefit" in mind (160). The last chapter of volume 1 takes the form of a whore biography titled "The STORY of POLLY GUNN, OTHERWISE POLLY CANNON" (138–47). This interpolation concludes the volume on a happy note, as the former prostitute affirms her "*contrite Heart*" and retires to a "Mansion of *Peace* and Tranquillity" (146). Polly Gunn's story, like Jack's own, attests that criminals can prosper, but the tales of two rogues encountered in Paris, Fanfaron and Maquereau, are less optimistic. Maquereau in particular resembles the protagonist, as a footman who "pass'd through many Services, and was remarkably dexterous in the *nice* Conduct of an Affair" (107–8). On his return to the city, Jack learns that Fanfaron has been "taken and *broke Alive* on the Wheel" as a punishment for murder (212). In *Jack Connor*, interpolations recalling criminal literature provide both parallel lives and counternarratives to the story of the protagonist.

In his travels, the servant Jack encounters criminals among his lower-order peers, but is also exposed to bad behavior among the gentry. In London, he works for a succession of masters whose names betray their characters, such as Lord Weakhead (125–27) and Sir Peter Shallow (154–60). He also dines at a tavern with a group of drunken gentlemen, an episode framed as "thirty Pages of the most *fashionable Oaths*, and refin'd *Bawdy Jokes*" (129). The crudely comic tenor of the gentlemen's exchange supports Dickie's conclusions about the tendency of eighteenth-century ramble novels to revel in the "delights of privilege," adopting an elite male perspective from which women or the lower orders were seen as fitting objects of abuse.[42] Sir Nicholas Royster boasts of tormenting his parents' tenants: "When I began to kill their *Dogs*, and brake their *Nets*, the Scoundrels complained to *Sir Joseph* . . . but when I was *Sixteen*, I shew'd them other Game, for D—— me if I didn't get their Daughters with Child by Dozens" (132). Dickie stresses the bawdy and unfeeling comedy of ramble fiction, but one of Chaigneau's themes is that the misdeeds of the gentry are not merely fun and games. *Jack Connor* refuses to countenance the idea that the powerful are above the law, equating them with proletarian criminals; for example, when Jack observes that "the *highest* and the *lowest* Class only vary in their *Vices* by the Manner of committing them" (105), or when Lord Truegood deplores the fact that "People could, with Justice, complain of the *Theft*, *Drunkenness*, and other Immoralities of their *Servants*, when they . . . too frequently gave Examples of *these Vices* themselves" (66). Truegood declares that nobles who run up debts to tradesmen commit a "*Robbery* of the blackest Kind" (66), and his words link the upper orders to the highwaymen featured elsewhere in the novel. Mackie has pinpointed the tendency in eighteenth-century discourse toward "making excuses" for gentlemen: "The rake's criminality is frequently not named as such" due to his "elite social status."[43] In *Jack Connor*, however, privileged vice is identified as criminal, an effort aided by the compiling of rogue biographies alongside the vignette of high society observed by Jack in the tavern.

As Truegood is made to denounce the crimes of the gentry, so other Irish characters are distinguished from the libertinism of London. An Irish gentleman at the tavern declines to accompany the rest to a brothel, and Jack comments approvingly that "*Mr. Fitzsimons* is a Man of more Understanding than to embarque in such an Exploit" (135–36). The Irishman Jack will eventually join the gentry himself, and the dissipated gentlemen he encounters in London are clearly inadequate examples of this station. Jack's life is instead shaped by the example, advice, and patronage of several mentors, including True-good, Kindly, and Colonel Manly. These mentors are all Protestant men, and their cumulative effect in the novel is to construct a model of exemplary Anglo-Irish masculinity for the hero to emulate, set out in interpolations such as the life story of Truegood (58–67) and two didactic letters from Kindly to Jack (95–97, 167). Kindly's second epistle has a particularly important role in Jack's life because he reads it after his encounter with the highwaymen, and it inspires him to mend his ways. Another interpolated text that functions similarly is a letter from Manly, "full of *good Instruction*" on how Jack should deport himself as an officer (199). Chaigneau's occupation as an army agent in Dublin would have made him familiar with military life. The "extra-fictional" register of this letter, to use Haslett's term, is confirmed by the fact that its prescriptions were used in a 1767 miscellany of military procedure.[44] The tellingly named Manly situates masculine worth partly on the battlefield, exhorting Jack to "drive every *Woman-ish Weakness* from your Heart" and reminding him that he is "a Man of *Property*, and now enlisted to fight the Cause of *Freedom*, and of *That* MONARCH who has ever supported it" (199–200). Martial heroics are part of the gentlemanly ideal, and even more important for Chaigneau is the sensible management of land and tenantry.

The landlord Truegood fulfils the function of a mentor and model for the protagonist, who will eventually emulate him by purchasing an estate in rural Ireland. Truegood is comparable in both name and narrative function to Fielding's Squire Allworthy, the country gentleman who adopts and raises Tom Jones. He differs from Allworthy because he is an exemplar not just for the hero, but for his tenants, and this marks *Jack Connor* as a novel of eighteenth-century Ireland. Chaigneau alludes to the "many Methods he practised to avoid *Drinking to Excess* himself, and preventing it in others" and his "many Schemes . . . to persuade the Natives into *Justice* and *Honesty*" (67). As Skeen has highlighted, the narrative of Jack's progress draws upon the genre of proposals and projects for the economic improvement of Ireland, which were written and read mostly by the country's Anglican landowners and clergymen.[45] An improving tract by Samuel Madden, *Reflections and Resolutions Proper for the Gentlemen of Ireland* (1738), exhorted Irish landlords to "oppose and discourage all ill Customs, that destroy Frugality, Thrift, and Industry in our Tenants," and to serve as exemplars themselves: "The Example of the Gentry, is the great Source of acting in all Countries; so it is remarkably true in Ireland."[46] *Jack Connor* draws upon the discourse of the dutiful landlord when Truegood counsels Jack to settle in Ireland: "Let me advise you to Purchase in that *Kingdom*, but in one of those Counties the least improv'd . . . You will build convenient Houses for the poor People" (232). Among the discourses of masculine or gentlemanly conduct drawn upon by Chaigneau, then, is the plan or project for Irish improvement, with its prescriptions for the conduct of landlords.

It can be reflected at this point that *Jack Connor* sets out a view of Irish masculinity that is completely opposed to fortune-hunter novels such as *Shelim O'Blunder*. In the latter, the essential inadequacy of the Irishman is seen in his avarice and attempts to deceive others as to his status and breeding, and his schemes are usually ineffectual. In the process, the very idea of Irish social mobility (or, more accurately, equality with the English) is dismissed as a mere rogue's scheme; the Irish will always be found out. The protagonist of *Jack Connor* effects marked and lasting social advancement, having begun the novel as a homeless vagrant—the clearest sign of its originality in the context of fortune-hunter stories. Though he is eventually (and conventionally) revealed to be the son of a lord, the novel overwhelmingly stresses education rather than innate qualities. For the majority of the narrative, Jack has no material advantages to draw upon; both his poverty and nationality motivate the novel's insistence on his learned accomplishments and morality. A range of male mentors, along with institutions such as the Protestant charter schools and British army, must be brought to bear upon Jack to give him the imprimatur of the gentleman. Masculine prestige is accordingly defined in terms of politeness and learning, and explicitly against the lawless and violent lower-class rogue or highwayman. The novel dramatizes a peculiarly Irish and Protestant brand of elite masculinity that stresses martial heroism and public-spirited governance.

A later ramble novel is, like *Jack Connor*, plotted in order to effect an explicit break between the Irish hero and criminal types or figures. *The Adventures of Patrick O'Donnell*, published in London in 1763, also features specific plot similarities with *Jack Connor* that imply a degree of influence. There are signs that the anonymous author was Irish, as the novel makes detailed references to places in the northeast of Ireland, such as Carrickfergus, Newry, Hillsborough, Loughbrickland, and Banbridge.[47] It is also dedicated to Thomas Newburgh of Ballyhaise, Co. Cavan, a landowner and poet.[48] Patrick is born to middling-sort Catholic parents in Cork. His profligate mother elopes with a lover, though she is reunited with Patrick at the novel's close. She marries "a wealthy merchant" in Lisbon before returning home upon her husband's death.[49] This chain of events mirrors the parting of Jack Connor from his mother, who also weds a merchant (this time in Cadiz) and then finds her son again at the end (217–19). Patrick is comparable to Jack as an essentially decent youth who is afforded various opportunities to sin; for instance, as part of a "club" of fellows in London: "I continued this life of folly for a year and a half, and was looked on by my companions, who were very numerous, as a compleat buck, a mighty blood, a jovial fellow, and a hearty cock."[50] The novel skeptically echoes the permissive discourse of sociable manliness, associated especially with young and unmarried men and liberating urban environments such as the coffeehouse or brothel.[51] But after Patrick falls in love with one Charlotte Worthy, "I resolved to amend my life, and forsake my follies; and by attending to my duties of a soldier and a man, my pride suggested, I might yet render myself worthy of my mistress."[52] Patrick's progress through the army to a happy marriage is certainly reminiscent of Jack Connor's, although his social rise is not so dramatic. But both novels stress Irish civility and trustworthiness in a wider British context through plots in which a poor and roguish protagonist improves himself, becoming worthy of the reader's esteem.

Patrick O'Donnell is emphatically not a criminal narrative, both in the sense that it shares more with novels such as *Tom Jones*, and in that it must repeatedly emphasize that Patrick is not a criminal.

Highwaymen appear frequently in the text; for instance, the Worthy family's coach is attacked by a band of "ruffians" in Hornsea Wood, providing an opportunity for Patrick to ride to their rescue. Later, the hero is himself robbed by highwaymen on the way to Cork. Desperate for cash to return to England and Charlotte, Patrick considers going "[u]pon the road" himself, his struggles presented in the form of a six-page monologue, at the end of which he resolves that "money, gained by wickedness, does not prosper." Instead, Patrick brings his robbers to justice by joining their gang and then turning on them in the midst of a robbery. With the help of the intended victims, the highwaymen are arrested and taken to be tried in Cork. The Irishman, in other words, is not only too upstanding to rob himself, but public-spirited enough to stop others doing so. Yet, of course, these episodes testify to the closeness between Patrick and the highwaymen: "the road" is a logical recourse for him when short of funds, and he is easily accepted into the gang, helped by the fact that their captain is an old acquaintance.[53] The insistent presence of the robber in this ramble novel is a reminder of prevailing views of Irishmen, encouraged by criminal biographies, which the novelist seemingly must engage with in order to banish. Plotlines in which Patrick fights off highwaymen and consigns them to jail exemplify a perceived need to underline that he is a different kind of Irishman. Although Patrick never breaks the law, he is automatically vulnerable to suspicion, especially given his Catholic background and lack of financial security. The novel must therefore draw lines between acceptable masculinity—the brawling and carousing in which Patrick indulges—and unacceptable criminality.

A forgotten novel like *The Adventures of Patrick O'Donnell* testifies to the existence of a patriotic strand of Irish writing within the wider tradition of midcentury ramble fiction. Irish novelists in this period turned the male-centered ramble plot to similar purposes to those pursued by contemporaneous Irish playwrights such as Thomas Sheridan and Charles Macklin. Though possibly influenced by *Jack Connor* in plot terms, *Patrick O'Donnell* does not share the political and economic scope of the earlier novel. The next section reflects on some neglected political undertones within *Jack Connor* that can be illuminated through a focused consideration of its central character and of attributes of the rogue such as disguise and masking.

Privacy, Identity, and Silence in *Jack Connor*

Through his novel, Chaigneau exhorts the Irish citizen—especially the elite male—to keep the improvement of their country in mind. From its very first reviews, *Jack Connor* has justly been read as a work of fiction engaged with national issues, in which "the author makes some agreeable excursions into the *political* world," and "takes frequent occasions to express his fondness for this country [Ireland] . . . to throw out hints for its advantage, and propose schemes for its improvement."[54] Hand has read *Jack Connor* as an "Irish 'problem' novel," in which "Ireland is presented as a dilemma: there is something wrong with it—socially, politically, economically. Corrective action can be taken, however, to make a better future."[55] Skeen also stresses the novel's public scope, aligning it with the improving project, and Ross refers to "Chaigneau's fervent dedication to the economic betterment of Ireland through agricultural improvement, better administration, and fairer taxation."[56] This section moves away from the novel's public and political overtones to demonstrate the importance of privacy, disguise, and secrecy within the text. Chaigneau might have had clear political agendas, but his characters are more than ciphers, exemplars, or mouthpieces for these; they are, at crucial points, inconsistent, private, or silent. Indeed, the novel begins by disclaiming a public scope and defining itself as a "Story of the *Calamities*, or *good Fortune of private Persons*" (41), and this definition of the novel invites further examination of the "private" character of Jack.

The power and influence of the Irish elites, as well as their morality, become a key issue in the narrative. Truegood's daughter Harriot tells her father, "I cannot but wonder at the vast Pains my Lord takes about *Ireland*, when, with all his Consideration, he cannot change the Nature of Things" (234). As this comment signals, *Jack Connor* is often skeptical about individual agency. For Skeen, the novel offers proposals for national improvement but also "hints at the postlapsarian impossibility of the projector's Ireland."[57] *Jack Connor* establishes a pessimistic view of providence alleviated by an optimistic romance ending, a narrative structure that is best seen in the context of contemporaries such as Smollett. In Jessica Richard's view, Smollett's novels endorse the doctrine of "special providence," in which the world is mostly understood as random and corrupt, though God occasionally intervenes to help the faithful. Ideas of special providence were formulated in response to skepticism about the existence of a "general providence" that reliably rewarded virtue and punished sin.[58] A Smollettian view of providence is discernible in *Jack Connor*, as Jack journeys through a mostly debased society, and learns that the good are not always rewarded. For instance, his prospects seem to be improving when he marries his first wife, Mrs. Gold, but her sudden death illustrates that "this World is not made for *permanent* and lasting Joys!" (196). The unfairness of the novel's "World" underlines the special nature of its providential ending. Jack finally looks back and discerns "the visible Hand of *Providence* conducting and leading me to the Fruition of the most *perfect Happiness* this World can afford" (237).

Truegood, who initially adopted Jack and has now consented to the marriage of Jack and his daughter, emerges as an embodiment of the occasional, "special" magnanimity of God. Truegood corresponds to Mikhail Bakhtin's trope of the "romantic secret benefactor" in the novel. Bakhtin detects traces of the romance genre in novels at moments of "the intrusion of nonhuman forces—fate, gods, villains" into the lives of characters.[59] Truegood's providential intervention in Jack's life constructs him as a figure of exceptional, deified power. But although he recalls the romance, he is geared to practical ends, as he stands for the possibility of an engaged, responsible Irish landowning class. He is described as extraordinary, a "View" of "what the *Nobility* ought *truly to be*, in Opposition to what they *really are*" (80). A prosperous country is glimpsed on his estate, where "all the Inhabitants and little Houses [are] so alter'd and so decent, that all seem'd Enchantment" (235). The landlord's capacity to improve the country is registered in a conversation between Jack and the Truegood family aboard a coach. The Lord declares that it is the "Duty of every *faithful Subject*, to throw out such Information and Hints to the *Government* as he judges of general Use" (234–35). His words are representative of eighteenth-century Irish patriotism in their "desire to contribute to the public benefit, to live up to one's responsibilities as a citizen."[60] Truegood also contributes to the development of the charter school system, showing that "Part of his Time was given to the Publick" (63). Truegood's public status and influence are exceptional within the world of this novel.

The true gentleman might be a public gentleman, but the protagonist of *Jack Connor* does not finally conform to this ideal. Indeed, Jack is repeatedly defined as a "private" individual, in terms of his low status and consequent lack of control over the course of his life. Chaigneau defines the novel as a "Story of the *Calamities*, or *good Fortune of private Persons*." The opening paragraphs distinguish *Jack Connor* from the register and sphere of romance, identifying the novel's form as a "BIOGRAPHY" that is "levell'd to the Sphere we act in" and opposed to "The Actions of *Monarchs*" (41). The novel's province is everyday "private" life rather than the realm of heroic deeds. A comparison between this passage and Smollett's preface to *Roderick Random* is instructive. Smollett prizes the "familiar scenes" of the novel over the "superstition" and "heathen mythology" of the "Romance."[61] Chaigneau instead opposes the biographical novel to "the History—of *Battles* and *Slaughter*." The counterpoint for *Jack Connor*, then, is not the mythic or fantastical, but the public, and though "History" might sometimes be "*wondrous strange*," it nevertheless encompasses real events in a way that Smollett's "Romance" does not. Speculating on the proper material of history, Chaigneau instances "a Glorious and a Wise *Prince*, triumphing over *Foreign* or *Domestick* Enemies" (41–42), a figure who brings to mind both William of Orange's Glorious Revolution, and the defeat of the Jacobites at Culloden by forces headed by Prince William Augustus, Duke of Cumberland.[62] After declaring that such public matters are beyond his scope, Chaigneau then defines *Jack Connor* as a narrative that "must sensibly affect every *private Reader*" (41–42). The difference between novel and romance, or biography and history, is one of private versus public realms. The novel is defined by its focus on ordinary or obscure people rather than monarchs or nobles, an opposition that invokes the distinction between Jack and Truegood. This opposition between public and private realms becomes a recurring element of *Jack Connor*.

During the narrative, the idea of Jack as a private person moves away from meaning simply lower status, and takes on connotations of secrecy. When he fights at Culloden, the narrator comments that "[m]y Task is only relative to the private Character of *Jack Connor* . . . in all those Pages on which *this History* is founded, I find little or no Traces of the Actions of the Times" (201–2). Chaigneau here invokes the framing fiction that his novel is based on "*a Bundle of Papers left him by a deceas'd Friend*" (39), the putative documentary records of Jack's life, and draws attention to the incomplete nature of these records, implying that Jack is so private as to be literally unknowable. Jack's enigmatic movements sometimes overlap with his roguish activities, as here: "A LITTLE more Time was spent in *Paris*, in Compliments on taking Leave . . . Those paid to Ladies, I am as ignorant of as the Reader" (226). The first section of this chapter drew attention to Chaigneau's use of a stock narrative of rogue travel, and Jack's progress through various countries and cultures is aided by his concealment of his Irish background. When he is banished from Ireland, Mr. Johnston advises him to soften his "*Irish* Manner of speaking" and renames him "JOHN CONYERS." This new, English name and identity, Johnston reasons, will avert prejudices against him in London (93). The recasting of Jack as Conyers is read by Skeen as a forecasting of national improvement: "The fact that Jack takes on a new name less than halfway through the first volume reminds us of the emphasis on fresh starts in the projector's Ireland—a place where people and places can be renamed, new methods applied . . . and old histories occluded."[63] However, Jack's change of name does not coincide with his reform, coming much earlier in the narrative than his sobering brush with the highway robbers.

The renaming of Jack as John Conyers adds to his status as a rogue by rendering his identity unstable and deceptive. His strategic naming makes him resemble Bakhtin's definition of the rogue, a figure who "can exploit any position that they choose, but only as a mask," or Head's Latroon, who has "a name for every month in the year" to evade the law.[64] When spying for the government, Dudley Bradstreet passes as an English nobleman called Oliver Williams, and also uses a different "travelling name," MacDonald.[65] Jack's first master, the Frenchman Mr. Champignon, dubs him "*Jean Conyer*" (99), and later, seeking work as a servant, "he took the Name of *Constant*" to give himself the appearance of constancy in the eyes of prospective employers (153). The narrator refers to Jack inconsistently as both "Jack" and "Conyers," and after he joins the army, also uses his military titles, "*Lieutenant Conyers*" (204) and "*Captain Conyers*" (216). Chaigneau's decision to construct his protagonist using the names he is known by in society, rather than always calling him "Jack Connor," stresses his temporary, socially directed and inauthentic persona, with his actual Irish name remaining undisclosed and private. Like his name, his nationality cannot be admitted, as when he tells his life story to an employer and "artfully avoided the Place of his Birth, or the least Hint of *Ireland*, as it might occasion Scandal" (176). Because of his inadmissible background, Jack becomes a protean figure comparable to the Irish rogue characters of the criminal narrative.

Jack's identity seems to be resolved and made public at the conclusion, when the newly wealthy "Captain Conyers" reveals to Truegood that he is Jack Connor, the beggar child adopted by the landlord. Ross reads this final scene as putting an end to secrecy: Jack "re-establishes for himself, as well as for others, the identity he has lost," and "reclaims the Irish identity prudence has suggested he conceal for so long."[66] But "prudence" remains the dominant factor, as Jack and Truegood agree to keep the hero's real name and past secret now that he is a gentleman, in order to avoid the class and national prejudices of "the *Ignorant*" (238). The effect is to present Ireland as finally, albeit regrettably, a taboo subject. Although it is clear that any prejudice against Jack is condemned as "*Ignorant*," it remains that the ending is one that stresses the privacy and illegitimacy of Irish identity. Some things, it seems, cannot be spoken openly, even in the enlightened spheres in which Jack is moving now, and in a novel that both acclaims and practices the articulation of patriotic opinions, this is significant. *Jack Connor* stresses improvement and conciliation between Ireland's religions and classes, but this register is not unanimous; private doubts and dissenting voices can be detected in the novel.

Jack Connor addresses its wider themes of Ireland's society and economy mainly via what the *Monthly Review* called "conversation-pieces"; for example, the protagonist's debates with his English neighbors during his first marriage (179–95), or Jack and the Truegoods's discussion aboard the coach (233–35). These conversations happen in public places, such as an inn in the former case, and address public issues such as taxation, the freedom of the press, and the state of Irish trade and agriculture. They represent the presence in the novel of a nonfictional discourse, standing in for the print culture of Chaigneau's Dublin, the "whirl of broadsides, pamphlets, and tracts addressing Irish economic conditions" referred to by Skeen.[67] In this, they can be read as imagined versions of the "Ascendancy public sphere" posited by Leerssen in eighteenth-century Ireland. Leerssen draws upon the work of Jürgen Habermas to define this sphere as constituted by printed exchange as well as socialization in clubs and coffeehouses: "any point where the minds and opinions of citizens can enter into communication and weigh matters of a non-private nature forms part of this public sphere." Before 1760, Ireland's public sphere was centered on Dublin and monopolized by Protestant, British, or patriot opinion, with the culture of Gaelic Ireland afforded scant opportunities for dissemination in print.[68] Leerssen's sense of an exclusive domain is reinforced by the tone of the discussions in *Jack Connor*. The conversation at the inn ends with Jack reading aloud Villeneuf's letter on the "*quiet* and *amenable*" state of the population. Chaigneau's representations of public discourse function to create an impression of understanding, as shown during the inn discussion. When the Englishman Sir John Dobson declares of the Irish that "we ought to give them no Trade, and make them pay some of our Taxes," Colonel Manly then comments reprovingly, "The best Way to make them pay some of our Taxes, is to put them in a Condition to do it" (191). In the sphere of British, upper-class, and here, masculine conversation, English chauvinism is neutralized by Manly's reminder of Irish poverty, and the colonel then gestures toward a common-sense solution. In this way, Chaigneau uses conversation scenes to project a confidence that his country can be improved and differences resolved. However, the exclusive nature of public discourse at this time is also registered in *Jack Connor*, as sensitive topics have the power to disturb the agreeable conversation.

The limits of the Ascendancy public sphere are tested during the exchange aboard the coach. Truegood advances an improving scheme to settle "Protestant *Swiss* or *Palatines*" on Irish farms, to which Jack replies thus: "As ENGLAND, *said the Captain*, has purchased that *Kingdom* by much Blood and Treasure, perhaps they are too severe in their Conduct towards it." He then argues that the English should "grant more Privileges" to Ireland, implying that projects such as Truegood's should be funded by the government. His words raise the ghost of conquest, "Blood and Treasure," and even though they highlight the costs to England rather than Ireland, they disturb the impression of harmony created thus far in this conversation. Truegood responds, "On this . . . I shall not argue, but take *Ireland* in General, and you will find them tolerably happy" (234). After the mention of conflict, the lord stresses peace, but his assurances contain a caveat: the people are not completely happy, but "tolerably" so. Villeneuf's letter is similarly equivocal: "Your Lordship will not expect Encomiums on the *Papists* of this Kingdom for their *firm* Attachment to a *Protestant Government*. No, my Lord, but they are *quiet* and *amenable* to it" (194). This is not a reassuring "quiet," because the fact of religious difference remains an obstacle to the people's loyalty. McBride has highlighted the error of assuming that Catholics in eighteenth-century Ireland were willing subjects because of the absence of large-scale insurrection, drawing attention to how an "outward posture of deference" could be belied by "everyday, local acts of insubordination."[69] When Chaigneau was writing, Ireland might have appeared increasingly peaceful, as forms of popular unrest such as banditry and agrarian protests were less prevalent than in the first two decades of the century.[70] However, as Timothy Watt has recently demonstrated, protests against taxation and so-called riot and rescue (seizure of confiscated goods from revenue officers and other officials) remained common in rural and urban

areas of Ireland until the 1760s.[71] Robbers continued to exist, such as
the notorious Freney, active in Kilkenny between 1744 and 1749.[72] The
national quietness referred to in the public-spirited conversations of
Jack Connor, then, is readable as a temporary state. The first section of
this chapter linked the reform of criminals to the diminution of the
threat of a Catholic rising in Ireland. However, the sporadic but persistent presence of low-level violence suggests that absence of rebellion
did not mean contentment. The ideal image of Ireland projected in
Jack Connor ignores crimes such as banditry and agitation. Nevertheless, mentions of past violence and present religious difference imply
that larger conciliation has not yet been fully effected.

If conversation in *Jack Connor* projects national harmony, then
silence represents tension, and the silence of Jack relates to his private identity and rogue status. From its first appearance, Chaigneau's
novel has been associated with the outspoken praise of Ireland. Jack
sometimes serves as a mouthpiece for such sentiments, as when he
critiques the labeling of criminals as Irish in London newspapers, yet
his presence in the novel is defined as much by reticence as it is by
patriotic speech. He remains quiet for most of the novel about his Irish
background, and is a silent listener (or reader) during the interpolated
speeches and letters of others. When he reads Villeneuf's letter, this
is viewed by Ross as "a lengthy and eloquent defence of Ireland and
its inhabitants," yet these opinions are not Jack's own, but those of his
former master.[73] Jack keeps a notable silence in one scene set in Paris,
in which he and his fellow officer Captain Thornton encounter Captain Magragh, of the Irish Brigades. Magragh declares that "'I love my
Countrymen, the *Irish*, and I love the *English* well enough, but, *Faith*
and *Sowle*, they are too hard upon us.' Captain *Thornton* observ'd a
peculiar Gravity in the Countenance of his Friend, and thought, that
by changing the Current of Conversation, to remove it. He try'd many
Ways, but *Conyers* seem'd lost in Thought. His Silence gave a serious Turn to the Company, and they broke up much sooner than was
intended" (215). Jack is seen from Thornton's perspective here, making him a private, inscrutable figure, the cause of his "peculiar Gravity" unknown. It transpires that he is silent because he has learned

from Magragh's speech that his long-lost mother is alive and married to the Irishman's uncle, a merchant in Cadiz. His mother represents the suppressed Catholic side of his Irish background, and his silence in the presence of the Englishman Thornton continues this suppression.

Magragh's words prompt us to reconsider the character of Jack. He is Captain Conyers, English gentleman and veteran of Culloden, but he is also Irish and is linked by marriage to Magragh, who, it is implied, fought for the Jacobites in the rebellion: "He told them of the vast Estate his Father lost in *Ireland*, and how near he was, the other Day, of recovering it" (214). What cannot quite be stated in this passage, in which Jack falls silent and the narrator withdraws from identification with him, is that the protagonist is reexamining his own identity. Sobered by Magragh's declaration that the English "are too hard upon us," he realizes that he is not just another English officer. As he grapples with a revived sense of his own Irishness, his public and private selves confront and contradict one another. The French setting of Jack's meeting with Magragh permits the articulation of pro-Jacobite sentiments that would be inadmissible in the Ascendancy public sphere. The novel's "conversation-pieces," or polite, disinterested debates on Irish issues, have the potential to shift into uncomfortable and compromised territory. The truncation of dialogue signals the limits of what can be said—and thus, of harmony and unanimity in Protestant Ireland.

Previous readings of *Jack Connor* have understandably emphasized the optimism of its narrative of improvement. Ross reads the novel as a progress toward a particularly Irish "stability," manifest both in Jack's "taking of his Irish name" and in "Ireland's material progress and current prosperity."[74] Hand writes that "the 'new' Jack Connor embraces the possibility and forward-thinking culture of the Irish Protestant elite, cutting himself off from his Gaelic, Catholic origins."[75] For these critics, Jack's renaming and moral reform orient the novel toward a positive future. Yet, as I have argued, the rogue of his early life remains present in Jack's continued use of assumed names. My analysis of public discourse in *Jack Connor* has contended that history remains troubling in the novel. References to crime and past conflict detract from the impressions of improvement and stability given by rational conversation. The power to improve the state of Ireland is invested in public figures such as Truegood. But the perspective remains with Jack, a protagonist who is necessarily subordinate to the Ascendancy's projects and ideologies, but who also stands far enough outside them to voice his misgivings.

The Irish Fortune Hunter in Fiction, 1750–1770

The conclusion of *Jack Connor* implies that an Irish background had the potential to undercut gentility, as Jack must remain in disguise as the English gentleman John Conyers, even after he has gained an estate. More widely, the fortune-hunter novels of the 1750s and 1760s presented the Irishman's social rise as worrying, improper, and problematic. Literary representations of penniless and felonious Irish gentlemen can be referred to a wider uncertainty over the worth of Irish titles in England, and the instability of elite prestige, position, and wealth in Ireland. The modulations of the fortune-hunting plot were shaped by socioeconomic and religious bias as much as by national prejudice. Such fictions, drawing on existing narrative patterns, could either end like criminal biographies, with legal punishment, or like ramble novels, with happy and secure marriage. The former, negative pattern is associated with the poor, disinherited Catholic protagonist, and the latter with the Protestant middling-sort or gentry. But some Irish novelists refused these conventions; Amory's *Life of John Buncle* can be read as a deliberate reversal of the fortune-hunter character.

Irish titles were often regarded as recently acquired or inferior in England because of Ireland's history of conquest, which meant that the ruling class was repeatedly supplemented with new arrivals from the sixteenth century onward. The descendants of ousted Gaelic and Old English noble families had a claim to nobility but little property or power. As Barnard explains, most peerages in eighteenth-century Ireland belonged to the descendants of planters who had arrived between 1530 and 1641, but the continued, unofficial prestige of the now-defunct Gaelic lordships "denied legitimacy to the hierarchy, headed by peers, which the English had imposed." The readiness of the Stuart kings in the early seventeenth century to hand out Irish lands and titles created an enduring sense of Irish peers as arrivistes.[76] This state of affairs is commented upon by the Irish writer Charles Johnston in his *Chrysal, or the Adventures of a Guinea* (1760–64). An English lady who profits from selling titles declares that an "Irish title was the constant refuge of those sons of fortune, who not being born in the rank of gentlemen, or having forfeited it by their villainies, were desirous of changing their names for sonorous titles," which "in reality only make them more exposed to the view, and consequently to the censure of the world."[77] An Irish title has become a hollow possession, vulnerable to "the censure of the world," and its possessor is likely to be taken for an adventurer or villain. In this climate, eighteenth-century literary representations of rogues expanded to encompass the Irish gentry.

Cromwell's wholesale confiscation and redistribution of lands in the 1650s again recomposed the landed elite and "left many old proprietors landless and in exile, some of them in England," a phenomenon that Hayton links to the creation of a new stereotype in English drama, "the miserable Irish pseudo-gentleman." By 1700, the dominant English stereotype of the Irishman had begun to travel "up the social scale," and the plays of George Farquhar inaugurate the idea of the Irishman as an "adventurous man-about-town." Playwrights mocked Irish gentlemen by tarring them with the supposed traits of the peasantry, such as drunkenness, lustfulness, and idleness. The attributes of the rogue Irish came to encompass Protestants of British ancestry, particularly as the power base of seventeenth-century arrivals settled and assumed an Irish identity. Hayton writes that "the amorous addresses of the fortune-hunter" are a version of the trope of Irish "peasant licentiousness."[78] Fortune hunting is a sign of the illegitimate or disinherited gentleman, as it involves making a figure in high society, but out of a practical need for financial security. Hayton identifies Farquhar's plays as the earliest literary representations of Irish fortune hunting, but Burke writes that the "first expanded treatment" of the trope comes in a 1717 poem by John Breval, *Mac-Dermot: or, the Irish Fortune-Hunter*.[79] In the case of Mac-Dermot, gentlemanly accomplishments are neatly combined with laboring origins, as a farmer's son is taught by a kindly baron to "forsake thy Father's Hutt / and in a pompous Liv'ry learn to Strutt."[80] Criminal narratives were a durable outlet for English anxieties about social interlopers, and the fortune-hunting Irishman recurs in fiction from at least the mid–seventeenth century. In Dublin, Latroon targets "wealthy and aged widows . . . such did I daily hunt out and visit by turns. I was not sparing of amorous expressions."[81] Betty Ireland's accomplice Will "passed for a Baronet, under the Name and Title of Sir G—— B——," a detail that glances at the suspicions over Irish titles.[82] The newsworthy careers of real Irishmen such as MacLaine and Bradstreet, both of whom operated in England, doubtless helped to solidify the trope in English readers' minds. Given such pretexts, it was unsurprising that the Irish fortune hunter should take up center stage in many English ramble novels of the 1750s and 1760s.

One fortune-hunter novel, *Shelim O'Blunder*, has been discussed already as an example of the criminal narrative plot. A further and very similar example is worthy of brief comment: John Oakman's *The Life and Adventures of Benjamin Brass* (1765). A programmatic work even by the standards of ramble fiction, *Benjamin Brass* carries the helpful subtitle "*An Irish Fortune-Hunter*," and the intended bride of the protagonist is given the name Mrs. Wealthy. Brass is the son of a Munster "brogue-maker" who "thought a gentleman's life was much preferable to that of making brogues."[83] He manages to marry Wealthy, but is humiliated when all of his new wife's creditors arrive at once to hound him. Unable to pay, Brass is taken by bailiffs and, like O'Blunder, ends the novel in debtor's prison.[84] The frequency in these fictions of financial mismanagement, overconsumption, and crippling debt is illustrative of anxieties that the city, particularly London, was an arena that enabled social mobility and fraudulent pretenses to status. Images of servants and maids who imitated the dress of their betters were reiterated by midcentury commentators such as Fielding.[85] The Irish fortune hunter was a version of such lower-order aspirants, and was often attacked for his fashionable trappings, or what the biographer of *A Complete History of James Maclean* calls an "extraordinary itch for a gay

Appearance."[86] Novels such as *Shelim O'Blunder* and *Benjamin Brass*, then, were primarily products of conservative English attitudes to commerce, social emulation, and the consequent risks of the marriage market. The poor, Catholic Irishman provides a convenient means of assuaging these worries through plots of exposure and punishment.

Other novels of the time instead adopted the romance plot of much male-centered ramble fiction, derived from exemplars such as *Gil Blas*, in which the rogue eventually prospers and settles into married life. In at least one case, this narrative was combined with Irish fortune hunting. *The Adventures of Dick Hazard* (1754) is a ramble novel, being both longer and, at three shillings, costlier than criminal-themed pamphlets.[87] The novel begins with the promise that Hazard will be "rescued from Despair, by many Examples of unexpected Assistance," which testify to "a providential Influence." The hero's father is a merchant in Cork who "enjoyed a considerable Fortune" and dispatches his son to Trinity College Dublin. Hazard fails to apply himself and is expelled from the university. He marries a widow to gain possession of her money before fleeing to England. There, he "did not wonder much at [his] seeming Rapidity of Success" in fortune hunting, given that he was "born in a Nation, the very Name of which implies Prosperity in Love." In London, he pretends to be in possession of "an estate of three thousand Pounds a Year in the County of *Westmeath*." Hazard's actions are often callous, as when he abandons his wife in Dublin, but the narrator assures us that he retains "a faithful Monitor within, that awakened Repentance." When his reform duly arrives, benefactors quickly intervene to stabilize his status; he discovers that his father, now deceased, has left him "his whole Fortune," and is forgiven by his loyal wife.[88] *Dick Hazard* thus combines a familiar focus on vice and crime with an optimistic frame narrative in which a young gentleman goes astray but is finally brought to a state of comfortable matrimony.

Hazard is reintegrated into affluent, urban society rather than undergoing the punishment of the law. Unlike O'Blunder, who is unable to effect his fortune-hunting schemes, he is popular with women, and is even welcomed back by the wife he first defrauded. It is hard to avoid the conclusion that it is Hazard's respectable beginnings that make him more acceptable within the fiction's xenophobic English perspective; he has acquired Irish charm, but avoided Irish vulgarity. In *Jack Connor*, Irish upward mobility remained illegitimate, possible only under conditions of secrecy. Jack has to pretend to be an English gentleman, whereas in the less tolerant world of *Shelim O'Blunder* and *Benjamin Brass*, Irish pretensions are dismissed as laughable. Meanwhile, Hazard hails from the Protestant Irish middling sort, and thus becomes eligible for an ending of happy stability. By the mid–eighteenth century, the Protestant Anglo-Irish saw themselves and were seen as Irish. Thus, Hayton argues, the Irish gentry were represented in literature through stereotypes previously applied only to the poor. But in the fortune-hunter novel, suspicious above all of social climbers, distinctions of class and religion within Ireland remained crucially important. Different kinds of stories could be told about higher-status Irishmen such as Hazard, who were allowed to attain (or rather, regain) wealth and status.

Differences of tone and ending between fortune-hunter novels do not change the fact that they unite poorer and richer, Catholic and Protestant Irishmen as rogues, vehicles for a basic, repetitive joke about national dishonesty and acquisitiveness. The ubiquity of this literary trope by the 1750s created a set of limiting expectations for Irish authors, such that any Irish character could be seen as a fortune hunter, and any plot of travel or adventure could be a criminal narrative. This situation is registered in Amory's *Life of John Buncle*, the supposed autobiography of a religious enthusiast and amateur scholar brought up in the west of Ireland. The skeletal structure used by Amory in *John Buncle* is thus that of the ramble novel; like Dick Hazard, Buncle attends Trinity College Dublin but does not complete his studies, and then departs for England. Distinctively, however, Buncle is driven not by worldly ambition but by his dissenting Unitarian faith, which causes him to fall out with his family and lose his allowance. In the preface to volume 1, the first-person narrator explains that "I say as little of myself, in my relation, as I can; and as much for true religion, and useful learning, as I was able." This intention is borne out in a narrative that tends to sideline the protagonist's actions in favor of interpolated material testifying to Amory's various academic and religious interests. Even so, the preface also seeks to preempt views of Buncle as an Irish rogue by signaling his "wandering life" and "wrong conduct," and contending that "by hard measure, I was compelled to be an adventurer, when very young." Buncle admits some small misdemeanors in his youth (brawling and drinking too much), but "these I now call wrong, and mention them only as samples of a rashness I was once subject to."[89] The preface to volume 1 thus registers a need, in this Irish novel, to acknowledge similarities to well-known rogue narratives, and to prove the hero's virtue.

Writing the early life of Buncle in volume 1, Amory combines the ramble plot with a deliberately unconventional character who is diametrically opposed to the fortune hunter in his intentions, attitudes to women, honesty, and moral scruples. After losing the support of his family, Buncle travels to England in order to stay with an old friend, Charles Turner, who resides in a remote, mountainous part of north Yorkshire. Shortly after he arrives, another friend counsels him to marry and proposes a possible match, the daughter of his neighbor. Buncle admits that "a fine northern girl and money down, are benefits not to be met with every day.—But at present, the object I must pursue is my university-friend, *Charles Turner*." In his quest to find Turner that takes up most of volume 1, Buncle encounters several young and unattached women. But these women are not viewed as economic or sexual prizes; instead, the narrator emphasizes their learning, attesting to "have met with many women, in my time, who, with very little reading, have been too hard for me on several subjects," and speculating that young women should be given "the laboured education the men have." Whereas fortune hunters such as Hazard pretend to have titles and estates, Buncle candidly admits his restricted situation to those he meets: "Ladies (I replied), necessity and curiosity united are the spring that move me over these mountains, and enable me to bear the hardships I meet with in these ways. Forced from home by the cruelties of a step-mother, and forsaken by my father on her account, I am wandering about the precipices of Richmondshire in search of a gentleman, my Friend." The prospect of fortune hunting is again dismissed when Buncle finally reaches Turner's house. His friend is away, and Buncle finds his sister to be both "a very great fortune" and interested in him. "[I]t was possible I might have got his sister," Buncle reflects, but "in his absence, I could not in honour make my addresses to her . . . for a man worth nothing to do this in her brother's house, without his leave, was a part I could not act, tho' by missing her I had been brought to beg my bread."[90] The option of a wealthy bride is considered, as with the earlier "fine northern girl," only to be rejected, this time for moral reasons. Leerssen argues that Macklin's *Love à La Mode* (1759) and *The True-Born Irishman* (1761) "created a new type" of "*counter*-Stage Irishman," "based on the inverted or re-valued typology of the older Stage Irishman."[91] I argue that a parallel intervention is effected here by Amory, in which Buncle is explicitly defined against the attributes of Irishmen in most other contemporary novels. His idiosyncratic identity, by turns ingenuous, bluntly honest, and zealous about dissenting theology or female learning, is formed in reaction to the roguishness and deceptiveness of the fortune hunter.

In volume 2 of *John Buncle*, published in 1766, Amory offered readers a still more unusual plotline in which Buncle marries six times and is bereaved of his wife on each occasion. I have argued elsewhere that this narrative, which brings Buncle far closer to the fortune hunter, derives from an attempt to combine a Christian faith in the sanctity of marriage with aristocratic, libertine attitudes to sexual pleasure.[92] Macklin's 1767 prologue to *The True-Born Irishman* complained that "Hibernia's sons" had long been "the jest and scandal of the comic scene." Buffoonish Irish characters were going out of fashion on the 1760s stage, but the fortune hunter remained a staple of the ramble novel.[93] For this reason, masculine virtue in *John Buncle* is primarily a matter of conduct toward women and in the marriage market. Writing with an awareness of the fortune-hunting plotline, Amory seeks to subvert it by making the Irish gentleman both pious and deliberately unconventional. *John Buncle* partakes in the patriotic trend within midcentury Irish fiction exemplified also by *Jack Connor* and *Patrick O'Donnell*. The common storyline in which an Irishman leaves home and travels to England enables this redressing of prejudice by enabling the hero to prove himself in a wider British social setting. These novels reveal a heightened concern with Irish masculinity, seen in ramble plots and male characters who are conspicuously virtuous.

†

John Buncle, Jack Connor, Dudley Bradstreet, Benjamin Brass, Dick Hazard . . . Any reader approaching the works discussed in this chapter might be forgiven for thinking that they are fairly similar, even formulaic texts. How different can the "Life" of one Irishman be from another's "History" or "Adventures"? In fact, these contemporaneous novels are starkly different from one another in terms of content, tone, form, and narrative perspective. The term "novel" will not even suffice for all of them, since at least one is the autobiography of a real man, Bradstreet. Many were inspired in plot terms by the well-known novels of Smollett, Lesage, and Fielding, but equally, they drew upon criminal biographies, as seen in the use of endings featuring legal punishment rather than happy marriage. *Shelim O'Blunder* and *Benjamin Brass* mock the Irish as hapless outsiders, and such judgments are based on social as much as ethnic considerations, as revealed by the happier fate of Dick Hazard, clearly seen from the same English perspective as a better class of Irishman. The blithe and predictable fortune-hunter novel shares little apart from its basic plot with *Jack Connor*, which is formally innovative and keen both to change English readers' perceptions and to intervene in Irish social and political debates in Ireland. *Jack Connor* stands out with its plotline of marked upward mobility, taking Jack from the margins of Irish society to its apex. But Chaigneau's fiction is comparable to contemporaneous novels, such as *Patrick O'Donnell* and *John Buncle*, which seek to formulate an ideal, polite Irish gentleman by means of distinguishing the hero from stock criminal types. The presence of robbers and highwaymen in these texts registers the overlap between the early Irish novel and the criminal narrative tradition. The era's masculine types and stock figures—rogues, fortune hunters, polite gentlemen—are both fundamental to midcentury Irish fiction and, paradoxically, inadequate for its purposes. Jack reforms, yet also remains a rogue in his silence, disguise, and masking, thus becoming emblematic of undertones of popular dissent and Jacobitism below the novel's façade of a peaceful and improving Ireland. Buncle, across the two volumes, both is and is not a fortune hunter, as the plot of reform, education, and maturation is exchanged for a deliberately eccentric character. In the end, close attention to the ramble fiction of the 1750s and '60s demonstrates that Chaigneau and Amory were not lone outliers in early Irish fiction; they find their place in a corpus of now-forgotten narratives by English, Irish, and anonymous authors, and derive much of their material and impetus from the continually vital repertoire of the rogue narrative.

4

Migratory Fictions
Charles Johnston and the Irish Novel in the 1780s

Charles Johnston was a prolific novelist by the standards of his day, writing in a varied range of styles and forms across some twenty-six years. The six novels attributed to him constitute an output unequaled by contemporaries such as Chaigneau and Amory, in an era in which most Irish authors published just a single work, as the Loebers point out. Johnston's first novel *Chrysal, or the Adventures of a Guinea* (1760–64) went through some twenty-four editions between 1760 and 1800; in terms of popularity, it was matched only by *Tristram Shandy* and *The Vicar of Wakefield* among eighteenth-century Irish novels.[1] An example of the "it-narrative" form, in which the protagonist is a sentient object or animal, *Chrysal* is narrated from the perspective of a gold guinea coin. It was followed by *The Reverie, or a Flight to the Paradise of Fools* (1762), which swapped the object narrator for a spirit, Ariel, who journeys through time and space giving the reader a view of human life as defined by folly and venality.[2] Johnston's next two novels are both described by Daniel Sanjiv Roberts as "orientalist fictions."[3] *The History of Arsaces, Prince of Betlis* (1774) is a historical novel set in ancient North Africa and the Middle East, while in *The Pilgrim, or a Picture of Life* (1775), a Chinese traveler pens a series of letters home about the

Parts of this chapter were previously published as "Migration, Nationality and Perspective in Charles Johnston's *The History of John Juniper* (1781)," *Eighteenth-Century Ireland* 32 (2017): 145–67.

strange land of Britain. In the 1780s, Johnston would add to his repertoire of it-narrative, historical, and epistolary fictions by turning to the ramble novel. His two last novels, *The History of John Juniper* (1781) and *The Adventures of Anthony Varnish* (1786), are little read today, but both are of considerable interest to the scholar of Irish literature.

Scott's influential *The Lives of the Novelists* discussed Johnston expressly as "the author of *Chrysal*," and refers only once to the "obscure and forgotten works" that he published afterward.[4] Modern critics of Johnston have likewise concentrated on his best-known and most-republished first novel.[5] Interpretations of Johnston as an Irish writer also tend to focus mainly on *Chrysal*, though Roberts offers a more careful and substantive analysis of all of Johnston's novels, and a 2013 critical edition of *Arsaces*, also edited by Roberts, furnishes us with the materials to assess this neglected Irish author's achievement more fairly.[6] In contrast to *Chrysal*, neither *John Juniper* nor *Anthony Varnish* went beyond a second edition.[7] That said, they afford a more central role to Irish people and places than any of Johnston's other works, and this chapter will bring them together as examples of the rogue narrative. *John Juniper* and *Anthony Varnish* are tales of the Irish in Britain, with a particular focus on Johnston's home city of London. The titular Juniper is born to Irish parents in the parish of St Giles, and Anthony Varnish migrates to the English capital to work as a servant. Johnston himself led a similarly migratory life. Born in Carrigogunnell, Co. Limerick, he was educated at Trinity College, Dublin, before moving to London sometime in the 1740s or 1750s. He trained at the Middle Temple before practicing as a barrister, then in 1782 left England for Calcutta, where he resided until his death.[8]

Johnston turned to the male-centered ramble novel several decades after this style had enjoyed its first flush of popularity with Fielding and Smollett. Authors of the 1780s continued to publish novels conforming to the pattern of masculine adventuring, and some were very successful: John Trusler's *Modern Times, or the Adventures of Gabriel Outcast . . . In Imitation of Gil Blas* went through six editions between 1785 and 1789.[9] Novels about Irish fortune hunters, however, seem in retrospect to have been a midcentury phenomenon, a natural extension of the criminal biographies that were most popular early in the century and losing currency by 1770. The unlamented demise of the fortune hunter might be attributed to wider fashions for sensibility, exemplified by the success of Mackenzie's *The Man of Feeling* (1771), which made stories about callous and unsympathetic men seem old-fashioned or distasteful. Developments in drama also contributed to changing fashions in the depiction of the Irish. Johnston was interested in the stage and wrote one play, *Buthred*, a heroic tragedy set in medieval Northumbria, which was performed at Covent Garden in the 1778–79 season.[10] Other playwrights took the lead from Charles Macklin in crafting patriotic stage Irishmen. Richard Cumberland's *The West-Indian* (1771) and *The Natural Son* (1785), for instance, both featured the popular character of Major Dennis O'Flaherty.[11] Indeed, plays that were not to the credit of Ireland could now elicit opprobrium. In January 1775, Richard Brinsley Sheridan's *The Rivals* was so badly received after its premiere at the Theatre Royal, Covent Garden, that Sheridan was forced to rewrite the play and present a new version, and a particular target of criticism was the blustering Irish gentleman Sir Lucius O'Trigger.[12] The fame of Macklin as an actor in the 1770s and 1780s, together with Irish contemporaries such as John Moody and John Henry Johnstone, both of whom often played Irish roles, doubtless contributed to the state of affairs by which open mockery of the Irish was no longer seen as acceptable.[13]

In this context, *John Juniper* might have seemed dated on first appearance, given that it focuses on an unlikable rogue who does not reform and spends most of the novel financially exploiting others. *The Monthly Review* commented that "*artful villainy* was the ruling principle" of Juniper's character, and criticized Johnston for not concluding the novel with due punishment: "But what (the Reader may ask) becomes of this 'most wonderful and surprising gentleman' at last? Is he hanged?"[14] *John Juniper*, then, resembles earlier criminal narratives that were unfashionable in an era of sentimental masculinity. Later readers of Johnston have also been baffled by *John Juniper*, "a highly disjointed tale of a particularly unattractive young waif" and "an extraordinarily mean-spirited book," according to Roger D. Lund.[15] This chapter offers a detailed reading of *John Juniper* that demonstrates that its conventional low comedy conceals a serious work of Irish fiction with neglected aspects of political satire and philosophical speculation. Juniper's criminal actions are in fact less important than the origins of his self, an issue that is the subject of frequent comment, as Johnston plays with the idea of Juniper's Irish parentage and supposed criminality. The idea that the rogue's personality is innate is belied by a contradictory emphasis on the power of education. Though set in Britain, *John Juniper* manifests a recurring interest in Irish affairs, and often highlights the unfairness of British attitudes to Ireland.

An orthodox, Protestant form of patriotism characterizes Johnston's novels, which speak out on behalf of Ireland while being generally suspicious of Catholicism and understanding the country as part of a larger imperial whole. The preface to *Chrysal* was dedicated to Prime Minister William Pitt and was signed "A Briton."[16] By 1780, patriots in the political sphere were increasingly inclined to demand greater autonomy for Ireland. An influential faction in the Dublin parliament campaigned for the lifting of restrictions on Irish trade within the British Empire. In 1782, in response to patriot pressure, the Irish parliament was granted legislative independence, meaning that new laws applying to Ireland no longer had to be approved in London.[17] But conservative-minded Protestants like Johnston were in an increasingly awkward position as a campaign grew to repeal the Penal Laws. The first Relief Act in 1778 granted property-owning Catholics rights of leasing and inheritance and relieved priests from the risk of arrest and imprisonment. More far-reaching reforms were granted in 1782.[18] During the American War of Independence (1775–83), a need for manpower necessitated the widespread recruitment of Irish Catholics into the British army.[19] The Relief Acts were not universally welcomed, and many Irish Protestants were staunch in their objections to the idea of Catholics bearing arms.[20] In London, meanwhile, sectarian animus exploded into the Gordon Riots of 1780, directed against the city's Catholic population. These events, motivated by opposition to the concessions of 1778, leave their mark on *John Juniper*, which features London's Irish Catholic underclass, and *Anthony Varnish*, which contains episodes of mob violence set in the city.

Anthony Varnish is commonly held to be Johnston's last novel, and is listed as such in nearly all bibliographical sources. However, Lund comments more circumspectly that the novel has been attributed to Johnston "on the basis of internal evidence," including its Irish setting.[21] This resort to the text's content has the effect of highlighting the comparative absence of external signs that Johnston might have written *Anthony Varnish*. The novel is not mentioned in primary sources on the novelist's life, and Johnston was probably already in India at the time of its publication.[22] Brief and crushing periodical reviews dismissed the novel's author as an unknown hack: "The *peep* has certainly been into St Giles's, for among such society alone he must have been an adept."[23] This chapter seeks to place the attribution on a firmer footing by marshaling the available bibliographical evidence and then considering possible connections between Johnston and the novel's dedicatee, the theater manager George Colman. More broadly, correspondences between *Anthony Varnish* and Johnston's earlier fiction are pursued. The novelist repeatedly utilized the device of an observing first-person narrator in order to satirize the foibles of society. In place of a coin, spirit, or Chinese traveler, *Anthony Varnish* is narrated by a rootless Irish orphan. Varnish wanders through Ireland and England, experiencing a society that is repeatedly callous and violent. On one level, his experiences reinforce the idea of the riotous "wild" Irish, but migrants to England like Varnish are also cast as victims of prejudice in the novel. *Anthony Varnish* was subtitled *A Peep at the Manners of Society*, and the review quoted above mockingly interpreted this "society" as that of St Giles, a down-at-heel district of London with a large Irish population, associated with crime and the seedier elements of the print trade. Indeed, the novel gives a detailed and sympathetic account of this sphere, as Varnish encounters other needy, displaced people, from the vagrant Irish to penniless authors. In doing so, the novel evokes both economic woes back home in Ireland,

and the difficulty for Irish immigrants in reestablishing a sustaining social and cultural community.

Political Satire and National Identity in *John Juniper*

Chrysal and *The Reverie* offer many salacious, thinly disguised caricatures of public figures, and *John Juniper* is partly a continuation of Johnston's brand of topical satire. Juniper is readable as a version of the journalist and politician John Wilkes (c. 1726–97), who was then the city chamberlain of London. *The Critical Review* guessed as much: "Just before the publication of this work, it was whispered round, that it contained the true history of a no less respectable personage than the celebrated John Wilkes, shadowed out under the character of Juniper Jack."[24] *John Juniper* can be framed as a satirical roman à clef that purports to reveal the disreputable origins of Wilkes. The novel references Wilkes's well-known squint when the infant Jack's mother, "stooping at the same instant to kiss him, started back in surprise and horrour, at seeing his eyes distorted into the strangest squint she had ever beheld."[25] His Irish mother runs an alehouse and is therefore known as *"Whisky Nan"* (1:4). Jack is soon orphaned when Whisky Nan is transported to America for her part in a libelous blackmail scheme, but fortunately, a more well-to-do English family, the Junipers, adopt him and raise him as their own. As an adult, he journeys around England, joining a troupe of actors in York, then returning to London, where he fortuitously encounters Whisky Nan, now returned from the colonies, and learns of his true parentage. He begins a career in politics, but fails to win a seat in Parliament and flees into exile in Wales, at which point the narrative ends. The conceit of Wilkes's hidden birth has a larger significance in the narrative given Johnston's own Irishness. Juniper's parents share both their nationality and their place of residence with Johnston, himself a migrant with an informed perspective on London's Irish diaspora that is evident from the novel. Nationality is also central to the story of Juniper, who spends his early life with the Catholic Irish but is then adopted by an English family. In considering his roguish tendencies, the novel invokes eighteenth-century theories of self-formation alongside the negative views of Irish national character available in criminal biographies.

John Juniper caricatures Wilkes as an ambitious and dangerous radical, a characterization looking back to his first rise to prominence in the 1760s. Early in the narrative, Whisky Nan expresses the hope that her son "might possibly rise in the world, as others had done from as low an origin" and become "a parliament-man" (1:9). Her wishes are borne out when her adult son attempts to "get into parliament": "He made it his business to mix with the people," because "the ladder of ambition must be fixed in the dirt, to prevent it slipping" (2:224). He begins to write and publish "slanders" in which "private virtue, even in the highest stations, was treated with contempt, as inconsistent with public abilities; and that respect, which is the indispensable support of government, trampled under foot; while the incendiary, who held the torch, gloried in the effects of that flame, as proof of his power" (2:226). The novel's deliberately vague references to subversive writing and mob violence invoke the controversy resulting from Wilkes's short-lived political weekly, the *North-Briton*. In April 1763, Wilkes was arrested for printing issue 45 of the periodical, which was received as a critique both of the ministry of Lord Bute and of King George III himself. In November the House of Commons ruled that the *North-Briton* constituted seditious libel, and Wilkes fled to France under threat of prosecution. This year witnessed the first public demonstrations in support of Wilkes, scenes that would be reprised in 1768, when Wilkes campaigned to become MP for Middlesex and "Wilkites" fought with opposing voters on the streets of London.[26] *John Juniper* sketches these turbulent events through the actions of the "incendiary" Juniper, a demonic figure whose flaming "torch" recalls the Wilkite riots.

Johnston had already utilized the *North-Briton* controversy as material in *Chrysal*, which offers a sketch of Wilkes's arrest for libel in the early 1760s. *Chrysal* advertises its loyalty to the king and establishment by describing Wilkes's writings as "disgraceful to himself, and dangerous to his country," though it also praises his "uncommon abilities."[27] But the portrayal of Wilkes in *John Juniper* constituted more than a reprisal of past battles. As the American Revolutionary War continued, British opponents of American independence attacked its egalitarian ethos, and the novel's critique of populist politics must be read in this light.[28] Wilkes was active in debates around the war, predicting several times in Parliament that the loss of the colonies was inevitable, and expressing support for their right to freedom from unjust taxation.[29] This aside, the novel's imagery of riots and flames would, for readers in 1781, have most immediately recalled the destructive Gordon Riots of the previous year. The Protestant Association, led by Lord George Gordon, marched to Westminster on June 2, 1780, to petition for the repeal of the 1778 Catholic Relief Act. When the government refused to debate their petition, enraged crowds attacked and set fire to chapels, Catholic-owned businesses, politicians' homes, and prisons.[30] The Gordon Riots would have reminded observers of earlier Wilkite disturbances, as the role of a firebrand politician—Wilkes, or Gordon—was seen as key in both cases. After the Gordon Riots, the government sought sympathizers among the opposition, and Wilkes came under suspicion; this was in fact groundless, as he was by then a respectable city chamberlain, and had actually participated in the defense of the Bank of England against rioters.[31] Nevertheless, Johnston's roman à clef, published the year after these tumultuous scenes, could have been intended as a timely reminder of the city chamberlain's radical past.

The satire on Wilkes in *John Juniper* orients itself around a central conceit: the exposure of his "true" parentage. Johnston plays on the supposed obscurity of Wilkes's middling-sort, commercial family (his father, Israel Wilkes, was a prosperous distiller in Clerkenwell) by inventing a backstory in which he is the illegitimate son of an Irish landlady.[32] The concocting of an Irish background for a public figure is not without precedent in fiction, seen also in the 1725 criminal biography *The Life and Glorious Actions of the Most Heroic and Magnanimous Jonathan Wilde*, discussed already. Another example, Edward Kimber's novel *The Juvenile Adventures of David Ranger* (1756), is a roman à clef about the English actor David Garrick (1717–79) that fictionalizes its subject both by making him Irish, and by changing his surname to that of his most famous role, Ranger in Benjamin Hoadly's *The Suspicious Husband*.[33] Kimber leaves readers with the image of Garrick as "the generous *Davy*" who "was in private life, all the great and amiable characters he so well personated upon the stage."[34] Kimber's conceit that Garrick is actually Irish serves as a humorous testament to his acting abilities, implying that Garrick has been playing the role of an Englishman all along. It is appropriate that Juniper is also a strolling player, and Johnston makes much of his ability to disguise himself, acclaiming "the astonishing power nature had given him over his eyes, and all the muscles of his face; any particular feature, or even the whole symmetry of which, he could vary in such a manner, as not only to disguise himself from all possibility of being known, but also to resemble any one he pleased" (1:84). The deceptive and variable identity conventional to the rogue narrative lends itself naturally to mock-lives of public figures, who can be celebrated (in Kimber's case) or libeled (as in Johnston's) by means of surreal narratives of hidden pasts and origins. Whether framed as criminal biographies (like *Jonathan Wilde*) or as novels, the Irish rogue narrative insistently blurs the lines between fact and fiction. The idea of Wilkes's secret parentage appropriately conjoins two of this novel's main concerns: the Irish and the development of identity. I will deal firstly with the text's depiction of the Irish in London.

Juniper "ascended into the world, out of a cellar in *Broad St Giles's*" (1:3). The parish of St Giles had been home to migrants from Ireland since Tudor times, and the early parts of the novel are dense with references to the city's Irish denizens.[35] Historical accounts of the Irish in eighteenth-century London have concentrated on poor Catholic laborers, constructing an image of a marginalized community who were associated with rioting and crime.[36] Recent studies focused on the networks of middling-sort and professional Irish Londoners have added more nuance to this picture.[37] Among Whisky Nan's associates is an Irish Catholic priest who has been "sent upon the *Mission* to *England*, where he piously exerted all his abilities to abuse the religion and laws of the country" (1:17). This character thus provides an excuse for Johnston to reiterate prejudices against Catholics recently granted legal freedoms. But the priest goes on to have an unexpectedly important role in the narrative, as he is later revealed to be the real father of the similarly villainous Juniper Jack (2:166). The novel also refers to a gang of Irish farm workers, "forty as clean, loose fellows as ever handled a hay-fork," refreshing themselves at Nan's cellar after participating in a fight at "Charing-Cross" (1:20). In the eighteenth century, agricultural laborers commonly migrated from Ireland to Britain to work during the harvest season.[38] The role of the cellar in these early scenes captures the way in which Irish-owned taverns and coffeehouses facilitated "shadowy networks" of shared nationality in eighteenth-century London.[39] But alongside the predictable company of priests and farmhands, Nan's social ties reach out to the middling-sort and elite Irish. When pursuing a scheme to blackmail various noblemen, she seeks the help of "a young gentleman belonging to the law, who had come over from Dublin, where he was a hackney clerk to the attornies" (1:21–22). Then, when her plot is discovered and she is sentenced to transportation, she tries to secure a pardon through a "fashionable young lady," "her dear friend and relation Miss *O'Kennelly*, whose interest with the great was such, that she had lately been able to save two condemned murtherers from the gallows" (1:33–34). This figure's "interest with the great" aligns her with the "community of privileged and influential Irish Catholics in London" whose existence is established by Bergin.[40] In the novel's early scenes, Nan's cellar acts as a locus for the Irish in London, who are not simply poor and marginalized, but able to draw upon connections to those of a higher status.

John Juniper thus gives a sense of the range of Irish people who were living in London during the century. That said, the plotline of Nan's scheme perpetuates the image of the criminal lower-class Irish that was established in Britain. And given that Nan's son grows up to pursue a rogue's career, ideas of inherited qualities then suggest themselves. Criminal biographies in the 1780s continued to retail anti-Irish prejudices, as can be seen in *The Life of Patrick Madan*, a cheap pamphlet published in the same year as *John Juniper*. Madan is born in a "country" that is "remarkable for a loose, disorderly, savage sett of beings, which she annually exports to her sister kingdom." After moving to

London, he is "impelled" "by a kind of *fatality*" into "*commencing robber at large.*"[41] Here, nationality is highlighted as the key factor in explaining Madan's crimes, implying that his disposition is predetermined. Johnston's novel, however, is more nuanced in its account of the development of the self. Previous readers of *John Juniper* such as Lund have argued that Juniper's predilection for vice is innate: "[Juniper] soon proves the ascendancy of nature over nurture when he tricks his Scots tutor and runs away from home."[42] Roberts also endorses the determinism of *John Juniper*: "The novel abounds in roguish escapades which are evidently linked with Jack's Irish blood though he remains oblivious of this until late in the story."[43] I argue, however, that *John Juniper* can be read as a critique of the concept of inherited qualities.

John Juniper repeatedly speculates upon the origins of Juniper's disposition. Like Smollett's Peregrine Pickle, the young boy torments his elders with practical jokes and mimicry, mocking his foster mother "by aping her *Frenchified* airs; which young as he was, he did with the most irresistible drollery; nature seeming to have sent him into the world, on purpose to burlesque every thing in it" (1:52).[44] The child's "advances in the sublime, and extensive science of mischief were so rapid," the narrator observes, that "they would have afforded the profound author of *Clio*, a stronger argument, in favour of *innate* ideas, than any of those that cost him so much labour to spin out of his own brain" (1:52). Johnston here references the Irish philosopher James Ussher's *Clio: Or, a Discourse on Taste* (1767), which argued that "there is, in several respects, an universal standard of taste in the soul of man, which, it is true, may be depraved or corrupted by education and habit, though it can never be wholly rooted out or stifled."[45] Ussher's thoughts on the existence of innate and ineluctable tastes are referenced in the novel—but importantly, in a skeptical fashion, being described as both labored and insubstantial ("so much labour to spin out of his own brain"). The undercutting of Ussher's theories here points to the novel's stance on the issue of Juniper's identity.

The reading of Juniper as a born rogue is troubled firstly by the fact that this belief is not taken seriously in the text, but is subject to mockery, primarily through the character of Juniper's superstitious mother. Noticing her son's squint, Nan declares, "his eyes turned every way at once, like those of a thief," and becomes convinced that her child is a "*changeling*," "the offspring of some foul fiend," details that gesture toward Irish "fairy" lore (1:13–14). But the narrator then reveals that the baby's squinting "proceeded from a ray of light shining constantly upon the point of his nose, through a crevice in the wall," a "determination" that is "most unphilosophically founded in fact" (1:17). Nan's misguided belief in her son's villainy is highlighted again when she returns from America and is reunited with him. She observes his rakish life with disapproval, yet is also "flattered to think that her hatred had proceeded from something like prescience, rather than injustice" (2:210). Her beliefs in fairies and "prescience" are dismissed in favor of empirical "fact," and thus, the idea that Juniper is born a "thief" is opened up to skepticism. Juniper himself seems to share his mother's fear of determinism, which is ultimately treated as comical. When he is still ignorant of his true parentage, he meets a patriotic Irishman who gives him the compliment, "I'll be hanged if you have not *Irish* blood in your veins," a suggestion that "made his flesh creep" (1:215). The suggestion of inherited nationality elicits fear, yet this is arguably neutralized by the final paragraph, which leaves us with an image of a credulous Juniper in old age: "If left a moment alone in the dark, he would burst out crying like a child, for fear of goblins, ghosts and devils" (2:259). Examination of the trope of superstition in *John Juniper* reveals a skeptical undercutting of the concepts of inherited vice and "*Irish* blood."

Johnston continues his attack on determinism in his account of the hero's upbringing by his foster parents, who are appalled that "the first words he ever attempted to articulate were *whore* and *rogue*" (1:47–48). The narrator entertains the idea that this denotes a criminal "nature": "The sentiments and language of his parents . . . which invariably descend to the offspring. But with due submission to better judgement, this opinion seems to be liable to some objections" (1:48). This determinist view is said to be composed of "metaphysical arguments" and "elaborate systems" and attributed to "the learned of a neighbouring nation" (1:49). Possibly implied here are the theories of French

Enlightenment scientists such as Georges-Louis Leclerc, the Comte de Buffon, regarded today as the foundation for the modern concept of genetic heredity. Buffon posited that individualized structures or molds, handed down from parent to child, lay behind intergenerational resemblances. These hypotheses lacked experimental evidence, leading many to dismiss them as fanciful, a reaction that is arguably registered here in the novel.[46] Johnston's narrator offers a more commonsense explanation for the child's swearing: having spent "the greatest part of his time in the kitchen, according to the invariable mode of *English* education . . . he must have learned the language and manners of servants." The narrator promotes exposure to servants as a rational explanation, "*founded in fact*" (1:49). Scorning both folk and scientific philosophies of heredity, the novel instead emphasizes the importance of education, from a Lockean perspective in which experiences and sensory impressions (the language of servants, the ray of light) produce the characteristics of the person.[47] In addition to the servants, Juniper's adoptive father, "a *buck* and a *bruiser*, too, in his day," gives him a "true *old English* education," teaching him to swear, fight, "eat cold beef, and drink strong beer for breakfast" (1:51–52). The repeated, satirical allusions to an "*English* education" function to offset any assumed hierarchy of morality or civility between the English and Juniper's Irish parents.

The evident importance of education in *John Juniper* would imply the possibility that criminals can acquire better principles and change their ways. It is fitting then that Whisky Nan returns after twenty-five years in America as a changed woman, having made "a true turn to piety" due to the attentions of a young slave girl who converts her from Catholicism to the Church of England (2:173). This story recalls Defoe's *Moll Flanders* (1722), in which the heroine is likewise transported to a plantation in Virginia and repents of her sins. However, *John Juniper* does not include any such moment of repentance for the protagonist—contrasting with midcentury novels like *Tom Jones*, *Peregrine Pickle*, or *Jack Connor*, with their redeemable male heroes. *John Juniper* thus invites another context with a different set of expectations: the criminal biography, which typically concluded with the criminal's execution. When Juniper is traveling across "the heath of

Hounslow, so celebrated in the records of justice" as the territory of highwaymen, he passes a "*gibbet*," which appears to him "as an omen inauspicious to his undertaking" (1:160). The possibility of a violent end is thereby set up, but only to be rejected. In the closing paragraphs, the narrator suspects that "critics" will question the "poetical justice" of Juniper's situation, then compares such moralizing objections to "those . . . who are offended with *Gay*, for not hanging *Macheath*" (2:256). This justifies a narrative in which a rogue escapes alive, as in John Gay's famous opera, and in contrast to the conventional ending of the criminal biography.

The novel's dispensing with the "poetical justice" of the gallows is consonant with its attitude to the concepts of fate and innate dispositions. In criminal biographies, such as those of Patrick Madan, Irish nationality is envisioned as predisposing the subject to a lawless existence that, according to the logic of the form, will result in capital punishment. But in *John Juniper*, the concept of innate qualities, in both traditional and scientific guises, is held up to interrogation. Ironically, it turns out that criminality is not Juniper's inheritance from his mother; the protagonist learns how to be a rogue in the house of his English foster parents. Johnston thus contests the representation of the Irish still current in criminal biography, not through any positive characterization of his hero, but more subtly, through critical reflections upon determinism.

Irish Patriotism in *John Juniper*

Thus far, *John Juniper* has been read as a satirical rogue biography in which the idea of Wilkes being Irish allows Johnston to question cultural associations between nationality and delinquency. More broadly, the novel can be read as an example of the patriotic strand in eighteenth-century Irish fiction, exemplified also by Chaigneau and Amory. Johnston's defense of Irish culture and civility is seen partly through a concern with Irish masculine virtue, comparable to earlier fiction and drama. Importantly, however, *John Juniper* demonstrates that this patriotic tendency is not incompatible with the rogue narrative; a desire to represent Ireland positively does not lead to the discarding of criminal characters. In fact, the rogue, with his characteristic deceptiveness and trickery, becomes an effective means of exposing the oppression of imperial subjects through satire.

The perennial discourse of Irish criminality was contested by Irish novelists and playwrights in the eighteenth century. *John Juniper* signals its awareness of this literary and historical context in the character of Doctor MacShane, who befriends Juniper in Somerset and gives an interpolated account of his life. MacShane is reminiscent of the *counter*-Stage Irishman in his stereotypical Hiberno-English speech, touchy reactions to jokes at his nation's expense, and strong morals: "The character of *MacShane* . . . was not marked more strongly by his blunders, than by sound sense, and true generosity of sentiment" (1:219). He hails from a noble family, whose "falling into decay, in the changes of time" impels him to enlist in "the *Irish* brigades, in the service of *France*" (1:219–20). France's Irish regiments, which were initially populated by Jacobite exiles, provided a career path for Catholic men throughout the eighteenth century.[48] In 1781, French armies were fighting on the side of the American colonies, meaning that anti-French feeling would have been high in Britain. But MacShane manifests no political sympathy with Britain's perennial enemies, and joins the Irish Brigades only due to his aristocratic disdain of trade (1:220). When he gets to France, he finds its soldiers to be "a set of the vilest out-casts of his country" who "complained of persecution at home, under the government, most favourable to freedom of any upon earth" (1:221). MacShane acclaims the liberal principles of the British government, voicing a brand of moderate loyalism that was associated with the Irish Catholic nobility rather than the poor. During the American war, the mainly aristocratic Catholic Committee emphasized their support of Britain with a view to securing the repeal of the remaining Penal Laws.[49] Johnston uses this positive Irish character to allude to Catholic hopes for "freedom" from the British government through his tale of service in France.

After leaving the Irish Brigades, Dr. MacShane is soon "*pressed into an English* man of war" that is headed for the East Indies (1:223). His transition from French to British service enacts a kind of reform analogous to that of Whisky Nan, and engages with contemporary debates around the Catholic presence in the British military. A primary aim of the 1778 Relief Act was to boost recruitment to the army in wartime by altering oaths of allegiance to make them less objectionable to Catholics.[50] Burke charts how the campaign for penal reform in the early 1780s sought to present Irish Catholics as a reliable military force, and how the prospect of Catholics bearing arms led to retaliatory propaganda from Irish Protestant writers.[51] Johnston's novel is therefore timely in presenting the Irish Catholic MacShane serving with distinction in the English navy. He volunteers to serve as surgeon's mate, and "the officers, whose esteem he had gained by the correctness and propriety of his conduct" promote him to surgeon, and again to the ship's agent (1:223). In this capacity, "he acquired a handsome fortune, with the fairest character, against his return to *Europe*" (1:224). Now wealthy, MacShane marries an English heiress, Miss Courtly. This narrative of MacShane's social success and acceptance through military service distinguishes *John Juniper* from conservative Protestant objections to Catholic relief. Moreover, in his nautical career, name, and nationality, MacShane also closely resembles an Irish character from Smollett's *Roderick Random*, the Irish ship's surgeon Mackshane. Smollett's Mackshane pursues a professional rivalry with Roderick to malicious extremes, having him "loaded with irons, and stapled to the deck, on pretence that I [Roderick] was a spy on board." He conspires with other sailors against Roderick, and moreover, is secretly a practicing Catholic.[52] Considering the earlier novel, it seems doubly deliberate that Johnston's MacShane behaves so laudably during his time aboard the English man-of-war. *John Juniper*, it can be argued, reworks Smollett's earlier, harsh depiction of the Irish to better reflect a moment in which Catholics were gaining greater legal rights.

Johnston's work previous to *John Juniper* manifests a recurrent interest in the international circulation of capital, seen most obviously in *Chrysal*, in which the guinea's adventures dramatize British commercial and imperial expansion.[53] *John Juniper* demonstrates a skeptical awareness of the workings of the colonial economy in an episode set on the Suffolk estate of Squire Mushroom, a landlord with property in India. The ambitious Juniper enters the nobleman's circle by posing as a Genoese "conjuror" called Gaffareni. His role as a court jester gives him the license to mock the squire, enabling the novel to satirize landlords with East Indian interests. Gaffareni claims that Mushroom is a "doctor" with marvelously effective "prescriptions" such as "fasting . . . by which you have the honour of having cured half a million of poor people of the head-ach for ever in *India*"—a clearly risky jest that the squire refutes, angrily denying responsibility for any "famine" (2:19–20). A likely allusion here is the Bengal famine of 1769–70, which began due to a drought and was exacerbated by the failure of the state to make enough food or funds available to the rural population.[54] At the time it was estimated that between a fifth and a third of Bengal's people had perished.[55] Gaffareni denounces Mushroom as "a *Nabob*; a self-made squire, sprung from a dunghill" (2:29). The stock figure of the "Nabob" registered public disapproval of the actions of East India Company agents such as Robert Clive. Nabob characters also feature in Johnston's previous two novels, *Arsaces* and *The Pilgrim*.[56] According to Stephen Gregg, anti-nabob satire is elicited by "a larger critique on the 'presumption' of the merchant-classes," as much as any opposition to the British enterprise in India.[57] Joseph Lennon offers a similar cautionary view of the radical potential of colonial satire in this period, focusing on "pseudo-oriental letters" that utilized the perspective of a foreign "other" to satirize British society. One of Lennon's examples is Johnston's epistolary *The Pilgrim*, written in the guise of Choang, a Chinese visitor to England. Lennon comments that these "critiques were satirical but rarely taken as subversive . . . such rhetorical 'writing back' did not represent mutiny or insubordination; it was merely comic."[58] Perhaps Juniper's comments about Mushroom are similarly neutralized by the unthreatening perspective of Gaffareni, a foreign and "comic" court entertainer. Yet further analysis reveals that the relationship of Juniper to Mushroom is precisely one of "insubordination."

Before the exchange quoted above, Juniper and Mushroom have planned to appear to fall out, so that Juniper can assist the landlord's electioneering scheme without being recognized as Mushroom's lackey (2:15). Yet their mock dispute becomes a real fight after Juniper's references to India: "There is no jest in tickling an old sore. This came so home to the squire, that it exceeded both his patience and presence of mind to bear it." Mushroom hurls "a silver ink-stand, at his head, with such force, that if he had not ducked from the blow, he would never after have wanted pill or prescription" (2:20). The prearranged boundaries of the exchange, as comic and hierarchical, are broken by the mention of "famine." The squire's extreme reaction, attacking Juniper with murderous "force" and then banishing him from the house, registers the challenge to his authority. Lennon writes that satires upon empire were "rarely taken as subversive," but here, Johnston dramatizes a reaction to anti-nabob satire that is anything but comfortable and good humored.

Mushroom expels Juniper with the words "his impudence shall cost him a hungry belly" (2:20), a punishment that aligns him with the starving Indians. Juniper is further positioned in this way—as a marginalized victim of colonialism—by subsequent events that bring his Irish identity into the frame. He sets himself up as a quack doctor on Mushroom's estate, hawking products to the tenants, including "*Batatas of Guinea*," the "nutritive qualities" of which, he tells his customers, "have been abundantly proved in our sister-kingdom of *Ireland*, where it is the only food left to the people by their absent landlords, who live so sumptuously among us" (2:25). The "absent landlords" indicted here can be counted among the critical portraits of the British colonial elite that "became commonplace in Irish writing during the American war," when a "vision of a corrupt and effeminate Britain [was] often contrasted with accounts of the rise of a manly Irish patriotism and virtue."[59] As he rails against the abstraction of absentee landlords, Juniper's words recall his parentage and thus, his kinship with the Irish poor he invokes.

It is significant that the novel voices its invective through its protagonist, and that he does so in disguise. His role-playing corresponds to Bakhtin's theory of the rogue in the picaresque novel: "They are life's maskers; their being coincides with their role, and outside this role they simply do not exist." For Bakhtin, the picaresque rogue is similar to the literary figure of the "fool" or jester, as both have the ability to "see the underside and the falseness in every situation"; "their entire function consists in . . . the making-public of specifically non-public spheres of life."[60] Juniper acts according to Bakhtin's definition of the rogue by posing as a conjuror and a doctor in order to expose "the underside" of the landlord's status and power, the hungry poor in India and Ireland. Bakhtin further offers a means of conceptualizing perspective in *John Juniper*. The archetypes of rogue and fool can function as a vehicle for the privileged, authorial viewpoint: "The novelist stands in need of some essential formal and generic mask that could serve to define the position from which he views life, as well as the position from which he makes that life public. And it is precisely here, of course, that the masks of the clown and the fool (transformed in various ways) come to the aid of the novelist."[61] The "position" that the novel takes up in these scenes sympathizes with the colonized poor in India and Ireland. The authorial viewpoint of *John Juniper* thus takes in critiques of British misrule alongside positive representations of Irish characters such as Dr. MacShane. Concomitantly, the blame for Juniper's criminality is transferred from his mother to a "true *old English* education." Throughout the novel, Juniper is an object of speculation as to the origins of his identity, and of censure for his vices. However, as he satirizes Squire Mushroom, he becomes the agent of, and mouthpiece for, the condemnation of crimes greater than his own.

Violence and Victimization in *Anthony Varnish*

The formation of the individual personality is a central theme of *John Juniper*, but in *Anthony Varnish*, characterization and identity are not foregrounded in the same way. Instead, the perspective is turned outward, as the narrator provides a vehicle for an extended survey of what the subtitle calls "the Manners of Society." *Anthony Varnish* presents, or exposes, Irish and English manners through a succession of what one reviewer termed "despicably vulgar scenes."[62] The scatological trickery and cruelty witnessed by Varnish was conventional to the ramble novel. *Anthony Varnish* thus seems to perpetuate the timeworn image of the wild Irish. As the narrator moves from Ireland to England, however, the Irish are revealed to be victims of violence and prejudice. But before the narrative is considered, some neglected aspects of Johnston's later life and career must be elucidated to shed further light on the novel's origins.

External evidence for the attribution of *Anthony Varnish* to Johnston relates mainly to the pseudonym under which the novel was originally issued, "An Adept," the same pseudonym that was used for *Chrysal*. However, all of Johnston's other novels were originally published as "by the Editor of Chrysal" or "the Editor of the Adventures of a Guinea." Why would Johnston have deviated from his long-standing custom of publishing as "the editor" of *Chrysal* to reassume an older literary alias? It should be noted that new editions of *Chrysal* in 1783 and 1785 kept "An Adept" current and visible, adding to the likelihood that it would have been associated with Johnston and making it a viable means of framing or marketing a new novel.[63] Johnston may also have published elsewhere as "An Adept," as two periodical articles bearing this name from 1777 and 1785 feature themes comparable to his novels.[64] A consideration of Johnston's networks and associations in London and India around the time that *Anthony Varnish* was likely written can further reinforce the attribution.

The novel is dedicated to a major figure in the theatrical world, George Colman the Elder, the manager of the Haymarket Theatre. The dedication expresses the wish that the novel may "make [Colman] laugh, in spite of the inroads of care, or the attacks of disease."[65] In 1784 and 1785, Colman had been prevented from working at the Haymarket by gout, and had traveled first to Bath and then Margate for his health. But in late 1785, he suffered a stroke that left him partially paralyzed.[66] A connection exists between Johnston and Colman that suggests why the novelist might have sought the theater manager's attention. This comes through the Sparks family of Irish actors, whom Johnston knew in London and Bombay. According to one biographer, Johnston helped a son of the actor Luke Sparks (1711–68) to secure a job in India: "A countryman, the respectable Luke Sparks, of Covent Garden Theatre, had a son appointed through his [Johnston's] influence to Bombay as a writer."[67] Sparks was a popular Irish actor who worked at Covent Garden from 1748 to his retirement in 1765. Colman went into management at Covent Garden two years later, in 1767. The letter calls the actor "a countryman" of Johnston's, hinting that both were part of a network based on shared nationality in London. Sparks and Johnston were of similar ages, the actor being eight years the elder. Both lived in Dublin in the 1730s and 1740s, and by 1750, they had both moved to London. The son of Luke Sparks that Johnston helped to an appointment seems to have been James Sparks, born in 1753. James was the younger of the actor's two sons, and Luke was worried about James's livelihood, and seeking positions for him, during his final years in the 1760s.[68] After his father's death, James had a brief career on the London stage, mainly at the Haymarket Theatre, where he appeared in 1779 and 1782.[69] Colman was the manager of the Haymarket throughout this period. The biography of Johnston cited already mentions that he and James kept up their association in India: "I saw Mr. Johnson at Bombay comfortably entertained in the house of old Luke Sparks's son, then a counsellor of that Presidency, in 1782."[70] By the time that Johnston might have been writing the novel, then, he possessed an ascertainable connection to Colman through James Sparks, who had acted at the Haymarket. The reasons for the choice of the theater manager can only be speculated. Certainly, Colman was an influential figure in literary circles, and it is possible that Johnston was seeking to make further inroads into the theater after his first play, *Buthred*, had been produced seven years previously. But the dedication of *Anthony Varnish* makes more sense when we realize that its likely author, Johnston, knew and helped others who were more entrenched in Colman's world, including an actor who had recently worked under him in London.

Beyond the bibliographical and biographical context of *Anthony Varnish*, the narrative certainly suggests that its author had experience of Ireland. Varnish is born in "a small cabin" in "Queen's County" (Co. Laois), the son, like Gil Blas or Jack Connor, of a retired soldier turned farmer (1:3). *Anthony Varnish* presents an immediate contrast with *John Juniper* in the virtuous upbringing and principles of its hero.

His childhood is idyllic and well regulated: "I was accordingly christened . . . with all due rites and solemn preparations. It were needless to recount all the little pleasantries and harmless jokes which passed in that rural, though friendly, circle upon the occasion" (1:15). The family's Protestantism is implicitly a factor in the hero's virtue, but it is not underlined as such. Indeed, it is possible to read *Anthony Varnish* without realizing the protagonist's faith, as seen in Hand's point that "Varnish is not identifiable as Irish or Anglo-Irish, Protestant or Catholic."[71] Much later, however, Varnish states that he "was educated agreeably to the established church" of his home country (3:9). Varnish's happy childhood is cut short when his parents' death "left me an orphan, at twelve years of age, to struggle with a base world in the best manner I was able" (1:20). Varnish is a passive observer who functions as a means of connecting together episodic accounts of the "base world" and anchoring the novel in a moral viewpoint. *Anthony Varnish* exhibits the process described by Mark Blackwell in which the heroes of mid-eighteenth-century novels become "mute and overlooked objects," "equivalent to the money and other objects that circulate . . . in contemporary it-narratives."[72] Hilary Jane Englert traces the observing narrators of such fictions to Lesage: "Novelists of the second half of the eighteenth century seized on the narrative device introduced by Lesage and popularised by Johnstone, organising their works around narrators with heightened awareness, an itinerant nature, and special capacities for surveillance." Englert refers here to *Chrysal* and to Lesage's *Le Diable Boiteux* (1707), in which the narrator is a devil who guides a young student through the corruptions of Madrid.[73] Yet this passage could equally well describe Johnston's *The Reverie*, in which the spirit Ariel endows the mortal narrator with the power of invisibility and promises him: "The walls of the closet shall be transparent to your eye; and the secret whisper sound distinctly in your ear."[74] The narrative technique of the itinerant eyewitness seems to have had a special appeal to Johnston, both early in his career and later on.

The strain of comic violence present in *Anthony Varnish* echoes the rogue narrative tradition. Grotesque practical jokes and scenes of accidental embarrassment abound in the novel; Varnish is apprenticed to the unpopular Doctor Calomel in Portarlington, and witnesses him being mercilessly tormented by the townspeople. An enemy of the doctor desires to "mortify him to that degree, as to oblige him to quit the town," and launches a convoluted trick that leaves the doctor lying drunk in a muddy street with sheep's entrails bound around his head (1:135–50). Elsewhere, an argument between two churchmen aboard a boat is interrupted by a seasick passenger, who "discharged . . . foetid liquids plump into the face of the angry Methodist" (2:105–6). The character of this violence recalls picaresque works such as Quevedo's *El Buscón*, in which Pablos is pelted with fruit by a carnival-day crowd and spat upon by a gang of students due to his servant status and criminal parents.[75] Such incidents are the stock-in-trade of ramble fiction, and betray the influence of "the picaresque and antiromance traditions" from *Lazarillo de Tormes* to *Peregrine Pickle* (1751).[76] The butts of the ritualized pranks perpetrated in *Anthony Varnish* are usually foreigners or members of religious minorities, or both; for example, the French Huguenot Calomel. Their humiliation, which often takes place in front of an amused audience, marks them as outside the pale of society. Jewish secondary characters are subjected to taunts and tricks in *Chrysal*, *John Juniper*, and *Anthony Varnish*; the particularly anti-Semitic character of all three novels adds to the sense that they share an author.[77]

Given the harsh treatment of national or religious difference in *Anthony Varnish*, and seeing as many of the novel's episodes of brutality take place in Ireland, this novel could also be read as reinforcing prejudices about the violent Irish. At one point, Varnish stays in a peasant cabin, where in the dark, he stumbles into a sleeping cattle drover. A brawl breaks out, causing the owner of the cabin to yell: *"Arrah, mun jowl*, you vagabonds, if you're not quiet, in no time at all at all, your souls to the devil, but I'll be after running the pitch-fork, up to the hilt, in every whore's son of ye" (1:208). The stereotyped Hiberno-English speech is joined by references to extortion and murder when the luckless Calomel receives a letter threatening to "carry you into the middle of the bog, and bury you alive" unless a sum of money is paid, signed "CORNELIUS CUT-THROAT, PETER PERDITION, AND PHELIM O'TAWNEY" (1:161–62). Menacing letters sent to landlords and other authority figures were a tactic of agrarian protest factions such as the Whiteboys and Rightboys in Ireland at the time.[78] In these scenes, *Anthony Varnish* transfers the distasteful picaresque humor of ramble fiction to Ireland, and in doing so, the novel often seems to reiterate timeworn tropes of Irish savagery.

Halfway through the narrative, Varnish moves from Ireland to England in the service of an army officer, yet the "despicably vulgar scenes" continue unabated. However, after Varnish's move to London, the tone of the violence becomes less slapstick and more dangerous and frightening, because pranks now give way to outbreaks of mob unrest. The eighteenth century was, in Shoemaker's words, "the most riotous century in London's history," seeing the Wilkite riots of the 1760s, various laborers' protests, and frequent smaller-scale disorder.[79] Soon after arriving in London, Varnish witnesses a crowd's treatment of a suspected pickpocket: "I followed the tattered cavalcade, who proceeded with their prisoner, close-guarded, to the water-side; where, after taking him to some neighbouring barges that were laden with coals, they plunged him, unrestrained by a single emotion of pity, into the sable stream" (2:198–99). In one sense, this is a scene straight out of ramble fiction, with public humiliation achieved via a dunking in the river. However, it also dramatizes the real practices of London crowds, who would administer vigilante justice to offenders themselves rather than resorting to the watch.[80] Soon afterward Varnish sees a friend of his being attacked by "a mob of people," and perceives this as an offense against class boundaries: "I was so enraged to see the only gentleman I had met with since my landing in England, who, in my opinion, possessed either tenderness or urbanity, treated in such a rude manner." Trying to intervene, Varnish only becomes a victim himself, as "my arms were pinioned behind me by the mob" (2:201–2). The treatment of the protagonist in this scene conveys the same anxiety about mass disorder as was present in *John Juniper*. The echoes of the 1780 riots are arguably also heard in this novel, published six years later.

Some of those rioting in eighteenth-century London were Irish; for example, the coal heavers whose protests over working conditions in 1768 contributed to British ideas of Irish belligerence.[81] Contemporary criminal biographies reiterated this image, as can be seen in another pamphlet-length biography of Patrick Madan that appeared in 1782, a year after the first: "About April, 1765, when our youth was but thirteen, he joined the riotous weavers of Spittlefields . . . and though very young, was remarkably active in the disturbance of Bloomsbury, when several of the horse-guards were terribly wounded."[82] In *Anthony Varnish*, however, the mob is very much an English creature that is viewed as strange and threatening by the newly arrived Irish migrant, who trembles at "the discordant groans of the millions that crouded the shores of old Thames" (2:200). Anthony's fright is suggestive of the fact that the ire of the London mob was periodically directed against the Irish migrants in the eighteenth century, as in 1736, when the lodging houses of migrant laborers working for lower wages than locals were pulled down.[83] The scenes of crowd violence here connote not the radicalism of disturbances like the Wilkite riots, but the London mob's victimization of Irish outsiders. After the comic punch-ups witnessed in Ireland, violence becomes a serious matter when the novel reaches London. *Anthony Varnish* derives much humor from scenes of low life in which social relations are never far from descending into conflict. This has the effect of reproducing stock views of the hotheaded Irish. The embarrassing of minority figures is likewise presented as humorous. However, the novel's pity for the powerless intensifies when Varnish reaches London, as a consequence of his own increasing marginality as an Irishman abroad.

Poverty and the Atomized Irish Diaspora in *Anthony Varnish*

The account of London's Irish denizens given in *Anthony Varnish* is fuller and less colored by anti-Catholicism than the view of St Giles in *John Juniper*. In *Anthony Varnish*, the migrant's lot is a dismal one, with benevolence having little power to alleviate hardship. The plight of migrants such as Varnish recalls both the Spanish picaresque and early modern anatomies of vagrancy. But any sense of a migrant community in London is now diminished; the connections between Irish people abroad that were charted in *John Juniper* are now absent. Though set largely in London and possibly written from India, *Anthony Varnish* betrays its Irish roots precisely through this narrative of vagrancy, which evokes the economic instability and patterns of emigration that characterized the second half of the eighteenth century in Ireland.

The novel's empathy for the victims of mob violence is consonant with its portraits of the Irish in England, who are cast as objects of prejudice, as when Varnish meets an Irish widow begging in London.[84] Moreover, preconceptions about national criminality are contested when the narrator arrives in Liverpool, as an officer of the port "saluted me with great incivility, and demanded to know where I was going with my trunk . . . honouring me with the familiar appellation of bog-trotting idle scoundrel" (2:128). The "familiar" insult of "idle scoundrel" accords with eighteenth-century views of Irish laborers as lazy or averse to regular, settled employment.[85] Varnish sails to Liverpool alongside several "Irish haymakers, or, what in that country are called, *spalpeens*, who were going over to England to perform the drudgeries of agriculture" (2:95). These "Irish haymakers" (briefly alluded to also in *John Juniper*) were a common feature of the eighteenth-century English countryside during harvest season. The prejudices that existed against them can be seen in an episode from Kimber's *David Ranger*. Two gentlemen in Lincolnshire are robbed by a pair of Irishmen who "were roaming from farm-house to farm-house to get work at the hay-harvest." The laborers murder one of the gentleman and later "meet with their deserved end at Tyburn."[86] Johnston's novels show a skeptical awareness of such prejudices and fears directed at Irish immigrants, as dramatized in one episode from *Chrysal*. A woman arrested for smuggling pleads with a justice of the peace, only to be dismissed as "one of those Irish thieves that come to rob us, and cut our throats . . . We shall never be well, till we have hanged you all." This episode is notably similar to the scene of the Irish widow in *Anthony Varnish*. In *Chrysal*, the Irish woman has been abandoned by her husband, left "to starve in a strange place, where nobody has any compassion for me," whereas in *Anthony Varnish* the woman's husband is dead after experiencing "misfortunes in a strange country" (3:237).[87] The parallels occur on the levels of vocabulary—England is "strange" in both—and of sentiments. *Chrysal* and *Anthony Varnish* present the Irish migrant as a needy object of sympathy, thus emerging as starkly different from English novels such as *David Ranger* and the biographies of Patrick Madan.

In its portrayals of Irish migrants, *Anthony Varnish* emphasizes their poverty rather than their brutality. A parallel movement takes place in the novel's rendering of a stock-character type, the impoverished "hack" writer. *The Critical Review* labeled the novel a "view of the manners of Grub-Street and St Giles's," referring to the London-set portion of the story, in which Varnish falls in with a set of small-time literary aspirants.[88] One of his new friends is a penniless poet, Mr. Crambo, a "figure of famine" who is first encountered on a bench in St James's Park, weeping over a sheaf of papers.[89] This sight inspires the narrator with the desire to "pour the balm of consolation into the wounds of the unfortunate" (3:16–18). This maudlin scene of neglected merit illustrates how the hack in later eighteenth-century writing became an object of sentimental feeling, a process Pat Rogers ascribes to a proto-Romantic "cult of artistic alienation." The sentimentalized hack was a departure from the connotations of the Grub Street writer in Augustan literature: dullness, plagiarism, and subversion. The areas of the capital most agitated by riots were centers of the cheap print trade such as St Giles and Drury Lane, and journalists were seen as responsible for exciting the mob after the Wilkite and Gordon riots.[90] Certainly, this association is made in *John Juniper*, which features the hero emulating Wilkes as a journalist and rabble-rouser. In *Anthony Varnish*, however, the hack is separated from violence as a symbol of need and virtue; Varnish calls Crambo "the best and most disinterested friend I had in the world" (3:161). The writers are seen as victims of prejudice; for example, when an actor mistakes Varnish for one of "the rhyme-weaving rascals" (3:48). The "general contempt he threw upon authors" causes Varnish to reflect upon "the calamities that are

hourly endured by men of the most sublime merit, virtue, and sensibility" (3:51). Such contempt is seen in the verdict on the novel given by
the *Critical Review*: "The author tells us he is an 'adept': we are sorry
for it, but 'we wish the man a dinner, and sit still.'"[91] The quotation
is from Alexander Pope's "Epistle to Dr Arbuthnot" (1735), in which
Pope condescendingly pictures the novelist Charles Gildon: "Yet then
did Gildon draw his venal quill; / I wish'd the man a dinner, and sate
still."[92] The conventional Augustan scorn for those who wrote for hire
is reiterated in the reviews of *Anthony Varnish*. But importantly, the
novel's "view of the manners of Grub-street" is detailed and nonjudgmental, as Crambo guides Varnish through his usual haunts, giving
a kind of hack's-eye view of the city, including "an accurate survey of
the furniture" in his "garret" (3:82). They also visit a wig seller's shop
(3:87–88), a pawnbroker's, and a "register-office" in Holborn where
Anthony looks for work in service (3:199–201). Hacks in *Anthony
Varnish* are distanced from the negative connotations of sedition and
dullness that they possess in earlier writing, and positioned as pitiable
outsiders, much like the Irish migrants encountered elsewhere.

In *Anthony Varnish*, poverty and hunger are the dominant attributes of both hacks and the London Irish. Crambo and his literary
friends are pictured in a night cellar, "sit[ting] down to the miserable
and cold remains of some ox-cheek and neck of beef, which they pres-
ently devoured with such speed as made me imagine, that a thousand
such men in a country would cause a general famine" (3:36). A similar
terminology of starvation is used to describe the unfortunate Irish
widow, whose children's faces are "sicklied over with the pale hand
of famine" (3:233). The theme of hunger in *Anthony Varnish* is comparable to the early picaresque. In *Lazarillo de Tormes*, Lazaro first
experiences life's harshness when working for a priest who rations him
to a diet of one onion every four days.[93] This plotline is echoed in the
young Varnish's experiences at "the oeconomic table of Dr. Calomel,"
where one meal becomes "a week's subsistence" (1:169). The doctor's
meanness is jarring after the earlier scenes of the Varnish family, in
which "good humour presided at the humble board," and represents
a picaresque process of exile from pastoral contentment into hardship

(1:15). Varnish is "left . . . to ramble on the face of the creation, in search of employment to procure me the means of living" (1:233). His forced entry into a commercial sphere of labor parallels the absorption of the underappreciated poet into London's book trade. For Crambo, the ideal but irrecoverable past is a literary golden age, figured in the parodic references to him as a follower of the Muses. Importantly, this idyll is Celtic as well as classical; Crambo is often dubbed a "bard," and the Irish connotations of this word are made explicit when we see Varnish walking down a London street, "humming over to myself a favourite tune of old Carolan, the Irish bard" (3:217). Turlough Carolan (1670–1738) is a particularly appropriate figure to invoke here, as one of the last Irish harpers and poets to operate in a traditional patronage system. Carolan was seen as a lone representative of a vanishing culture, and was dubbed "The Last Irish Bard" by Goldsmith in a 1760 eulogy written for *British Magazine*.[94] Varnish and the hacks, as devalued, urban bards, represent an Irish cultural decline, as community—whether the family, or the structures of patronage that supported Gaelic musicians—gives way to embattled economic self-sufficiency.

Ross has dubbed *Anthony Varnish* "a very early emigration narrative," and the novel returns to accounts of Irish characters impelled to leave home by hardship.[95] Emigration from Ireland is represented as a process of exile and fracture; there is no sense that Varnish is entering an Irish community in London. The ruin of Varnish's family after the death of his parents is paralleled in the tale of the Irish widow in London, whose husband "experienced a sad reverse; and, falling into misfortunes in a strange country, it speedily broke his heart, and he left that disconsolate woman pregnant with these children" (3:237). In London, Varnish meets a former soldier "from a reputable family in the north of Ireland" who has returned from fighting in America and is now unable to financially support his family. After listening to his tale, the narrator "sympathised with his misfortunes, and begged to know if I could serve him, before I recollected I had not even the power to assist myself" (3:97–99). This bleak encounter typifies the way in which social connections have no sustaining power in *Anthony Varnish*. The

Irish networks sketched in *John Juniper* are absent from the London of Johnston's last novel, in which migrants are atomized figures, brought together by chance meetings but unable to aid one another.

The displacement of these vagrant figures evokes the larger developments and crises that caused emigration from Ireland to increase in the second half of the eighteenth century. Traveling through Kildare, Varnish meets a man who "had formerly been a considerable farmer in that county; but, one misfortune happening upon the back of another had reduced him at last to a state of extreme indigence" (1:235). Famine in Ireland was not a live issue in 1786, but the outbreaks of the 1740s and crop failures of 1756–57 were still within living memory. Food shortages and inconsistent economic growth meant that the eviction of tenants remained a customary feature of rural life, and many of those evicted left the country for good. From the 1770s, the Ulster linen industry entered recession, precipitating the migration of much of its workforce to Britain.[96] The stories of material decline in *Anthony Varnish* project an image of Ireland at odds with the narrative of economic improvement plotted in Chaigneau's *Jack Connor*. The two novels begin similarly, as the child of Irish farmers is orphaned. However, they differ in that Jack is saved by Lord Truegood's intervention, whereas Varnish continues his homeless, wandering progress for the rest of the novel. *Anthony Varnish* does not feature the landlord class at all, and thus lacks the powerful benefactors that are crucial to Chaigneau's optimistic projection of the kingdom. Irish society in *Anthony Varnish* is typified by insecurity and destitution rather than benevolence.

The novel's pessimism is highly reminiscent of the outlook of Johnston's earlier *Chrysal*, which features a story in which an English nobleman discovers that a branch of his family exists in "a neighbouring dependant kingdom." He travels to Ireland, where he finds "that the family was reduced, by revolutions of government, and the calamity of the times, to two poor, low-bred, illiterate women, who had been married to mechanics of the meanest rank." The family's fate is described as a "melancholy . . . instance of the instability of human grandeur," but also has a more specifically Irish significance as a consequence of "revolutions of government" (implicitly, either the Cromwellian interregnum or the later Williamite wars).[97] The pessimism of *Chrysal* relates both to the permanence of material stability and to the possibility of virtue. The novel "portrayed a world characterised, always and everywhere, by man's propensity to vice," in Ross's words.[98] Particularly, the lure of gold (represented by the guinea) is shown repeatedly to have a powerful corrupting effect on characters, overcoming their willpower and conscience.[99] *Anthony Varnish* has more faith in human morality than *Chrysal*, and its ending affirms that the virtuous can be rewarded, as Varnish wins the affections of his master's daughter Jessie and settles down in solvent marriage. His final reflections valorize the power of benevolence, advising readers to "look . . . with an eye of kindness upon the weaknesses of each other" (3:269). However, despite the praise of "kindness," more widely this novel implies that little can be done to alleviate poverty and suffering. The story of the soldier, who is bankrupted due to the injustices of the legal system, inspires Varnish to declare that "we are born to suffer much more than to enjoy" (3:139). His words betray that his own happy ending is an incidence of special providence that goes against the grain of the novel. In *Anthony Varnish*, unpromising circumstances override the choice of morality, and the virtuous meet the same fate as the villainous.

The forces that rule Johnston's narratives are economic rather than providential. This is affirmed in the closing scenes of volume 2 when Varnish, reduced to destitution, makes a heartfelt speech to his "last guinea" that is the novel's clearest reminder of *Chrysal*: "Thy influence, more potent than the blandishments of beauty, can turn aside the stream of justice . . . Alas, how ineffectual is merit, if not supported by your smiles!" (2:238–39). Just as the guinea is personified, humans become objects of commercial forces—in *Chrysal*, due to the coin's power to make its owners lust after gold, and in *Anthony Varnish*, as origins exert a defining influence on the course of life. The latter novel's emigration plot dramatizes the effects of Ireland's unsettled economy on its poorest inhabitants. Varnish realizes the injustice of the economic order as he asks the guinea, "If Providence . . . meant you as a blessing, why were you distributed with so unequal a hand?" However, the radical implications of his revelation are hastily defused: "But, on the contrary, my reason assures me, that you were sent us as a curse . . . to shake the peace of society." He then relinquishes "avarice and ambition" and resolves to be "obedient to the dictates of morality" (2:239–40). Varnish's move from recognizing inequality to disclaiming "ambition" shows his difference from the status-craving rogue Juniper. His choice of a subordinate, unthreatening "morality" implicitly leads to the reward of his lucrative marriage. This success is a special case in this pessimistic novel, in which the good usually go hungry. As such, *Anthony Varnish* ends up reaffirming the order of an "unequal" society. But at the same time, it confronts the reader with that inequality, dramatizing the plight of the atomized migrant exiled from home and family.

†

The extended depictions of life in rural Ireland and St Giles given in *Anthony Varnish* are a product of its formal strategy of an observing, nonparticipating narrator. *John Juniper*, on the other hand, puts the protagonist and his identity at the center of the action. The characterization of Juniper is motivated by contradictory impulses: to denounce demagoguery and lambast Wilkes and the American revolutionaries but also to defend the Irish from the charge of criminal tendencies. In *Anthony Varnish*, fears about popular sedition are less prominent, resulting in a more compassionate treatment of the urban poor, perhaps indicating a subsiding of anxieties as the Gordon Riots receded into the past. These two novels are united in countering assumptions of Irish criminality. Given *John Juniper*'s determinist narrative of failed ambition, its sideswipes at ideas of heredity risk incoherence; however, these function to cast Juniper as an England-raised, rather than Irish-born, rogue. The text's agenda becomes clearer as it revises the wicked Irish character of Mackshane from Smollett's *Roderick Random* into the noble Dr. MacShane. Similarly, *Anthony Varnish* highlights the prejudice that the Irish encounter in England. Its depictions of disorderly crowds in London recall the anti-Irish riots that recurred in the capital during the eighteenth century. These scenes in *Anthony Varnish* form part of a sentimental strain of pity for the marginal, and are consonant with its ending praise of "kindness." However, sympathy has little power to alleviate poverty in a novel that repeatedly emphasizes financial misfortune and displacement, themes that evoke the history of Irish laboring-class migration to England. The novel stresses factors of economic decline and famine, running counter to discourses of improvement during the period.

Varnish's adventures and encounters with other displaced characters leave him with a pessimistic outlook, as he learns that divine providence has little power to reward the good. The emphasis in *Anthony Varnish* on the instability of fortune is strongly reminiscent of the earlier works by Johnston treated here. Furthermore, the traveling servant Varnish comes to resemble the inanimate object narrator of *Chrysal*. In a climactic scene, he rejects avarice, accepting his status rather than aspiring to any higher station. *Anthony Varnish* can only empathize with the poor and hungry, whereas *John Juniper* can critique the colonial basis of famine in veiled references to events in India and rural Ireland. The caustic satire voiced by the rogue in *John Juniper* can be opposed to the mute witnessing offered in *Anthony Varnish*. In this sense, the latter novel scales back the radical aspects of the rogue narrative, even as it offers a more positive rendering of the Irish protagonist. I have contended that these two novels of the 1780s share an outlook with Johnston's earlier *Chrysal*. All three works sympathize with poverty and with the Irish experience of marginality, but remain convinced that hardship and conflict are inevitable, and are apprehensive about class confusion. *John Juniper* and *Anthony Varnish* stand as testament to the continued vitality of the Irish rogue narrative in a decade of Irish migration to Britain, mass unrest in London, and war abroad.

I have concentrated on these two novels at such length out of the conviction that their significance, both within Irish literary studies and more widely, has not been adequately recognized. *John Juniper* and *Anthony Varnish* seem like outliers in the 1780s, in a way that *Jack Connor* was not in the 1750s, in their unflinching concentration on low life, violence, and poverty. Midcentury novelists exploited the materials of

popular criminal literature, but authors like Chaigneau were understandably concerned to demonstrate the distance between their Irish
characters and the underworld of robbery and the gallows. But by
1780, forms like the Ordinary's *Account* and highwayman biography
were less popular. In fiction, the 1780s have been associated with the
continuing prominence of sentimental fiction and the rise of the novel
of manners, after Frances Burney's *Evelina* (1778) and *Cecilia* (1782).[100]
Contemporary ramble novels were dispensing with the Smollettian
tone of bawdy comedy and cruel pranks. Examples include the anonymous *The Minor, or History of George O'Nial* (1786) and Maria Hunter's
Fitzroy, or Impulse of the Moment (1792). A romance plot reminiscent of
Tom Jones is common to these novels, in which adventure is resolved in
marriage. Both center on sympathetic Irish heroes from the middling
sort or lower gentry who are educated at Trinity College Dublin. The
merchant's son George Fitzroy proves himself to be a deserving match
for Charlotte Beauclerk despite the machinations of other suitors.[101]
Suspense in *The Minor* is derived from the threatened loss of the protagonist O'Nial's inheritance, an estate in Co. Tyrone.[102] These late
eighteenth-century Irish novels eschew fortune hunter and rogue
character types. A similar brand of masculinity is present in another
Irish-authored novel, Elizabeth Hervey's *The History of Ned Evans*
(1796). The plot centers on the virtuous, upstanding son of a poor
Welsh curate who discovers that he is the rightful heir to an estate and
title in Ireland.[103] Indeed, it is a short step from novels such as *Fitzroy*
and *Ned Evans* to Maria Edgeworth's *Ennui* (1809), *The Absentee* (1812),
and *Ormond* (1817), all biographical coming-of-age novels about men
from the Anglo-Irish elite. Johnston's last two novels instead prompt
us to look back across more than a century of prose narratives about
Ireland. *John Juniper* and *Anthony Varnish* were products of a migratory life, and refuse to return their heroes to Ireland or grant them
lasting stability. Instead, Johnston narrates the breakdown of the Irish
family and community. These two narratives of criminal and vagrant
mobility invoke not only the Irish fiction of the mid–eighteenth century, but the durable rogue narratives of Head and his successors.

Conclusion

Reassessing Early Irish Fiction,
Tracing the Legacies of the Rogue

Rogue Narratives as Irish Fiction

After taking account of the rogue narratives considered in this book, we can draw new conclusions about the development of Irish fiction. Rogue narratives are a neglected yet important element within writing from Ireland. Moreover, they add to our knowledge of the development and diversity of prose fiction in the eighteenth century, and they influence our view of the Irish writing that came after 1800. The earliest works of fiction about Ireland suggest that stories of migration and diaspora are at least as important to what we today call "the Irish novel" as stories with Irish settings. The Irish rogue as a cultural trope has been interpreted simplistically in the past as either an iconoclastic "hero" or a wild Irish "brute" (to use Faller's terms). But close attention to fiction published between 1660 and 1790 overturns this binary and demonstrates that the rogue character was a capacious metaphor in Irish writing, adaptable to different historical circumstances, and coming to stand for the Protestant gentry as well as the Catholic lower orders. It remains difficult to talk confidently about the many early and obscure works that I have discussed as Irish novels, given that so much of the period's fiction comes to us as anonymous and London-published. However, this study highlights and brings together an important collection of Irish novelists between 1750 and 1790 who rebuked English views of their country from an informed perspective through the use of the rogue narrative. If noticed at all, these novelists have been treated by previous critics as outliers or isolated precursors to the more coherent nineteenth-century Irish novel. Instead, I contend that these eighteenth-century writers constituted a shared tradition with common influences.

I have chosen to end in the 1780s, rather than extending my study up to the 1800 Act of Union, from a sense that after the French Revolution, new political realities and generic crosscurrents begin to make themselves felt in Irish fiction, which would have necessitated more space to cover than this book allows. The 1790s witnessed both "a growth in radical politics on the island" and an expansion in the readership for "popular fiction about Ireland," meaning that the Irish national tale came into its own.[1] National tales, in the words of Miranda Burgess, are "the earliest Irish novels centrally concerned with definitions and descriptions of Ireland." Distinctively, they attempt "to provide an overview of a national community."[2] Katie Trumpener's *Bardic Nationalism* (1997), a study of the development of the Irish novel alongside its British cousins, groups Chaigneau, Amory, and Johnston as authors of a "nationally inflected picaresque." Trumpener views the picaresque "travelling fiction" of these authors as a precursor to the national tale and historical novel, forms that show the collective development of a community through time.[3] This is a useful distinction in that it captures certain characteristics of the rogue narrative, such as its travel plot and focus on an individual, which distinguish it from the national tale focused on a bounded social group. But more widely, I argue that conceptions of Irish fiction derived from the national tale delimit understandings of earlier writing, leading to an emphasis on place, geography, and community at the expense of character, and obscuring the ways in which "picaresque" fictions, those concentrating on mobile protagonists exiled from home, can have national significance.

Recent assessments of seventeenth- and early eighteenth-century Irish fiction concentrate on representations of the space of Ireland. Ross maps the Irish locales of *Vertue Rewarded* (1693) and Butler's *Irish Tales* (1716), and comments on the former novel's choice of a provincial setting, the Tipperary town of Clonmel. *Vertue Rewarded* and *Irish*

Tales are distinguished from contemporary English novels because they are "not concerned with the movement of populations *out of* Ireland to other lands but about the inhabitants of other lands coming *into* Ireland, whether as raiders or invaders."[4] Equally, however, a plot of the Irish leaving their country behind for adventures elsewhere is inaugurated by *The English Rogue* and continues into the criminal narrative and the novels of Chaigneau and Johnston. Studies of Head are exemplary in that they pay close attention to his renderings of particular Irish places but take little account of the significance of migration in his work. Rankin draws attention to the "resonance[s]" of the Irish country towns visited by Latroon, Baltinglass and Ballymore Eustace, contending that Head "chooses his locations with care" and "demonstrates a true sense for *dinnseanchas*: the lore of the local."[5] Head's play *Hic et Ubique* is set wholly in Dublin, and was moreover written and performed there. The play's strong, sustained sense of the city and its Protestant settler culture is a factor in the critical attention paid to this text by Rankin, Wheatley, and others.[6] The setting of *Hic et Ubique* seems to make it a more recognizably Irish work than traveling fictions such as *The English Rogue* or *The Floating Island*. Rogue narratives usually follow a single protagonist through many societies, rather than aspiring to represent a particular one in any depth. Chapter 2 argued that Irish rogues are more often protean than typical of their original cultures. Nevertheless, the rogue fictions analyzed in this study abundantly demonstrate that texts set mostly outside of Ireland can still have considerable relevance to the history of Irish literature.

Early criminal narratives suggest that the first Irish fictions were migratory, even diasporic, in character. Early Irish fiction's engagement with migrant populations and diasporic contexts has not yet been widely recognized, as demonstrated by Tony Murray's *London Irish Fictions*, which does not mention any novels published before 1900, and states that "[a]t the turn of the twentieth century, London Irish characters begin to appear in fiction as well as drama."[7] Yet many of the authors studied here, from Head to Amory and Johnston, pursued their careers in London. A large number of the subjects of criminal biographies also made London their destination, from the Popish Plot informer David Fitzgerald to highwaymen such as James Carrick and James MacLaine; more fully fictional texts (*Jonathan Wilde, Betty Ireland*, the fortune-hunter novel *John Juniper*) are insistently drawn to London as the locus of criminal literature. Head's Latroon suggests the Spanish ladrón in name, and travels as far as the East Indies, emulating the colonial English in his global adventuring. France and Spain are the destinations for O'Divelley in *The Irish Rogue* and Chaigneau's Jack Connor, and in both cases, the countries connote radical religious and political kinships. Irish novels such as *John Juniper* and *Anthony Varnish* take views of London that open onto contemporary issues of public order and radical politics. Rogues might travel abroad, but Ireland is constantly present through the people they encounter. Here and elsewhere, Irish novels repeatedly feature the trope of the unexpected meeting with a figure from one's homeland or past, who then relates their story. Examples analyzed here include Jack Connor with Captain Magragh (and then his with his own mother), Juniper and Dr. MacShane, and Varnish and the beggar woman. These chance encounters between the isolated and displaced do not add up to what Burgess calls a "national community," but they nevertheless become charged with meaning and illuminate or reveal hidden aspects of the hero's identity and nationality.

Mid-eighteenth-century Irish novelists such as Chaigneau, Amory, and Johnston are too often positioned as antecedents to a more developed, truly "national" mode of writing, as seen in Trumpener's view of them as precursors to the fiction of the Romantic period. National tales, it is argued, took on the earlier ramble style of fiction and utilized it to describe Irish locales with a deeper sense of their cultural history: "In the late eighteenth century, the writers of picaresque novels become interested . . . in the differences between the places passed through."[8] The "picaresque" is of interest to Trumpener when it surveys and analyzes places and cultures, but is at the same time less able to represent these locales than the national tale and historical novel. Trumpener defines the picaresque here simply as a travel narrative, but it is important to remember that the earliest Spanish picaresque fictions centered on a poor, marginalized pícaro. In the texts examined here, the geographical itineraries of rogues are often secondary to their interior, moral, and spiritual dimensions. The first criminal narratives presented rogues as figures for the Irish national character, and these rogues emerge as complex and multilayered figures rather than buffoons or savages. *Jack Connor* permits glimpses of a private sphere that encompasses Jack's rogue side, his concealed nationality, and his silence on public matters. In *John Juniper*, contradictory discourses about the constitution of identity emerge in the course of an Irish rogue's upbringing in London. The complexities of individual identity in such novels are not remote from questions of national history and politics. Earlier criminal narratives such as *The Irish Rogue* imply that rogues cannot shed their essential disposition, which refers back to their birthplace. But the portraits of national character in criminal fictions and biographies are unexpectedly various, as the focus on one protagonist in travels through many societies allows stereotypically national characteristics to be discarded and multiplied. In turn, this tradition of fiction from Head to Cosgrave, combining a travel narrative with protean characterization, furnishes later novelists with a blueprint with which they can craft tales of rogues that reform or ascend the social ladder.

In criminal narratives, "wild Irish" stereotypes ultimately dissolve as rogues assimilate into various classes and cultures. The Irish rogue's national and political significance is therefore far from straightforward or stable. Past critical accounts of rogues and criminals in Irish culture view this trope as originating in popular folklore. Maureen Waters identifies the "figure of the outlaw or the dispossessed" as "one of the great archetypes of Irish literature" with its source in "Irish ballads and folktales." Waters finds that "[t]he rogue literature of England and the continent, with the exception of *Gil Blas*, which Carleton read at a young age, apparently had little impact" on Irish fiction.[9] The fiction analyzed here proves that the opposite was true. Before 1790, Irish fiction was far from a self-sufficient national tradition; Head wrote an "English" version of Mabbe's translation of *Guzmán de Alfarache*, later Dublin biographers such as Cosgrave drew upon Smith's English collections, and the male-centered ramble novel looked to Lesage,

Smollett, and Fielding. Waters stresses the anticolonial aspects of rogues, who "held out the possibility of change, of rescue, of driving out the English settlers," and Ó Ciardha refers to the Irish outlaw as "a nationalist icon."[10] But when we consider a broader range of narratives, the usual assumptions about the cultural or political significance of the Irish rogue cannot be sustained. The fictions analyzed here reveal that rogue narratives are able to contain a broader range of "Irish" characters. The representation of the Protestant Anglo-Irish as rogues endured from the 1660s until the mid–eighteenth century, as a view of English settlers as degenerate developed into the stereotype of the Irish upper orders as a counterfeit gentry. In *The English Rogue*, *The Miss Display'd*, or *Betty Ireland*, the Protestant English in Dublin are represented in the terms of the picaresque and whore biography. Mid-eighteenth-century English novels such as *Shelim O'Blunder*, *Dick Hazard*, and *Benjamin Brass* represent Irish gentlemen as ambitious and unscrupulous, in the style of earlier criminal narratives. These novelists may have seized upon the *succès de scandale* caused in 1749 and 1750 by MacLaine, a Protestant Irishman from a respectable family who was seen as a fine gentleman in London. Certainly, biographies of MacLaine from 1750 differ noticeably from earlier highwayman lives due to their focus on fortune hunting. The earliest of the formulaic fortune-hunter novels, *Shelim O'Blunder*, appeared only a year after MacLaine's death, and it is possible that English novelists were attempting to capitalize upon this notorious and recent criminal case.

Tracing such patterns and resemblances takes us away from a stable sense of "Irish fiction." The midcentury vogue for fortune-hunter novels is comparable to the earlier trend for tales of nationalized (French, German, or Scottish) "rogues"; both were developments centered in the English print trade that produced works about Irish characters. Some simply gave an Irish gloss to preexisting stories, as when celebrities like Jonathan Wild and David Garrick were framed as Irish by opportunistic comic fictions. I hope to have shown, however, that a range of works written between 1660 and 1790 are "Irish" in a more than superficial sense. Of course, novels such as *Jack Connor* and *John Buncle* are already recognized as such, but they existed alongside and share much with forgotten Irish narratives such as *The Life and Uncommon Adventures of Capt. Dudley Bradstreet* and *The Adventures of Patrick O'Donnell*. Johnston has likewise now gained a place within discussions of Irish fiction, though his two most overtly Irish novels, *John Juniper* and *Anthony Varnish*, are still too often passed over, the first for esthetic reasons and the second because of its uncertain authorship. My close reading of these two novels has accordingly emphasized similarities to Johnston's better-known *Chrysal*, as well as their shared narratives of crime and vagrancy, informed views of Irish diaspora in Britain, and moments of Irish patriotism. *John Juniper* recasts a rogue character from *Roderick Random*, Dr. Mackshane, in more ideal terms, for instance. The reversal of the pejorative "Irish rogue" image, a tactic also used by Chaigneau, advertises national allegiance in a conspicuous way, but Johnston's concentration on themes of hunger and famine, displacement and decline, is no less redolent of his Irish background.

Despite their differences, Chaigneau and Johnston were part of broader trends in the 1750–90 period, as can be illustrated when they are compared to the forgotten ramble fiction of their day. The concern with Irish masculinity, criminality, and civility in their novels points to a dynamic literary interchange between early Irish fiction and the popular literature of England and Ireland. When Irish novelists such as Chaigneau, Johnston, and the author of *Patrick O'Donnell* decided to write about their native country, they used the materials available in criminal biography: highway robbery, Jacobite dissent, the ever-present threat of the gallows, and the narrative of sin and penitence. Rebels and robbers appear in these novels, but must eventually be dispelled or distanced. Similarly, Amory's *John Buncle* suggests the possibility of fortune hunting for Buncle, in self-conscious and comic fashion, but has him steadfastly maintain his morals. Historians of the criminal biography such as Shoemaker and McKenzie find that by the 1780s, the form became unpopular with middling-sort English readers.[11] But my case study of Johnston implies that criminal biographies retained their appeal for novelists in this decade, when readers in London could still choose between one-shilling pamphlet lives of felons like Patrick Madan and unsentimental ramble novels of low life. The criminal tradition was both present and generative for John-ston in *John Juniper*, which is centrally concerned with the origins of criminality, and *Anthony Varnish*, with its narrative of destitution and itinerancy comparable to Head's writings.

The novels of Chaigneau, Johnston, and their contemporaries, then, are shortchanged by existing broad surveys, positioned too often as early, isolated, incipient precursors to a more fully developed and uniquely "national" mode of Irish fiction. They constitute, in themselves, a tradition within Irish literature, developed by multiple novelists across most of four decades. These rogue narratives can be differentiated from the national tale in terms of their focus on indi-viduals over communities. Nevertheless, they evidence a serious and informed investment in Irish affairs and a recurrent agenda, recog-nized by reviewers and imitated by contemporaries, to write a more affirmative, complex, and nuanced kind of story about Ireland.

Rogue Narratives and Eighteenth-Century Fiction in English

The issues explored in my chapters have, like so many Irish rogues, ranged beyond the space of Ireland. As such, this research foregrounds neglected aspects of the development of fiction in English during the seventeenth and eighteenth centuries. Accounts of early fiction cen-tered on the picaresque are inadequate to the range of prose writing that is now available to us from the long eighteenth century. Critics of the picaresque cleave to an established canon of worthy novels, based on criteria of integrated form and psychological complexity, as well as more basic expectations of a fiction concentrating on an economically marginalized subject. As such, the picaresque framework delimits the attention that can be paid to biographies or memoirs of real crimi-nals, and seems a poor fit for ramble novels about the gentry or high society. The choice of rogue narrative as an organizing concept in this study instead allows connections to be noted between many more texts, some biographical or factual in basis, but all concerned with the Irish and brought together by characteristic plots of crime, travel, and social mobility, as well as an interest in nationality and masculinity. It is established that major British novelists such as Defoe, Smollett, and Fielding exploited cheaper crime-themed fiction.[12] My approach, by prioritizing Irish fiction, goes beyond the tendency seen here to orient arguments about the significance of criminal narrative toward the same few authors. Previous critics such as Richetti, Faller, and Gladfelder have read novels alongside popular forms such as the criminal and whore biography, but the tendency of these forms to turn rogues into national emblems has not been investigated. This study revisits the relationship between criminal biography and the emerging novel by emphasizing the importance of national identity. Head's fiction and "Irish" criminal narratives published between 1680 and 1750 are multifaceted in their views of identity, going beyond simple mockery or national stereotyping. Through these texts, a recognizable, suggestive, and malleable character type, the "Irish rogue," was made available to midcentury novelists.

My later chapters consider the uses that novelists after 1750 made of the rogue narrative. For Keymer, writing in 2002, the 1750s were "a crucial decade in the history of the novel," and yet "[n]o deep trawl of the kind so illuminatingly performed by Jerry C. Beasley on the output of fiction between *Pamela* and *Tom Jones* has been undertaken for the 1750s."[13] The publication of Dickie's *Cruelty and Laughter* in 2011 would go a long way toward rectifying this state of affairs, drawing attention to the many "forgotten bestsellers" to be published between 1750 and 1770. My study advances this work, not only through a focus on Irish aspects, but through supplementing Dickie's distant survey of fictional trends with close readings of chosen works such as *Jack Connor*, *John Juniper*, and *Anthony Varnish*. I hope that a more nuanced assessment of ramble fiction can thus emerge, as opposed to Dickie's stressing of its formulaic nature, crudity, and reliance on "filler," which inevitably creates an impression of this fiction as undifferentiated (provoking, at one point, the despairing question: "How bad are these books?").[14] For Dickie, the significance of the ramble novel is essentially negative, a sobering reminder of the cruelty of eighteenth-century social relations. By concentrating on selected works of ramble fiction, I have shown that this framework was also used to write novels that were both compassionate and serious. Even as Irish novelists deployed the stock figures of the criminal, rake, prostitute, or fortune hunter, they did so in order to contest prejudices against the migrant or socially mobile Irish, or to engage critically with discourses of economic improvement, masculinity, gentility, and identity. Moreover, this study has argued for an expanded sense of the evolution of ramble novels by highlighting their resemblances to preexisting criminal narratives. Equally, it can be pointed out that the male-centered ramble novel did not decline or expire after 1770, enduring into the 1780s and 1790s to be taken up by Irish authors such as Johnston, Hunter, and Hervey. Later examples of this durable style, both English and Irish, would merit further study, and the ramble novel should be integrated with accounts of the development and decline of the criminal biography in the later eighteenth century, as well as the rise of sentimental "man of feeling" novels.

Developments after 1790

In nineteenth-century Ireland, the outlaw continued to be enlisted as a national emblem. Changing literary trends meant that, in the main, Irish authors were no longer writing works recognizable as ramble novels, but the rogue remained an intertextual presence, with novels making numerous references and allusions to the ever-popular *Gil Blas* and to Cosgrave's and Freney's tales of Irish highwaymen. Like their forebears, nineteenth-century Irish novelists utilized the rogue as a figure of miseducation and impropriety, opposed to the gentleman.

A few of the works analyzed here, such as *John Buncle* and *Chrysal*, enjoyed a high profile during the early nineteenth century.[15] Cahalan concludes however that such early Irish novels "established no tradition recognizable either during their period or for a long time since."[16] In retrospect, the establishment of characteristic strategies, narratives, and concerns for fiction writing in Ireland is discernible in the decades between 1750 and 1790. Edgeworth famously satirized the eighteenth-century Irish gentry in *Castle Rackrent* (1800), written shortly before the Act of Union, and subtitled *An Hibernian Tale, Taken from Facts, and from the Manners of the Irish Squires, before the Year 1782*. Despite its subtitle, *Castle Rackrent* has overwhelmingly been interpreted as an originating point, a text that influences and anticipates future novels, as opposed to an echo or culmination of past fiction. It was Edgeworth's first novel, and one bound up with the new century and political state in which Ireland was soon to find itself; it has been read as "the first regional novel, the first socio-historical novel, the first Irish novel, the first Big House novel."[17] Yet the novelty of *Castle Rackrent* lies not in its social and historical milieu, but in its form, a first-person, vernacular account of several generations of one family. Edgeworth's next three novels to feature Irish settings—*Ennui* (1809), *The Absentee* (1812), and *Ormond* (1817)—would adopt a more conventional biographical shape, following a young Anglo-Irish gentleman from youth to maturity. In *Ennui*, for example, the idle and dissolute Lord Glenthorn is deprived of his estate and forced to commence legal studies, but eventually regains his status through career success. These novels evidence a shared interest in masculine education and maturation that is comparable to Irish ramble fiction from *Jack Connor* to Hunter's *Fitzroy* and Hervey's *Ned Evans*.

Though remote in their social milieu from the rogue narrative, Edgeworth's Irish novels often present dutiful and inadequate types of masculinity by invoking fictional archetypes. In *Ormond*, the titular hero reads *Tom Jones* and Richardson's *Sir Charles Grandison* (1753). The latter novel "inspired him with virtuous emulation" and "made him ambitious to be a *gentleman* in the best and highest sense of the word," and thus "counteracted in his mind the effect of Tom Jones," with its less ideal hero, who is "an adventurer, a spendthrift, and a rake."[18] For Clíona Ó Gallchoir, *Ormond* "contains distinct echoes" of the tales in Cosgrave's *Irish Highwaymen*, and Ormond himself possesses "a number of the features of possibly the most popular character in eighteenth- and nineteenth-century literature in Ireland—the 'Irish Rogue,'" for example, his passionate nature and early exile from home. However, Ormond eventually matures to become "not a rebel or a felon, but a perfect husband and gentleman."[19] In Ó Gallchoir's reading, *Ormond* echoes or invokes the Irish criminal narrative as a negative counterpoint; it can be added that this is a conventional strategy within early Irish fiction, opening up the possibility of repositioning *Ormond* as a late (or long-eighteenth-century) manifestation of the rogue narrative. Edgeworth's Irish novels, then, evidence the continued closeness of the outlaw and the polite gentleman as versions of Irish masculinity. The still-common view of *Castle Rackrent*, published auspiciously in the year of the Act of Union, as the first Irish novel obscures the clear kinships between Edgeworth's other Irish tales and the eighteenth-century ramble fictions considered in this study.

The criminal biographies of Cosgrave and Freney acquired a long-lasting popular readership in Ireland during the nineteenth century, and were joined by more original biographies of Irish outlaws. One such text, *The Life and Adventures of John Connor* (1785), is largely made up of borrowings from *Jack Connor* and *Roderick Random*, illustrating the fact that disparities in length and price have long functioned to disguise basic similarities in content between popular criminal biography and what we now know as the novel. The life of Connor was reprinted in Dublin in 1821, and was mentioned as common children's reading fare by Thomas Moore in his novel *The Memoirs of Captain Rock* (1824).[20] Criminal biography enjoyed contrasting fortunes in the late eighteenth century, going into decline in England but being more widely disseminated in Ireland.[21] However, less attention has been paid to the ways in which diverse literary and cultural mediums in the nineteenth century continued to draw upon the corpus of rogue and criminal literature. In both Britain and Ireland, changing fashions in genre and esthetics obscured a continuing fascination with contemporary or historic crime.

In the Romantic period, Gothic and sublime currents leading to a fascination with wild, mountainous landscapes and their denizens encouraged Irish writers to draw upon the history and continuing reality of banditry in rural Ireland. The seventeenth-century Italian painter Salvator Rosa, known for his picturesque landscapes featuring gangs of brigands, or banditti, inspired a vogue for such landscapes in eighteenth-century English painting, travel writing, and fiction. Anne Radcliffe's influential Gothic novel *The Mysteries of Udolpho* (1794) featured a band of Italian brigands.[22] In Ireland, the exotic and Gothic trope of the bandit was imbued with historic and local resonances. Banditry was a continuing reality in Ireland at this time, as James G. Patterson has shown in a historical study of rural crime between 1798 and 1804.[23] John O'Keeffe's comic opera *The Castle of Andalusia*, published in Cork in 1783, included among its dramatis personae a gang of Spanish banditti, and in 1795, O'Keeffe premiered *The Wicklow Mountains*, in which a character named Redmond O'Hanlon is a member of a secret agrarian faction. Irish associations of mountainous terrain with toryism are brought to the fore by O'Keeffe, who references a real seventeenth-century bandit who had entered folkloric status through criminal biography.[24] Artists in Ireland were also seeking Rosa-esque vistas; an engraving by one J. B. Harraden, exhibited at Parliament House, Dublin, in January 1802, was titled *A View Near the Devil's Glen, Ireland. After Salvator Rosa.* The engravings and watercolors in this exhibit were framed as "views taken from the new military roads" built in Wicklow in the aftermath of the 1798 rebellion, and some of their prospects were populated by soldiers and rebel bands. Finola O'Kane compares these works to the plays of O'Keeffe in their engagement with post-1798 Irish history through picturesque esthetics.[25] The cultural presence of Irish rural crime in the Romantic period could be investigated further. The major Irish Romantic novelist Sydney Owenson, Lady Morgan, was also the author of a biography of Rosa (1824), which perpetuated the legend of the artist's "captivity by the banditti" of the Abruzzi mountains and "temporary (and it is said voluntary) association with these fearful men."[26] Regina Maria Roche, the most successful Irish Gothic novelist of the early nineteenth century, wrote *The Discarded Son, or Haunt of the Banditti* (1807), which is set partly in Ireland.[27] William Lane's London-based Minerva Press published Roche and many other Irish authors, and issued dozens of Gothic novels utilizing similar imagery and themes between 1790 and 1820.[28] Comparisons between these Romantic fictionalizations of banditry and the earlier rogue narratives studied here would add to our knowledge of continuities in popular fiction before and after 1800.

Dublin-published criminal narratives such as *Irish Highwaymen* and *James Freney* had a demonstrable impact on Irish novelists of the nineteenth century, and presented ideal material for historical novels about decades past. Carleton referenced them directly, writing disapprovingly in his story "The Hedge School" (1830) that "[e]ulogiums on murder, robbery and theft were read with delight in the histories of Freney the Robber, and the Irish Rogues and Rapparees" by pupils in rural schools.[29] Carleton's professed suspicion of criminal biography did not stop him from rewriting a story made famous by Cosgrave in his novel *Redmond Count O'Hanlon, the Irish Rapparee* (1862). The English novelist William Thackeray read and enjoyed Freney's memoirs during a visit to Ireland in 1842, commenting upon "the noble *naïveté* and simplicity of the hero as he recounts his own adventures." The tone and narrative of *James Freney* were a formative influence on Thackeray's *The Memoirs of Barry Lyndon, Esq.* (1856), a tale of an eighteenth-century Irishman's social mobility, military service, and marriage to a wealthy heiress.[30] The nineteenth-century ubiquity of criminal tales, then, meant that they became suggestive resources for novelists both in Ireland and more widely. Thackeray, like earlier authors, seems to have quickly made the connection between the outlaw or robber and the fortune-hunting adventurer within civilized society.

It would be easy to dismiss Victorian novels such as *Barry Lyndon* and *Redmond Count O'Hanlon* as further imaginings of Ireland as a "bandit country," typified by its most infamous criminals. Yet the early memoirs and biographies of O'Hanlon and Freney remained popular with lower-class Irish readers because of their ambivalence, the ease with which these men's violent acts could be spun into tales of witty rogues defying authority. And it seems now that one of the most enduring and least-known permutations or manifestations of this popular folklore was in the Irish novel. From the earliest known works of fiction, Ireland was evoked in the terms of the rogue narrative: displacement, hunger, crime, and deception. The potential of the clever, adaptable rogue to contradict stereotypes of Irish foolishness and barbarism is present in texts from the seventeenth century, and is refined to produce patriotic Irish novels in the mid– to late eighteenth century. Authors from Head to Johnston looked to the models available in Spanish, French, and British fiction, while also exploiting local materials such as anatomies and accounts of real crime. This established a formal premise that is observable also in the nineteenth-century Irish novel. Fictional forms changed, with picaresque and ramble styles giving way to national tales and Gothic and historical fiction, but the memory and reality of crime continued to fascinate and provide a spur for fictions evoking the complexities of Ireland's past and present.

Notes

Bibliography

Index

Notes

Introduction

1. Simon Carswell, "Ireland's Call: From 'Bandit Country' to Brexit's Frontier," *The Irish Times*, March 18, 2017, https://www.irishtimes.com/news/politics/ireland-s-call-from-bandit-country-to-brexit-s-frontier-1.3014496; James Conor Patterson, "Bandit Country," *The Tangerine* 7 (November 2018): 10–15.

2. Merlyn Rees, statement issued after ambush at Drummuckavall, Co. Armagh, November 22, 1975. Quoted in Toby Harnden, *Bandit Country: The IRA and South Armagh* (London: Hodder and Stoughton, 1999), 50–51. Rees later addressed "the security problem in South Armagh" in the 1970s in his memoirs: "The army's responses had not been inhibited by the ceasefire; the bandit country was simply hard to deal with." Merlyn Rees, *Northern Ireland: A Personal Perspective* (London: Methuen, 1985), 245–46.

3. Éamonn Ó Ciardha, "The Early Modern Irish Outlaw: The Making of a Nationalist Icon," in *People, Politics and Power: Essays on Irish History 1660–1850*, ed. James Kelly, John McCafferty, and Charles Ivar McGrath (Dublin: University College Dublin Press, 2009), 51–69.

4. Jim McCallen, *Stand and Deliver: Stories of Irish Highwaymen* (Cork: Mercier Press, 1993); Stephen Dunford, *The Irish Highwaymen* (Dublin: Merlin, 2000); Michael Holden, *Freney the Robber: The Noblest Highwayman in Ireland* (Cork: Mercier Press, 2009).

5. Ray Cashman, "The Heroic Outlaw in Irish Folklore and Popular Literature," *Folklore* 111, no. 2 (October 2000): 191–215 (193).

6. Douglas Sirk (dir.), *Captain Lightfoot* (1955); Michael Cimino (dir.), *Thunderbolt and Lightfoot* (1977); Tony Tracy, "*Captain Lightfoot* (1955): Caught Between a Rock (Hudson) and a Rapparee," in *Screening Irish-America: Representing Irish-America in Film and Television*, ed. Ruth Brady (Dublin: Irish Academic Press, 2009), 193–210 (193, 200–201); Jake Scott (dir.), *Plunkett & Macleane* (1999); Andrea McKenzie, "Maclaine [Maclean], James (1724–1750), Highwayman," in *Oxford Dictionary of National Biography* (Oxford: Oxford University Press), online database, accessed February 5, 2019, https://doi.org/10.1093/ref:odnb/17637.

7. Michael Delahaye, "Irish or Australian, Hero or Villain, the Ned Kelly Legend Lives On," *The Irish Independent*, November 4, 2012, https://www.independent.ie/lifestyle/irish-or-australian-hero-or-villain-the-ned-kelly-legend-lives-on-28826785.html.

8. S. J. Connolly, *Religion, Law and Power: The Making of Protestant Ireland* (Oxford: Clarendon Press, 1992), 264–78.

9. Holden, *Freney the Robber*, 10.

10. James Sharpe, *Dick Turpin: The Myth of the English Highwayman* (London: Profile Books, 2004).

11. Ó Ciardha, "Early Modern Irish Outlaw," 51.

12. Frank Wadleigh Chandler, *The Literature of Roguery*, 2 vols. (New York: Houghton Mifflin, 1907), 2:392.

13. Terry Eagleton, *Heathcliff and the Great Hunger: Studies in Irish Culture* (London: Verso, 1995), 154.

14. Chandler, *Literature of Roguery*, 2:387–97 (388).

15. On Sterne, see, for example, Ian Watt, *The Rise of the Novel: Studies in Defoe, Richardson, and Fielding* (London: Chatto and Windus, 1957), 290–95, and Ronald Paulson, *Satire and the Novel in Eighteenth-Century England* (New Haven: Yale University Press, 1967), 245–71. On Congreve and Swift, see Michael McKeon, *The Origins of the English Novel, 1600–1740* (Baltimore: Johns Hopkins University Press, 1987), 61–63, 338–56.

16. Ian Campbell Ross, "*The Triumph of Prudence over Passion*: Nationalism and Feminism in an Eighteenth-Century Irish Novel," *Irish University Review* 10, no. 2 (1980): 232–40; "An Irish Picaresque Novel: William Chaigneau's *The History of Jack Connor*," *Studies: An Irish Quarterly Review* 71, no. 283 (1982): 270–79; "Thomas Amory, *John Buncle* and the Origins of Irish Fiction," *Éire-Ireland* 18, no. 3 (1983): 71–85; "Rewriting Irish Literary History: The Case of the Irish Novel," *Etudes Anglaises* 39, no. 4 (1986): 383–99; James M. Cahalan, *The Irish Novel: A Critical History* (Dublin: Gill and Macmillan, 1988), 11–13; Ian Campbell Ross, "Introduction to Fiction before 1800," in *The Field Day Anthology of Irish Writing*, ed. Seamus Deane (Derry: Field Day, 1991), 1:682–88.

17. See *Virtue Rewarded, or the Irish Princess*, ed. Anne Markey and Ian Campbell Ross (Dublin: Four Courts Press, 2010); Sarah Butler, *Irish Tales, or Instructive Histories for the Happy Conduct of Life*, ed. Aileen Douglas, Markey, and Ross (Dublin: Four Courts Press, 2010); Thomas Amory, *The Life of John Buncle, Esq.*, ed. Moyra Haslett (Dublin: Four Courts Press, 2011); Elizabeth Sheridan, *The Triumph of Prudence Over Passion*, ed. Douglas and Ross (Dublin: Four Courts Press, 2011); Charles Johnston, *The History of Arsaces, Prince of Betlis*, ed. Daniel Sanjiv Roberts (Dublin: Four Courts Press, 2014).

18. Rolf Loeber and Magda Loeber, with Anne Mullin Burnham, *A Guide to Irish Fiction, 1650–1900* (Dublin: Four Courts Press, 2005), 171–72, 578–79.

19. Loeber and Loeber, introduction to *Guide to Irish Fiction*, xlix–cv (lvii).

20. Deana Rankin, "Kinds of Irishness: Henry Burnell and Richard Head," in *A Companion to Irish Literature*, ed. Julia M. Wright, 2 vols. (Chichester: Wiley-Blackwell, 2010), 1:108–24 (110).

21. Deana Rankin, *Between Spenser and Swift: English Writing in Seventeenth-Century Ireland* (Cambridge: Cambridge University Press, 2005), 162.

22. Jonathan Pritchard, "Head, Richard (c. 1637–1686?)," in *Oxford Dictionary of National Biography* (Oxford: Oxford University Press), online database, accessed February 5, 2019, https://doi.org/10.1093/ref:odnb/12810.

23. Moyra Haslett, "The Rise of the Irish Novel," in *The Oxford History of the Novel in English, Volume 1: Prose Fiction in English from the Origins of Print to 1750*, ed. Thomas Keymer (Oxford: Oxford University Press, 2017), 486–99 (493).

24. Seamus Deane, foreword to *Guide to Irish Fiction*, ed. Loeber and Loeber, xvii–xxii (xxii).

25. Brean Hammond and Shaun Regan, *Making the Novel: Fiction and Society in Britain, 1660–1789* (Basingstoke: Palgrave Macmillan, 2006), 16, 21, 32–44.

26. John Wilson Foster, introduction to *The Cambridge Companion to the Irish Novel*, ed. Foster (Cambridge: Cambridge University Press, 2006), 1–21 (3–5).

27. Markey and Ross, introduction to *Virtue Rewarded*, 9–30 (11).

28. Hammond and Regan, *Making the Novel*, 7; Lennard Davis, *Factual Fictions: The Origins of the English Novel* (New York: Columbia University Press, 1987), 25.

29. Aileen Douglas, "The Novel before 1800," in *Cambridge Companion to the Irish Novel*, ed. Foster, 22–38 (22–25).

30. Ian Campbell Ross, "Prose in English 1690–1800: From the Williamite Wars to the Act of Union," in *The Cambridge History of Irish Literature*, ed. Margaret Kelleher and Philip O'Leary, 2 vols. (Cambridge: Cambridge University Press, 2005), 1:232–81 (269–74).

31. Anne Fogarty, "Literature in English 1550–1690: From the Elizabethan Settlement to the Battle of the Boyne," in *Cambridge History of Irish Literature*, ed. Kelleher and O'Leary, 1:140–90 (179–80).

32. Derek Hand, *A History of the Irish Novel* (Cambridge: Cambridge University Press, 2011), 38, 54.

33. Katie Trumpener, *Bardic Nationalism: The Romantic Novel and the British Empire* (Princeton: Princeton University Press, 1997), 131–37.

34. Harry Sieber, *The Picaresque* (London: Methuen, 1977), 5.

35. Peter N. Dunn, *Spanish Picaresque Fiction: A New Literary History* (Ithaca, NY: Cornell University Press, 1993), 5, 29.

36. Howard Mancing, "The Protean Picaresque," in *The Picaresque: Tradition and Displacement*, ed. Giancarlo Maiorino (Minneapolis: University of Minnesota Press, 1996), 273–91 (285–86).

37. Claudio Guillén, *Literature as System: Essays toward the Theory of Literary History* (Princeton: Princeton University Press, 1971), 75–84.

38. Francisco Rico, *The Spanish Picaresque Novel and the Point of View*, trans. Charles Davis and Harry Sieber (Cambridge: Cambridge University Press, 1984), 70–81; Mancing, "Protean Picaresque," 283–84; J. A. Garrido Ardila, "Origins and Definition of the Picaresque Genre," in *The Picaresque Novel in Western Literature*, ed. Garrido Ardila (Cambridge: Cambridge University Press, 2015), 1–23 (15–16). See also Fernando Lázaro Carreter, *Lazarillo de Tormes en la Picaresca* (Barcelona: Ariel, 1972); Florencio Sevilla, *La Novela Picaresca* (Madrid: Castalia, 2001); and Antonio Rey Hazas, *Deslindes de la Novela Picaresca* (Malaga: University of Malaga Press, 2003).

39. Dale B. J. Randall, *The Golden Tapestry: A Critical Survey of Non-Chivalric Spanish Fiction in English Translation, 1543–1657* (Durham, NC: Duke University Press, 1963), 57–58.

40. Richard Bjornson, *The Picaresque Hero in European Fiction* (Madison: University of Wisconsin Press, 1977), 139–42, 161, 207.

41. Alain-René Lesage, *The History and Adventures of Gil Blas of Santillane*, trans. unknown (London: Jacob Tonson, 1716).

42. Tobias Smollett, preface to *The Adventures of Roderick Random*, ed. O. M. Brack (Athens: University of Georgia Press, 2012), 3–5 (4).

43. Ross, "An Irish Picaresque Novel," 275.

44. Jenny Mander, "Picaresque Itineraries in the Eighteenth-Century French Novel," in *Picaresque Novel*, ed. Garrido Ardila, 157–83 (162–63).

45. Walter Scott, "Le Sage," in *Lives of the Novelists* (Philadelphia: H. C. Carey et al, 1825), 1:42–80 (71).

46. Dunn, *Spanish Picaresque Fiction*, 6.

47. Robert Alter, *The Rogue's Progress: Studies in the Picaresque Novel* (Cambridge, MA: Harvard University Press, 1964); Alexander Parker, *Literature and the Delinquent: The Picaresque Novel in Spain and Europe, 1599–1753* (Edinburgh: Edinburgh University Press, 1967); Stuart Miller, *The Picaresque Novel* (Cleveland, OH: Case Western Reserve University Press, 1967); Frederick Monteser, *The Picaresque Element in Western Literature* (Tuscaloosa: University of Alabama Press, 1975); Sieber, *The Picaresque*.

48. J. A. Garrido Ardila, "The Picaresque Novel and the Rise of the English Novel," in *Picaresque Novel*, ed. Garrido Ardila, 113–39 (133).

49. O. M. Brack and Leslie A. Chilton, introduction to, *The Adventures of Gil Blas of Santillane*, by Alain-René Lesage, ed. Brack and Chilton, trans. Tobias Smollett (Athens: University of Georgia Press, 2011), xvii–xxix (xxi).

50. Robert Giddings, *The Tradition of Smollett* (London: Methuen, 1967); Robert Spector, *Tobias Smollett* (New York: Twayne, 1968); G. S. Rousseau, "Smollett and the Picaresque: Some Questions about a Label," *Studies in Burke and His Time* 12 (1971):

1886–904; Paul-Gabriel Boucé, "Smollett's Pseudo-Picaresque: A Response to Rousseau's Smollett and the Picaresque," *Studies in Burke and His Time* 14 (1972): 73–79.

51. John Skinner, *Constructions of Smollett: A Study of Genre and Gender* (Plainsboro, NJ: Associated University Presses, 1996), 23–24, 119–40.

52. Nicholas Seager, *The Rise of the Novel: A Reader's Guide to Essential Criticism* (Basingstoke: Palgrave Macmillan, 2012), 46–88.

53. Jerry C. Beasley, *Tobias Smollett, Novelist* (Athens: University of Georgia Press, 1998), 12–13, 21.

54. Leslie A. Chilton, "Smollett, the Picaresque and Two Medical Satires," in *New Contexts for Eighteenth-Century British Fiction: "Hearts Resolved and Hands Prepared": Essays in Honour of Jerry C. Beasley*, ed. Christopher D. Johnson (Newark: University of Delaware Press, 2011), 173–82 (174, 228).

55. Mancing, "Protean Picaresque," 277.

56. Guillén, *Literature as System*, 85, 93.

57. Guillén, *Literature as System*, 74; Garrido Ardila, "Rise of the English Novel," 131.

58. Garrido Ardila, "Rise of the English Novel," 124.

59. Monteser, *Picaresque Element*, 45–46; Parker, *Delinquent*, 100.

60. Walter L. Reed, "The Continental Influence on the Eighteenth-Century Novel: 'The English Improve What Others Invent,'" in *The Oxford Handbook of the Eighteenth-Century Novel*, ed. J. A. Downie (Oxford: Oxford University Press, 2016), 73–87 (74–75).

61. Simon Dickie, *Cruelty and Laughter: Forgotten Comic Literature and the Unsentimental Eighteenth Century* (Chicago: University of Chicago Press, 2011), 251–54, 259. For other accounts of ramble fiction, see Dickie, "Tobias Smollett and the Ramble Novel," in *The Oxford History of the Novel in English, Volume 2: English and British Fiction 1750–1820*, ed. Karen O'Brien and Peter Garside (Oxford: Oxford University Press, 2015), 92–108; Dickie, "Novels of the 1750s," in *Eighteenth-Century Novel*, ed. Downie, 252–63.

62. Dunn, *Spanish Picaresque Fiction*, 11.

63. Paul Salzman, *English Prose Fiction, 1558–1700: A Critical History* (Oxford: Oxford University Press, 1985), 205.

64. A. L. Beier, *Masterless Men: The Vagrancy Problem in England, 1560–1640* (London: Methuen, 1985), 7–8.

65. Linda Woodbridge, *Vagrancy, Homelessness, and English Renaissance Literature* (Urbana: University of Illinois Press, 2001), 42.

66. Craig Dionne and Steve Mentz, introduction to *Rogues and Early Modern English Culture*, ed. Dionne and Mentz (Ann Arbor: University of Michigan Press, 2004), 1–30 (2).

67. Kathleen Pories, "The Intersection of Poor Laws and Literature in the Sixteenth Century: Fictional and Factual Categories," in *Framing Elizabethan Fictions:*

Contemporary Approaches to Early Modern Narrative Prose, ed. Constance C. Relihan (Kent, OH: Kent State University Press, 1996), 17–40 (36–38).

68. Woodbridge, *Vagrancy*, 29.

69. Beier, *Masterless Men*, 8.

70. Thomas Harman, *A Caveat or Warning for Common Cursitors* [1566], in *The Elizabethan Underworld: A Collection of Tudor and Early Stuart Tracts and Ballads*, ed. A. V. Judges (Oxford: Routledge, 2002), 61–118 (80–81).

71. Harman, *Caveat*, 114–15; Richard Head, *The English Rogue Described, in the Life of Meriton Latroon* (London: Francis Kirkman, 1667), 47–53.

72. Anne J. Cruz, "Sonnes of the Rogue: Picaresque Relations in England and Spain," in *The Picaresque: Tradition and Displacement*, ed. Maiorino, 248–72 (263–67).

73. Woodbridge, *Vagrancy*, 160.

74. Hal Gladfelder, *Criminality and Narrative in Eighteenth-Century England* (Baltimore: Johns Hopkins University Press, 2001), 22–24.

75. Harman, *Caveat*, 113.

76. Beier, *Masterless Men*, 62–65, 161–62.

77. Brooke A. Stafford, "Englishing the Rogue, 'Translating' the Irish: Fantasies of Incorporation and Early Modern English National Identity," in *Rogues and Early Modern English Culture*, ed. Dionne and Mentz, 312–37 (314–15, 327–30).

78. Edmund Spenser, *A View of the State of Ireland. From the First Printed Edition (1633)*, ed. Andrew Hadfield and Willy Maley (Oxford: Blackwell, 1997), 149.

79. Paul Brown, "'This Thing of Darkness I Acknowledge Mine': *The Tempest* and the Discourse of Colonialism," in *Political Shakespeare: Essays in Cultural Materialism*, ed. Alan Sinfield and Jonathan Dollimore (Manchester: Manchester University Press, 1994), 48–71 (50).

80. Kevin Kenny, *Ireland and the British Empire* (Oxford: Oxford University Press, 2004), 1–8.

81. Brown, "'This Thing of Darkness,'" 50–55.

82. Leah Orr, "*The English Rogue*: Afterlives and Imitations, 1665–1741," *Journal for Eighteenth-Century Studies* 38, no. 3 (September 2015): 361–76 (366).

83. Head, *English Rogue* (1667), initial pages unnumbered (4 of 4).

84. Richard Head, *The English Rogue Containing a Brief Discovery of the Most Eminent Cheats, Robberies and Other Extravagancies* (London: J. Blare, 1688), 1.

85. Paul Salzman, "Travelling or Staying In: Spain and the Picaresque in the Early 1620s," *The Yearbook of English Studies* 41, no. 1 (2011): 141–55.

86. *The Irish Rogue, or the Comical History of the Life and Actions of Teague O'Divelley* (London: Geo. Conyers, 1690), 109.

87. Laura J. Rosenthal, *Infamous Commerce: Prostitution in Eighteenth-Century British Literature and Culture* (Ithaca, NY: Cornell University Press, 2006), 162–63.

88. Head, *The English Rogue* (1667), 15.

89. Beier, *Masterless Men*, 64.

90. Niall Ó Ciosáin, *Print and Popular Culture in Ireland, 1750–1850* (Basingstoke: Macmillan, 1997), 84–99; Peter Linebaugh, *The London Hanged: Crime and Civil Society in the Eighteenth Century*, 2nd ed. (London: Verso, 2003), 288–332.

91. George Fidge, *The English Gusman; or the History of that Unparallel'd Thief James Hind* (London: George Latham, 1652).

92. Philip Rawlings, introduction to *Drunks, Whores and Idle Apprentices: Criminal Biographies of the Eighteenth Century* (London: Routledge, 1992), 1–35 (23–24, 115).

93. Linebaugh, *The London Hanged*, 91–92, 288.

94. Lynn Hollen Lees, *Exiles of Erin: Irish Migrants in Victorian London* (Manchester: Manchester University Press, 1979), 45, 56.

95. "J. W.," "James Carrick, a Highwayman," in *A Full and Compleat History of the Lives, Robberies, and Murders, of all the Most Notorious Highwaymen* (London: J. Hodges, 1742), 158–62 (158).

96. Ian McBride, *Eighteenth-Century Ireland: The Isle of Slaves* (Dublin: Gill & Macmillan, 2009), 184–88, 223–26.

97. Kate Loveman, "'Eminent Cheats': Rogue Narratives in the Literature of the Exclusion Crisis," in *Fear, Exclusion and Revolution: Roger Morrice and Britain in the 1680s*, ed. Jason McElligott (Aldershot: Ashgate, 2006), 108–22.

98. Tim Hitchcock and Robert Shoemaker, *London Lives: Poverty, Crime and the Making of a Modern City, 1690–1800* (Cambridge: Cambridge University Press, 2015), 70–93.

99. Ó Ciosáin, *Print and Popular Culture*, 88–89.

100. Lincoln B. Faller, *Turned to Account: The Forms and Functions of Criminal Biography in Late Seventeenth and Early Eighteenth-Century England* (Cambridge: Cambridge University Press, 1987), 3–4, 12.

101. D. W. Hayton, *The Anglo-Irish Experience, 1680–1730: Religion, Identity and Patriotism* (Woodbridge: Boydell Press, 2012), 2.

102. Patrick Parrinder, *Nation and Novel: The English Novel from Its Origins to the Present Day* (Oxford: Oxford University Press, 2006), 46; Jerry C. Beasley, *Novels of the 1740s* (Athens: University of Georgia Press, 1982), 87.

103. Faller, *Turned to Account*, 47. Editions of *The English Rogue* from the 1680s and 1720s cost a shilling: *The English Rogue, or Witty Extravagant Described in the Life of Meriton Latroon* (London: J. Back, 1688); *The English Rogue, or Witty Extravagant Described in the Life of Meriton Latroon* (London: T. Norris, 1723). So did two texts cited thus far, *The Irish Rogue* (1690) and 'J. W.', *Most Notorious Highwaymen* (1742). All prices are taken from title pages. Elsewhere, if a primary text's price is available, it is given upon the first citation.

104. Rawlings, *Drunks, Whores and Idle Apprentices*, 3–4.

105. These novels all originally retailed for six shillings: Smollett's *Roderick Random* (1748) and *Ferdinand Count Fathom* (1753); Chaigneau's *Jack Connor* (1752); Amory's *John Buncle*, vol. 1 (1756); and Johnston's *Chrysal* (1760). On Smollett, see Ashley Marshall, *The Practice of Satire in England, 1658–1700* (Baltimore: Johns Hopkins University Press, 2013), 311. See also "The History of Jack Connor," *The Monthly Review* 6 (June 1752): 447–49 (447); Haslett, Notes to Amory, *John Buncle*, ed. Haslett, 270–335 (271); "Chrysal; Or, the Adventures of a Guinea," *The Critical Review* 9 (May 1760): 419.

106. John Richetti, *Popular Fiction before Richardson: Narrative Patterns, 1700–1739* (Oxford: Clarendon Press, 1969), 35, 38–47.

107. For example, Rosenthal, *Infamous Commerce*; *Whore Biographies, 1700–1825*, ed. Julia Peakman, Alexander Pettit, and Patrick Spedding, 8 vols. (London: Pickering and Chatto, 2006).

108. Robert Shoemaker, "The Street Robber and the Gentleman Highwayman: Changing Perceptions of Robbery in London, 1690–1800," *Cultural and Social History* 3, no. 4 (2006): 381–405; Andrea McKenzie, "From True Confessions to True Reporting? The Decline and Fall of the Ordinary's Account," *The London Journal* 30, no. 1 (2005): 55–70 (65).

109. McKeon, *Origins of the English Novel*, 383; Beasley, *Novels of the 1740s*, 115.

110. Faller, *Turned to Account*; Lincoln B. Faller, *Crime and Defoe: A New Kind of Writing* (Cambridge: Cambridge University Press, 1993); Gladfelder, *Criminality and Narrative*; Erin Mackie, *Rakes, Highwaymen, and Pirates: The Making of the Modern Gentleman in the Eighteenth Century* (Baltimore: Johns Hopkins University Press, 2009).

111. James Raven gives a total of 95 new works of fiction published in the 1730s, 210 in the 1740s, and 238 in the 1750s. Raven, introduction to *British Fiction, 1750–1770: A Chronological Check-List of Prose Fiction Printed in Britain and Ireland*, ed. Raven (Plainsboro, NJ: Associated University Presses, 1987), 1–42 (9–10).

112. Ross, "Prose in English, 1690–1800," in *Cambridge History of Irish Literature*, ed. Kelleher and O'Leary, 268–69.

113. Dickie, *Cruelty and Laughter*, 250–61 (253–54).

114. Dickie, *Cruelty and Laughter*, 252.

115. Hayton, *Anglo-Irish Experience*, 16–17.

116. Joep Leerssen, *Mere Irish and Fíor-Ghael: Studies in the Idea of Irish Nationality, Its Development and Literary Expression Prior to the Nineteenth Century* (Cork: Cork University Press/Field Day, 1995), 108.

117. Hand, *History of the Irish Novel*, 38–40.

118. Rosenthal, *Infamous Commerce*, 158–80.

119. Geoffrey Sill, "Developments in Sentimental Fiction," in *Eighteenth-Century Novel*, ed. Downie, 426–39 (427, 432–33).

120. Dickie, *Cruelty and Laughter*, 250.

121. Vic Gatrell, *City of Laughter: Sex and Satire in Eighteenth-Century London* (London: Atlantic Books, 2006), 110–36; Helen Berry, "Rethinking Politeness in Eighteenth-Century England: Moll King's Coffee House and the Significance of 'Flash Talk,'" *Transactions of the Royal Historical Society* 11 (December 2001): 65–81; Erin Mackie, "The Perfect Gentleman: Boswell, the *Spectator* and Macheath," *Media History* 14, no. 3 (2008): 353–72.

122. Gatrell, *City of Laughter*, 129.

123. David O'Shaughnessy, "'Rip'ning Buds in Freedom's Field': Staging Irish Improvement in the 1780s," *Journal for Eighteenth-Century Studies* 38, no. 4 (2015): 541–54 (543).

124. Leerssen, *Mere Irish and Fíor-Ghael*, 124.

125. Leerssen, *Mere Irish and Fíor-Ghael*, 119–20.

126. David O'Shaughnessy, "Making a Play for Patronage: Dennis O'Bryen's *A Friend in Need Is a Friend Indeed* (1783)," *Eighteenth-Century Life* 39, no. 1 (2015): 183–211 (201).

127. J. O. Bartley, *Teague, Shenkin and Sawney: Being an Historical Study of the Earliest Irish, Welsh and Scottish Characters in English Plays* (Cork: Cork University Press, 1954). See also G. C. Duggan, *The Stage Irishman: A History of the Irish Play and Stage Characters from the Earliest Times* (New York: B. Blom, 1969).

128. Hand, *History of the Irish Novel*, 38–39.

129. Leerssen, *Mere Irish and Fíor-Ghael*, 311–13.

130. Hayton, *Anglo-Irish Experience*, 46–47.

131. Moyra Haslett, "Experimentalism in the Irish Novel, 1750–1770," *Irish University Review* 41, no. 1 (Spring/Summer 2011): 63–79 (73). Special Issue on "Irish Fiction, 1660–1830," ed. Haslett, Aileen Douglas, and Ian Campbell Ross.

1. The Irish Writing of Richard Head

1. Chandler, *Literature of Roguery*, 1:211–12, 214.

2. Matthew Steggle, "Richard Head's *The Floating Island* (1673) Plagiarizes Thomas Powell," *Notes and Queries* 52, no. 3 (2005): 325–27; Margaret C. Katanka, "Goodman's *Holland's Leaguer* (1632)—Further Examples of the Plagiarism of Richard Head," *Notes and Queries* 21, no. 11 (November 1974): 415–17; C. W. R. D. Moseley, "Richard Head's *The English Rogue*: A Modern Mandeville?," *The Yearbook of English Studies* 1, no. 1 (1971): 102–7; Allen H. Lanner, "Richard Head's Theophrastan Characters," *Notes and Queries* 17, no. 7 (July 1970): 259.

3. William Winstanley, *The Lives of the Most Famous English Poets* (London: H. Clark, 1687), 207–9. See also Gerard Langbaine, *The Lives and Characters of the English Dramatick Poets* (London: William Turner, 1699), 68; Pritchard, "Head, Richard." Our knowledge of Head's Irish birth and early life derives from Winstanley,

and at least one modern scholar, Margaret C. Katanka, has argued for the reliability of this biography. Winstanley's account of Head was not based on Edward Phillips's *Theatrum Poetarum* (1675), as were the majority of the biographies in the volume, but on personal knowledge. One concrete connection between the two men is that Winstanley describes writing a prefatory verse for *The English Rogue*, and these same lines, quoted in the biography, appear in an edition of the text. See Margaret C. Katanka, "Richard Head, 1637(?)–1686(?), A Critical Study," (PhD diss., University of Birmingham, 1975), 3–4; Winstanley, *Famous English Poets*, 208–9; Head, *The English Rogue Described* (London: Francis Kirkman, 1668), initial pages unnumbered (6 of 8).

4. Christopher J. Wheatley, *Beneath Ïerne's Banners: Irish Protestant Drama of the Restoration and Eighteenth Century* (Notre Dame: University of Notre Dame Press, 1999), 15–28; Rankin, *Between Spenser and Swift*, 187–90; "Kinds of Irishness," in *Companion to Irish Literature*, ed. Wright; "'An Outlandish Miss': The Geography of 'Vertue' in Three Seventeenth-Century Irish Novels," *Irish University Review* 41, no. 1 (Spring/Summer 2011): 21–40; Barbara Freitag, *Hy Brasil: The Metamorphosis of an Island from Cartographic Error to Celtic Elysium* (Amsterdam: Rodopi, 2013), 134–54.

5. Salzman, *English Prose Fiction*, 221–40; Parrinder, *Nation and Novel*, 47–50.

6. Orr, "Afterlives and Imitations"; Betty Joseph, "The Political Economy of *The English Rogue*," *The Eighteenth Century* 55, no. 2–3 (Summer/Fall 2014): 175–92.

7. Paul Salzman, "Alterations to *The English Rogue*," *The Library: A Quarterly Journal of Bibliography*, 6th series, no. 4 (1982): 49–56 (49–50, 55).

8. Francis Kirkman, preface to *The English Rogue Continued, in the Life of Meriton Latroon and Other Extravagants . . . The Second Part* (London: Francis Kirkman, 1671), initial pages unnumbered (1–3, 10 of 18).

9. Chandler, *Literature of Roguery*, 211.

10. Pritchard, "Head, Richard."

11. Only one performance of the play is recorded, which took place privately, "in an unnamed inn in the Quays area of the city." Rankin, *Between Spenser and Swift*, 187–88.

12. Wheatley, *Beneath Ïerne's Banners*, 19–21.

13. T. C. Barnard, *Improving Ireland?: Projectors, Prophets and Profiteers, 1641–1786* (Dublin: Four Courts Press, 2008), 19–20.

14. Richard Head, *Hic et Ubique, or the Humours of Dublin*, in *Irish Drama of the Seventeenth and Eighteenth Centuries*, ed. Christopher J. Wheatley and Kevin Donovan, 2 vols. (Bristol: Thoemmes, 2003), 1:85–146 (107–8, 132).

15. Head, *Hic et Ubique*, 142.

16. Spenser, *View of the State of Ireland*, 69–70.

17. Fynes Moryson, "Of the Commonwealth of Ireland," in *Shakespeare's Europe: Unpublished Chapters of Fynes Moryson's Itinerary*, ed. Charles Hughes (London:

Sherratt and Hughes, 1903), 185–260 (254, 249). Moryson's *Itinerary* was published in 1617, but he then added further chapters to the manuscript, including the material on Ireland quoted here, between 1617 and 1620: Hughes, introduction to *Shakespeare's Europe*, i–xlvi (xl–xli).

18. Head, *Hic et Ubique*, 100.

19. Wheatley and Donovan, ed., *Irish Drama*, 82.

20. Seventeenth-century meanings of "phlegmatic" included: "Having, showing, or characteristic of the temperament formerly believed to result from a predominance of phlegm among the bodily humours; not easily excited to feeling or action; stolidly calm, self-possessed, imperturbable; (with pejorative connotation) sluggish, apathetic, lacking enthusiasm." "Phlegmatic, adj.," *Oxford English Dictionary* (Oxford: Oxford University Press), online database, accessed May 6, 2019, https://www.oed.com/view/Entry/142540?redirectedFrom=phlegmatic.

21. Head, *The English Rogue Described* (London: Kirkman, 1667), 11. The corrected edition of 1667 has been chosen as this chapter's main text, rather than the earlier editions, because the additions made to this edition are relevant to my purposes; for instance, chapter 2, "A short account of the insurrections of the Irish, anno. 1641," which does not appear earlier than 1667. For a summary of the expurgations and additions, see Salzman, "Alterations to *The English Rogue*." All further references to this edition will be given parenthetically. Parts of this edition are paginated wrongly. In cases of erroneous pagination, I have given firstly the page number actually printed, then the correct page number in square brackets.

22. Richard Head, preface to *The English Rogue Described, in the Life of Meriton Latroon, a Witty Extravagant* (London: Francis Kirkman, 1666), pages unnumbered (7–8 of 12).

23. The first two sentences of this passage were added to the 1667 edition and do not appear earlier. See Head, *English Rogue* (1666), 4.

24. *Lazarillo, or, The Excellent History of Lazarillo de Tormes, the Witty Spaniard* (London: W. Leake, 1653), 1–2.

25. Mateo Alemán, *The Rogue, or the Life of Guzmán de Alfarache*, trans. James Mabbe, 4 vols. [1622–23] (London: Constable and Co., 1924), 1:90–91.

26. Staffan Müller-Wille and Hans-Jörg Rheinberger, "Heredity: The Formation of an Epistemic Space," in *Heredity Produced: At the Crossroads of Biology, Politics, and Culture, 1500–1870*, ed. Müller-Wille and Rheinberger (Cambridge, MA: Massachusetts Institute of Technology Press, 2007), 3–34 (4).

27. Rawlings, *Drunks, Whores and Idle Apprentices*, 18.

28. Flux was "an early name for dysentery": "Flux, n.," in *Oxford English Dictionary* (Oxford: Oxford University Press), online database, accessed May 6, 2019, https://www.oed.com/view/Entry/72249?rskey=b50P1h&result=1&isAdvanced=false.

29. Spenser, *View of the State of Ireland*, 57.

30. Helen M. Burke, "'Integrated as Outsiders': Teague's Blanket and the Irish Immigrant 'Problem' in Early Modern Britain," *Éire-Ireland* 46, no. 1–2 (2011): 20–42 (26–29); Mairead Dunlevy, *Dress in Ireland*, 2nd ed. (Cork: Collins Press, 1999), 93.

31. Spenser, *View of the State of Ireland*, 101.

32. Barnard, *Improving Ireland?*, 13.

33. Kathleen M. Noonan, "'Martyrs in Flames': Sir John Temple and the Conception of the Irish in English Martyrologies," *Albion: A Quarterly Journal Concerned with British Studies* 36, no. 2 (Summer 2004): 223–55 (231).

34. Rankin, "Geography of 'Vertue,'" 25, 30.

35. Rankin, "Geography of 'Vertue,'" 30.

36. Brown, "'This Thing of Darkness,'" 50–55.

37. Philip Lawson, *The East India Company: A History* (London: Longman, 1993), 19–44.

38. Moseley, "*The English Rogue*: A Modern Mandeville?," 102–7.

39. Lawson, *East India Company*, 27–28, 34, 40.

40. Parrinder, *Nation and Novel*, 49.

41. Clare Carroll, *Circe's Cup: Cultural Transformations in Early Modern Writing About Ireland* (Cork: Cork University Press/Field Day, 2001), 15–18.

42. Spenser, *View of the State of Ireland*, 13, 93.

43. Nicholas Canny, *Making Ireland British, 1580–1650* (Oxford: Oxford University Press, 2003), 461–62, 469–73.

44. Kathleen M. Noonan, "'The Cruell Pressure of an Enraged, Barbarous People': Irish and English Identity in Seventeenth-Century Policy and Propaganda," *The Historical Journal*, 41, no. 1 (March 1998): 151–77 (151, 159).

45. Noonan, "'Martyrs in Flames,'" 234–35.

46. Sir John Temple, *The Irish Rebellion: Or, An History of the Beginnings and First Progresse of the General Rebellion Raised within the Kingdom of Ireland* (London: R. White, 1646), 40, 7, 9–10.

47. McKeon, *Origins of the English Novel*, 95–96.

48. The same text appears in Temple, *Irish Rebellion*, 14.

49. Noonan, "'Cruell Pressure,'" 161.

50. Faller, *Turned to Account*, 126.

51. Head, *English Rogue* (1666), initial pages unnumbered (14 of 17). This verse was signed "A. B." and so was presumably not written by Head.

52. Harold Weber, "Rakes, Rogues, and the Empire of Misrule," *Huntington Library Quarterly* 47, no. 1 (Winter 1984): 13–32 (28).

53. Rankin, "Kinds of Irishness," 121.

54. On the brat, see Dunlevy, *Dress in Ireland*, 39. *Brechan* is defined as "a Highland plaid," with the first citation as 1771 and possible derivations from Scots Gaelic,

Irish, and Welsh: "Brechan, n.," in *The Dictionary of the Scots Language/Dictionar o the Scots Leid*, accessed May 6, 2019, http://www.dsl.ac.uk/entry/snd/brechan.

55. Noonan, "'Cruell Pressure,'" 169–72.

56. On the publication history of *The English Rogue*, see Moseley, "*The English Rogue*: A Modern Mandeville?," 102. On the authorship of parts 3 and 4, see Pritchard, "Head, Richard," and Salzman, *English Prose Fiction*, 223.

57. Kirkman, preface to *The English Rogue . . . Second Part* (1671), 10–11.

58. McKeon, *Origins of the English Novel*, 95–96.

59. Head, *English Rogue* (1666), 130 [399].

60. Richard Head and Francis Kirkman, *The English Rogue Continued, in the Life of Meriton Latroon, and Other Extravagants . . . The Fourth Part* (London: Francis Kirkman, 1680), 324.

61. Kirkman, preface to *The English Rogue . . . Second Part* (1671), 16.

62. Kirkman, preface to *The English Rogue . . . Second Part* (1671), 1–3.

63. Pritchard, "Head, Richard."

64. Winstanley, *Famous English Poets*, 208.

65. Head, preface to *English Rogue* (1666), initial pages unnumbered (4 of 12).

66. Kirkman, preface to *The English Rogue . . . Second Part* (1671), 1.

67. Pritchard, "Head, Richard"; Salzman, "Alterations to the English Rogue," 49.

68. Richard Head, "The Author's Epistle and Apology to His Ingenious Friend N. W., Esq.," *Proteus Redivivus, or the Art of Wheedling* (London: W. D., 1675), initial pages unnumbered (5 of 14).

69. Kirkman, *The English Rogue . . . Second Part* (1671), 11.

70. *The Life and Death of the English Rogue* (London: Charles Passinger, 1679).

71. *The English Rogue* (London: J. Back, 1688), title page.

72. Orr, "Afterlives and Imitations," 371–72; *The English Rogue* (London: T. Norris, 1723), title page.

73. *The English Rogue* (Back, 1688), 3. See also *The English Rogue* (Gosport, J. Philpott, 1710), 50; *The English Rogue* (London: T. Norris, 1723), 2; and *The English Rogue* (London: Henry Woodgate & Samuel Brooks, 1759), 4.

74. *The English Rogue* (Back, 1688), 78–87.

75. Temple's *The Irish Rebellion* reads, "Many English being strangely degenerated into Irish affections and customes," 14.

76. "Jeremy Sharp," *The English Rogue, or the Life of Jeremy Sharp, Commonly Called Meriton Latroon* (London: T. Read, 1741), 13, 18, 177, 190.

77. Richard Head and Francis Kirkman, *The Original English Rogue; Described in the Life of Meriton Latroon. In Two Parts* (Manchester: John Radford, 1786).

78. Orr, "Afterlives and Imitations," 373.

79. Freitag, *Hy Brasil*, 1.

80. Richard Head, *The Western Wonder, or, O Brazeel, an Inchanted Island Discovered . . . to Which is Added, a Description of a Place, Called, Montecapernia* (London: N. C., 1674).

81. Richard Head, *O-Brazile or The Inchanted Island Being a Perfect Relation of the Late Discovery, and Wonderful Dis-Inchantment of an Island on the North of Ireland . . . Communicated by a Letter from London-Derry, to a Friend in London* (Edinburgh: n.p., 1675).

82. Freitag, *Hy Brasil*, 134–54 (135).

83. Jonathan Scott, *When the Waves Ruled Britannia: Geography and Political Identities, 1500–1800* (Cambridge: Cambridge University Press, 2011), 102; Katanka, "Richard Head, 1637(?)–1686(?), A Critical Study," 17.

84. Richard Head, *The Floating Island, or, a New Discovery Relating the Strange Adventure on a Late Voyage from Lambethana to Villa Franca, Alias Ramallia* (London: "Published by Franck Careless, one of the Discoverers," 1673), 1, 3.

85. Jacqueline Watson and Joey Takeda, "Ram Alley," in *The Map of Early Modern London*, ed. Janelle Jenstad (University of Victoria, June 20, 2018), accessed January 15, 2019, mapoflondon.uvic.ca/RAMA1.html; Robert Somerville, *The Savoy: Manor, Hospital, Chapel* (London: Duchy of Lancaster, 1960). For a detailed explanation of the urban topography of *The Floating Island*, see Katanka, "Richard Head, 1637(?)–1686(?), A Critical Study," 210–20.

86. Head, *The Floating Island*, 8.

87. Winstanley, *Famous English Poets*, 208.

88. Head, *The Western Wonder*, 8, 24–35.

89. Head, preface to *The Floating Island*, pages unnumbered (1 of 2).

90. Head, *The Floating Island*, 17–18, 27, 31, 33–34.

91. Rankin, "Geography of 'Vertue,'" 31–32; Katanka, "Goodman's *Holland's Leaguer*."

92. Richard Head, *The Miss Display'd, with all her Wheedling Arts and Circumventions* (London: n.p., 1675), 5, 39, 132–33.

93. Head, *The Miss Display'd*, 132.

94. Rosenthal, *Infamous Commerce*, 8.

95. Raymond Gillespie, "Richard Head's *The Miss Display'd* and Irish Restoration Society," *Irish University Review* 34, no. 2 (2004): 213–28 (218–22).

96. Rankin, "Geography of 'Vertue,'" 32.

97. Head, preface to *The Miss Display'd*, pages unnumbered (2–3 of 4).

98. Head, *The Miss Display'd*, 94, 92.

99. Rankin, "Geography of 'Vertue,'" 37.

100. Melissa Hope Ditmore, ed., *Encyclopaedia of Prostitution and Sex Work*, 2 vols. (Westport, CT: Greenwood Press, 2006), 1:211.

101. Nicholas Goodman, *Holland's Leaguer* (London: Richard Barnes, 1632), pages unnumbered (4 of 49).

2. Ireland in Popular Criminal Literature, 1680–1750

1. Shoemaker, "The Street Robber and the Gentleman Highwayman," 385–86; Rawlings, *Drunks, Whores and Idle Apprentices*, 1–2.

2. *The French Rogue: Or, the Life of Monsieur Ragoue de Versailles* (London: A. Boddington, 1694); *The Scotch Rogue: Or, the Life and Actions of Donald Macdonald* (London: Robert Gifford, 1706); *The German Rogue: Or, The Life and Merry Adventures, Cheats, Stratagems, and Contrivances of Tiel Eulespiegle* (London: n.p., 1720).

3. Gladfelder, *Criminality and Narrative*, 35.

4. Dickie, *Cruelty and Laughter*, 259.

5. *The Irish Rogue* (1690), title page.

6. Hand, *History of the Irish Novel*, 29.

7. *The Irish Rogue* (1690), 3.

8. Niall Ó Ciosáin, "The Irish Rogues," in *Irish Popular Culture, 1650–1850*, ed. James S. Donnelly and Kerby A. Miller (Ballsbridge: Irish Academic Press, 1997), 78–96 (80, 84).

9. *The Irish Rogue* (1690), 69.

10. John Gibney, *The Shadow of a Year: The 1641 Rebellion in Irish Memory and History* (Madison: University of Wisconsin Press, 2013), 47–48.

11. *The Irish Rogue* (1690), 109–10.

12. Hayton, *Anglo-Irish Experience*, 14.

13. *The Irish Rogue* (1690), 109. See, for example, the following: "The [Irish] people are thus enclined, religious, franke, amorous, irefull . . . delighted with wars"; Richard Stanyhurst, "The Description of Ireland," in *Holinshed's Irish Chronicle, the History of Ireland from the First Inhabitants Thereof, Unto the Yeare 1509*, ed. Liam Miller and Eileen Power (Dublin: Dolmen Press, 1979), 3–116 (112). This passage compares closely with *The Irish Rogue*: "The Inclination of the Irish, says he, is to be superstitiously Religious, Frank, Amorous, Ireful . . . delighting in Branglings and War" (109–10).

14. *The Irish Rogue* (1690), 102, 120, 137–38.

15. "To the Reader," *The Irish Rogue*, initial pages unnumbered (1 of 3).

16. *The Irish Rogue* (1690), 176.

17. Elizabeth Cellier, *The Matchless Rogue; Or, a Brief Account of the Life of Don Thomazo* (London: Printed for Elizabeth Cellier, 1680); Anon., *Don Tomazo, or the Juvenile Rambles of Thomas Dangerfield* (London: William Rumbald, 1680); Loveman, "'Eminent Cheats,'" 115–17. Loveman suggests that the second biography, *Don Tomazo*, is by Dangerfield himself.

18. *Don Tomazo*, 4.

19. Samuel Fannin, "The Irish Community in Eighteenth-Century Cadiz," in *Irish Migrants in Europe after Kinsale, 1602–1820*, ed. Thomas O'Connor and Mary Ann Lyons (Dublin: Four Courts Press, 2003), 135–48; Patricia O'Connell, "The Early Modern Irish College Network in Iberia, 1590–1800," in *The Irish in Europe, 1580–1815*, ed. Thomas O'Connor (Dublin: Four Courts Press, 2001), 49–64 (49–50).

20. McBride, *Eighteenth-Century Ireland*, 185.

21. Preface to *Don Tomazo*, initial pages unnumbered (2–3 of 5).

22. See *The Irish Rogue* (1690), 172–75. The same episode appears in the contemporary *The Pleasant Adventures of the Witty Spaniard, Lazarillo de Tormes*, trans. unknown (London: J. Leake, 1688), 109–15.

23. Thomas Shadwell, *The Lancashire Witches*, in *The Complete Works of Thomas Shadwell*, ed. Montague Summers, 5 vols. (London: Fortune Press, 1927), 4:99–188 (187–88); John Gibney, *Ireland and the Popish Plot* (Basingstoke: Palgrave Macmillan, 2009), 5–6.

24. Hayton, *Anglo-Irish Experience*, 7.

25. Shadwell, *Lancashire Witches*, 168–69.

26. *The Irish Rogue* (1690), 139–43.

27. Leerssen, *Mere Irish and Fíor-Ghael*, 94–97.

28. Richetti, *Popular Fiction before Richardson*, 59.

29. *The Irish Rogue* (1690), 5.

30. *The Irish Rogue, or the Comical History of the Life and Actions of Darby O Brolaghan* (Dublin: James Dalton, 1740), 3, 13. The editing of the text is piecemeal, however, with references to the Irish as "naturally mistrustful" and "thievish" retained, along with the material taken from Stanyhurst's "Description of Ireland," *The Irish Rogue* (1740), 38, 43, 60–65.

31. Leerssen, *Mere Irish and Fíor-Ghael*, 37.

32. Spenser, *View of the State of Ireland*, 55, 96.

33. *The Irish Rogue* (1690), 2.

34. Ó Ciosáin, *Print and Popular Culture*, 89.

35. *The Wild-Irish Captain, or Villany Display'd* (London: n.p., 1692), 5.

36. John Gibney, "An Irish Informer in Restoration England: David Fitzgerald and the 'Irish Plot' in the Exclusion Crisis, 1679–81," *Éire-Ireland* 42, no. 3–4 (2007): 249–76 (274).

37. J. Paul Hunter, *Before Novels: The Cultural Contexts of Eighteenth-Century English Fiction* (New York: W. W. Norton, 1990), 181.

38. *The Wild-Irish Captain*, 20.

39. Gibney, "Irish Informer," 254–56, 272–74.

40. *The Irish Evidence Convicted by their Own Oaths* (London: William Inghal, 1682), 4.

41. Gibney, "Irish Informer," 272–74.

42. Hunter, *Before Novels*, 181–82.

43. *The Wild-Irish Captain*, 9–10.

44. Gladfelder, *Criminality and Narrative*, 72–77.

45. *The Wild-Irish Captain*, 17, 30, 20.

46. R. F. Foster, *Modern Ireland, 1600–1972* (London: Penguin, 1989), 119.

47. *The Wild-Irish Captain*, 22.

48. J. M. Beattie, *Policing and Punishment in London 1660–1750: Urban Crime and the Limits of Terror* (Oxford: Oxford University Press, 2004), 160–61.

49. Gladfelder, *Criminality and Narrative*, 229–31.

50. Beattie, *Policing and Punishment*, 232–42.

51. Gerald Howson, *Thief-Taker General: The Rise and Fall of Jonathan Wild* (London: Hutchinson, 1970), 319.

52. *The Life and Glorious Actions of the Most Heroic and Magnanimous Jonathan Wilde* (London: H. Whitridge, 1725), title page, 4, 56.

53. *Jonathan Wilde*, 19.

54. Foster, *Modern Ireland*, 3, 38.

55. *Jonathan Wilde*, 21–24, 29, 47.

56. *Jonathan Wilde*, 4–5, 11, 17–18.

57. Jerry White, "Pain and Degradation in Georgian London: Life in the Marshalsea Prison," *History Workshop Journal* 68, no. 1 (2009): 69–98 (73–74).

58. *Jonathan Wilde*, 24.

59. Ó Ciosáin, *Print and Popular Culture*, 93.

60. James Kelly, ed., *Gallows Speeches from Eighteenth-Century Ireland* (Dublin: Four Courts Press, 2001).

61. Paul Lorrain, *A Narrative or, the Ordinary of Newgate's Account of What Passed between Him and James Sheppard* (Dublin: n.p., 1718). See also *A Narrative of all the Robberies, Escapes, &c. of John Sheppard* (Dublin: Rider and Harbin, 1724).

62. Mary Pollard, *Dublin's Trade in Books, 1550–1800* (Oxford: Clarendon Press, 1989), 1–17, 224.

63. Voltaire, *The History of Charles XII. King of Sweden. In Eight Books* (Dublin: George Golding, 1735), 162.

64. Kelly, introduction to *Gallows Speeches*, 11–69 (37–38).

65. Ó Ciosáin, *Print and Popular Culture*, 87–88. T. C. Barnard finds that "by the 1730s, there were indications of compilations aimed more specifically at Irish audiences, now large enough to be worth cultivating." T. C. Barnard, "Print Culture 1700–1800," in *The Irish Book in English, 1550–1800*, ed. Raymond Gillespie and Andrew Hadfield (Oxford: Oxford University Press, 2005), 34–58 (49).

66. John Cosgrave, *A Genuine History of the Lives and Actions of the Most Notorious Irish Highwaymen, Tories and Rapparees* (Dublin: C. W., 1747), 166. All further citations are to this edition.

67. T. W. Moody, "Redmond O'Hanlon (c. 1640–1681)," *Proceedings and Reports of the Belfast Natural History and Philosophical Society* 1, no. 1 (1935–36): 17–33 (23–25).

68. *The Life and Death of the Incomparable and Indefatigable Tory Redmond O Hanlyn* (Dublin: John Skinner, 1682), 23, 9, 4.

69. Neal Garnham, *The Courts, Crime and the Criminal Law in Ireland, 1692–1760* (Dublin: Irish Academic Press, 1996), 188–90. Popular support for tories did not necessarily mean that biographies of Irish highwaymen had a predominantly lower-class readership in the late seventeenth and eighteenth centuries. Ó Ciosáin concludes that such biographies were more probably read by the Catholic gentry and by middle-class tenant farmers. Figures like O'Hanlon became widely known and idealized by the tenantry, however, as can be gauged from the use of their biographies as school texts and their presence in oral culture by the late eighteenth century. Ó Ciosáin, "The Irish Rogues," 83, 91–92.

70. Head, *English Rogue* (1667), 230.

71. *Redmond O Hanlyn*, 4–5, 16.

72. Canny, *Making Ireland British*, 417.

73. Raymond Gillespie, *Seventeenth-Century Ireland: Making Ireland Modern* (Dublin: Gill and Macmillan, 2006), 24.

74. Foster, *Modern Ireland*, 122.

75. Mary Pollard, ed., *A Dictionary of Members of the Dublin Book Trade 1550–1800* (London: Bibliographical Society, 2000).

76. Cosgrave, *Irish Highwaymen*, 91.

77. Garnham, *Courts, Crime and the Criminal Law*, 188–92; John Cosgrave, *A Genuine History of the Lives and Actions of the Most Notorious Irish Highwaymen, Tories and Rapparees* (Dublin: Richard Cross, 1782).

78. Ó Ciosáin, *Print and Popular Culture*, 91.

79. Cosgrave, *Irish Highwaymen*, 9–10, 16, 92, 108.

80. Ó Ciosáin provides a helpful table of the sources of Cosgrave's collection in "The Irish Rogues," 84.

81. Alexander Smith, *The Second Volume of the History of the Lives of the Most Notorious High-Way Men* (London: J. Morphew and A. Dodds, 1714), 133–44; *A Compleat History of the Lives and Robberies of the Most Notorious Highway-men*, 2 vols. (London: Sam Briscoe, 1719), 2:236–42.

82. Ó Ciosáin, *Print and Popular Culture*, 88–89.

83. Faller, *Turned to Account*, 144.

84. Cosgrave, *Irish Highwaymen*, 45–46.

85. "J. W.," *Most Notorious Highwaymen*, title page.

86. Cosgrave, *Irish Highwaymen*, 64–68. The same biographical details feature in the London-published collection, with the exception of Butler's learning Spanish and Italian. See "J. W.," *Most Notorious Highwaymen*, 123–26. Cartouche was a

notorious Parisian criminal executed in 1721. See *The Life and Actions of Lewis Dominique Cartouche* (London: J. Roberts, 1722). An earlier biography of Butler appears
in Smith, *Highway-Men* (1719), 2:341–52. But the 1742 collection was more likely to
have been Cosgrave's source, as its biography features specific details not included in
Smith, which Cosgrave reuses, such as "Lord Galway's Regiment" and Butler team-
ing up with Cartouche. See "J. W.," *Most Notorious Highwaymen*, 123–24.

87. Cosgrave, *Irish Highwaymen*, 77–78, 69–70.

88. "J. W.," *Most Notorious Highwaymen*, 155–62. The lives of Mulhoni and
Carrick were first published in James Carrick, *A Compleat and True Account of all the
Robberies Committed by James Carrick, John Malhoni, and their Accomplices* (London: J.
Peele, 1722). However, Cosgrave's biography more resembles that of 1742 in its ab-
breviated style as well as in its wording.

89. Cosgrave, *Irish Highwaymen*, 76; "J. W.," *Most Notorious Highwaymen*, 157.

90. "J. W.," *Most Notorious Highwaymen*, 155.

91. Cosgrave, *Irish Highwaymen*, 72.

92. Faller, *Turned to Account*, 52–56.

93. Hayton, *Anglo-Irish Experience*, 17–18.

94. The *English Short Title Catalogue* has records of ten editions published between c. 1740 and c. 1800: http://estc.bl.uk, search: "Secret History of Betty Ireland."
The earliest are *The Secret History of Betty Ireland* (London: M. Read, 1740[?]), http://
estc.bl.uk/N22256; *The Secret History of Betty Ireland* (London: n.p., 1741), http://estc.
bl.uk/N22254. See also *The Secret History of Betty Ireland*, 10th ed. (London: John
Lever, c. 1765), title page.

95. *The Secret History of Betty Ireland* (Dublin: George Golding and Christopher Goulding, 1742), title page. All further citations are to this edition.

96. Daniel Defoe, *The Fortunes and Misfortunes of the Famous Moll Flanders*
[1722], ed. G. A. Starr (Oxford: Oxford University Press, 1998), 210.

97. "The German Princess, a Cheat, Jilt, and Thief," in Smith, *Highway-Men*
(1719), 1:236–47 (236–37).

98. *Betty Ireland*, 5.

99. Rosenthal, *Infamous Commerce*, 11.

100. *Betty Ireland*, 6–7.

101. *Betty Ireland*, 10, 17.

102. Rosenthal, *Infamous Commerce*, 7.

103. *Betty Ireland*, 17.

104. Eliza Haywood, *Fantomina and Other Works*, ed. Alexander Pettit, Margaret
Case Croskery, and Anna C. Patchias (Peterborough: Broadview, 2004), 41–43.

105. *Betty Ireland*, 17–21.

106. Head, *The Miss Display'd*, 125.

107. Hayton, *Anglo-Irish Experience*, 18.

108. Head, *The Miss Display'd*, initial pages unnumbered (2 of 4).

109. Head, *The Miss Display'd*, 5.

110. *Betty Ireland*, 72.

111. Hayton, *Anglo-Irish Experience*, 17–18.

112. *Betty Ireland*, 95–96.

113. *Betty Ireland*, 85, 87.

114. Hayton, *Anglo-Irish Experience*, 15.

115. Sir Richard Cox, *The True Life of Betty Ireland, with her Birth, Education and Adventures, Together with Some Account of her Elder Sister Blanch of Britain* (Dublin: Peter Wilson, 1753). See also *The Tryal of Roger for the Murder of Lady Betty Ireland* (Dublin: n.p., 1756); *Memoirs of the Right Honourable Lady Betty Ireland, with a Particular Account of her Eldest Son Roger, Jemmy Gripe, and Fox, the Jugler* (Dublin: George Timberfoot, 1756). See also Jacqueline Hill, "'Allegories, Fictions, and Feigned Representations': Decoding the Money Bill Dispute, 1752–56," *Eighteenth-Century Ireland/Iris an Dá Chultúr* 21 (2006): 66–88.

116. Jonathan Swift, *The Story of the Injured Lady* [1746], in *Swift's Irish Writings*, ed. Carole Fabricant and Robert Mahony (Basingstoke: Palgrave Macmillan, 2011), 3–9.

117. McKenzie, "Maclaine [Maclean], James."

118. Hitchcock and Shoemaker, *London Lives*, 202.

119. Preface to *The Genuine Account of the Life and Actions of James Maclean* (London: W. Falstaff, 1750), iii–iv.

120. *A Complete History of James Maclean, the Gentleman Highwayman* (London: Charles Corbett, 1750), title page.

121. Fifield Allen, *An Account of the Behaviour of Mr. James Maclaine from the Time of his Condemnation to the Day of his Execution* (London: J. Noon and A. Millar, 1750), title page, 10.

122. Allen, 20–25; *Genuine Account*, 31–33; *Complete History*, 55–62.

123. *Genuine Account*, 6, 11. The use of a long dash in place of specifying MacLaine's nationality suggests either that the Irish assurance trope was so well known as not to need stating fully, or (interestingly) that there was a perceived need at the time to tone down explicitly anti-Irish references.

124. Howson, *Thief-Taker General*, 172.

125. Shoemaker, "The Street Robber and the Gentleman Highwayman," 386.

126. Hitchcock and Shoemaker, *London Lives*, 204.

127. *Genuine Account*, 10.

128. *Complete History*, 5, 65.

129. Andrea McKenzie, "The Real Macheath: Social Satire, Appropriation, and Eighteenth-Century Criminal Biography," *Huntington Library Quarterly* 69, no. 4 (2006): 581–605 (600–602).

130. Shoemaker, "The Street Robber and the Gentleman Highwayman," 404.

131. *Genuine Account*, 9–33; *Complete History*, 12.

132. *Complete History*, 10–11.

133. Rosenthal, *Infamous Commerce*, 158–62.

134. *Complete History*, 7, 50–51.

135. McKenzie, "Real Macheath," 589–90.

136. Rosenthal, *Infamous Commerce*, 162.

137. *Complete History*, 11, 14, 67.

138. *Complete History*, 18; *Genuine Account*, 11.

139. *Genuine Account*, 22.

3. Crime and Irishness in Ramble Fiction, 1750–1770

1. Norma Clarke, *Brothers of the Quill: Oliver Goldsmith in Grub Street* (Cambridge, MA: Harvard University Press, 2016), 182–91.

2. *An Essay on the New Species of Writing Founded by Mr. Fielding: With a Word or Two upon the Modern State of Criticism* (London: W. Owen, 1751), 16.

3. Francis Coventry, *The History of Pompey the Little*, ed. Nicholas Hudson (Peterborough, Ontario: Broadview Press, 2008), 41.

4. Cahalan, *Irish Novel*, 11.

5. Ian Campbell Ross, introduction to *The History of Jack Connor*, by William Chaigneau, ed. Ross (Dublin: Four Courts Press, 2013), 11–32 (11–14).

6. Haslett, "Experimentalism in the Irish Novel," 76.

7. Catherine Skeen, "Projecting Fictions: *Gulliver's Travels, Jack Connor*, and *John Buncle*," *Modern Philology* 100, no. 3 (February 2003): 330–59 (348–53).

8. Ross, "An Irish Picaresque Novel"; Ross, "Irish Fiction before the Union," in *The Irish Novel in the Nineteenth Century*, ed. Jacqueline Belanger (Dublin: Four Courts Press, 2005), 34–52 (42–45); Hand, *History of the Irish Novel*, 39–42; Trumpener, *Bardic Nationalism*, 131–37.

9. Dickie, *Cruelty and Laughter*, 251–55, 259.

10. Dickie, *Cruelty and Laughter*, 257; Raven, *British Fiction*, 65; "The History of Jack Connor," *The Monthly Review* 6 (June 1752): 447. Haslett, Notes to Amory, *John Buncle*, 271.

11. *The Adventures of Shelim O'Blunder, Esq.* (London: H. Carpenter, 1751), title page, 2, 9, 31, 48.

12. Ross, introduction to *Jack Connor*, 14; Chaigneau, *The History of Jack Connor*, vol. 2, 3rd ed. (Dublin: Abraham Bradley, 1753).

13. *The Life and Adventures of John Connor, Commonly Called, Jack the Batchelor* (Dublin: William Jones, 1785).

14. Ian Campbell Ross, "Novels, Chapbooks, Folklore: The Several Lives of William Chaigneau's Jack Connor, Now Conyers; Or, John Connor, Alias Jack the

Batchelor, the Famous Irish Bucker," *Eighteenth-Century Ireland/Iris an dá Chultúr* 30 (2015): 60–86 (71).

15. Chaigneau, *The History of Jack Connor*, ed. Ross, 46. Further references to *Jack Connor* are to this edition and will be given parenthetically in this chapter.

16. Head, *The English Rogue* (1667), 8; *The Irish Rogue* (1690), 5; *The Wild-Irish Captain*, 5; Smith, *Notorious High-Way Men* (1714), 133–34.

17. On attitudes to Irish migrants in England, see Linebaugh, *The London Hanged*, 292–94.

18. Head, *The English Rogue* (1667), 23.

19. Rawlings, *Drunks, Whores and Idle Apprentices*, 19.

20. McBride, *Eighteenth-Century Ireland*, 27, 181–85, 187–88.

21. Cosgrave, *Irish Highwaymen*, 43, 49.

22. Ross, introduction to *Jack Connor*, 19.

23. Faller, *Turned to Account*, 3–4, 126–27.

24. *The Irish Rogue* (1690), 181; *Redmond O Hanlyn*, 22–23; *Jonathan Wilde*, 61–62.

25. Éamonn Ó Ciardha, *Ireland and the Jacobite Cause, 1685–1766: A Fatal Attachment* (Dublin: Four Courts Press, 2001), 272.

26. Leerssen, *Mere Irish and Fíor-Ghael*, 312–13.

27. Hand, *History of the Irish Novel*, 41.

28. Ross, "Novels, Chapbooks, Folklore," 71.

29. Nicholas Mooney, *The Life of Nicholas Mooney, Alias Jackson* (Dublin: Elizabeth Golding and James Esdall, 1752).

30. Ó Ciosáin, *Print and Popular Culture*, 96.

31. Dudley Bradstreet, *The Life and Uncommon Adventures of Capt. Dudley Bradstreet* (Dublin: S. Powell, 1755), 85, 335–41.

32. Bradstreet, *Life*, 135–50; Patrick M. Geoghegan, "Bradstreet, Dudley," in *Cambridge Dictionary of Irish Biography* (Cambridge: Cambridge University Press), online database, accessed May 9, 2019, http://dib.cambridge.org/viewReadPage.do?articleId=a0876.

33. Bradstreet, *Life*, 135–36, 157–58, 174, 128.

34. Bradstreet, *Life*, 184; Murray G. H. Pittock, "Elphinstone, Arthur, Sixth Lord Balmerino and Fifth Lord Coupar (1688–1746), Jacobite Army Officer," in *Oxford Dictionary of National Biography* (Oxford: Oxford University Press, 2009), online database, accessed April 8, 2019, https://doi.org/10.1093/ref:odnb/8741; William C. Lowe, "Boyd, William, Fourth Earl of Kilmarnock (1705–1746), Jacobite Army Officer," in *Oxford Dictionary of National Biography* (Oxford: Oxford University Press), online database, accessed April 8, 2019, https://doi.org/10.1093/ref:odnb/3117.

35. Bradstreet, *Life*, 186–87, 184.

36. *The History of Jack Connor*, 2 vols. (London: William Johnston, 1753); *The History of Jack Connor . . . The Fourth Edition*, 2 vols. (Dublin: Hulton Bradley, 1766).

37. Philip Carter, *Men and the Emergence of Polite Society, Britain 1660–1800* (Harlow: Longman, 2001), 100.

38. Mackie, *Rakes, Highwaymen and Pirates*, 169, 172.

39. *Monthly Review* 6 (June 1752): 447–49 (448).

40. Lesage, *Gil Blas*, ed. Brack and Chilton, 215–53, 454–81.

41. Lesage, *Gil Blas*, ed. Brack and Chilton, 255–66.

42. Dickie, *Cruelty and Laughter*, 130–34, 261–62.

43. Mackie, *Rakes, Highwaymen, and Pirates*, 35.

44. Ross, introduction to *Jack Connor*, 29. See also Thomas Simes, *The Military Medley, Containing the Most Necessary Rules and Directions for Attaining a Competent Knowledge of the Art* (Dublin: S. Powell, 1767), 153.

45. Skeen, "Projecting Fictions," 331, 348–51.

46. Samuel Madden, *Reflections and Resolutions Proper for the Gentlemen of Ireland, as to Their Conduct for the Service of Their Country* (Dublin: R. Reilly, 1738), 46–47.

47. However, the novel does not appear to have been published in Dublin. Only two London editions survive: *The Adventures of Patrick O'Donnell, in His Travels through England and Ireland* (London: J. Williams, 1763), *The Adventures of Patrick O'Donnell . . . the Second Edition* (London: J. Williams, 1763). For place-names, see the second edition, 11, 17, 23, 62. All further citations are to this second edition.

48. Dedication to *Patrick O'Donnell*, vi–viii. Ballyhaise, Newburgh's estate, is mentioned on page 191 of the novel. On Newburgh, see Andrew Carpenter, *Verse in English from Eighteenth-Century Ireland* (Cork: Cork University Press, 1998), 319, and Michael Talbot, "Thomas Newburgh and his Poem on Handel's Blindness," *The Handel Institute Newsletter* 2, no. 2 (Autumn 2018): 7–10.

49. *Patrick O'Donnell*, 55–61, 238.

50. *Patrick O'Donnell*, 152.

51. See Gatrell, *City of Laughter*, 110–36.

52. *Patrick O'Donnell*, 180.

53. *Patrick O'Donnell*, 183–88, 208, 210–16, 228–36, 217.

54. *Monthly Review* 6 (1752), 447–48.

55. Hand, *History of the Irish Novel*, 41.

56. Ross, "Novels, Chapbooks, Folklore," 68.

57. Skeen, "Projecting Fictions," 352.

58. Jessica Richard, *The Romance of Gambling in the Eighteenth-Century British Novel* (Basingstoke: Palgrave Macmillan, 2009), 78.

59. Mikhail Bakhtin, *The Dialogic Imagination: Four Essays*, trans. Caryl Emerson and Michael Holquist (Austin: University of Texas Press, 1981), 94–96.

60. Leerssen, *Mere Irish and Fíor-Ghael*, 300.

61. Smollett, *Roderick Random*, 3.

62. W. A. Speck, "William Augustus, Prince, Duke of Cumberland (1721–1765), Army Officer," in *Oxford Dictionary of National Biography* (Oxford: Oxford University Press), online database, accessed April 8, 2019, https://doi.org/10.1093/ref:odnb /29455.

63. Skeen, "Projecting Fictions," 350.

64. Bakhtin, *Dialogic Imagination*, 159, 162; Head, *The English Rogue* (1667), 294.

65. Bradstreet, *Life*, 132, 146.

66. Ross, "An Irish Picaresque Novel," 277; introduction to *Jack Connor*, 32.

67. Skeen, "Projecting Fictions," 331.

68. Joep Leerssen, *Hidden Ireland, Public Sphere* (Galway/Dublin: Arlen House, 2002), 33, 36, 12.

69. McBride, *Eighteenth-Century Ireland*, 243.

70. Garnham, *Courts, Crime and the Criminal Law*, 186–209.

71. Timothy Watt, *Popular Protest and Policing in Ascendancy Ireland, 1691–1761* (Martlesham, Suffolk: Boydell Press, 2018), 129–56.

72. Bridget Hourican, "Freney, James," in *Cambridge Dictionary of Irish Biography* (Cambridge: Cambridge University Press), online database, accessed May 9, 2019. http://dib.cambridge.org/viewReadPage.do?articleId=a3372.

73. Ross, "An Irish Picaresque Novel," 277.

74. Ross, "An Irish Picaresque Novel," 277.

75. Hand, *History of the Irish Novel*, 41.

76. T. C. Barnard, *A New Anatomy of Ireland: The Irish Protestants, 1649–1770* (New Haven: Yale University Press, 2003), 21–23.

77. Charles Johnston, *Chrysal, or the Adventures of a Guinea*, ed. Kevin Bourque, 2 vols. (Kansas City: Valancourt Books, 2011), 1:259.

78. Hayton, *Anglo-Irish Experience*, 15, 18–19.

79. Helen M. Burke, "Crossing Acts: Irish Drama from George Farquhar to Thomas Sheridan," in *Companion to Irish Literature*, ed. Wright, 129–41 (137).

80. *Mac-Dermot: Or, the Irish Fortune-Hunter. A Poem* (London: E. Curll, 1717), 5.

81. Head, *The English Rogue* (1667), 243.

82. *Betty Ireland*, 85–87.

83. John Oakman, *The Life and Adventures of Benjamin Brass. An Irish Fortune-Hunter*, 2 vols. (London: W. Nicoll, 1765), 1:4–5.

84. Oakman, *Benjamin Brass*, 2:238–62.

85. Dror Wahrman, *The Making of the Modern Self: Identity and Culture in Eighteenth-Century England* (New Haven: Yale University Press, 2004), 202–5.

86. *Complete History*, 65.

87. Raven, *British Fiction*, 96.

88. *The Adventures of Dick Hazard* (London: W. Reeve, 1754), 3, 47–49, 63, 187, 240–43.

89. Amory, preface to *John Buncle*, ed. Haslett, 45–47.

90. Amory, *John Buncle*, ed. Haslett, 102, 168–69, 224, 227–28.

91. Leerssen, *Mere Irish and Fíor-Ghael*, 124.

92. Joe Lines, "Contesting Masculinities in Thomas Amory's *The Life of John Buncle, Esq.* (1756–66)," *Journal for Eighteenth-Century Studies* 41, no. 3 (September 2018): 447–63.

93. Leerssen, *Mere Irish and Fíor-Ghael*, 120, 124.

4. Migratory Fictions

1. Loeber and Loeber, introduction to *Guide to Irish Fiction*, xciv, xcv. On editions of *Chrysal*, see Bourque, introduction to *Chrysal*, by Johnston, ed. Bourque, 1:vii–li (x).

2. Charles Johnston, *The Reverie, or a Flight to the Paradise of Fools*, 2 vols. (Dublin: Dillon Chamberlaine, 1762), 1:3–4.

3. Daniel Sanjiv Roberts, "A 'Teague' and a 'True Briton': Charles Johnstone, Ireland and Empire," *Irish University Review* 41, no. 1 (2011): 133–50 (134, 140).

4. Scott, *Lives of the Novelists*, 1:142–43.

5. *The Secret Life of Things: Animals, Objects, and It-Narratives in Eighteenth-Century England*, ed. Mark Blackwell (Lewisburg, PA: Bucknell University Press, 2007), 147–61, 242–64.

6. On *Chrysal*, see Ross, "Introduction to Fiction before 1800," 684–85; Douglas, "The Novel before 1800," 32–33; Hand, *History of the Irish Novel*, 53–54. See also Roberts, "Charles Johnstone, Ireland and Empire"; Johnston, *Arsaces*, ed. Roberts.

7. *John Juniper* received a London edition and a Dublin edition, both in 1781. *Anthony Varnish* was published in London in 1786 and 1789. The 1789 edition was reviewed, although no copy survives: *Index to Book Reviews in England, 1775–1800*, ed. Antonia Forster (London: British Library, 1997), 226. See also "The Adventures of Anthony Varnish; Or, a Peep at the Manners of Society," *English Review, or, an Abstract of English and Foreign Literature* 14 (December 1789), 471. *Anthony Varnish* was also translated into French and German during the 1780s, with these translations published in Paris and Leipzig, respectively: Loeber and Loeber, *Guide to Irish Fiction*, 666–67.

8. Daniel Sanjiv Roberts, "A Biographical Note," in *Arsaces*, by Johnston, ed. Roberts, 225–33.

9. Antonia Forster and James Raven, eds., *The English Novel 1770–1829: A Bibliographical Survey*, 2 vols. (Oxford: Oxford University Press, 2000), 1:365.

10. C. B. Hogan, ed., *The London Stage, 1660–1800, Part 5: 1776–1800* (Carbondale: Southern Illinois University Press, 1960), 220–21, 228; Charles Johnston,

Buthred: A Tragedy, as It Is Acted at the Theatre-Royal in Covent-Garden (London: F. Newbery, 1779).

11. Leerssen, *Mere Irish and Fíor-Ghael*, 124–27.

12. Michael Cordner, introduction to *The School for Scandal and Other Plays*, by Richard Brinsley Sheridan, ed. Cordner (Oxford: Oxford University Press, 1998), vii–xlv (vii–ix).

13. Frances Clarke and Sinéad Sturgeon, "Macklin, Charles"; Clarke, "Moody (Cochran), John"; Patrick M. Geoghegan, "Johnstone, John Henry," in *Cambridge Dictionary of Irish Biography* (Cambridge: Cambridge University Press), online database, accessed May 6, 2019, http://dib.cambridge.org/viewReadPage.do?articleId=a5912; http://dib.cambridge.org/viewReadPage.do?articleId=a5240; http://dib.cambridge.org/viewReadPage.do?articleId=a4316.

14. "*The History of John Juniper, Esq., Alias Juniper Jack*," *Monthly Review* 66 (January–June 1781): 131–33 (131, 132).

15. Roger D. Lund, "Charles Johnstone," in *The Dictionary of Literary Biography, Vol. 39: British Novelists, 1660–1800*, ed. Martin Battestin (Detroit: Gale Research, 1985), 293–300 (299).

16. Johnston, *Chrysal*, ed. Bourque, 1:5–6.

17. Daniel Carey, "Intellectual History: William King to Edmund Burke," in *The Princeton History of Modern Ireland*, ed. Richard Bourke and Ian McBride (Princeton: Princeton University Press, 2016), 193–216 (206).

18. Colin Haydon, *Anti-Catholicism in Eighteenth-Century England* (Manchester: Manchester University Press, 2003), 204.

19. McBride, *Eighteenth-Century Ireland*, 347–59.

20. Thomas Bartlett, *The Fall and Rise of the Irish Nation: The Catholic Question, 1690–1830* (Gill and Macmillan, 1992), 82–91.

21. Lund, "Charles Johnstone," 299.

22. John Ferrar, *The History of Limerick* (Limerick: A. Watson and Co., 1787), 368–69; "W. P.," "Anecdotes of the Author of 'Chrysal,'" *The Gentleman's Magazine* (July 1807): 631; "Conservator," "An Account of the Life and Writing of Charles Johnston, Esq.," *The European Magazine, and London Review* 57 (March 1810): 214–16; John Palmer Jr., "Anecdotes and Letters of Charles Johnston," *The Gentleman's Magazine* (August 1836): 135–40.

23. "The Adventures of Anthony Varnish; Or, a Peep at the Manners of Society," *The Town and Country Magazine* 18 (September 1786): 485.

24. "The History of John Juniper, Esq. Alias Juniper Jack," *The Critical Review* 52 (July 1781): 480.

25. Charles Johnston, *The History of John Juniper, Esq. Alias Juniper Jack*, 2 vols. (Dublin: S. Price et al., 1781), I: 16–17. All further references to this text will be given in parentheses. On Wilkes's squint, see Audrey Williamson, *Wilkes: A Friend*

to Liberty (London: Allen and Unwin, 1974), 13. On first publication (London: R. Baldwin, 1781), this novel was priced at nine shillings: See Forster and Raven, eds., *The English Novel 1770–1829*, 1:304.

26. Peter D. G. Thomas, *John Wilkes: A Friend to Liberty* (Oxford: Oxford University Press, 1996), 27–28, 72–76.

27. Johnston, *Chrysal*, ed. Bourque, 2:278–316 (284).

28. Wahrman, *Making of the Modern Self*, 228–37.

29. Thomas, *John Wilkes*, 159–75.

30. Ian Haywood and John Seed, introduction to *The Gordon Riots: Politics, Culture and Insurrection in Late Eighteenth-Century Britain*, ed. Haywood and Seed (Cambridge: Cambridge University Press, 2012), 1–18.

31. Nicholas Rogers, "The Gordon Riots and the Politics of War," in *The Gordon Riots*, ed. Haywood and Seed, 21–45 (31–32).

32. Arthur H. Cash, *John Wilkes: The Scandalous Father of Civil Liberty* (New Haven: Yale University Press, 2006), 5–10.

33. Dickie, *Cruelty and Laughter*, 260.

34. Edward Kimber, *The Juvenile Adventures of David Ranger*, 2 vols. (London: P. Stevens, 1756), 2:283.

35. Lees, *Exiles of Erin*, 56.

36. See Lees, *Exiles of Erin*, and Linebaugh, *The London Hanged*, 288–332.

37. See Craig Bailey, *Irish London: Middle-Class Migration in the Global Eighteenth Century* (Liverpool: Liverpool University Press, 2013) and the essays in David O'Shaughnessy, ed., *Eighteenth-Century Life* 39, no. 1 (2015), special issue on "Networks of Aspiration: The London Irish of the Eighteenth Century."

38. Donald M. MacRaild, *The Irish Diaspora in Britain, 1750–1939* (Basingstoke: Palgrave Macmillan, 2010), 17.

39. T. C. Barnard, "The Irish in London and the London Irish, ca. 1660–1780," *Eighteenth-Century Life* 39, no. 1 (2015): 14–40 (28). On Irish-owned taverns, see also John Bergin, "Irish Catholics and their Networks in Eighteenth-Century London," *Eighteenth-Century Life* 39, no. 1 (2015): 66–102 (88–89).

40. Bergin, "Irish Catholics and their Networks," 92.

41. *The Life of Patrick Madan* (London: Alexander Hogg, 1781), 11–13. According to the title page, this text was priced at one shilling.

42. Lund, "Charles Johnstone," 299.

43. Roberts, "Charles Johnstone, Ireland and Empire," 143.

44. Tobias Smollett, *The Adventures of Peregrine Pickle*, ed. O. M. Brack Jr. and W. H. Keithley (Athens: University of Georgia Press, 2013), 72, 90, 146.

45. James Ussher, *Clio: or, a Discourse on Taste* (London: T. Davies, 1767), 7.

46. François Jacob, *The Logic of Life: A History of Heredity*, trans. Betty E. Spillmann (London: Penguin, 1989), 73–82.

47. Wahrman, *Making of the Modern Self*, 186–87.

48. McBride, *Eighteenth-Century Ireland*, 185–88.

49. David A. Wilson, *United Irishmen, United States: Immigrant Radicals in the Early Republic* (Ithaca, NY: Cornell University Press, 1998), 15; Vincent Morley, *Irish Opinion and the American Revolution* (Cambridge: Cambridge University Press, 2002), 133.

50. Haywood and Seed, introduction, *Gordon Riots*, 2.

51. Helen M. Burke, "The Catholic Question, Print Media, and John O'Keeffe's *The Poor Soldier* (1783)," *Eighteenth-Century Fiction* 27, no. 3–4 (2015): 419–48.

52. Smollett, *Roderick Random*, ed. Brack, 145–54.

53. See Aileen Douglas, "Britannia's Rule and the It-Narrator," in *The Secret Life of Things*, ed. Blackwell, 147–61.

54. For comparable depictions of famines in Johnston's earlier fiction, see Johnston, *Arsaces*, ed. Roberts, 26, 100, 112.

55. Sugata Bose, *Peasant Labour and Colonial Capital: Rural Bengal since 1770* (Cambridge: Cambridge University Press, 1993), 17–19.

56. See Johnston, *Arsaces*, ed. Roberts, 106; *The Pilgrim, or a Picture of Life*, 2 vols. (London: T. Cadell and W. Flexney, 1775), 1:61–63, 116–21.

57. Stephen Gregg, "Representing the Nabob: India, Stereotypes and Eighteenth-Century Theatre," in *Picturing South Asian Culture in English: Textual and Visual Representations*, ed. Tasleem Shakur and Karen D'Souza (Liverpool: Open House Press, 2003), 19–31 (22).

58. Joseph Lennon, *Irish Orientalism: A Literary and Intellectual History* (Syracuse, NY: Syracuse University Press, 2004), 123–26.

59. Padhraig Higgins, *A Nation of Politicians: Gender, Patriotism and Political Culture in Late-Eighteenth-Century Ireland* (Madison: University of Wisconsin Press, 2010), 14.

60. Bakhtin, *Dialogic Imagination*, 159–61.

61. Bakhtin, *Dialogic Imagination*, 161.

62. "The Adventures of Anthony Varnish; or, a Peep at the Manners of Society," *The European Magazine and London Review* 11 (January 1787): 255.

63. "An Adept," *Chrysal, or the Adventures of a Guinea*, 4 vols. (London: R. Baldwin et al., 1783); "An Adept," *Chrysal, or the Adventures of a Guinea*, 4 vols. (London: J. Watson et al., 1785).

64. "An Adept," "On Wigs," *The Weekly Miscellany, or Instructive Entertainer* 9 (1 December 1777): 205–6; "An Adept," "Man of Six Thousand Years," *The Edinburgh Magazine, or Literary Miscellany* (February 1785): 92–93. For further detail, see Joe Lines, "Charles Johnston and the Attribution of *The Adventures of Anthony Varnish* (1786)," *Notes and Queries* 63, no. 1 (March 2016): 91–94.

65. "An Adept," *The Adventures of Anthony Varnish, or a Peep at the Manners of Society* (London: William Lane, 1786), v–xii (vii). All further citations will be to this

edition and will be given parenthetically. On first publication, this novel was priced at seven shillings and sixpence. See Forster and Raven, eds., *The English Novel 1770–1829*, 1:382.

66. Olive Baldwin and Thelma Wilson, "Colman, George, the Elder," in *Oxford Dictionary of National Biography* (Oxford: Oxford University Press), online database, accessed 6 May 2019, https://doi.org/10.1093/ref:odnb/5976.

67. "W. P.," "Anecdotes of the Author of Chrysal," 631.

68. Philip H. Highfill, Kalman A. Burnim, and Edward A. Langhans, "Luke Sparks," in *A Biographical Dictionary of Actors, Actresses, Musicians, Dancers, Managers & Other Stage Personnel in London, 1660–1800* (Carbondale: Southern Illinois University Press, 1991), 14:211–14 (212–13).

69. Highfill, Burnim, and Langhans, "James Sparks," in *Biographical Dictionary*, 14:210–11.

70. "W. P.," "Anecdotes of the Author of Chrysal," 631.

71. Hand, *History of the Irish Novel*, 54.

72. Mark Blackwell, "Disjecta Membra: Smollett and the Novel in Pieces," *The Eighteenth Century* 52, no. 3–4 (2011): 423–42 (433).

73. Hilary Jane Englert, "Occupying Works: Animated Objects and Literary Property," in *Secret Life of Things*, ed. Blackwell, 218–41 (220).

74. Johnston, *The Reverie*, 1:5.

75. Francisco de Quevedo, *The Swindler (El Buscón)*, in *Two Spanish Picaresque Novels*, trans. Michael Alpert (Harmondsworth: Penguin, 1969), 90–91, 107.

76. Dickie, *Cruelty and Laughter*, 48.

77. Johnston, *Chrysal*, ed. Bourque, 1:346–51; *John Juniper*, 1:159–75; *Anthony Varnish*, 1:55–66.

78. McBride, *Eighteenth-Century Ireland*, 315.

79. Robert Shoemaker, *The London Mob: Violence and Disorder in Eighteenth-Century England* (London: Hambledon, 2007), 111.

80. Shoemaker, *London Mob*, 28–32.

81. Linebaugh, *London Hanged*, 306–17.

82. "A Gentleman of the Inner-Temple," *Authentic Memoirs of the Life, Numerous Adventures, and Remarkable Escapes, of the Celebrated Patrick Madan* (London: A. Milne, 1782), 6. According to the title page, this text was priced at one shilling.

83. Shoemaker, *London Mob*, 128, 264.

84. Ross, "Irish Fiction before the Union," 46–47.

85. Linebaugh, *London Hanged*, 292–94.

86. Kimber, *David Ranger*, 2:200–201.

87. Johnston, *Chrysal*, ed. Bourque, 1:155.

88. "The Adventures of Anthony Varnish; Or, a Peep at the Manners of Society," *Critical Review* 62 (August 1786), 149.

89. Johnston's *The Reverie* also features a writer called Crambo, introduced as "that favourite of the muses": *The Reverie*, 1:103, 111. This phrasing foreshadows the descriptions of his fellow writer in *Anthony Varnish*, who is both a "retainer of the Muses" and a "follower of the Muses" (3:69, 170). Crambo's reappearance in *Anthony Varnish* would fit with Johnston's practice of reusing characters in different novels. In *Chrysal* we meet Mr. Poundage, a nobleman's steward (1:74–75), and in *John Juniper*, Squire Mushroom's steward is called Poundage (2:18). *Anthony Varnish* features an actor, Buskin (3:43), who shares his name with an actor from *John Juniper* (2:59–74).

90. Pat Rogers, *Grub Street: Studies in a Subculture* (London: Methuen, 1972), 116–17, 351.

91. *Critical Review* 62 (August 1786), 149.

92. Alexander Pope, *The Works of Alexander Pope*, ed. Whitwell Elwin (London: John Murray, 1882), 3:241–74 (253).

93. *Lazarillo de Tormes*, in *Two Spanish Picaresque Novels*, trans. Alpert, 38–39.

94. Oliver Goldsmith, "The History of Carolan, the Last Irish Bard," *The British Magazine, or Monthly Repository* 1 (July 1760): 418–19; Harry White, "Carolan, Turlough (Ó Cearbhalláin, Toirdhealbhach)," in *Cambridge Dictionary of Irish Biography* (Cambridge: Cambridge University Press), online database, accessed 9 May 2019, http://dib.cambridge.org/viewReadPage.do?articleId=a1492.

95. Ross, "Irish Fiction before the Union," 46.

96. MacRaild, *Irish Diaspora in Britain*, 18–19, 92–93.

97. Johnston, *Chrysal*, ed. Bourque, 1:181.

98. Ross, "Introduction to Fiction before 1800," 684.

99. Douglas, "Britannia's Rule and the It-Narrator," 151.

100. Caroline Franklin, "The Novel of Sensibility in the 1780s," in *English and British Fiction, 1750–1820*, ed. Garside and O'Brien,164–81.

101. Maria Hunter, *Fitzroy; Or, Impulse of the Moment*, 2 vols. (London: William Lane, 1792).

102. *The Minor; Or History of George O'Nial*, 2 vols. (London: William Lane, 1786).

103. Elizabeth Hervey, *The History of Ned Evans*, ed. Helena Kelly (London: Pickering and Chatto, 2010).

Conclusion

1. Claire Connolly, *A Cultural History of the Irish Novel, 1790–1829* (Cambridge: Cambridge University Press, 2012), 5.

2. Miranda Burgess, "The National Tale and Allied Genres, 1770s–1840s," in *Cambridge Companion to the Irish Novel*, ed. Foster, 39–59 (39–40).

3. Trumpener, *Bardic Nationalism*, 131–37.

4. Ian Campbell Ross, "Mapping Ireland in Early Fiction," in *Irish University Review* 41, no. 1 (2011): 1–20 (5, 9, 11–12).

5. Rankin, "Geography of 'Vertue'," 28.

6. Wheatley, *Beneath Ïerne's Banners*, 15–28; Rankin, *Between Spenser and Swift*, 187–90, and "Kinds of Irishness."

7. Tony Murray, *London Irish Fictions: Narrative, Diaspora and Identity* (Liverpool: Liverpool University Press, 2012), 30–31.

8. Trumpener, *Bardic Nationalism*, 131–37 and introduction, xii.

9. Maureen Waters, *The Comic Irishman* (Albany: State University of New York Press, 1984), 5, 28.

10. Waters, *Comic Irishman*, 32; Ó Ciardha, "Early Modern Irish Outlaw."

11. Shoemaker, "The Street Robber and the Gentleman Highwayman"; McKenzie, "From True Confessions to True Reporting."

12. See Beasley, *Novels of the 1740s*, 85–125; Rosenthal, *Infamous Commerce*, 70–96, 154–78.

13. Thomas Keymer, *Sterne, the Moderns, and the Novel* (Oxford: Oxford University Press, 2002), 53.

14. Dickie, *Cruelty and Laughter*, 265.

15. *Chrysal* was included in Walter Scott's anthology of novels, *Ballantyne's Novelists Library* (1821–24). See Bourque, introduction to Chrysal, x. *John Buncle* was republished twice during the 1820s and praised by several Romantic-era writers. See Haslett, introduction to *John Buncle*, 32.

16. Cahalan, *Irish Novel*, 13.

17. Kathryn J. Kirkpatrick, introduction to *Castle Rackrent*, by Maria Edgeworth, ed. George Watson (Oxford: Oxford University Press, 2008), vii–xxxvi (vii–viii).

18. Maria Edgeworth, *Ormond: A Tale* (Belfast: Appletree Press, 1992), 56.

19. Clíona Ó Gallchoir, *Maria Edgeworth: Women, Enlightenment and Nation* (Dublin: University College Dublin Press, 2005), 150–51.

20. Ross, "Novels, Chapbooks, Folklore," 82.

21. Hitchcock and Shoemaker, *London Lives*, 272; Ó Ciardha, "Early Modern Irish Outlaw."

22. Richard W. Wallace, *The Etchings of Salvator Rosa* (Princeton: Princeton University Press, 1979), 113–20.

23. James G. Patterson, *In the Wake of the Great Rebellion: Republicanism, Agrarianism and Banditry in Ireland after 1798* (Manchester: Manchester University Press, 2008).

24. John O'Keeffe, *The Castle of Andalusia, a Comic Opera* (Cork: J Sullivan, 1783); *The Wicklow Mountains*, in *The Dramatic Works of John O'Keeffe* (London: T. Woodfall, 1798), 2:108–91.

25. Finola O'Kane, "Ireland: A New Geographical Pastime?," in *Ireland: Cross-roads of Art and Design, 1690–1840*, ed. William Laffan, Christopher P. Monkhouse, and Leslie Fitzpatrick (Chicago: Art Institute of Chicago, 2015), 77–96 (90–92).

26. Lady Morgan, *The Life and Times of Salvator Rosa* (London: David Bryce, 1855), 43.

27. Loeber and Loeber, eds., *Guide to Irish Fiction*, 1138.

28. One study finds that the Minerva Press published nineteen titles featuring the terms "bandit" or "banditti" and seventeen mentioning Ireland between 1790 and 1820. See Deborah Anne McLeod, "The Minerva Press" (PhD diss., University of Alberta, 1997), 99–102. On the Minerva Press and Irish authors, see Loeber and Loeber, introduction to *Guide to Irish Fiction*, ed. Loeber and Loeber, xci, and Christina Morin, "Irish Gothic Goes Abroad: Cultural Migration, Materiality and the Minerva Press," in *Traveling Irishness in the Long Nineteenth Century*, ed. Marguérite Corporaal and Christina Morin (Basingstoke: Palgrave Macmillan, 2017), 185–204.

29. William Carleton, *Traits and Stories of the Irish Peasantry*, ed. Barbara Hayley, 2 vols. (Gerrard's Cross, Buckinghamshire: Colin Smythe, 1990), 1:271–324 (313).

30. Andrew Sanders, introduction to *The Memoirs of Barry Lyndon, Esq.*, by William Thackeray, ed. Sanders (Oxford: Oxford University Press, 2008), vii–xxii (ix–x).

Bibliography

Primary Sources

Note: The list of primary sources is organized alphabetically by author or pseudonym. Anonymous works are listed under their titles.

"An Adept." *The Adventures of Anthony Varnish, or a Peep at the Manners of Society.* 3 vols. London: William Lane, 1786.

————. "Man of Six Thousand Years." *The Edinburgh Magazine, or Literary Miscellany*, February 1785.

————. "On Wigs." *The Weekly Miscellany, or Instructive Entertainer* 9 (1 December 1777): 205–6.

"The Adventures of Anthony Varnish; Or, a Peep at the Manners of Society." *The Critical Review* 62 (August 1786): 149.

"The Adventures of Anthony Varnish; Or, a Peep at the Manners of Society." *The Town and Country Magazine* 18 (September 1786): 485.

"The Adventures of Anthony Varnish; Or, a Peep at the Manners of Society." *The European Magazine and London Review* 11 (January 1787): 255.

"The Adventures of Anthony Varnish; Or, a Peep at the Manners of Society." *English Review, or, an Abstract of English and Foreign Literature* 14 (December 1789): 471.

The Adventures of Dick Hazard. London: W. Reeve, 1754.

The Adventures of Patrick O'Donnell, in His Travels through England and Ireland. London: J. Williams, 1763.

The Adventures of Patrick O'Donnell, in His Travels through England and Ireland, the Second Edition. London: J. Williams, 1763.

The Adventures of Shelim O'Blunder, Esq. London: H. Carpenter, 1751.

Alemán, Mateo. *The Rogue, or the Life of Guzmán de Alfarache.* Translated by James Mabbe [1622–23]. 4 vols. London: Constable and Co., 1924.

Allen, Fifield. *An Account of the Behaviour of Mr. James Maclaine from the Time of his Condemnation to the Day of his Execution.* London: J. Noon and A. Millar, 1750.

Amory, Thomas. *The Life of John Buncle, Esq.* Vol. I [1756]. Edited by Moyra Haslett. Dublin: Four Courts Press, 2011.

"The Author of Chrysal." "The Temple of the Sun; an Oriental Tale." *The Edinburgh Magazine and Review* 3 (January 1775): 73–77.

Bradstreet, Dudley. *The Life and Uncommon Adventures of Capt. Dudley Bradstreet.* Dublin: S. Powell, 1755.

Butler, Sarah. *Irish Tales, or Instructive Histories for the Happy Conduct of Life* [1716]. Edited by Aileen Douglas, Anne Markey, and Ian Campbell Ross. Dublin: Four Courts Press, 2010.

Carleton, William. *Traits and Stories of the Irish Peasantry* [1830]. Edited by Barbara Hayley. 2 vols. Gerrard's Cross, Buckinghamshire: Colin Smythe, 1990.

Carrick, James. *A Compleat and True Account of All the Robberies Committed by James Carrick, John Malhoni, and Their Accomplices.* London: J. Peele, 1722.

Cellier, Elizabeth. *The Matchless Rogue; Or, a Brief Account of the Life of Don Thomazo.* London: Elizabeth Cellier, 1680.

Chaigneau, William. *The History of Jack Connor* [1752]. Edited by Ian Campbell Ross. Dublin: Four Courts Press, 2013.

———. *The History of Jack Connor.* 2 vols. London: William Johnston, 1753.

———. *The History of Jack Connor.* 3rd ed. 2 vols. Dublin: Abraham Bradley, 1753.

———. *The History of Jack Connor.* 4th ed. 2 vols. Dublin: Hulton Bradley, 1766.

"Chrysal; Or, the Adventures of a Guinea." *The Critical Review* 9 (May 1760): 419.

A Complete History of James Maclean, the Gentleman Highwayman. London: Charles Corbett, 1750.

"Conservator." "An Account of the Life and Writing of Charles Johnston, Esq." *The European Magazine, and London Review* 57 (March 1810): 214–16.

Cosgrave, John. *A Genuine History of the Lives and Actions of the Most Notorious Irish Highwaymen, Tories and Rapparees.* Dublin: C. W., 1747.

———. *A Genuine History of the Lives and Actions of the Most Notorious Irish Highwaymen, Tories and Rapparees.* Dublin: Richard Cross, 1782.

Coventry, Francis. *The History of Pompey the Little* [1751]. Edited by Nicholas Hudson. Peterborough, Ontario: Broadview Press, 2008.

Cox, Sir Richard. *The True Life of Betty Ireland, with her Birth, Education and Adventures, Together with Some Account of her Elder Sister Blanch of Britain.* Dublin: Peter Wilson, 1753.

Defoe, Daniel. *The Fortunes and Misfortunes of the Famous Moll Flanders* [1722]. Edited by G. A. Starr. Oxford: Oxford University Press, 1998.

Don Tomazo, or the Juvenile Rambles of Thomas Dangerfield. London: William Rumbald, 1680.

Edgeworth, Maria. *Castle Rackrent* [1800]. Edited by George Watson. Introduction by Kathryn J. Kirkpatrick. Oxford: Oxford University Press, 2008.

———. *Ennui* [1809]. In *Castle Rackrent and Ennui*, edited by Marilyn Butler. London: Penguin, 1992.

———. *Ormond: A Tale* [1817]. Belfast: Appletree Press, 1992.

An Essay on the New Species of Writing Founded by Mr. Fielding: With a Word or Two upon the Modern State of Criticism. London: W. Owen, 1751.

Ferrar, John. *The History of Limerick.* Limerick: A. Watson and Co., 1787.

Fidge, George. *The English Gusman; or the History of that Unparallel'd Thief James Hind.* London: George Latham, 1652.

The French Rogue: or, the Life of Monsieur Ragoue de Versailles. London: A. Boddington, 1694.

Freney, James. *The Life and Adventures of James Freney.* Dublin: S. Powell, 1754.

"A Gentleman of the Inner-Temple." *Authentic Memoirs of the Life, Numerous Adventures, and Remarkable Escapes, of the Celebrated Patrick Madan.* London: A. Milne, 1782.

The Genuine Account of the Life and Actions of James Maclean. London: W. Falstaff, 1750.

The German Rogue: Or, The Life and Merry Adventures, Cheats, Stratagems, and Contrivances of Tiel Eulespiegle. London: n.p., 1720.

Goldsmith, Oliver. "The History of Carolan, the Last Irish Bard." *The British Magazine, or Monthly Repository* 1 (July 1760): 418–19.

Goodman, Nicholas. *Holland's Leaguer.* London: Richard Barnes, 1632.

Harman, Thomas. *A Caveat or Warning for Common Cursitors* [1566]. In *The Elizabethan Underworld: A Collection of Tudor and Early Stuart Tracts and Ballads*, edited by A. V. Judges, 61–118. Oxford: Routledge, 2002.

Haywood, Eliza. *Fantomina* [1725]. In *Fantomina and Other Works*, edited by Alexander Pettit, Margaret Case Croskery, and Anna C. Patchias. Peterborough: Broadview, 2004.

Head, Richard. *The Canting Academy, or the Devils Cabinet Opened.* London: F. Leach, 1673.

———. *The English Rogue Described, in the Life of Meriton Latroon, a Witty Extravagant.* London: Francis Kirkman, 1666.

———. *The English Rogue Described, in the Life of Meriton Latroon, a Witty Extravagant.* London: Francis Kirkman, 1667.

———. *The English Rogue Described, in the Life of Meriton Latroon, a Witty Extravagant.* London: Francis Kirkman, 1668.

———. *The English Rogue Described, in the Life of Meriton Latroon, a Witty Extravagant.* London: Francis Kirkman, 1672.

———. *The English Rogue Described, in the Life of Meriton Latroon, a Witty Extravagant.* London: Francis Kirkman, 1680.

———. *The Floating Island, or, a New Discovery Relating the Strange Adventure on a Late Voyage from Lambethana to Villa Franca, Alias Ramallia.* London: "Published by Franck Careless, one of the Discoverers," 1673.

———. *Hic et Ubique, or the Humours of Dublin* [1663]. In *Irish Drama of the Seventeenth and Eighteenth Centuries*, edited by Christopher J. Wheatley and Kevin Donovan, vol. 1, 85–146. 2 vols. Bristol: Thoemmes, 2003.

———. *The Miss Display'd, with All Her Wheedling Arts and Circumventions.* London: n.p., 1675.

———. *O-Brazile or The Inchanted Island Being a Perfect Relation of the Late Discovery, and Wonderful Dis-Inchantment of an Island on the North of Ireland . . . Communicated by a Letter from London-Derry, to a Friend in London.* Edinburgh: n.p., 1675.

———. *Proteus Redivivus, or the Art of Wheedling.* London: W. D., 1675.

———. *The Western Wonder, or, O Brazeel, an Inchanted Island Discovered . . . to Which is Added, a Description of a Place, Called, Montecapernia.* London: N. C., 1674.

Head, Richard, and Francis Kirkman. *The English Rogue Continued in the Life of Meriton Latroon, and Other Extravagants . . . The Third Part.* London: Anne Johnson, 1674.

———. *The Life and Death of the English Rogue.* London: Charles Passinger, 1679.

————. *The English Rogue Continued in the Life of Meriton Latroon, and Other Extravagants . . . The Fourth Part.* London: Francis Kirkman, 1680.

————. *The English Rogue, or, Witty Extravagant Described in the Life of Meriton Latroon.* London: J. Back, 1688.

————. *The English Rogue Containing a Brief Discovery of the Most Eminent Cheats, Robberies and Other Extravagancies.* London: J. Blare, 1688.

————. *The English Rogue, or, Witty Extravagant Described in the Life of Meriton Latroon.* Gosport, J. Philpott, 1710.

————. *The English Rogue, or, Witty Extravagant Described in the Life of Meriton Latroon.* London: T. Norris, 1723.

————. *The English Rogue, or, Witty Extravagant Described in the Life of Meriton Latroon.* London: Henry Woodgate and Samuel Brooks, 1759.

————. *The Original English Rogue; Described in the Life of Meriton Latroon. In Two Parts.* Manchester: John Radford, 1786.

Hervey, Elizabeth, *The History of Ned Evans* [1796]. Edited by Helena Kelly. London: Pickering and Chatto, 2010.

"The History of Jack Connor." *The Monthly Review* 6 (June 1752): 447–49.

"The History of John Juniper, Esq., Alias Juniper Jack." *The Critical Review* 52 (July 1781): 480.

"The History of John Juniper, Esq., Alias Juniper Jack." *The Monthly Review* 66 (January–June 1781): 131–33.

Holinshed, Raphael, and Richard Stanyhurst. *Holinshed's Irish Chronicle, the History of Ireland from the First Inhabitants Thereof, Unto the Yeare 1509* [1577]. Edited by Liam Miller and Eileen Power. Dublin: Dolmen Press, 1979.

Hunter, Maria. *Fitzroy; or, Impulse of the Moment.* 2 vols. London: William Lane, 1792.

The Irish Evidence Convicted by their Own Oaths. London: William Inghal, 1682.

The Irish Rogue, or the Comical History of the Life and Actions of Darby O Brolaghan. Dublin: James Dalton, 1740.

The Irish Rogue, or, the Comical History of the Life and Actions of Teague O'Divelley. London: Geo. Conyers, 1690.

Johnston, Charles. *Buthred: A Tragedy, as It Is Acted at the Theatre-Royal in Covent-Garden.* London: F. Newbery, 1779.

————. *Chrysal, Or the Adventures of a Guinea.* 4 vols. London: R. Baldwin et al., 1783.

———. *Chrysal, Or the Adventures of a Guinea.* 4 vols. London: J. Watson et al., 1785.

———. *Chrysal, Or the Adventures of a Guinea* [1760–64]. Edited by Kevin Bourque. 2 vols. Kansas City: Valancourt Books, 2011.

———. *The History of Arsaces, Prince of Betlis* [1774]. Edited by Daniel Sanjiv Roberts. Dublin: Four Courts Press, 2014.

———. *The History of John Juniper, Esq., Alias Juniper Jack.* 2 vols. Dublin: S. Price et al., 1781.

———. *The History of John Juniper, Esq., Alias Juniper Jack.* 3 vols. London: R. Baldwin, 1781.

———. *The Pilgrim, or a Picture of Life.* 2 vols. London: T. Cadell and W. Flexney, 1775.

———. *The Reverie, or a Flight to the Paradise of Fools.* 2 vols. Dublin: Dillon Chamberlaine, 1762.

"J. W." *A Full and Compleat History of the Lives, Robberies, and Murders, of all the Most Notorious Highwaymen.* London: J. Hodges, 1742.

Kimber, Edward. *The Juvenile Adventures of David Ranger.* 2 vols. London: P. Stevens, 1756.

Kirkman, Francis. *The English Rogue Continued, in the Life of Meriton Latroon and Other Extravagants . . . The Second Part.* London: Francis Kirkman, 1671.

Langbaine, Gerard. *The Lives and Characters of the English Dramatick Poets.* London: William Turner, 1699.

Lazarillo, or, The Excellent History of Lazarillo de Tormes, the Witty Spaniard. Translated by David Rowland. London: W. Leake, 1653.

Lazarillo de Tormes [1554]. In *Two Spanish Picaresque Novels*, translated by Michael Alpert, 23–79. Harmondsworth: Penguin, 1969.

Lesage, Alain-René. *The Adventures of Gil Blas of Santillane* [1715–35]. Edited by O. M. Brack and Leslie A. Chilton. Translated by Tobias Smollett. Athens: University of Georgia Press, 2011.

———. *The History and Adventures of Gil Blas of Santillane.* Translator unknown. London: Jacob Tonson, 1716.

The Life and Actions of Lewis Dominique Cartouche. London: J. Roberts, 1722.

The Life and Adventures of John Connor, Commonly Called, Jack the Batchelor. Dublin: William Jones, 1785.

The Life and Death of the Incomparable and Indefatigable Tory Redmond O Hanlyn. Dublin: John Skinner, 1682.

The Life and Glorious Actions of the Most Heroic and Magnanimous Jonathan Wilde. London: H. Whitridge, 1725.

The Life of Patrick Madan. London: Alexander Hogg, 1781.

Lorrain, Paul. *A Narrative or, the Ordinary of Newgate's Account of What Passed between Him and James Sheppard.* Dublin: n.p., 1718.

Mac-Dermot: Or, the Irish Fortune-Hunter. A Poem. London: E. Curll, 1717.

Madden, Samuel. *Reflections and Resolutions Proper for the Gentlemen of Ireland, as to Their Conduct for the Service of Their Country.* Dublin: R. Reilly, 1738.

Memoirs of the Right Honourable Lady Betty Ireland, with a Particular Account of her Eldest Son Roger, Jemmy Gripe, and Fox, the Jugler. Dublin: George Timberfoot, 1756.

The Minor; Or History of George O'Nial. 2 vols. London: William Lane, 1786.

Mooney, Nicholas. *The Life of Nicholas Mooney, Alias Jackson.* Dublin: Elizabeth Golding and James Esdall, 1752.

Morgan, Lady [Sydney Owenson]. *The Life and Times of Salvator Rosa.* London: David Bryce, 1855.

Moryson, Fynes. "Of the Commonwealth of Ireland" [1617–20]. In *Shakespeare's Europe: Unpublished Chapters of Fynes Moryson's Itinerary*, edited by Charles Hughes, 185–260. London: Sherratt and Hughes, 1903.

A Narrative of all the Robberies, Escapes, &c. of John Sheppard. Dublin: Rider and Harbin, 1724.

Oakman, John. *The Life and Adventures of Benjamin Brass. An Irish Fortune-Hunter.* 2 vols. London: W. Nicoll, 1765.

O'Keeffe, John. *The Castle of Andalusia, a Comic Opera.* Cork: J. Sullivan, 1783.
———. *The Dramatic Works of John O'Keeffe.* 4 vols. London: T. Woodfall, 1798.

Palmer Jr., John. "Anecdotes and Letters of Charles Johnston." *The Gentleman's Magazine*, August 1836.

The Pleasant Adventures of the Witty Spaniard, Lazarillo de Tormes. London: J. Leake, 1688.

Pope, Alexander. *The Works of Alexander Pope.* Edited by Whitwell Elwin. 4 vols. London: John Murray, 1882.

Quevedo, Francisco de. *The Swindler (El Buscón)* [1626]. In *Two Spanish Picaresque Novels*, translated by Michael Alpert, 83–214. Harmondsworth: Penguin, 1969.

The Scotch Rogue: Or, the Life and Actions of Donald Macdonald. London: Robert Gifford, 1706.

The Secret History of Betty Ireland. London: M. Read, 1740[?].

The Secret History of Betty Ireland. London: n.p., 1741.

The Secret History of Betty Ireland. Dublin: George Golding and Christopher Goulding, 1742.

The Secret History of Betty Ireland. London: John Lever, 1765.

Shadwell, Thomas. *The Amorous Bigot* [1690]. In *The Complete Works of Thomas Shadwell*, edited by Montague Summers, 5:13–76. 5 vols. London: Fortune Press, 1927.

———. *The Lancashire Witches* [1682]. In *The Complete Works of Thomas Shadwell*, edited by Montague Summers, 4:99–188. 5 vols. London: Fortune Press, 1927.

"Sharp, Jeremy." *The English Rogue, or the Life of Jeremy Sharp, Commonly Called Meriton Latroon*. London: T. Read, 1741.

Sheridan, Elizabeth. *The Triumph of Prudence Over Passion* [1781]. Edited by Aileen Douglas and Ian Campbell Ross. Dublin: Four Courts Press, 2011.

Simes, Thomas. *The Military Medley, Containing the Most Necessary Rules and Directions for Attaining a Competent Knowledge of the Art*. Dublin: S. Powell, 1767.

Smith, Alexander. *A Compleat History of the Lives and Robberies of the Most Notorious Highway-Men*. 2 vols. London: Sam. Briscoe, 1719.

———. *The Second Volume of the History of the Lives of the Most Notorious High-Way Men*. London: J. Morphew and A. Dodds, 1714.

Smollett, Tobias. *The Adventures of Peregrine Pickle* [1751]. Edited by O. M. Brack Jr. and W. H. Keithley. Athens: University of Georgia Press, 2013.

———. *The Adventures of Roderick Random* [1748]. Edited by O. M. Brack. Athens: University of Georgia Press, 2012.

Spenser, Edmund. *A View of the State of Ireland. From the First Printed Edition (1633)*. Edited by Andrew Hadfield and Willy Maley. Oxford: Blackwell, 1997.

Swift, Jonathan. *The Story of the Injured Lady* [1746]. In *Swift's Irish Writings*, edited by Carole Fabricant and Robert Mahony. Basingstoke: Palgrave Macmillan, 2011.

Temple, Sir John. *The Irish Rebellion: Or, an History of the Beginnings and First Progresse of the General Rebellion Raised within the Kingdom of Ireland*. London: R. White, 1646.

Thackeray, William. *The Memoirs of Barry Lyndon, Esq.* [1856]. Edited by Andrew Sanders. Oxford: Oxford University Press, 2008.

The Tryal of Roger for the Murder of Lady Betty Ireland. Dublin: n.p., 1756.

Ussher, James. *Clio: Or, a Discourse on Taste*. London: T. Davies, 1767.

Vertue Rewarded, or the Irish Princess [1693]. Edited by Anne Markey and Ian Campbell Ross. Dublin: Four Courts Press, 2010.

Voltaire. *The History of Charles XII. King of Sweden. In Eight Books*. Dublin: George Golding, 1735.

The Wild-Irish Captain, or Villany Display'd. London: n.p., 1692.

Winstanley, William. *The Lives of the Most Famous English Poets*. London: H. Clark, 1687.

"W. P." "Anecdotes of the Author of 'Chrysal.'" *The Gentleman's Magazine*, July 1807.

Secondary Sources

Alter, Robert. *The Rogue's Progress: Studies in the Picaresque Novel*. Cambridge, MA: Harvard University Press, 1964.

Bailey, Craig. *Irish London: Middle-Class Migration in the Global Eighteenth Century*. Liverpool: Liverpool University Press, 2013.

Bakhtin, Mikhail. *The Dialogic Imagination: Four Essays*. Translated by Caryl Emerson and Michael Holquist. Austin: University of Texas Press, 1981.

Baldwin, Olive and Thelma Wilson. "Colman, George, the Elder." In *Oxford Dictionary of National Biography*. Oxford: Oxford University Press, 2009. https://doi.org/10.1093/ref:odnb/5976.

Barnard, T. C. *Improving Ireland?: Projectors, Prophets and Profiteers, 1641–1786*. Dublin: Four Courts Press, 2008.

———. "The Irish in London and the London Irish, ca. 1660–1780." *Eighteenth-Century Life* 39, no. 1 (2015): 14–40.

———. *A New Anatomy of Ireland: The Irish Protestants, 1649–1770*. New Haven, CT: Yale University Press, 2003.

Bartlett, Thomas. *The Fall and Rise of the Irish Nation: The Catholic Question, 1690–1830*. Gill and Macmillan, 1992.

Bartley, J. O. *Teague, Shenkin and Sawney: Being an Historical Study of the Earliest Irish, Welsh and Scottish Characters in English Plays*. Cork: Cork University Press, 1954.

Beasley, Jerry C. *Novels of the 1740s*. Athens: University of Georgia Press, 1982.

———. *Tobias Smollett, Novelist*. Athens: University of Georgia Press, 1998.

Beattie, J. M. *Policing and Punishment in London, 1660–1750: Urban Crime and the Limits of Terror.* Oxford: Oxford University Press, 2004.

Beier, A. L. *Masterless Men: The Vagrancy Problem in England, 1560–1640.* London: Methuen, 1985.

Belanger, Jacqueline, ed. *The Irish Novel in the Nineteenth Century: Facts and Fictions.* Dublin: Four Courts Press, 2005.

Bergin, John. "Irish Catholics and their Networks in Eighteenth-Century London." *Eighteenth-Century Life* 39, no. 1 (2015): 66–102.

Berry, Helen. "Rethinking Politeness in Eighteenth-Century England: Moll King's Coffee House and the Significance of 'Flash Talk'." *Transactions of the Royal Historical Society* 11 (December 2001): 65–81.

Bjornson, Richard. *The Picaresque Hero in European Fiction.* Madison: University of Wisconsin Press, 1977.

Blackwell, Mark. "Disjecta Membra: Smollett and the Novel in Pieces." *The Eighteenth Century* 52, no. 3–4 (Autumn/Winter 2011): 423–42.

Blackwell, Mark, ed. *The Secret Life of Things: Animals, Objects, and It-Narratives in Eighteenth-Century England.* Lewisburg, PA: Bucknell University Press, 2007.

Bose, Sugata. *Peasant Labour and Colonial Capital: Rural Bengal since 1770.* Cambridge: Cambridge University Press, 1993.

Boucé, Paul-Gabriel. "Smollett's Pseudo-Picaresque: A Response to Rousseau's Smollett and the Picaresque." *Studies in Burke and His Time* 14 (1972): 73–79.

Brown, Paul. "'This Thing of Darkness I Acknowledge Mine': *The Tempest* and the Discourse of Colonialism." In *Political Shakespeare: Essays in Cultural Materialism*, edited by Alan Sinfield and Jonathan Dollimore, 48–71. Manchester: Manchester University Press, 1994.

Burgess, Miranda. "The National Tale and Allied Genres, 1770s–1840s." In *The Cambridge Companion to the Irish Novel*, edited by John Wilson Foster, 39–59. Cambridge: Cambridge University Press, 2006.

Burke, Helen M. "The Catholic Question, Print Media, and John O'Keeffe's *The Poor Soldier* (1783)." *Eighteenth-Century Fiction* 27, no. 3–4 (2015): 419–48.

———. "Crossing Acts: Irish Drama from George Farquhar to Thomas Sheridan." In *A Companion to Irish Literature*, 2 vols., edited by Julia M. Wright, 1:129–412. Chichester: Wiley-Blackwell, 2010.

———. "'Integrated as Outsiders': Teague's Blanket and the Irish Immigrant 'Problem' in Early Modern Britain." *Éire-Ireland* 46, no. 1–2 (2011): 20–42.

Cahalan, James M. *The Irish Novel: A Critical History*. Dublin: Gill and Macmillan, 1988.

Canny, Nicholas. *Making Ireland British, 1580–1650*. Oxford: Oxford University Press, 2003.

Carey, Daniel. "Intellectual History: William King to Edmund Burke." In *The Princeton History of Modern Ireland*, edited by Richard Bourke and Ian McBride, 193–216. Princeton: Princeton University Press, 2016.

Carroll, Clare. *Circe's Cup: Cultural Transformations in Early Modern Writing About Ireland*. Cork: Cork University Press/Field Day, 2001.

Carswell, Simon. "Ireland's Call: From 'Bandit Country' to Brexit's Frontier." *The Irish Times*, March 18, 2017. https://www.irishtimes.com/news/politics /ireland-s-call-from-bandit-country-to-brexit-s-frontier-1.3014496.

Carpenter, Andrew. *Verse in English from Eighteenth-Century Ireland*. Cork: Cork University Press, 1998.

Carter, Philip. *Men and the Emergence of Polite Society, Britain 1660–1800*. Harlow: Longman, 2001.

Cash, Arthur H. *John Wilkes: The Scandalous Father of Civil Liberty*. New Haven, CT: Yale University Press, 2006.

Cashman, Ray. "The Heroic Outlaw in Irish Folklore and Popular Literature." *Folklore* 111, no. 2 (October 2000): 191–215.

Chandler, Frank Wadleigh. *The Literature of Roguery*. 2 vols. New York: Houghton Mifflin, 1907.

Chilton, Leslie A. "Smollett, the Picaresque and Two Medical Satires." In *New Contexts for Eighteenth-Century British Fiction: "Hearts Resolved and Hands Prepared": Essays in Honour of Jerry C. Beasley*, edited by Christopher D. Johnson, 173–82. Newark: University of Delaware Press, 2011.

Cimino, Michael, dir. *Thunderbolt and Lightfoot*. 1977.

Clarke, Frances. "Moody (Cochran), John." In *Cambridge Dictionary of Irish Biography*. Cambridge: Cambridge University Press, 2009. http://dib .cambridge.org/viewReadPage.do?articleId=a5912.

Clarke, Frances and Sinéad Sturgeon. "Macklin, Charles." In *Cambridge Dictionary of Irish Biography*. Cambridge: Cambridge University Press, 2009. http://dib.cambridge.org/viewReadPage.do?articleId=a5240.

Clarke, Norma. *Brothers of the Quill: Oliver Goldsmith in Grub Street*. Cambridge, MA: Harvard University Press, 2016.

Connolly, Claire. *A Cultural History of the Irish Novel, 1790–1829*. Cambridge: Cambridge University Press, 2012.

Connolly, S. J. *Religion, Law and Power: The Making of Protestant Ireland*. Oxford: Clarendon Press, 1992.

Cordner, Michael. Introduction to *The School for Scandal and Other Plays*, by Richard Brinsley Sheridan, vii–xlv. Edited by Michael Cordner. Oxford: Oxford University Press, 1998.

Cruz, Anne J. "Sonnes of the Rogue: Picaresque Relations in England and Spain." In *The Picaresque: Tradition and Displacement*, edited by Giancarlo Maiorino, 248–72. Minneapolis: University of Minnesota Press, 1996.

Davis, Lennard. *Factual Fictions: The Origins of the English Novel*. New York: Columbia University Press, 1987.

Delahaye, Michael. "Irish or Australian, Hero or Villain, the Ned Kelly Legend Lives On." *The Irish Independent*, November 4, 2012. https://www.independent.ie/lifestyle/irish-or-australian-hero-or-villain-the-ned-kelly-legend-lives-on-28826785.html.

Dickie, Simon. *Cruelty and Laughter: Forgotten Comic Literature and the Unsentimental Eighteenth Century*. Chicago: University of Chicago Press, 2011.

———. "Novels of the 1750s." In *The Oxford Handbook of the Eighteenth-Century Novel*, edited by J. A. Downie, 252–63. Oxford: Oxford University Press, 2016.

———. "Tobias Smollett and the Ramble Novel." In *The Oxford History of the Novel in English, Volume 2: English and British Fiction 1750–1820*, edited by Karen O'Brien and Peter Garside, 92–108. Oxford: Oxford University Press, 2015.

Ditmore, Melissa Hope, ed. *Encyclopaedia of Prostitution and Sex Work*. 2 vols. Westport, CT: Greenwood Press, 2006.

Douglas, Aileen. "Britannia's Rule and the It-Narrator." In *The Secret Life of Things: Animals, Objects, and It-Narratives in Eighteenth-Century England*, edited by Mark Blackwell, 147–61. Lewisburg, PA: Bucknell University Press, 2007.

———. "The Novel before 1800." In *The Cambridge Companion to the Irish Novel*, edited by John Wilson Foster, 22–38. Cambridge: Cambridge University Press, 2006.

Douglas, Aileen, Moyra Haslett, and Ian Campbell Ross, eds. *Irish University Review* 41, no. 1 (Spring/Summer 2011). Special issue on "Irish Fiction, 1660–1830."

Downie, J. A., ed. *The Oxford Handbook of the Eighteenth-Century Novel*. Oxford: Oxford University Press, 2016.

Duggan, G. C. *The Stage Irishman: A History of the Irish Play and Stage Characters from the Earliest Times*. New York: B. Blom, 1969.

Dunford, Stephen. *The Irish Highwaymen*. Dublin: Merlin, 2000.

Dunlevy, Mairead. *Dress in Ireland*. 2nd ed. Cork: Collins Press, 1999.

Dunn, Peter N. *Spanish Picaresque Fiction: A New Literary History*. Ithaca, NY: Cornell University Press, 1993.

Eagleton, Terry. *Heathcliff and the Great Hunger: Studies in Irish Culture*. London: Verso, 1995.

Englert, Hilary Jane. "Occupying Works: Animated Objects and Literary Property." In *The Secret Life of Things: Animals, Objects, and It-Narratives in Eighteenth-Century England*, edited by Mark Blackwell, 218–41. Lewisburg, PA: Bucknell University Press, 2007.

Faller, Lincoln B. *Crime and Defoe: A New Kind of Writing*. Cambridge: Cambridge University Press, 1993.

———. *Turned to Account: The Forms and Functions of Criminal Biography in Late Seventeenth and Early Eighteenth-Century England*. Cambridge: Cambridge University Press, 1987.

Fannin, Samuel. "The Irish Community in Eighteenth-Century Cadiz." In *Irish Migrants in Europe after Kinsale, 1602–1820*, edited by Thomas O'Connor and Mary Ann Lyons, 135–48. Dublin: Four Courts Press, 2003.

Fogarty, Anne. "Literature in English 1550–1690: From the Elizabethan Settlement to the Battle of the Boyne." In *The Cambridge History of Irish Literature*. 2 vols., edited by Margaret Kelleher and Philip O'Leary, 1:140–90. Cambridge: Cambridge University Press, 2005.

Forster, Antonia, ed. *Index to Book Reviews in England, 1775–1800*. London: British Library, 1997.

Forster, Antonia, and James Raven, eds. *The English Novel 1770–1829: A Bibliographical Survey*. 2 vols. Oxford: Oxford University Press, 2000.

Foster, John Wilson, ed. *The Cambridge Companion to the Irish Novel*. Cambridge: Cambridge University Press, 2006.

Foster, R. F. *Modern Ireland, 1600–1972*. London: Penguin, 1989.

Franklin, Caroline. "The Novel of Sensibility in the 1780s." In *The Oxford History of the Novel in English, Volume 2: English and British Fiction 1750–1820*, edited by Peter Garside and Karen O'Brien, 164–81. Oxford: Oxford University Press, 2015.

Freitag, Barbara. *Hy Brasil: The Metamorphosis of an Island from Cartographic Error to Celtic Elysium*. Amsterdam: Rodopi, 2013.

Garnham, Neal. *The Courts, Crime and the Criminal Law in Ireland, 1692–1760*. Dublin: Irish Academic Press, 1996.

Garrido Ardila, J. A., ed. "Origins and Definition of the Picaresque Genre." In *The Picaresque Novel in Western Literature*, edited by Garrido Ardila, 1–23. Cambridge: Cambridge University Press, 2015.

———. "The Picaresque Novel and the Rise of the English Novel." In *The Picaresque Novel in Western Literature*, edited by Garrido Ardila, 113–39. Cambridge: Cambridge University Press, 2015.

———. *The Picaresque Novel in Western Literature*. Cambridge: Cambridge University Press, 2015.

Garside, Peter, and Karen O'Brien, eds. *English and British Fiction, 1750–1820*. Oxford: Oxford University Press, 2015.

Gatrell, Vic. *City of Laughter: Sex and Satire in Eighteenth-Century London*. London: Atlantic Books, 2006.

Geoghegan, Patrick M. "Johnstone, John Henry." *Cambridge Dictionary of Irish Biography*. Cambridge: Cambridge University Press, 2009. http://dib.cambridge.org/viewReadPage.do?articleId=a4316.

———. "Bradstreet, Dudley." *Cambridge Dictionary of Irish Biography*. Cambridge: Cambridge University Press, 2009. http://dib.cambridge.org/viewReadPage.do?articleId=a0876.

Gibney, John. *Ireland and the Popish Plot*. Basingstoke: Palgrave Macmillan, 2009.

———. "An Irish Informer in Restoration England: David Fitzgerald and the 'Irish Plot' in the Exclusion Crisis, 1679–81." *Éire-Ireland* 42, no. 3–4 (2007): 249–76.

———. *The Shadow of a Year: The 1641 Rebellion in Irish Memory and History*. Madison: University of Wisconsin Press, 2013.

Giddings, Robert. *The Tradition of Smollett*. London: Methuen, 1967.

Gillespie, Raymond. "Richard Head's *The Miss Display'd* and Irish Restoration Society." *Irish University Review* 34, no. 2 (2004): 213–28.

———. *Seventeenth-Century Ireland: Making Ireland Modern*. Dublin: Gill and Macmillan, 2006.

Gillespie, Raymond, and Andrew Hadfield, eds. *The Irish Book in English, 1550–1800*. Oxford: Oxford University Press, 2005.

Gladfelder, Hal. *Criminality and Narrative in Eighteenth-Century England*. Baltimore: Johns Hopkins University Press, 2001.

Gregg, Stephen. "Representing the Nabob: India, Stereotypes and Eighteenth-Century Theatre." In *Picturing South Asian Culture in English:*

Textual and Visual Representations, edited by Tasleem Shakur and Karen D'Souza, 19–31. Liverpool: Open House Press, 2003.

Guillén, Claudio. *Literature as System: Essays toward the Theory of Literary History*. Princeton: Princeton University Press, 1971.

Hammond, Brean, and Shaun Regan. *Making the Novel: Fiction and Society in Britain, 1660–1789*. Basingstoke: Palgrave Macmillan, 2006.

Hand, Derek. *A History of the Irish Novel*. Cambridge: Cambridge University Press, 2011.

Harnden, Toby. *Bandit Country: The IRA and South Armagh*. London: Hodder and Stoughton, 1999.

Haslett, Moyra. "Eccentricity, Originality, and the Novel: *Tristram Shandy*, Volumes I and II." In *Reading 1759: Literary Culture in Mid-Eighteenth-Century Britain and France*, edited by Shaun Regan, 169–86. Lewisburg, PA: Bucknell University Press, 2013.

———. "Experimentalism in the Irish Novel, 1750–1770." *Irish University Review* 41, no. 1 (Spring/Summer 2011): 63–79.

———. Introduction to *The Life of John Buncle, Esq.*, vol. I, by Thomas Amory, 11–37. Edited by Moyra Haslett. Dublin: Four Courts Press, 2011.

———. "The Rise of the Irish Novel." *In The Oxford History of the Novel in English, Volume 1: Prose Fiction in English from the Origins of Print to 1750*, edited by Thomas Keymer, 486–99. Oxford: Oxford University Press, 2017.

Haydon, Colin. *Anti-Catholicism in Eighteenth-Century England*. Manchester: Manchester University Press, 2003.

Hayton, D. W. *The Anglo-Irish Experience, 1680–1730: Religion, Identity and Patriotism*. Woodbridge: Boydell Press, 2012.

Haywood, Ian and John Seed, ed. *The Gordon Riots: Politics, Culture and Insurrection in Late Eighteenth-Century Britain*. Cambridge: Cambridge University Press, 2012.

Higgins, Padhraig. *A Nation of Politicians: Gender, Patriotism and Political Culture in Late-Eighteenth-Century Ireland*. Madison: University of Wisconsin Press, 2010.

Highfill, Philip H., Kalman A. Burnim, and Edward A. Langhans. *A Biographical Dictionary of Actors, Actresses, Musicians, Dancers, Managers & Other Stage Personnel in London, 1660–1800*, vol. 14. Carbondale: Southern Illinois University Press, 1991.

Hill, Jacqueline. "'Allegories, Fictions, and Feigned Representations': Decoding the Money Bill Dispute, 1752–56." *Eighteenth-Century Ireland/Iris an Dá Chultúr* 21 (2006): 66–88.

Hitchcock, Tim and Robert Shoemaker. *London Lives: Poverty, Crime and the Making of a Modern City, 1690–1800.* Cambridge: Cambridge University Press, 2015.

Hogan, C. B., ed. *The London Stage, 1660–1800, Part 5: 1776–1800.* Carbondale: Southern Illinois University Press, 1960.

Holden, Michael. *Freney the Robber: The Noblest Highwayman in Ireland.* Cork: Mercier Press, 2009.

Hourican, Bridget. "Freney, James." In *Cambridge Dictionary of Irish Biography.* Cambridge: Cambridge University Press, 2009. http://dib.cambridge.org/viewReadPage.do?articleId=a3372.

Howson, Gerald. *Thief-Taker General: The Rise and Fall of Jonathan Wild.* London: Hutchinson, 1970.

Hunter, J. Paul. *Before Novels: The Cultural Contexts of Eighteenth-Century English Fiction.* New York: W. W. Norton, 1990.

Jacob, François. *The Logic of Life: A History of Heredity.* Translated by Betty E. Spillmann. London: Penguin, 1989.

Jenstad, Janelle, ed. *The Map of Early Modern London.* University of Victoria, June 20, 2018. https://mapoflondon.uvic.ca/.

Joseph, Betty. "The Political Economy of *The English Rogue*." *The Eighteenth Century* 55, no. 2–3 (Summer/Fall 2014): 175–92.

Katanka, Margaret C. "Goodman's *Holland's Leaguer* (1632)—Further Examples of the Plagiarism of Richard Head." *Notes and Queries* 21, no. 11 (November 1974): 415–17.

———. "Richard Head, 1637(?)–1686(?), A Critical Study." PhD diss., University of Birmingham, 1975.

Kelleher, Margaret, and Philip O'Leary, eds. *The Cambridge History of Irish Literature.* 2 vols. Cambridge: Cambridge University Press, 2005.

Kelly, James, ed. *Gallows Speeches from Eighteenth-Century Ireland.* Dublin: Four Courts Press, 2001.

Kenny, Kevin. *Ireland and the British Empire.* Oxford: Oxford University Press, 2004.

Keymer, Thomas. *Sterne, the Moderns and the Novel.* Oxford: Oxford University Press, 2002.

Lanner, Allen H. "Richard Head's Theophrastan Characters." *Notes and Queries* 17, no. 7 (July 1970): 259.

Lawson, Philip. *The East India Company: A History*. London: Longman, 1993.

Lázaro Carreter, Fernando. Lazarillo de Tormes *en la Picaresca*. Barcelona: Ariel, 1972.

Leerssen, Joep. *Hidden Ireland, Public Sphere*. Galway/Dublin: Arlen House, 2002.

———. *Mere Irish and Fíor-Ghael: Studies in the Idea of Irish Nationality, Its Development and Literary Expression Prior to the Nineteenth Century*. Cork: Cork University Press/Field Day, 1995.

Lees, Lynn Hollen. *Exiles of Erin: Irish Migrants in Victorian London*. Manchester: Manchester University Press, 1979.

Lennon, Joseph. *Irish Orientalism: A Literary and Intellectual History*. Syracuse, NY: Syracuse University Press, 2004.

Linebaugh, Peter. *The London Hanged: Crime and Civil Society in the Eighteenth Century*. 2nd ed. London: Verso, 2003.

Lines, Joe. "Charles Johnston and the Attribution of *The Adventures of Anthony Varnish* (1786)." *Notes and Queries* 63, no. 1 (March 2016): 91–94.

———. "Contesting Masculinities in Thomas Amory's *The Life of John Buncle, Esq.* (1756–66)." *Journal for Eighteenth-Century Studies* 41, no. 3 (September 2018): 447–63.

Loeber, Rolf and Magda Loeber with Anne Mullin Burnham, eds. *A Guide to Irish Fiction, 1650–1900*. Dublin: Four Courts Press, 2005.

Loveman, Kate. "'Eminent Cheats': Rogue Narratives in the Literature of the Exclusion Crisis." In *Fear, Exclusion and Revolution: Roger Morrice and Britain in the 1680s*, edited by Jason McElligott, 108–22. Aldershot: Ashgate, 2006.

Lowe, William C. "Boyd, William, Fourth Earl of Kilmarnock (1705–1746), Jacobite Army Officer." *Oxford Dictionary of National Biography*. Oxford: Oxford University Press, 2009. https://doi.org/10.1093/ref:odnb/3117.

Lund, Roger D. "Charles Johnstone." In *The Dictionary of Literary Biography*, edited by Martin Battestin, vol. 39:1, 293–300. Detroit: Gale Research, 1985.

Mackie, Erin. "The Perfect Gentleman: Boswell, the *Spectator* and Macheath." *Media History* 14, no. 3 (2008): 353–72.

———. *Rakes, Highwaymen, and Pirates: The Making of the Modern Gentleman in the Eighteenth Century*. Baltimore: Johns Hopkins University Press, 2009.

MacRaild, Donald M. *The Irish Diaspora in Britain, 1750–1939*. Basingstoke: Palgrave Macmillan, 2010.

Maiorino, Giancarlo, ed. *The Picaresque: Tradition and Displacement*. Minneapolis: University of Minnesota Press, 1996.

Mancing, Howard. "The Protean Picaresque." In *The Picaresque: Tradition and Displacement*, edited by Giancarlo Maiorino, 273–91. Minneapolis: University of Minnesota Press, 1996.

Mander, Jenny. "Picaresque Itineraries in the Eighteenth-Century French Novel." In *The Picaresque Novel in Western Literature*, edited by J. A. Garrido Ardila, 157–83. Cambridge: Cambridge University Press, 2015.

Marshall, Ashley. *The Practice of Satire in England, 1658–1700*. Baltimore: Johns Hopkins University Press, 2013.

McBride, Ian. *Eighteenth-Century Ireland: The Isle of Slaves*. Dublin: Gill & Macmillan, 2009.

McCallen, Jim. *Stand and Deliver: Stories of Irish Highwaymen*. Cork: Mercier Press, 1993.

McKenzie, Andrea. "From True Confessions to True Reporting? The Decline and Fall of the Ordinary's Account." *London Journal* 30, no. 1 (2005): 55–70.

———. "Maclaine [Maclean], James (1724–1750), Highwayman." In *Oxford Dictionary of National Biography*. Oxford: Oxford University Press, 2009. https://doi.org/10.1093/ref:odnb/17637.

———. "The Real Macheath: Social Satire, Appropriation, and Eighteenth-Century Criminal Biography." *Huntington Library Quarterly* 69, no. 4 (2006): 581–605.

McKeon, Michael. *The Origins of the English Novel, 1600–1740*. Baltimore: Johns Hopkins University Press, 1987.

McLeod, Deborah Anne. "The Minerva Press." PhD diss., University of Alberta, 1997.

Miller, Stuart. *The Picaresque Novel*. Cleveland, OH: Case Western Reserve University Press, 1967.

Monteser, Frederick. *The Picaresque Element in Western Literature*. Tuscaloosa: University of Alabama Press, 1975.

Moody, T. W. "Redmond O'Hanlon (c. 1640–1681)." *Proceedings and Reports of the Belfast Natural History and Philosophical Society* 1, no. 1 (1935–36): 17–33.

Morin, Christina. "Irish Gothic Goes Abroad: Cultural Migration, Materiality and the Minerva Press." In *Traveling Irishness in the Long Nineteenth*

Century, edited by Marguérite Corporaal and Christina Morin, 185–204. Basingstoke: Palgrave Macmillan, 2017.

Morley, Vincent. *Irish Opinion and the American Revolution*. Cambridge: Cambridge University Press, 2002.

Moseley, C. W. R. D. "Richard Head's *The English Rogue*: A Modern Mandeville?" *The Yearbook of English Studies* 1 (1971): 102–7.

Müller-Wille, Staffan, and Hans-Jörg Rheinberger, eds. *Heredity Produced: At the Crossroads of Biology, Politics, and Culture, 1500–1870*. Cambridge, MA: Massachusetts Institute of Technology Press, 2007.

Murray, Tony. *London Irish Fictions: Narrative, Diaspora and Identity*. Liverpool: Liverpool University Press, 2012.

Noonan, Kathleen M. "'The Cruell Pressure of an Enraged, Barbarous People': Irish and English Identity in Seventeenth-Century Policy and Propaganda." *The Historical Journal* 41, no. 1 (March 1998): 151–77.

———. "'Martyrs in Flames': Sir John Temple and the Conception of the Irish in English Martyrologies." *Albion: A Quarterly Journal Concerned with British Studies* 36, no. 2 (Summer 2004): 223–55.

Ó Ciardha, Éamonn. "The Early Modern Irish Outlaw: The Making of a Nationalist Icon." In *People, Politics and Power: Essays on Irish History 1660–1850*, edited by James Kelly, John McCafferty, and Charles Ivar McGrath, 51–69. Dublin: University College Dublin Press, 2009.

———. *Ireland and the Jacobite Cause, 1685–1766: A Fatal Attachment*. Dublin: Four Courts Press, 2001.

Ó Ciosáin, Niall. "The Irish Rogues." In *Irish Popular Culture, 1650–1850*, edited by James S. Donnelly and Kerby A. Miller, 78–96. Ballsbridge: Irish Academic Press, 1997.

———. *Print and Popular Culture in Ireland, 1750–1850*. Basingstoke: Macmillan, 1997.

O'Connell, Patricia. "The Early Modern Irish College Network in Iberia, 1590–1800." In *The Irish in Europe, 1580–1815*, edited by Thomas O'Connor, 49–64. Dublin: Four Courts Press, 2001.

Ó Gallchoir, Clíona. *Maria Edgeworth: Women, Enlightenment and Nation*. Dublin: University College Dublin Press, 2005.

O'Kane, Finola. "Ireland: A New Geographical Pastime?" In *Ireland: Crossroads of Art and Design, 1690–1840*, edited by William Laffan, Christopher P. Monkhouse, and Leslie Fitzpatrick, 77–96. Chicago: Art Institute of Chicago, 2015.

Orr, Leah. "*The English Rogue*: Afterlives and Imitations, 1665–1741." *Journal for Eighteenth-Century Studies* 38, no. 3 (September 2015): 361–76.

O'Shaughnessy, David, ed. *Eighteenth-Century Life* 39, no. 1 (2015). Special issue on "Networks of Aspiration: The London Irish of the Eighteenth Century."

O'Shaughnessy, David. "Making a Play for Patronage: Dennis O'Bryen's *A Friend in Need Is a Friend Indeed* (1783)." *Eighteenth-Century Life* 39, no. 1 (2015): 183–211.

———. "'Rip'ning Buds in Freedom's Field': Staging Irish Improvement in the 1780s." *Journal for Eighteenth-Century Studies* 38, no. 4 (2015): 541–54.

Parker, Alexander. *Literature and the Delinquent: The Picaresque Novel in Spain and Europe, 1599–1753*. Edinburgh: Edinburgh University Press, 1967.

Parrinder, Patrick. *Nation and Novel: The English Novel from Its Origins to the Present Day*. Oxford: Oxford University Press, 2006.

Patterson, James Conor. "Bandit Country." *The Tangerine* 7 (November 2018): 10–15.

Patterson, James G. *In the Wake of the Great Rebellion: Republicanism, Agrarianism and Banditry in Ireland after 1798*. Manchester: Manchester University Press, 2008.

Paulson, Ronald. *Satire and the Novel in Eighteenth-Century England*. New Haven, CT: Yale University Press, 1967.

Peakman, Julia, Alexander Pettit, and Patrick Spedding, eds. *Whore Biographies, 1700–1825*. 8 vols. London: Pickering and Chatto, 2006.

Pittock, Murray G. H. "Elphinstone, Arthur, Sixth Lord Balmerino and Fifth Lord Coupar (1688–1746), Jacobite Army Officer." In *Oxford Dictionary of National Biography*. Oxford: Oxford University Press, 2009. https://doi.org/10.1093/ref:odnb/8741.

Pollard, Mary, ed. *A Dictionary of Members of the Dublin Book Trade, 1550–1800*. London: Bibliographical Society, 2000.

———. *Dublin's Trade in Books, 1550–1800*. Oxford: Clarendon Press, 1989.

Pories, Kathleen. "The Intersection of Poor Laws and Literature in the Sixteenth Century: Fictional and Factual Categories." In *Framing Elizabethan Fictions: Contemporary Approaches to Early Modern Narrative Prose*, edited by Constance C. Relihan, 17–40. Kent, OH: Kent State University Press, 1996.

Pritchard, Jonathan. "Head, Richard (c. 1637–1686?)." In *The Oxford Dictionary of National Biography*. Oxford: Oxford University Press, 2009. https://doi.org/10.1093/ref:odnb/12810.

Randall, Dale B. J. *The Golden Tapestry: A Critical Survey of Non-Chivalric Spanish Fiction in English Translation, 1543–1657*. Durham, NC: Duke University Press, 1963.

Rankin, Deana. *Between Spenser and Swift: English Writing in Seventeenth-Century Ireland*. Cambridge: Cambridge University Press, 2005.

———. "Kinds of Irishness: Henry Burnell and Richard Head." In *A Companion to Irish Literature*, 2 vols., edited by Julia M. Wright, 1:108–24. Chichester: Wiley-Blackwell, 2010.

———. "'An Outlandish Miss': The Geography of 'Vertue' in Three Seventeenth-Century Irish Novels." *Irish University Review* 41, no. 1 (Spring/Summer 2011): 21–40.

Raven, James, ed. *British Fiction, 1750–1770: A Chronological Check-List of Prose Fiction Printed in Britain and Ireland*. Plainsboro, NJ: Associated University Presses, 1987.

Rawlings, Philip. *Drunks, Whores and Idle Apprentices: Criminal Biographies of the Eighteenth Century*. London: Routledge, 1992.

Reed, Walter L. "The Continental Influence on the Eighteenth-Century Novel: 'The English Improve What Others Invent.'" In *The Oxford Handbook of the Eighteenth-Century Novel*, edited by J. A. Downie, 73–87. Oxford: Oxford University Press, 2016.

Rees, Merlyn. *Northern Ireland: A Personal Perspective*. London: Methuen, 1985.

Rey Hazas, Antonio. *Deslindes de la Novela Picaresca*. Malaga: University of Malaga Press, 2003.

Richard, Jessica. *The Romance of Gambling in the Eighteenth-Century British Novel*. Basingstoke: Palgrave Macmillan, 2009.

Richetti, John. *Popular Fiction before Richardson: Narrative Patterns, 1700–1739*. Oxford: Clarendon Press, 1969.

Rico, Francisco. *The Spanish Picaresque Novel and the Point of View*. Translated by Charles Davis and Harry Sieber. Cambridge: Cambridge University Press, 1984.

Roberts, Daniel Sanjiv. "A 'Teague' and a 'True Briton': Charles Johnstone, Ireland and Empire." *Irish University Review* 41, no. 1 (Spring/Summer 2011): 133–50.

Rogers, Nicholas. "The Gordon Riots and the Politics of War." In *The Gordon Riots: Politics, Culture and Insurrection in Late Eighteenth-Century Britain*, edited by Ian Haywood and John Seed, 21–45. Cambridge University Press, 2012.

Rogers, Pat. *Grub Street: Studies in a Subculture*. London: Methuen, 1972.

Rosenthal, Laura J. *Infamous Commerce: Prostitution in Eighteenth-Century British Literature and Culture*. Ithaca, NY: Cornell University Press, 2006.

Ross, Ian Campbell. "Introduction to Fiction before 1800." In *The Field Day Anthology of Irish Writing*, 3 vols., edited by Seamus Deane, 1, 682–88. Derry: Field Day, 1991.

———. Introduction to *The History of Jack Connor*, by William Chaigneau, 11–34. Edited by Ian Campbell Ross. Dublin: Four Courts Press, 2013.

———. "Irish Fiction before the Union." In *The Irish Novel in the Nineteenth Century: Facts and Fictions*, edited by Jacqueline Belanger, 34–52. Dublin: Four Courts Press, 2005.

———. "An Irish Picaresque Novel: William Chaigneau's *The History of Jack Connor*." *Studies: An Irish Quarterly Review* 71 (Autumn 1982): 270–79.

———. "Mapping Ireland in Early Fiction." *Irish University Review* 41, no. 1 (Spring/Summer 2011): 1–20.

———. "Novels, Chapbooks, Folklore: The Several Lives of William Chaigneau's Jack Connor, Now Conyers; Or, John Connor, Alias Jack the Batchelor, the Famous Irish Bucker." *Eighteenth-Century Ireland/Iris an dá chultúr* 30 (2015): 60–86.

———. "Prose in English 1690–1800: From the Williamite Wars to the Act of Union." In *The Cambridge History of Irish Literature*, 2 vols., edited by Margaret Kelleher and Philip O'Leary, 1, 232–81. Cambridge: Cambridge University Press, 2005.

———. "Rewriting Irish Literary History: The Case of the Irish Novel." *Etudes Anglaises* 39, no. 4 (1986): 383–99.

———. "Thomas Amory, *John Buncle* and the Origins of Irish Fiction." *Eire-Ireland* 18, no. 3 (1983): 71–85.

———. "*The Triumph of Prudence over Passion*: Nationalism and Feminism in an Eighteenth-Century Irish Novel." *Irish University Review* 10, no. 2 (Autumn 1980): 232–40.

Rousseau, G. S. "Smollett and the Picaresque: Some Questions about a Label." *Studies in Burke and His Time* 12 (1971): 1886–904.

———. *Tobias Smollett: Essays of Two Decades*. Edinburgh: T. and T. Clark, 1982.

Salzman, Paul. "Alterations to *The English Rogue*." *The Library: A Quarterly Journal of Bibliography*, 6th series, no. 4 (1982): 49–56.

———. *English Prose Fiction, 1558–1700: A Critical History*. Oxford: Oxford University Press, 1985.

———. "Travelling or Staying In: Spain and the Picaresque in the Early 1620s," *The Yearbook of English Studies* 41, no. 1 (2011): 141–55.

Scott, Jake, dir. *Plunkett & Macleane*. 1999.

Scott, Jonathan. *When the Waves Ruled Britannia: Geography and Political Identities, 1500–1800*. Cambridge: Cambridge University Press, 2011.

Scott, Walter. *Lives of the Novelists*. 2 vols. Philadelphia: H. C. Carey et al., 1825.

Seager, Nicholas. *The Rise of the Novel: A Reader's Guide to Essential Criticism*. Basingstoke: Palgrave Macmillan, 2012.

Sevilla, Florencio. *La Novela Picaresca*. Madrid: Castalia, 2001.

Sharpe, James. *Dick Turpin: The Myth of the English Highwayman*. London: Profile Books, 2004.

Shoemaker, Robert. *The London Mob: Violence and Disorder in Eighteenth-Century England*. London: Hambledon, 2007.

———. "The Street Robber and the Gentleman Highwayman: Changing Perceptions of Robbery in London, 1690–1800." *Cultural and Social History* 3, no. 4 (2006): 381–405.

Sieber, Harry. *The Picaresque*. London: Methuen, 1977.

Sill, Geoffrey. "Developments in Sentimental Fiction." In *The Oxford Handbook of the Eighteenth-Century Novel*, edited by J. A. Downie, 426–39. Oxford: Oxford University Press, 2016.

Sirk, Douglas, dir. *Captain Lightfoot*. 1955.

Skeen, Catherine. "Projecting Fictions: *Gulliver's Travels*, *Jack Connor*, and *John Buncle*." *Modern Philology* 100, no. 3 (February 2003): 330–59.

Skinner, John. *Constructions of Smollett: A Study of Genre and Gender*. Plainsboro, NJ: Associated University Presses, 1996.

Somerville, Robert. *The Savoy: Manor, Hospital, Chapel*. London: Duchy of Lancaster, 1960.

Speck, W. A. "William Augustus, Prince, Duke of Cumberland (1721–1765), Army Officer." In *The Oxford Dictionary of National Biography*. Oxford: Oxford University Press, 2009. https://doi.org/10.1093/ref:odnb/29455.

Spector, Robert. *Tobias Smollett*. New York: Twayne, 1968.

Stafford, Brooke A. "Englishing the Rogue, 'Translating' the Irish: Fantasies of Incorporation and Early Modern English National Identity." In *Rogues and Early Modern English Culture*, edited by Craig Dionne and Steve Mentz, 312–37. Ann Arbor: University of Michigan Press, 2004.

Steggle, Matthew. "Richard Head's *The Floating Island* (1673) Plagiarizes Thomas Powell." *Notes and Queries* 52, no. 3 (2005): 325–27.

Talbot, Michael. "Thomas Newburgh and his Poem on Handel's Blindness." *The Handel Institute Newsletter* 2, no. 2 (Autumn 2018): 7–10.

Thomas, Peter D. G. *John Wilkes: A Friend to Liberty*. Oxford: Oxford University Press, 1996.

Tracy, Tony. "*Captain Lightfoot* (1955): Caught Between a Rock (Hudson) and a Rapparee." In *Screening Irish-America: Representing Irish-America in Film and Television*, edited by Ruth Brady, 193–210. Dublin: Irish Academic Press, 2009.

Trumpener, Katie. *Bardic Nationalism: The Romantic Novel and the British Empire*. Princeton: Princeton University Press, 1997.

Wahrman, Dror. *The Making of the Modern Self: Identity and Culture in Eighteenth-Century England*. New Haven, CT: Yale University Press, 2004.

Wallace, Richard W. *The Etchings of Salvator Rosa*. Princeton: Princeton University Press, 1979.

Waters, Maureen. *The Comic Irishman*. Albany: State University of New York Press, 1984.

Watt, Ian. *The Rise of the Novel: Studies in Defoe, Richardson, and Fielding*. London: Chatto & Windus, 1957.

Watt, Timothy. *Popular Protest and Policing in Ascendancy Ireland, 1691–1761*. Martlesham, Suffolk: Boydell Press, 2018.

Weber, Harold. "Rakes, Rogues, and the Empire of Misrule." *Huntington Library Quarterly* 47, no. 1 (Winter 1984): 13–32.

Wheatley, Christopher J. *Beneath Iërne's Banners: Irish Protestant Drama of the Restoration and Eighteenth Century*. Notre Dame: University of Notre Dame Press, 1999.

Wheatley, Christopher J, and Kevin Donovan, eds. *Irish Drama of the Seventeenth and Eighteenth Centuries*. 2 vols. Bristol: Thoemmes, 2003.

White, Harry. "Carolan, Turlough (Ó Cearbhalláin, Toirdhealbhach)." In *The Cambridge Dictionary of Irish Biography*. Cambridge University Press, 2009. http://dib.cambridge.org/viewReadPage.do?articleId=a1492.

White, Jerry. "Pain and Degradation in Georgian London: Life in the Marshalsea Prison." *History Workshop Journal* 68, no. 1 (2009): 69–98.

Williamson, Audrey. *Wilkes: A Friend to Liberty*. London: Allen & Unwin, 1974.

Wilson, David A. *United Irishmen, United States: Immigrant Radicals in the Early Republic*. Ithaca, NY: Cornell University Press, 1998.

Woodbridge, Linda. *Vagrancy, Homelessness, and English Renaissance Literature*. Urbana: University of Illinois Press, 2001.

Wright, Julia M., ed. *A Companion to Irish Literature*. 2 vols. Chichester: Wiley-Blackwell, 2010.

Index

agrarian agitation, 129–30, 163–64, 187
American War of Independence, 144, 148, 155–56
Amory, Thomas, 6, 27, 136–39, 184
anti-Catholicism, 46–53, 72–84, 91, 148–51
antisemitism, 163
Armagh, 1–2, 82, 85, 87

bailiffs, 82–83
Balf, Richard, 88, 107
Banbridge, 121
banditry. *See* highway robbery
Boyd, William (fourth Earl of Kilmarnock), 113–14
Boyle, Roger, 6–8
Bradstreet, Dudley, 112–15, 127, 134
Brasil, legend of, 35, 60–64
Burney, Frances, 174
Butler, James, 89
Butler, Sarah, 6, 176–77

capital punishment, 22–23, 50, 81, 89, 90, 95, 113–14, 117, 143, 150, 153–54, 166
Carleton, Mary, 92
Carleton, William, 2, 4, 179, 188
Carolan, Turlough, 169

Carrick, James, 23, 89–90, 96–97
Carrickfergus, 121
Cavan, 121
Cellier, Elizabeth, 207n17
Chaigneau, William, 4, 6, 9, 10–11, 27, 103–32
Colman, George (the elder), 145, 160–61
colonial sea voyage, 42–45, 60–64
Connor, John (pirate), 106, 186
Cork, 94, 122, 135
Cosgrave, John, 3–4, 24, 84–91, 185, 188
criminal anatomy, 15–19, 54, 60, 63, 83, 117; dictionaries of thieves' cant, 16–17, 59; Irish featured in, 17–18
criminal biographies, 22–26, 69–71, 77–91, 95–99, 106, 112, 150–51; 165; fiction as element of, 24–26, 81–84, 148–49; and London, 22–24, 77–84, 150–51, 165; and the novel, 25, 103, 105–15, 117, 121–22, 150–51, 165, 180–81, 185–88; Ordinary of Newgate's *Accounts*, 22–23, 25, 85; price of, 25, 96, 106; published in Dublin, 70–71, 84–91, 112–15, 186; readership, 24–25, 41–42, 50, 210n69; and religion, 22–23, 24, 50, 54–55, 91–97, 110, 112
Culloden, Battle of, 110, 125

251

Joe Lines studied for a PhD in English at Queen's University, Belfast. He has published articles in *Journal of Eighteenth-Century Studies, Eighteenth-Century Ireland, Notes and Queries,* and *Romantic Textualities.*